A THORNY ROSE ...

Without warning Annie stopped and bent to look at the ground, and Rik almost tripped over her.

"What is this leafy plant called?" she asked, unaware.

"Trillium. Earlier in the summer they have white flowers," he answered, looking appreciatively at the shapely bottom thrust up toward him.

"Must be pretty." She looked over her shoulder, and her mouth tightened to a straight line as she realized what he'd been staring at.

Tough. The woman had a nice ass, and if she was going to point it at him like that, he was going to look. He glared back.

"When you're not being obnoxious, are you sort of a nice guy? Or do I just bring out all your sterling qualities at once?" she asked.

"Obnoxious? What do you expect? I said you can work here, but I'm not gonna pretend to be happy about it. And you might think about being a little nicer to the guy who owns the private property you're standing on."

"Oh, no. Don't you go there," she retorted. "You've got a pretty nice butt yourself, but I'm not kissing it."

A reluctant smile tugged at Rik's mouth at that little zinger.

Other Avon Contemporary Romances by
Michelle Jerott

ABSOLUTE TROUBLE

ALL NIGHT LONG

MICHELLE JEROTT

AVON BOOKS ◆ NEW YORK

This is a work of fiction. Names, characters, places, and incidents either are the product of the author's imagination or are used fictitiously. Any resemblance to actual events, locales, organizations, or persons, living or dead, is entirely coincidental and beyond the intent of either the author or the publisher.

AVON BOOKS, INC.
1350 Avenue of the Americas
New York, New York 10019

Copyright © 1999 by Michele Albert
Inside cover author photo by Edwin E. Proctor
Published by arrangement with the author
Library of Congress Catalog Card Number: 99-94809
ISBN: 0-380-81066-2
www.avonbooks.com/romance

First Avon Books Printing: October 1999

AVON TRADEMARK REG. U.S. PAT. OFF. AND IN OTHER COUNTRIES, MARCA REGIS-TRADA, HECHO EN U.S.A.

Printed in the U.S.A.

WCD 10 9 8 7 6 5 4 3 2 1

In memory of Lena and Elmer Renier: Grandma and Grandpa, thanks for so many wonderful times at the farm. Some days I can close my eyes and still see the wind rippling through the hay-fields, smell the baking bread, and hear you yelling, *"Allez!"*

PROLOGUE

September 12, 1832, Youngstown, Ohio: Oh, how I long for Peace, for an end to this Great Unknown. Find our son, Dear Sir, wherever he may be. Ease a Mother's broken heart, and bring my Boy home again.

—MRS. AUGUSTINA HUDSON,
COPY OF A LETTER TO COLONEL ZACHARY TAYLOR

April 13

Mr. Rurik Magnusson
Black Hollow Farm
Magnusson Road
Warfield, Wisconsin

Dear Mr. Magnusson,

You don't know me, but I fervently hope you will take a moment to read my letter and consider the request you'll find herein. As you'll see by the enclosed book, I am a photographer/writer of documentary stories with a picture-intensive format—that is, your basic coffee-table books.

For the past ten or so years, I've been working on a story involving the 1832 confrontation in Wisconsin known as the Black Hawk War. A particular incident is of importance to me, and I have firm evidence it involved an area of your land, which is now referred to as Black Hawk's Hollow. I am writing to request your permission to research and photograph this area. My work is nondisruptive and will only require as much time as it takes me to take pictures, make notes, and follow through with research in local museums and libraries.

I feel quite strongly about bringing this story to its close. I'd like to schedule the trip for July, and therefore would appreciate a response as soon as possible. Please feel free to contact me with any questions or concerns you may have.

Sincerely,
Annora Beckett, Author & Photographer
The Romance of Route 66, *Hanneman Press*

April 24

Ms. Annora Beckett
85 W. Chesterfield Street, #3B
Columbus, Ohio

Dear Ms. Beckett,

I do own a couple acres of woods called Black Hawk's Hollow, but old Chief Black Hawk never came anywhere near it, no matter what local legends say. Coming here would be a waste of time, so save yourself the trouble. I'm sending back your book. Nice job.

Regards,
R. Magnusson

April 30

Dear Mr. Magnusson,

My apologies for not being clearer. I'm not researching Chief Black Hawk, but the journey of a young officer who fought in the war. Since this area of your land is mentioned several times in my primary sources, I would very much like to visit the landmark. Again, I assure you the nature of my work is not invasive. I'm sending another book, this one chronicling a race-car driver's season on the circuit. I think you'll see my work is inquisitive and honest, but never exploitive.

Please reconsider my request.

Sincerely,
Annora Beckett

May 10

Ms. Beckett,

Thanks for asking my permission first, but the Hollow is on grazing land for my dairy herd and I don't want strangers upsetting their routine. July isn't good for me, anyway. I'm returning your book again. Looks nice, but I don't have time to read it, and I make a point to never keep gifts with strings attached.

R. Magnusson

May 30

Dear Mr. Magnusson,

Pardon the tardy response, but I've been on the road a lot lately. Part of the job, I'm afraid. I also wasn't sure how to respond to your last letter. In my years of freelancing, I've worked with rodeo riders, long-haul truckers, train conductors, race-car drivers, military history reenactors, and fishermen and trappers in the Louisiana bayous, to name just a few. In addition, I've written pieces for national magazines which have required me to follow historic journeys, such as the Mormons' westward trek, old cattle-drive routes, and the trail taken by the Cherokees during their relocation. As a professional, I'm more than willing to work with you until we reach terms that meet your satisfaction.

I'm sorry you feel the books I sent came with some sort of "strings" attached. Because I cannot present my case to you in person, I had hoped examples of my work would impress upon you the sincerity of my intentions and the depth of my dedication. My only purpose is to take photographs that will complement the text of my book.

I can promise that you—and your cows—won't even know I'm around. If my books are not proof enough of my intentions, I can offer you monetary compensation, one-half payable upon my arrival at the Hollow and the remainder due upon completion of my project. I often provide cash payments to those I work with, especially if I'll require a few hours of their time. No strings attached to this offer, Mr. Magnusson. Think of me as a contractor, if it helps, and I'm hiring you to help me complete an ongoing project.

Also, if July is not good for your schedule, I can make August, but would prefer not to wait much longer. Please be assured that my intentions are sincere and legitimate. I anxiously await your response.

Sincerely,
Annora Beckett

June 10

Ms. Beckett,

You sure are stubborn but have convinced me that you are serious. I'm not so sure about this money thing. Sounds like a bribe to me. How long will you need to be at the Hollow? The farm keeps me busy, and I don't want a bunch of people around, getting in my way.

Rik

June 15

Rik,

This will have to be brief, as I'm leaving for a short assignment soon. Your last letter made me laugh, because I'm usually not so pushy. I'm persistent only because I feel strongly about completing this story. You could say it's been a dream of mine for many years. I also laughed at the word "bribe," and it seems I'm not the only one here who's rather stubborn. The money is NOT a bribe and the amount is negotiable to a certain extent. We can talk about this more later, if you wish. As for how long I'd be at the Hollow, I estimate the project will take six to eight weeks to complete. I'm a stickler for doing thorough research. I can also assure you that only I, a suitcase, and a lot of camera equipment will arrive at your place. Which reminds me, if you agree to let me come to the Hollow, I'll need a place to stay. Are there any decent hotels or bed-and-breakfasts in or near Warfield?

I trust all is well with you. I've heard on the news the Midwest hasn't been getting much rain lately. I hope that's not causing you too much worry.

Please respond as soon as you can, so I can begin making travel plans.

Warmly,
Annie Beckett

June 23

Ms. Beckett,

Hope your assignment went well. Rain would be great, but it doesn't look like we'll get any soon. Since you won't give up and since July isn't much worse than any other time, I grant you permission to work at the Hollow and research your book. But only if it won't cause trouble. As for the money, I guess a little extra is always welcome. I don't know about hotels. I tore out some pages from the phone book for you. Let me know when you'll arrive. The door's always open, but I'll need to tie up the dog in the yard. He bites. I'm in the barn by six every morning and often don't get in until after dark, so if you need me, leave a note by the coffeemaker. I'll find you.

Rik

June 28

Rik,

I am delighted everything worked out. My plane arrives in Madison on July 20. And, yes, do tie up your dog—I've been chased by more than my fair share of those creatures. I PROMISE there will be no trouble. Girl Scout's honor! As for the money, I'm willing to offer you a compensation of $3,000. I hope this will meet with your approval. I'm on the road again until July 19, so I won't have time to talk with you before I arrive in town. You can't change your mind now!

Oh, and thanks for the list of hotels. Not much to choose from, but I'll make do. Hope you get a little rain soon.

Annie

CHAPTER ONE

June 27, 1832, Dixon's Ferry, Illinois: We are preparing to march and so I must be brief, or I shall miss the post. I have read your last letter and beg you, Dear Mother, not to fear for my health. The weather holds warm and clear, and wild game is plentiful (Father would be keen to hunt here!). Indeed, I am in most excellent spirits! The Beauty of this land leaves me in much wonderment, and I am sending you these little sketches so you may see, through my eyes, the blue rivers and swaying grasses growing as high as my chest. Give my sisters my love and tell Emily the shirt is splendid, that I wear it with great pride and I hope to be home for Christmas to settle A Matter most dear to her sweet heart. With Affection, Your Obedient Son, Lewis.

—LIEUTENANT LEWIS HUDSON,
TO HIS MOTHER, AUGUSTINA

"Ow!"

Rik Magnusson sucked in his breath as his bare toe hit a warped porch plank. He jerked straight at the stab of pain—and sloshed hot coffee over his hand.

"Dammit!"

His curse cut across the hushed quiet of dawn and

7

startled a pair of mourning doves coo-cooing on the porch rail into flight. If stubbing a toe wasn't enough to bring him wide-awake at five-thirty in the morning, the hot coffee made sure of it.

Wiping his hand dry on his jeans, Rik scowled at the board and reminded himself, as he had umpteen times already this summer, that he needed to fix the damn thing as soon as he could find a little extra time and money.

With a last muttered curse, he limped to the far side of the wide porch and hitched himself up to straddle the railing. Leaning back against a carved post, he sipped his coffee and watched the early rays of sun spread a soft, golden glow across his 220 acres of land.

In the low light, the bare, bone-dry patches amid his hay were less noticeable, although nothing could hide the fact the corn was at least a foot shorter than it should've been by now—or that it wouldn't take more than a single spark to start a flash fire just about anywhere.

At the click of paws on wood, Rik glanced down to see his collie, Buck, trotting toward him.

"But you gotta admit," he said, putting his cup aside to ruffle the long fur on the dog's neck, "it's still the prettiest sight in the world."

To Buck, fields were nothing more than good places to nose out mice, so his bright eyes and lolling tongue likely meant he wanted his food bowl filled. Or that he hoped Rik would play a game of fetch on the way to the barn.

"Maybe later, boy," he said. Buck replied with an excited, snuffling bark.

Sitting back again, Rik breathed in deeply, taking in the familiar scent of sweet hay on the morning breeze. The breeze also carried with it a lowing from the barn, reminding him it was nearly time to get off his butt and begin the morning's chore of milking his herd of forty cattle. Once he finished there, he'd start repairs on the garage roof, fix the radiator on the John Deere—they didn't make tractors like they used to—and after a quick lunch, he'd feed the Belgian horses and give them their daily practice before he had to milk the cows again.

Just a day's work at Black Hollow Farm.

For now, though, he enjoyed the luxury of letting the minutes drift by as he nursed his coffee and ate a tart Macintosh from one of his own trees, which he sliced with a pocketknife.

Man, this was the life. No time clock to beat, no one to tell him when to work or how. Farming wasn't for guys who needed quick profits and instant results, or who didn't like ruining their designer shirts with sweat, but the job sure had its moments.

Like now. Even when he was an old, old man, he wanted to look across his land and feel the satisfaction like this, warm and deep in his belly.

As his father always used to say: *You earn what's yours, and no man can ever take that away.*

Not without a fight, anyway—and if he smelled trouble on this dry, hot wind, he'd just work that much harder to keep it away. He'd done it before.

Which brought to mind that pesky writer, and her carrot-on-a-stick offer of money. He never should've agreed to let her come. It didn't set right, not from the very start.

With sudden determination, Rik straightened.

"Hell, we don't need her money," he informed

Buck, who cocked his ears forward. "And Magnussons never beg."

The dog swished his soft brush of a tail against the porch. Then he rolled to his back, paws curled, and whined, eyes begging.

Rik grinned, shaking his head as he rubbed the dog's belly. "Except for Magnusson mutts, that is."

Patting the dog a last time, Rik glanced again at the sky, where the gray had given way to blue. His eye tagged the time close to six. Time to get to work.

But he had a telephone call to make first, and set everything aright once more.

God, what a life.

Smothering a yawn at the early hour, Annie Beckett picked her way through the cases and trunks scattered across her living room floor.

She hadn't bothered to unpack after flying in from Santa Fe yesterday, since she had to head right back to Columbus International Airport tomorrow morning. Half the cases lay open, awaiting a pretrip equipment check—a tedious chore, but there was no way she'd ever risk losing the photograph of the century due to a scratched lens or dead batteries.

In the small island kitchen Annie put water on to boil, then pulled a mug from the cupboard. She tore open a Constant Comment tea packet, filling the room with the pungent smell of orange and cinnamon.

Yawning again, she quickly sorted through a mound of mail lying jumbled on the counter. The usual bills, which she'd pay ahead by several months and post before hitting the road; a few letters, which she separated from the pile so she could write back while at the airport or in-flight; and the letters from her Wisconsin farmer, scrawled on notepaper from Dow's Feed and Seed.

Rurik Magnusson.

What a name for some guy who likely wore dirty overalls, sported a farmer's tan, and chewed tobacco; a contrary old coot who, as his blunt notes told her, lived alone and zealously guarded his solitude and comfortable routines.

While waiting for the water to boil, she took the mail into the living room and sat cross-legged on the floor next to her desk. She pulled a leather attaché toward her, placed the mail in the front compartment, then opened her file cabinet drawer and began packing her files on the Hudson project.

With any luck, this would be the last time she'd ever have to pack them.

The irony never failed to touch her: that while searching for her mother and her own past, she'd found Lieutenant Lewis Hudson instead.

Lewis was actually family: a tie of blood existed between them, and Annie's admiration for Gussie Hudson's tireless thirty-year search for her lost son had bound that tie into a knot.

Such a shame that her own mother hadn't inherited even a smidgen of her ancestress's maternal instincts.

Just as the teakettle whistled, the phone rang. Annie looked at her watch in disbelief. Anybody calling this early was either a wrong number or someone she didn't want to talk to.

She headed to the kitchen, letting the answering machine take the call. As she turned off the stove, a deep, unfamiliar male voice filled the small room.

"Yeah, Miz Beckett, this is Rik Magnusson at Black Hollow Farm."

Annie froze, her fingers tightening on the kettle's handle.

"I'm calling about your visit. Something's come up, and I can't have you come by. Sorry for the short notice and for any trouble this causes with your ticket. I'd, uh, be willing to pay you for it, if you can't get a refund." The man hesitated, then added with finality, "Good-bye."

The tape beeped and began rewinding as Annie swore softly and slammed the kettle back down on the stove.

The wishy-washy worm! After all her efforts to appease him, how dare he screw her over?

Well, she wouldn't let Magnusson stop her that easily.

CHAPTER TWO

July 20, 1832, Michigan Territory: I should fight for this land were it mine. Cyrus calls me a philosophizing Fool, but I cannot help but feel a profound sympathy for our Enemy.

—LIEUTENANT LEWIS HUDSON,
FROM A LETTER TO HIS MOTHER, AUGUSTINA

Annie lost her way twice before she found Magnusson Road, and now, driving slowly behind a road-hogging tractor piloted by an overalled gnome, she read the mailboxes planted along the rough, narrow road.

"Bingo!"

She squinted against the early evening sun at a mailbox with the name MAGNUSSON painted in square, black letters. Below it, in a fancier script, were the words: *BLACK HOLLOW FARM.*

She turned onto the bumpy gravel drive. The house and outbuildings were about a half mile off the road, with most of the house hidden behind towering pines and oak trees that looked as if they'd been around since the Cretaceous period.

"Oh, my," she murmured as she brought her rental compact to a halt in the yard, in front of the biggest Victorian farmhouse she'd ever seen.

With its peeling white paint and spacious sprawl, resulting from a time when extended families still lived together under one roof, the house oozed atmosphere. She almost expected an ample-hipped, big-bosomed woman to walk out onto the porch, wiping flour-dusted hands clean on her apron, and invite her inside for coffee and apple pie.

Annie switched off the car engine, peering up at the two-story house—nearly three, with that tall attic. Dairy farming must pay better than she'd thought.

With any luck, Farmer Magnusson would be home. She'd decided against calling ahead, since experience had taught her that people were less likely to be difficult if they had to look her in the eye.

She got out of the car and surveyed the neatly mown rolling lawn, the clothesline hung with towels flapping lazily in the breeze, and fields of sweet-smelling alfalfa.

The place was as quiet, as peaceful, as a shrine.

"Well, Lewis," she said softly. "I'm here."

Here, right where the frontier US Army had camped on a hot July night in 1832. No farmhouses or picturesque red barns existed then; only prairie valleys, bluffs, and virgin forest. Right here, Lewis had written his last letter, its tone tense and weary. Here, he'd spent the last hours of his life, and here, if her hunch was correct, he'd been killed.

A shiver took her, but she dismissed it and turned back to the house. Its wide, pleasant porch even came complete with a rocking chair and swing.

"God, how Norman Rockwell can you get?" she said out loud, oddly fascinated by this Victorian monstrosity before her.

But after hours in airports and on planes, she

wouldn't mind kicking off her sandals and curling up on that swing with a cold lemonade, listening to ice cubes clink against the glass as they melted. How nice it would feel to press a cool, sweating glass against her forehead.

Wisconsin in July was as hot as a Louisiana bayou. The humidity glued her ivory silk shell and navy cotton batik skirt to her skin—and the heat didn't do much to help settle the ball of worry roiling in her stomach.

But the time had long since passed for second thoughts.

Annie opened the car trunk and removed her Nikon 35mm camera—Old Faithful—and slipped the strap over her head, glad to have its familiar weight around her neck.

She walked up the porch steps and, although fairly certain no one was home, raised a hand to knock on the old-fashioned screen door. But just before she banged on the wood, a loud barking erupted behind her.

Dog!

Nasty, barking, biting, snarling creatures!

With a shriek, Annie yanked open the screen door and let it slam shut behind her. A knee-high missile of gold-and-white fur with snapping teeth skidded to a halt at the door and set up a furious barking.

This wasn't good—Magnusson was bound to be just a wee bit annoyed at finding her there to begin with, much less parked inside his house.

"Hush," she snapped, although the dog was only doing what dogs do. "Stop it! For God's sake, you'll pop out your eyeballs if you carry on like that."

She planted her fists on her hips and stared hard at

the collie. He barked again, but his tail swished a little.

"Where's your rotten master, hmmm?"

The dog growled, tail gyrating like a boat rotor.

"Now there's mixed signals for you," Annie said with a sigh, turning to look around her temporary sanctuary.

From what she could see from the entry hall, the inside of the house looked a lot like the outside. Well lived in and quaintly old-fashioned, with beautiful woodwork and architectural detailing from a bygone era. A bit overdone for her taste, but still impressive.

The pine plank flooring could stand some polishing, though, to make it gleam warm and golden. Too bad the window shades were drawn. She wanted to open them, to let the sunshine stream through the glass and brighten the hall, and touch the cool wooden floor with its warm fingers of light.

The dog, which had been growling nonstop, barked and dashed off so abruptly its nails skittered on the porch.

Now what?

Gravel crunched under footsteps coming fast and hard. Annie stepped back from the door in alarm.

"Buck, shut up!"

At that curt, deep voice, she took yet another step back. Some sort of tussle between man and dog ensued on the porch, a chain jangled, and then the screen door slammed open.

"Who the hell are you?"

Annie's mouth opened, but no words squeaked past her dry throat.

A tall man stood before her, framed in the open doorway and silhouetted by the strong sun, filling her entire field of vision with broad, bare shoulders and red-gold hair gleaming like fire. Then he stepped farther into the hall and she met ice-blue eyes in a sun-browned face with reddish beard stubble and a mustache that needed a trim as badly as his hair.

A barbarian god fallen from Valhalla.

Her stomach made a little flutter of dread—along with something else.

"I asked you a question, lady. You got five seconds to answer before I toss you outside."

His jeans and boots were filthy, and as he stood glaring at her he used his shirt to wipe dirt and sweat from his face and chest—a supple, lithely powerful chest.

Good God, please don't let *this* be her contrary old coot!

"I'm here to see Rik Magnusson," Annie said at last.

"You're looking at him." The silence lengthened until understanding flooded his remarkable eyes. He treated her to an unsubtle once-over before his gaze locked on hers again. For an instant, something hot and angry and aware shimmered between them. "You're that damned writer."

"Yes. Annie Beckett," she answered, fighting the urge to back away from his too-forward stare or pull the clinging silk away from her skin. "I wrote and told you when I'd arrive. Remember?"

"And I left a message on your answering machine that you couldn't come. You should've—"

"I wasn't home to receive it," she interrupted, the lie slipping out easily. "I've gone to considerable trouble for this trip, and we had a deal, Mr. Magnusson. I honored my end. I expect you to honor yours."

His eyes narrowed. "Sorry, but as I said on the phone, something's come up."

Sure. Like he had to braid his mustache. Or go sharpen his ax.

Annie pulled an envelope out of her purse. "And here I am, come all this way with a check for fifteen hundred dollars." He looked down briefly, then raised his gaze to hers. "It has your name on it, Mr. Magnusson, so you may as well take it."

He didn't move.

Fine. She'd been stonewalled by the very best; she'd just shift her tactics.

Annie let her hand fall to her side. "Look. We're not off to a very good start, and I'm sorry. I have a job to do here and once it's done, I'll be on my way again. I'm not sure what you expected, but as you can see, I'm just an ordinary woman with a small suitcase and a big camera."

She laughed a little at her joke. He didn't.

Wonderful. Humor-impaired; not her favorite kind of human. Gathering her courage, she stepped forward—close enough to feel the heat radiating from his bare skin and close enough to see the mingled red-and-gold hairs on his chest.

Taking a deep breath, she extended her hand. "Let's start from scratch. Hello, I'm Annie Beckett, and I'm pleased to meet you, Mr. Magnusson. I'm looking forward to taking pictures at the Hollow. Please, let's work together."

Magnusson hesitated for a long moment, but finally took her hand in a firm grip. His skin was work-roughened, and he pumped her hand once before dropping it. Brief as it was, the contact left Annie very aware that she stood before a half-naked man with hot skin and eyes like ice.

After a brief, awkward silence, punctuated by the frenzied barking outside, Annie said, "So . . . are you going to invite me the rest of the way in or throw me to the dog?"

Something flickered across his face—embarrassment, she hoped—before he gave a nod. "Come on in."

Annie's knees went rubbery with relief, and she started after him, only to wait while he wrestled free of his work boots. Fascinated, she watched the play of his back muscles as he yanked at the ties.

The scents of sweat and barnyard hit her. Honest smells, and not exactly unpleasant, but she couldn't help taking a step back.

At her movement he turned, then stood straight and tall with a quiet, unapologetic pride. "I didn't think you'd show up or else I'd have made sure I was squeaky-clean. I'll go wash up before we talk."

"It's no problem," she said quickly. "I'm used to men who smell of hard work and hard play."

"Is that so?"

Again, Magnusson ran a slow, assessing gaze over her and Annie felt a sudden urge to tidy her frizzy braid and smooth the wrinkles from her travel-rumpled clothing.

"I'm gonna wash up anyway," he said, running a hand through his hair. "Maybe you don't care that I smell like shit, Miz Beckett, but I sure do."

He walked away without giving Annie a chance to respond, and she eyed his long legs and lean, sun-browned back. She was an artist, trained to see beauty—and, boy, did he have a beauty of a behind in those tight, dusty jeans. Firm muscles, a roundness so neatly outlined beneath worn denim that any woman would consider giving that rear a proprietary pat—if only it weren't attached to six feet and 180 pounds of testy male.

Letting out a soft sigh of appreciation, Annie followed him into a large kitchen—one of the fussiest, maiden-lady-aunt kitchens she'd ever seen. The walls were a riot of Victorian cabbage roses in muted tones of mauve, maroon, and hunter green, and an old, hand-hewn china cabinet displayed a collection of antique china in a gold-rimmed, delicate rose pattern. What had to be vintage Irish lace curtains topped a wide bay window over the sink.

She couldn't imagine any man spending time in a kitchen like this, much less cooking in it, and she badly wanted to take a picture of Rik Magnusson standing against the counter, all that lean, rapacious male beauty juxtaposed against rampant femininity.

Then she noticed Magnusson returning her stare. He stood in the bathroom doorway, just off the kitchen. "What's with the camera?"

Annie realized she held it in the ready-aim-shoot position. "It goes where I go. In fact, I always feel a little naked without it."

Poor choice of words. As a heated embarrassment spread through her, Magnusson's gaze lowered to her breasts, where the damp silk let all the world know she wore a lacy bra embroidered with white seed pearls.

When his gaze returned to her face again, he said coolly, "I don't want you taking any pictures in my house."

"That's a shame. It's a lovely room."

He hesitated as if he meant to say more, then scowled. "You look hot. Take what you want from the fridge to drink. There's soda, iced tea, and juice."

"And milk?" she asked, making a last stab at humor.

Magnusson didn't smile back. "Always milk," he said, then shut the bathroom door with a bang.

Sagging back against the counter with both relief and resentment, Annie glared at the door. Having Thor the Thunder God crash her Rockwellian idyll was *not* what she'd anticipated.

The sound of the shower cut across her thoughts, and at once her mental camera provided a vivid shot of water rivulets running down the lines of Rik Magnusson's strong, tanned body.

She closed her eyes—not that it helped much. God, what was wrong with her? Even if he was gorgeous and she hadn't slept with a man since the last ice age, such thoughts were just plain unprofessional.

Maybe she *should* get something cold to drink, after all. Annie headed toward the refrigerator, decorated with a motley collection of advertising magnets and a few whimsical cows. These last must have been gifts, because the man of the house didn't strike her as the whimsical sort, no matter what his kitchen looked like.

Annie grabbed a diet 7UP and peeked out at the other rooms. An old-fashioned parlor, situated opposite a steep, dark staircase, was all she could see clearly, but what incredible lines this old house possessed! Her fingers practically twitched to capture the geometry of tall, stately windows and pocket doors, the lushly extravagant curves of plaster cornices and scrolled woodwork. And, most interesting of all, the walls were crowded with framed antique photographs.

The water shut off and Annie tiptoed back to sit at the table. When the bathroom door opened, she straightened.

Magnusson walked out, toweling his hair dry—and still bare-chested, to her dismay. The scent of damp air, shampoo, and strong soap followed him.

"I'll grab a shirt, then we can talk about what to do with you."

Annie frowned at his retreating back. Just her luck he was the difficult type, and a shower hadn't improved his mood at all.

She'd finished off the soda before Magnusson returned. He wore a short-sleeved blue T-shirt tucked into clean jeans, and plain white athletic socks.

No-nonsense and utilitarian, nothing flashy. But the shirt's color warmed his eyes and emphasized his red-gold hair and tanned skin. The knit, wash-worn and thin, fit him as if it were tailored to each line of muscle and sinew. His long, lean build reminded her of cats—twitchy-tailed cats with unblinking eyes. Under his regard, Annie shifted in her chair.

"Where would you like me to put your check?" she asked, before he had a chance to say anything.

"Leave it on the counter." He fetched a soda for himself, but instead of sitting at the table, he leaned back against the counter, forcing her to look up at him.

The pop of the can and a carbonated hiss sounded in the following silence.

"Too bad you didn't check your messages before

coming all this way and spending all that money," he said at length.

"Maybe, but the fact is that I *am* here, so why not just agree to work together?" She stood and propped the white envelope against the coffeemaker. "Or do you want to see me squirm a little first because you're mad?"

Magnusson stared at her for a moment longer, then took a deep swallow of his soda. "Just letting you know where I stand on this. I don't want you here."

"And I don't like getting screwed over," she retorted.

His mustache hitched up on one side, either in a smile or a sneer. "Glad we cleared the air. Now, I'm a busy man, Miz Beckett"—he bit out her last name in two staccato syllables, like gunshots—"and I don't want you causing me any trouble or upsetting my dog."

Outside, the collie continued his barking and growling.

"And I don't like people thinking they can just walk into my house whenever they feel like it." He paused, his mustache turning down in a frown. "But I guess you're right. Since you're here anyway, I may as well take you to the Hollow."

A little bubble of hope rose at this grudging offer. Maybe he wasn't such a bad sort, after all. "I'd like that, thank you."

"But first let's get one more thing straight. If you give me any reason to think you've not been up-front with me about what you want here, I'll boot your behind right off my property. Don't even think I won't do it."

Annie managed a smile, even though she'd upset his dog, invaded his house, and been anything but up-front with him. For now, what he didn't know wouldn't hurt him.

"Warning noted, Mr. Magnusson. Shall we go?"

CHAPTER THREE

April 6, 1832, Jefferson Barracks, St. Louis: It is Politics, this War. It is about Profit, and Power. A man Wants, and thus the end shall justify the means. Old Hickory may Want all he wishes. He may Want the lead mines. He may Want the Sac subdued. But I Want a horse—chastising a mounted Enemy is difficult for even the most dedicated soldier if he shall lack a mount. Congress does not Want to pay the players, yet demands a performance. I am asked to deliver the Impossible, but I swore an Oath to serve my Country and I shall uphold that Oath.

—LIEUTENANT LEWIS HUDSON,
FROM A LETTER TO HIS MOTHER, AUGUSTINA

Rik stared at the bossy bit standing in his kitchen, then turned and grabbed his keys off the counter, ignoring the white envelope propped against his coffeemaker.

He stalked from the kitchen, well aware he was acting like a jerk. Miz Annie Beckett hadn't really done anything wrong, except upset his peace and quiet, leave him feeling like a beggar, and spring on him an unwelcome surprise.

Dammit, she was pretty. Dark, curly hair, exotic-looking eyes, straight eyebrows, and an unexpectedly wide smile.

Needing a moment to reorder his thoughts, Rik headed to the entryway. While he yanked on his dress boots, the thump of thick-soled footsteps sounded on the floor behind him. When the woman followed him outside to the porch, Buck started barking, and she yelped in alarm.

Rik glanced over his shoulder. She stood with her back to the railing, leaning away from the dog, a position which pulled the fabric of her blouse tight over a right nice pair of breasts. He looked away just as she turned to him, eyes wide with alarm.

"Buck, down," he ordered in a warning tone, and the dog flopped down, laid his nose on crossed paws, and heaved a gusty sigh, as if saying: *You never let me have any fun*!

Rik walked down the porch steps toward the detached garage, where his white dually pickup and horse trailers were parked, leaving the woman to follow.

Nope, not at all what he'd expected. Her letters said she'd been working on her project for "years," so he'd pictured her older and stern-looking. Sweet young things like her should be at home giving promising smiles to a husband and tucking little kids into bed, not roaming alone around the countryside and accepting rides from strange men.

The air inside the garage smelled musty, thick with the scents of old gasoline and oil, and as a sudden heat prickled his skin, Rik pulled at his shirt. He climbed into the truck and barely waited until she'd done the same before cranking the ignition. The pickup started with the roar of a well-maintained engine, and he backed out of the garage.

When he took off in a spin of gravel, she grabbed for the door handle. "I'm not in any hurry."

"I am. The sooner I get you to the Hollow, the sooner I can get back to work."

He sped along the narrow road and around a corner, barely touching the brakes, and her knuckles whitened. "Relax, Miz Beckett. I've been driving these roads for years, you know."

"And you can still die on these roads, you know. Slow down!"

"No point. We're here." Rik took a sharp left onto a deeply rutted dirt road, then brought the truck to a swaying halt before a locked metal gate with a NO TRESPASSING sign sporting an editorial bullet hole smack in the middle of the O.

"It's as far as I drive. We'll walk the rest of the way."

She gazed ahead at the grassy field leading to a wooded, rocky patch of land that, in Rik's opinion, wasn't much to get excited about. Then she climbed out of the truck and walked ahead. In the sunlight her hair shone like polished mahogany, and the creases of her skirt skimmed the curves of her bottom.

After a moment Rik followed her, wishing he'd brought along another soda. Man, it was hot.

"Has the land here ever been farmed or homesteaded?"

"Nope."

"So these hills, all bristling with pine, maple, and oak, are as untouched as when he was here."

She talked like a bad movie—and who the hell was "he"?

"The Hollow's still up a bit. Go on."

Inside the woods, the light faded, and the heavy heat eased. The place smelled dank and earthy, reminding him of hazy, long-ago summer days spent at the Hollow, hiding with his brothers as they ogled *Playboy* magazines and guzzled Grandpa Ed's homemade root beer.

Without warning, Annie Beckett stopped and bent to look at the ground, and Rik almost tripped over her.

"What are these leafy plants called?" she asked, unaware.

"Trillium. Earlier in the summer they have white flowers," he answered, scowling at the shapely bottom thrust up toward him.

"Must be pretty." She looked over her shoulder, and her mouth tightened to a straight line as she realized what he'd been staring at.

Tough. The woman had a nice ass, and if she was going to point it at him like that, he was going to look. A twig snapped behind them, and she jerked upright, unease replacing her look of annoyance. "What was that?"

"Don't worry. The only wild animals around here are the Nelson boys down the road." Rik rubbed his palm over his jaw, eyeing her. "But you can probably handle them just fine, being so used to men and all."

She looked at him as if he'd spoken in a foreign language, then made a noise of disgust. "When you're not being obnoxious on purpose, are you sort of a nice guy? Or do I just bring out all your sterling qualities at once?"

"Obnoxious? What do you expect? I said you can work here, but I'm not gonna pretend to be happy about it. And you might think about being a little nicer to the guy who owns the private property you're standing on."

"Oh, no. Don't you go there," she retorted, her cheeks bright red. "You've got a pretty nice butt yourself, but I'm not kissing it."

A reluctant smile tugged at Rick's mouth at that little zinger. She stared at him as if waiting for something, then shook her head and marched away, hips swishing from side to side with each forceful step.

He watched her and her swishes for a moment longer. "Hey, hold up—where you going? This here's Black Hawk's Hollow, Miz Beckett."

"Please." She stopped and looked back over her shoulder. "Do my ears a favor and call me Annie."

Closing a hand over the camera hanging around her neck, she slowly walked around. As far as Rik could tell, no rock or leaf bud or sapling went unexamined—or untouched.

She stopped, aimed the camera at the trillium, and clicked a shot with a satisfied smile.

Rik watched her, frowning. Even if he didn't want her around getting in his way, he *had* bailed out on her at the last minute. It wouldn't hurt to give her a chance.

"So it really is a hollow." Her words broke across his thoughts. "A wooded coulee nestled within the embrace of a jagged outcropping of brownish red rock and carpeted with brown leaves and green, spade-shaped trillium."

She talked like she was dictating to a tape or reading from an encyclopedia, and eyed the Hollow in the same way she'd stared at him earlier, camera in hand, as if he were a bowl of fruit to arrange and photo-graph.

Weird chick.

"What kind of rock formation is this?"

"Beats me. I'm a farmer, not a geologist."

She sent him a cool look, then ran her hands over the rock. Her fingers were long, with short, unpainted nails, and she traced the grooves and cracks, touching its dips and rises as if it were a lover's body.

Enough of that! He'd better get back to work, in-stead of standing there like a fool checking out some strange woman who was likely to be nothing but a pain in the butt for the next few weeks.

But he bet her fingers would be soft and strong, and she'd be one bossy handful in bed.

"Hard . . . smooth," she said, oblivious to his thoughts. "Can't be sandstone. This isn't a glacial re-gion, is it?"

Glacial would be good, right about now. He pulled at his damp shirt again. "Glaciers didn't get this far south."

"Any caves around here?"

"Some. Not on the Hollow, though, if that's what you mean."

"How about lead mines?"

"You know your stuff," he said, impressed. "Most of the lead mines were south of here, at places like Mineral Point and Galena. What are you getting at? You're not digging holes or anything, are you?"

"I'm just asking questions," she said quickly. "Right now, I'm doing a history of the area and gath-ering details. If old Chief Black Hawk was hiding be-hind a tree, people want to know if it was a burr oak or a red pine. When you're re-creating worlds, you need to get the details right."

"I told you Black Hawk and his band didn't stop here."

"But the army did."

"According to the family stories, yeah. Fire circles from the camp were still around when old Ole built the first house."

"Ole?"

"The first Magnusson here. He bought the land in 1844, years after the war."

"Your family's lived here for over a hundred and fifty years?" When he nodded, she whistled and said, "Wow. Impressive."

The bright interest in her eyes made him uncomfortable. He took a step back. "I've got work to do."

"Then go on. I'd like to stay and take a few shots. I'll head back on my own."

Rik eyed her skirt and earth-mama sandals. "It's a long walk."

She arched a brow. "I'm used to walking, and I'm not the helpless, fragile sort."

No kidding. She'd already moved away from him, camera in hand, when he said, "You got a watch on?"

"Of course!"

"Good. I'll be back in an hour to pick you up."

"You don't—"

"Just be ready in an hour. The sun will be setting by then, and the woods get dark pretty fast. I don't like the idea of you out here alone." She'd probably fall off the bluff or something, then sue him. As Rik backed away, he called, "And you better watch out for the Wailing Woman."

She turned sharply. The tower of rock behind her

blocked out the sun, wrapping her in shadows so that he couldn't clearly see her face. "Wailing Woman?"

"Our local ghost."

Her smile flashed bright and wide. "A ghost! That's exactly the sort of detail I'm looking for. Have you seen it?"

Rik stopped. Full of surprises, this Annie Beckett. "Nope. But some of my family have, and my old man saw her once."

"Can I pick your brains later about the family stories?"

"Do you believe in ghosts?"

"No, I don't, but that's not what I asked you."

Rik laughed. "You sure can try, Miz Beckett."

"Annie!"

"Okay—Annie. Now I've got a question for you. What's this about, anyway? What are you looking for?"

"As I told you in my letters, I'm following the journey of an infantry officer who disappeared in 1832."

"You didn't say anything about the disappearing part," Rik said.

She blinked. "Only because it was too complicated to go into in a few letters."

Sounded cagey to him. "So who was he? Somebody important?"

Annie hesitated, then said, "No."

Puzzled, he asked, "It's not going to change history or anything?"

"No." Her voice had gone cool again. "My angle on this project is that it's a unique human interest story."

"Sounds like a lot of trouble for nothing."

"Depends on what you call nothing. Lieutenant

Lewis Hudson was an only son. His mother doted upon him, his father wanted him to go into politics, and his four younger sisters adored him. He was crazy in love with a girl named Emily, whose father didn't want her to marry a frontier army officer."

With each quiet word, she'd walked closer. The breeze fluttered her flowery skirt and ruffled strands of dark hair that had escaped her braid—but those warm, woodsy brown eyes had turned hard and sharp, startling him into silence.

"He came from an Ohio family who'd made their fortune in mining iron ore, then went to West Point and graduated in the top ten of his class. He was only twenty-two when the army claimed he deserted. I don't believe that, any more than I believe a man's life is 'nothing.' "

"No need to get mad," Rik said, turning away, suddenly impatient to get back to work. "I figure I've got a right to know what you're up to. Just go on and do your thing and leave me alone to do mine. That's all I ask."

Annie watched Magnusson trot down to his truck, negotiating rocks, branches, and ruts with an easy grace. Too bad. She wanted to see him fall flat on his red-necked, bad-tempered butt.

Nothing was going as she'd anticipated. And the nerve of that man, insinuating she'd better kiss up because he had something she wanted!

With a sigh of frustration, she sat on the ground, cool and giving beneath her, and leaned back against the rough rock of the Hollow.

What on earth was the key to this man's cooperation?

Only money came to mind, though he didn't appear hard up for cash. Still, he'd avoided touching the check she'd held out to him, and when she'd written to him, it had all been no, no, no—right up until she offered money.

Of course he must need money; *everybody* needed money at some time, for one thing or another.

The easiest, most convenient way to handle this would be to board with Magnusson—a kind of option she'd resorted to often enough in the past—and offer him a weekly rental fee too attractive to refuse. It'd tip the scales of control back in her direction, if only a little, and give him a reason to be magnanimous.

Annie peered through the canopy of tree branches toward the sky. Okay. So her plan was a bit underhanded. But he wasn't playing nice, either, and it wasn't as if boarding with him would be a breeze. He was uncouth, and he didn't appear to like her much, even if she had caught him eyeing her bottom.

"Lewis, Lewis," she said, rubbing her brows. "You better be here. If you really did desert and run off with some Indian cutie, I'll be pretty ticked off."

As the last echo of her voice died away, smothered in the silence of the woods, a sudden chill stole over her. She glanced at the dense brush and brittle spread of brown leaves, at massive old trees and the dried, rotting hulks of dead ones . . . but saw nothing worrisome. No wisps of wailing specters anywhere.

The light was fading, that was all. Annie rubbed briskly at her prickly goose bumps, then stood. Time to get to work.

First she roved around to get a feel for the area: up and down the bluff, then along sloping fields and a patch of grassy prairie that lay outside the woods. She followed the progress of a shallow creek as it gurgled around rocks and through the tangled, exposed roots of trees. Lastly, she climbed the rocky incline of the Hollow again, surveying the land as far as the eye could see.

So quietly beautiful—these checkerboard fields colored in green and gold and black earth, the pockets of woods tucked into seams between fields and rolling hills, all cross-hatched by country roads and winding, nourishing veins of streams. She glimpsed other farmhouses, other barns flanked by tall silos, and tiny dots of cattle in the pastures. Cows and more cows, as if Holsteins outnumbered humans in this part of Wisconsin. America's Dairy Land was living up to its reputation.

But no traces of war remained. Whatever pain and suffering had occurred here in 1832, it had left no mark.

Almost no mark, anyway.

The cost of war touched me but a little, for long ago my innocence died at that place they now call Black Hawk's Hollow.

The truth she'd come for was here: she could feel it in her bones.

Annie wondered what the Hollow had looked like when Lewis was here. Hilly, of course, with acres upon acres of trees and valleys, and seas of tall grasses and wildflowers undulating like waves in the breeze. Wild, and untouched.

In her mind, she heard words—words in faded ink on brittle paper, memorized long ago—and as always, she "heard" these in a young man's deep, pleasant voice: *I have tried to preserve a bloom. I know not what it is called, but its blue color reminds me of your eyes. When*

I see these flowers, I think of you and such thoughts, Dearest Emily, help me keep faith during these tedious days and nights. I am pleased your father warms to the idea of our marriage, but of course he is right to be so concerned. It is no life for a delicate soul.

The long-ago "bloom" Lewis had sent to his sweetheart, Emily Oglethorpe, had been a bright blue chicory flower.

It grew in fields or along ditches, so Annie made her way toward the road. Before long, she spotted several chicory plants growing beside a thicket of frothy Queen Anne's lace.

Camera in hand, she walked around the flowers, taking in details and angles, colors and textures. The sky, under a setting sun, had faded to a delicate pinkish purple.

Satisfied with the light, she got down on her belly in the dirt, twisting her body to the angle she needed for the perfect picture of a wild chicory's periwinkle flower, its simple little face tipped toward the fading sun.

To be safe, she snapped another six shots from several other angles, then stood and brushed dust and grass from her skirt and blouse. Almost absently, she plucked a blossom in memory of the blue-eyed sweetheart who'd never married her dashing young officer or subjected her delicate soul to a life on the frontier.

Annie tucked the flower into her hair, then glanced at her watch. Almost time to go. She turned toward the road and in the distance spotted a white truck cresting a hill.

She perched on the gate, watching as Magnusson turned off the road and drove toward her, bouncing along the uneven ground. He parked, leaving the engine idling.

"Hey," he called as he opened the door and jumped to the ground, sending up puffs of dust beneath his boots. "Let's go."

Annie slipped down from the fence. "Thanks for picking me up. You really didn't have to, but I appreciate it."

He tipped his head to one side, frowning a little, and Annie noticed his shirt was the exact same blue color of a chicory blossom. "You got a weed in your hair."

She sighed and said, "It's a pretty *flower*."

Without waiting for a response, Annie climbed up into the truck. After a moment Magnusson slid into his seat, put the truck in gear, and sent them lurching slowly toward the road.

Although he didn't speak, she was still aware of his solid male presence beside her, and scooted closer to the door. Several long seconds passed before she risked a quick, discreet peek at him. Her gaze settled on his hands; on long fingers with half-moons of dirt beneath the nails and reddish hair on his forearms and hands that almost glowed in the golden light.

She eyed her dusty legs and dirt-smudged skirt, the blouse glued to her skin again by perspiration—and she wore a weed in her hair, as he'd so kindly pointed out.

Oh, well. Getting ravished by Vikings wasn't on her agenda, anyway. "Mr. Magnusson?"

"Call me Rik. It's shorter."

"You live alone, don't you?"

He hesitated, then said, "Mostly."

Not the answer she'd hoped for, but close enough.

"I bet you put in some long days working your farm, which leaves that big house empty most of the time."

The tips of his mustache turned down. "Get to the point."

"I have a proposition for you."

His gaze lingered on her mouth before moving to a point below her face, then back to the road. "No offense, but I'm not interested."

The air inside the truck had grown hot and tense, and her skin flushed with anger—his intent, no doubt. Annie counted to five before saying calmly, "I'd like to pay you to rent a room at your place."

"Forget it."

"I'm offering because it'll save me a lot of travel time between my hotel and the Hollow." And the Black Hawk Inn was expensive, so moving on-site would save her money, too. When he still said nothing, she added dryly, "That means the sooner I finish my work, the sooner you can get rid of me."

Another moment's hesitation. Then, "No."

"Two hundred fifty dollars a week. That's some easy money, Mr. Magnusson . . . Rik. What do you say to that?"

He didn't answer and remained quiet for so long that Annie feared she'd misread him. Maybe money wasn't the key to this man's cooperation, after all.

When he halted the truck at a stop sign at the top of a hill, he turned toward her. "Do you always offer to move in with strange men, Miz Beckett?"

"If it's necessary, yes. My work takes me all over the country, often where there are no hotels or bed-and-breakfasts." He continued to stare at her, and she added, "I'm used to living with strangers. And my instincts about people are quite good."

His brows shot upward. "Yeah? And what do your instincts tell you about me?"

"That you're a decent guy, and can be trusted to do the right thing." God, she hoped so, anyway.

"Anything else?"

"You don't like me very much."

"I don't like surprises," he said after a moment.

Trying not to sound desperate, she asked, "But will you at least think about it?"

He put the truck back in gear and turned the corner. Several nerve-wracking moments passed before he glanced her way, and said, "Yeah."

CHAPTER FOUR

March 10, 1832, Youngstown, Ohio: I am busy making plans. Plans, plans and more plans! You shall like them, I vow, as you are a prominent and most vital part of each! I am planning Trousseaus. I am planning names for the lovely little Children we shall have. Oh, so many, many plans and you are so very far, far away.

—MISS EMILY OGLETHORPE,
FROM A LETTER TO LIEUTENANT LEWIS HUDSON

The next day, Annie left the Black Hawk Inn for the town of Warfield with a two-pronged attack in mind. First, she wanted to contact any locals familiar with the area's history, and second, she meant to dig up what dirt she could about Rik Magnusson.

The mom-and-pop restaurants, traditional gathering places for longtime natives, headed her list. If she turned up nothing there, she'd try bars, then farming businesses and, lastly, beauty salons. A man who looked like Rik had surely made an impression on the female population of this small town.

After cruising the streets, Annie chose Ruth's Restaurant, which happened to be a block from Dow's Feed and Seed.

She parked across from the small brick building and as she opened the restaurant door, clanging cow bells announced her arrival. It might not look like much from outside, but the rough-hewn interior, crowded with tables covered by bright red table-cloths, was cozy and cheery.

Mouth-watering scents of frying eggs, buttery toast, and brewing coffee tempted Annie as she made her way toward a lunch counter, and sat on a squeaky red-vinyl stool.

"I'll be right with you!" the counter waitress called, and Annie nodded in acknowledgment.

Swiveling on the stool, she looked over the mish-mash of antiques mounted on the paneled walls: horse collars, plow blades, saws, arrowheads, and household items like advertising tins and rolling pins. The restaurant owner also did a little side business selling local crafts, such as handmade wooden cows wearing bows and dried flowers, green-and-gold Green Bay Packers souvenirs, and a shelf full of wooden boxes painted in a colorful, abstract floral style she recognized as rosemaling.

A large number of antique photos also hung on the walls, showing stone-faced people standing outside white farmhouses. Above the cash register was a ro-manticized lithograph of Chief Black Hawk himself.

A fine, fierce old fellow, this Ma-ka-tai-me-she-kia-kiak, whose shaved head, spiked scalp lock, and mul-titude of ear hoops rivaled any punk rocker's regalia. Black Hawk had fought beside Tecumseh, and allied himself with the British when America's breadbasket still belonged to jolly old England. In his old age, he and his band of Sauk and Fox led the frontier US Army on quite a chase, before the army trapped him at the Bad Axe River and slaughtered hundreds of his people, including women and children.

"Okay, here's a menu for you."

The waitress's voice broke across Annie's grim thoughts, and she turned to see a friendly, round face with several chins. "Thanks."

"And a little coffee. I'll be right back to get your order."

While she waited, Annie sipped her coffee and glanced around again. With the main breakfast rush over, only a few tables were occupied. A fortyish waitress with darkly dyed hair stood nearby, taking orders from a group of boisterous, flirtatious grandpa types. She laughed and flirted right back as she scribbled on her tablet, then power-walked toward the kitchen, elbows pumping and thick-soled shoes squeaking on the floor.

The counter waitress returned, whipped out her tablet, and said, "Good morning! What can I get for you today?"

"A big stack of pancakes . . . no, wait. Since I'm in Wisconsin, how about a huge, gooey cheese omelet." Her stomach growled in anticipation of a real, artery-clogging breakfast. "Maybe a little pancake on the side. And an extra helping of bacon."

Her waitress didn't bat an eyelash at an order that would bring most truck drivers to their knees. "Want your syrup heated up?"

"Yes, please, that sounds wonderful. Thank you."

Halfway through her breakfast, Annie managed to strike up a conversation with the waitress, who rarely stopped moving and whose name badge, pinned to a brown-polyester uniform blouse over a generous bosom, identified her as MILLIE.

"A writer and photographer, huh?" Millie said as she vigorously wiped down chrome napkin dispensers. "Isn't that something. Are you in town for long?"

"A few months, maybe. I'm still learning my way around. Do you mind if I ask a few questions?"

"Go right ahead. Always pleased to help out a visitor."

"I'm basing my work over at Black Hollow Farm. Do you know where that is?"

"Sure do. That's Rik Magnusson's place."

"Do you know him?"

Millie chuckled. "Since he was a baby. His folks were neighbors of ours, back when my husband and I still had our farm."

"Did somebody say Rik Magnusson?" A young waitress, busy filling a coffeepot, turned and grinned at Annie. "I saw him the other day at the grocery store. He was feeling up cantaloupes in the produce aisle and I nearly had an orgasm on the spot!"

Coughing a little, Annie set down her coffee cup as Millie frowned, and said, "Jodie, what have I told you about saying things like that in front of the customers!"

"Well, it's the truth," the young woman said, her expression partly contrite, partly obstinate.

Annie turned to the blond, buxom Jodie. "Let me take a wild guess here: you think he's attractive."

"Oh, God, yes," Jodie said with a dramatic sigh. "But the Iceman's too busy to give a girl like me a second look. Always polite, always says hello, but I swear, I'd have to be a porn queen or something to get his attention. And here I am in this ugly uniform. Now tell me, do I look sexy to you?"

The kitchen counter bell dinged as the rough-voiced

cook yelled out a number, and Jodie dashed off to fill her order, saving Annie from trying to form a tactful response.

Catching the embarrassed look on Millie's face, she laughed. "Don't worry. I'm not at all offended."

"Young girls these days—I just don't understand them. The things they say, I swear!" Millie shook her head but after a moment, she smiled. "She's right about Rik being a hard worker, though. Even when he was just a little tyke, I remember him toddling after his pa and helping with chores. What did you say you're doing over at his place?"

"I'm researching the Black Hawk War."

"You've come to the right place," Millie said, refilling Annie's cup for the bazillionth time. "Around these parts, Black Hawk is something of a celebrity."

"I've noticed."

The cow bells on the door jangled again. Annie glanced behind her to see a well-dressed, dark-haired man departing with a wave and a laugh directed toward the Grandpa Gang.

"Why are you asking all these questions about Rik?"

Annie turned back to Millie and detected a hint of motherly suspicion in the woman's eyes. "I've offered to rent a room at his house. Just checking him out in case he agrees. You know, make sure he's not a serial killer or hiding any crazy wives in his attic."

Millie's plucked eyebrows shot toward her hairline. "Oh, my good gracious, no! A more decent, honest, hardworking young man you won't find anywhere. He's a sweetheart."

Sweetheart? "He's certainly a . . . very up-front type of individual."

Millie gave her a shrewd look. "He keeps to himself, that one. I'm surprised he agreed to a boarder."

"He hasn't yet." But enough of Rik; *he* wasn't item number one on her agenda. "Millie, who could I talk to about the history of the area?"

"Try the historical society. Go six blocks toward the park, then turn right on Main Street. But you could talk to Rik, too. His family's been here since Genesis."

"I'll keep that in mind. Thanks, Millie."

She paid her bill, an amount so low for so much food that she recalculated the check twice. After waving good-bye to Millie, she set out to find the historical society.

Main Street, with its brick and wooden false-front buildings and towering old oaks, hadn't changed much over the past century. She almost expected to see a horse and buggy come smartly along, and hear the clip-clop of shod hooves instead of a pickup truck full of rowdy teenage boys blasting rock music.

Very different from the bustling cities she was used to—but still nice, in its own way.

The Warfield Historical Society and Museum was housed in an elegant old building with decorative stonework and a carved plaque proudly proclaiming: EST 1883. This time, a door chime announced her arrival. She stood in the entryway before what must be an old hotel desk, judging by its many small letter compartments. After a few moments, a shuffling sound heralded the arrival of a short old lady with gray pin curls of a faintly bluish tint.

"Hello, hello! How can I help you today?"

Annie handed the woman her business card. "My name is Annie Beckett, and I'm researching the Black Hawk War. I was hoping you might help me contact people who are knowledgeable about the area's history."

The old lady blinked. "Oh, my. Well. Yes, I suppose so. Would you like to sit down?" She peered at the business card, nodded to herself, then shuffled to the desk. "A writer? My, how fascinating. I've always wanted to write myself. I used to dabble in poetry, but that was back in the thirties. Quite some time ago."

Smiling, Annie said, "I tried poetry once, but wasn't very good at it. Is there somebody I could talk to about the town's history?"

"Why, yes. Of course! That's my job, to help people who are looking for information. I'm well-acquainted with Chief Black Hawk. I went to the centennial celebration of the Bad Axe Battle, you know. But I was quite young then, only seventeen."

Annie's interest sharpened. "Maybe we can talk about that some time. Are you interested in history?"

"Most certainly! My father taught history at the university in Madison, and I've been volunteering here at the society for twenty-five years."

"That's a long time. You must really love the job."

The old lady beamed. "Why, yes. Yes, I do."

"I'm sorry, but I didn't catch your name."

"Oh, dear ... how rude of me." She laid a blue-veined hand across her starched blouse in a courtly, old-fashioned gesture. "I'm Mrs. Michlowski."

"Pleased to meet you, Mrs. Michlowski."

"Now, you want to speak with Mr. Decker. He's the president of the society. He'll be in soon to sign a few checks I've prepared." With an air of importance, the old lady hauled out an oversize ledger checkbook. "We're nonprofit, of course, but there are still bills to be paid. Might you perhaps be interested in making a contribution?''

Annie held back her grin. The old dear was good at her job of wheedling donations from stray visitors. ''I'd be happy to.''

The old lady smiled again. She was lovely, her facial structure dainty and shining with an inner radiance undimmed by age—and Annie had to check herself as she reached for her camera, remembering she'd left it behind.

''Then you sit right there while I gather our literature for you. It'll be only a moment before Mr. Decker arrives. Ten o'clock sharp, Monday through Saturday. He's never late.''

While the delicately mercenary Mrs. Michlowski went in search of her ''literature,'' Annie sat back. She glanced at her watch. Only five minutes or so before this Mr. Decker arrived. She was still sitting alone, staring at a glass display case full of ladies' gloves, when the wall clock began chiming the hour and the door swung open with an airy tinkle of bells.

A vaguely familiar man walked in. Dark-haired, wearing a suit. Annie frowned, then remembered she'd seen him leaving Ruth's Restaurant.

''Hello. Have you been helped?'' he asked politely.

He was about the same age as Rik Magnusson. Mid-thirties, but already with wings of gray in his hair. His quiet, academic good looks reminded her of college professors.

''Yes, I have, thank you. Mrs. Michlowski has gone to fetch me some literature.''

The man smiled and held out his hand. ''Owen Decker. I'm pleased to say that Betty is one of our most valuable assets. She's like a Girl Scout with cookies: nobody ever says no."

Laughing, Annie stood and shook his hand. "Annie Beckett, Mr. Decker. You're actually the person I'm here to see."

"Well, then, why don't we head into my office."

She followed him down the narrow hall, which smelled dry and dusty like a museum, and her every step on the creaky wooden floor echoed up to the high, pressed-tin ceiling. His office was warm and inviting, flooded with light and scented with beeswax. Every inch of wood in the room, from floor to furniture and shelves, gleamed with a high polish. After he'd seated her in a leather desk chair, he signed checks for Mrs. Michlowski while Annie signed a check over to the historical society. Then Mrs. Michlowski left, quietly closing the door behind her.

"So. What exactly can I do for you, Ms. Beckett?"

"Please, call me Annie." She gave him a warm smile. "I'm interested in the activity of the US Army in this area in 1832. I'm not looking only for historical facts; I'm also interested in legends, folklore. Ghost stories. Anything of that nature will help."

Decker nodded as she spoke. "I can give you the number of a friend of mine at the county courthouse. I also know a few other people you might want to talk to. In fact, I'm something of a Black Hawk War buff myself. What are you researching?"

"I'm writing about an infantry officer from the Fighting Sixth."

The man leaned toward her across his neat desk, interest lighting his dark eyes. "You've got your work cut out for you. There's not much available in the way of resources."

"Tell me about it." Used to encountering blank looks or boredom on this subject, Annie found Owen Decker's interest a pleasant surprise. "My primary sources are personal ones. His life is well documented up until his disappearance."

"Disappearance, huh? Sounds like a live one." Decker grinned. "A mystery?"

She eyed him, faintly uneasy with all this cheerful interest. It was probably nothing, but it made her feel protective of Lewis. "Maybe, maybe not. He was last reported seen in this area, and I'm hoping to turn up something."

"Any area in particular?"

"Black Hawk's Hollow was mentioned in my later sources, so I'm focusing my work at Rik Magnusson's farm. Do you know him?"

Decker sat back, chair springs creaking. "I know him."

Annie waited, but when Decker didn't elaborate, she said, "I plan on talking with Mr. Magnusson myself, but I'm waiting for a moment when he has a little free time."

"Given you the brush-off, has he?" Decker asked with a smile.

She raised a brow. "Why do you say that?"

"Because Rik's not much of a people person. But I tell you what, if you can get him to talk, he may give you some of those answers you're looking for. His family's owned land around here for years."

"Since 1844. I did get that much out of him," Annie said, then shrugged. "He's somewhat ambivalent about my work, so I've been reluctant to discuss it."

Decker leaned forward again. "You can talk to me about it all you want. Like I said, the war is something of a hobby of mine and I'm glad someone's willing to take a serious crack at it. The war deserves more than the passing glance it's gotten in history books."

"I may take you up on your offer, Mr. Decker; thank you."

"Just call me Owen. No need to be so formal."

Annie smiled as she stood, pleased at this unexpected stroke of luck. Maybe finding Lewis, and what happened to him, wouldn't be such an impossible task after all. "I have a couple of stops to make this morning, so I'd better move along. Could you give me the name of your friend in the courthouse, and your number, too? We can make an appointment to meet, perhaps this Friday."

"That'd be fine." He took out a pad of paper and a pen, then began flipping through a rotary file. As he wrote, he said, "We can meet here. I try to spend at least an hour every day here at the office, and we have a collection of Black Hawk–era artifacts you might want to look at."

"I'd love to, and thanks again for your help." She hesitated, remembering Magnusson's terse warning of the day before. "But between you and me, Owen, you shouldn't say anything about this yet. Mr. Magnusson is concerned about privacy issues, and I don't want any curiosity-seekers with metal detectors and shovels wandering around his property, looking for buried treasure. You understand how troublesome rumors can be and how easily they're started."

He looked at her for a long moment. "I surely do."

"Come on, girl," Rik crooned. "Give me a kiss."

Rubbery wet lips bumped the top of his head in an equine smooch. As a reward, Rik scratched the hairy chin of his four-year-old Belgian mare. "That's my girl. How are you doing today, eh? Didn't notice you limping."

The horse blew out a breath and shook her big head, and Rik laughed at the almost-human gesture. He gave her chestnut flank a light slap and the mare trotted off to join her companions, white tail flaring. He watched her trot, focusing on her white-furred socks, and detected no break in her gait. Venus had turned out a little lame a few days ago, but she seemed back to normal.

For the past eight years, he'd raised and trained Belgian draft horses. The sight of six big horses marching around a show arena at the fair, in perfect sync with each other and in full finery, was a guaranteed crowd-pleaser. From time to time, he also let them flex their muscle at local horse-pulls. Brutus, his youngest gelding, had racked up a number of wins over the past few years.

"Hey, Brutus," he called, then whistled for the horse to come to him.

With surprising grace for a two-thousand-pound animal, Brutus galloped toward the fence, hooves kicking up clumps of dirt. The ground beneath Rik's feet shook at the gelding's approach.

Rik grinned as he slipped Brutus an apple slice. "Think you're pretty smart, don't you?"

Brutus slobbered all over Rik's hand in greedy appreciation.

The midafternoon training sessions started with games and treats; then it was time to get down to business. The horses were hired for a wedding this weekend, and while he preferred Venus for such events, her first foaling was three weeks off, so he'd have to take his older mare, Marigold, instead.

Rik first worked separately with each horse, rewarding their responses to commands and smoothly performed high-stepping marches. After several warm-ups, he hitched the team to a cart. Then he climbed up to the buckboard, took the reins, and ordered the team to march together with military precision around the barnyard.

Although the horses responded quickly to commands—he had the blue ribbons to prove it—Rik remained firm about daily practice. He enjoyed the work so much that he wasn't sure who looked forward to the afternoons most.

Dairy farming might be his job, but his little pocket of paradise was right here, raising these gentle giants.

After practice, Rik turned the horses loose to roam the pasture and perched on a fence rail, watching as they wandered along, nibbling grass and sweet clover. The sun beat down on him, and he dragged off his T-shirt to wipe the sweat from his face and neck. Time to check the tanks. In weather like this, the stock needed plenty of fresh water. Then he'd get himself a little water, too.

Damn, it was hot.

A nice, gentle rain shower would be nice, even if it wouldn't save much of this year's feed crop. Like last year, he'd have to shell out a small fortune for winter feed, which would put a damn-ugly bite in the money he'd saved for year-end property taxes.

Brutus trotted playfully in the field, tossing his head so that his pale mane fluttered in the breeze, acting just like a six-year-old on a sugar overload. Rik smiled. Brutus lacked the dignity of the older geldings. Vanguard, Tiberius, and Napoleon liked to arrange themselves under shady trees like bronze statues on an old-time war monument.

His smile faded and he looked away from the horses. The quickest way to prevent his cash-flow problem from becoming a crisis would be to sell off several Belgians, but the thought made his gut knot.

Anything but that. It might cost him a dent to his pride, but hell, he'd let a stranger under his roof if it was the lesser of two evils.

No Magnusson ever took a handout, not even during the Depression. You got two hands to work with, you got everything you need.

He couldn't remember how often he'd heard his father say those words, self-satisfied pride ringing in his voice. His old man had never understood that times had changed; that what worked for a man fifty years ago didn't work now. Big business was king, and Rik had survived only because he was too pigheaded to give up.

He slid off the fence and headed toward the galvanized-steel water tank in the barnyard. He'd been angry yesterday—and bad-tempered. His mother, were she still alive, would've rapped her knuckles against his head to remind him how a gentleman should behave around a lady.

Rik eyed his dusty boots and jeans, the dirt under his nails and deeply grained into the whorls of his fingertips. Erik and Lars, with their fancy jobs, were the "gentlemen" of the family. Even Ingrid had married a city man before moving to Kansas, and the closest she came to her roots these days was cutting grass with a John Deere riding mower.

Still, three out of four wasn't so bad for all his mother's efforts to raise a decent crop of kids. Farming wasn't a life for big dreamers, anyway.

With the water-tank levels checked out, he was heading for the far pasture when a distant thread of frantic barking reached him.

He glanced toward the house. The milk truck had already come and gone, and Buck always ignored the mailman. Visitors were rare and would've known better than to drop by during work hours, anyway, so who—

Annie.

Come for her answer. With a shake of his head, Rik turned and walked back to the house, stepping up his pace when he remembered he hadn't tied up Buck. When he arrived in the yard he found the woman still sitting in her car, looking annoyed, while Buck guarded the porch.

The collie raced down the steps to greet him, rising on his hind feet to place his paws on Rik's chest. Rik gave the dog a rough, affectionate petting.

"Sorry to have to do this, Buck."

He walked toward the garage, whistling for the dog. By the time Buck figured out what was up, he couldn't dart away quickly enough. After Rik hooked the chain to the dog's collar, Buck looked at him as if he'd just lost his best friend in the world.

Man, he hated that.

"Hey," Rik said quietly. "I'll make it up to you later, boy. Just sit and be good for me."

He made his way back to the house, where Annie waited for him on the porch. His breath caught at the sight of her. She wore a white blouse and a black skirt, with flat-heeled shoes and no hose. Not a sexy outfit, but it showed off her curves and nice, long legs.

Great. Just what he needed, having a beautiful

woman underfoot when he smelled like shit and probably looked worse.

"Buck's never bitten anyone," Rik said, coming slowly up the steps. "I just said so in my letter to warn you off. He barks a lot, but he won't hurt you."

She didn't look convinced. "Discretion is the better part of valor when facing an animal with lots of sharp teeth. The car was only a little hot. It's a good thing you arrived when you did, though. I was getting ready to lay on the horn. The view's nice, but—"

"I figure you've come for an answer."

She blinked. "You've had time to think it over."

And he hadn't come up with one good reason why he should turn her away. He hated taking her money, but pride wasn't worth risking even a single one of his Belgians.

"So?" she asked after a moment, her tone impatient. "Is it yes or no? Two hundred fifty dollars a week, and I swear I'll be so quiet you won't even know I'm around."

Now that, he seriously doubted. He'd know she was around, every second of the day. Sudden perspiration dotted his forehead, the skin beneath his mustache. He took a quick breath and said, "Okay. You got yourself another deal, Miz Beckett."

She sighed. "If we're going to share the same house, do you think you can call me Annie? And please, don't look like you've just been given a death sentence," she said as he walked past. "But thank you, Rik. I mean that."

Her touch, feather-light and warm, came on the back of his shoulder—unexpected, unasked for, unwanted—and he stopped short, muscles stiffening.

At once, she pulled her hand away. "I'm sor—"

"Forget it." He cut her off, hot with embarrassment, but didn't turn to look at her where she stood in the open doorway. "You're letting in flies. Either come in or get out."

CHAPTER FIVE

April 6, 1832, Jefferson Barracks, St. Louis: Wearing
this uniform, I had hoped to render honorable service
to my Country and conduct myself in such a manner
as to make you and Father proud. But there is little
Honor in what we must now do and when I am
called upon to prove my mettle in Battle, I pray I shall
do what is right.

—LIEUTENANT LEWIS HUDSON,
FROM A LETTER TO HIS MOTHER, AUGUSTINA

Rik Magnusson didn't like to be touched?

Annie curled her hand into a fist, fingers tingling
from his tensed heat. Slowly letting out her breath,
she shut the door.

While she stood in uneasy silence, he moved forward again and worked free of his boots.

"I'll go wash up, then we'll talk," Rik said at length.
His eyes held no emotion, but a dark red color stained
his cheeks.

Annie only nodded, then followed Rik to the
kitchen. While he took a shower, she hauled her
equipment cases from the car and stacked them near
the door, out of the way. After that she leaned against
the counter by the sink, gazing out the window to-

ward Rik's fields, at their alternating ribbons of corn, alfalfa, and soybeans.

He joined her a short while later, finger-combing his hair. "There's a room in the attic. I lived up there myself for a while. It has a bathroom and kitchen. I can't promise the stove and fridge still work, but I can fix them if they don't."

"Sounds fine."

"Come on. This way."

For the first time, she made it past the kitchen. But since his shower-dampened knit shirt did nothing to disguise his tense muscles, Annie didn't ask about the knickknacks and trinkets she glimpsed in passing, or about all those old family pictures. She'd bet he could rattle off the names and histories of every one of them.

"Most of the house stays closed up," Rik said as he led her up very steep stairs boxed in by dark-paneled walls.

"Why?"

"Maid service is outta my price range, that's why."

Even if she'd wanted to, she couldn't avoid watching the muscles of his rear and thighs flex with each step upward.

Vikings—the man always made her think of ravishing Vikings.

Rik muttered something she didn't quite catch, then added, "I'm just warning you I don't have much to offer."

Huh—on an elemental level, he had plenty to offer.

While her silly heart thumped away, Annie glared at his butt. Window-shopping; that's all this was. Liking, admiring—maybe even a little tingle of real wanting—but nothing more.

"Rik, I've lived in tents, semi trucks, and a swamp shack with snakes," she said, as they passed the second story and made a sharp turn where the stairs abruptly narrowed. "Cobwebs and dust won't bother me, and I know how to run a vacuum."

Rik stopped on the last step and pushed open a small door. He flicked on a light, then stood aside. She walked past him, close enough to smell the strong soap he used.

"Will this be okay?" He motioned at the attic that had been converted to a studio apartment, with odd angles, a low ceiling, and two charming round turrets.

Annie smiled, pleasantly surprised. "It's perfect, Rik."

And bigger than her room at the inn, although that one, decorated with ruthless perfection, would be at home amid the pages of any country magazine.

No such designer touches here. The walls, ceiling, and bare wooden floor were painted white, and the only spot of color was the faded blue curtains on the windows of each turret. The furnishings were similarly sparse: a small table with two chairs, a dorm-style refrigerator, and an old gas stove.

But no bed.

As if he'd read her mind, Rik said, "I can bring up a bed."

"I don't want to be a bother. Maybe I should just stay in another room?"

"You've got more space and privacy up here. The rooms on the second floor are small."

It sounded like an order, so Annie didn't argue. She glanced back at the narrow staircase. "Can you get a mattress up here?"

"It'll take some maneuvering, but I can bring one up now if you want."

"I'm sorry to keep interrupting your work like this."

Rik shrugged, and it struck her then how his tall, broad-shouldered body dominated the room. Only the middle of the attic had a ceiling high enough for him to stand upright. If he'd lived up here, it must've been as a boy.

"I'm just reshingling the garage roof, and it's not like I gotta worry about rain anytime soon. The next milking's after supper."

Despite his words, his tone sharpened with irritation. Feeling guilty, she almost asked him not to bother—but didn't. "Okay. I'll stay here. I need to go collect my things from the inn, but I can be back in an hour. I'll write you a check then."

Their gazes met, and she could've sworn a shadow of discomfort crossed his face. He shifted. "You don't have to do that. I'll take your word for it."

Unnerved by that mesmerizing blue stare, Annie looked away. "Thanks for the trust, but I'd prefer to pay in advance."

"It's got nothing to do with trust," Rik said. "You want to be here pretty bad, so I figure I couldn't budge you even with dynamite."

That snapped her gaze back to his face. She smiled without humor. "It's refreshing to know exactly where I stand in your estimation, Rik. Yes, I believe this will work out just fine."

As it turned out, she wrapped up her packing quicker than anticipated, leaving her enough time to stop at the local market to buy groceries—and a box of dog treats.

She could get by without winning over Rik Magnusson, but she needed to wiggle into the good graces of that dog of his.

As expected, the chained collie greeted her arrival with a barrage of barking. Annie parked in the shadiest spot she could find. She unrolled the window, letting in a blast of hot, thick air, then tossed a bone-shaped treat into the grass.

Buck sniffed it once before he flopped down and went to work: *crunch-crunch-craaack.* Annie shuddered. Then, armed with the box, she opened the car door a crack. The dog looked up, but didn't move.

"Nice doggy."

Buck watched her as he gobbled a few last crumbs. She stepped closer. The dog raised his head, ears alert. His tail thumped. Cursing the perspiration dampening her palm, Annie held out another treat, letting the dog sniff her hand and prepared to jump back at the first hint of a growl. But the dog took the bone from her almost daintily, then licked her fingers as she stroked his soft coat.

Devil-dog disarmed!

No longer fearing he'd rip out her throat, she grabbed her suitcase and grocery bag from the car and went toward the house.

Once inside the kitchen, she set her bag on the table and called, "Rik? You home?"

No answer. He was probably off repairing that roof he'd mentioned, so she hauled her suitcase up the stairs, humming to herself.

As promised, Rik had set up a twin bed for her in the middle of the room, between the windows. He'd left a pillow, blanket, and a neatly folded pile of linens on the mattress—along with a key. Beside the bed sat a rotating floor fan.

Thankful, she turned it on. The attic was warmer than the rest of the house. If not for all the surrounding shade trees, it would've been ungodly hot.

Annie spied her stack of equipment cases in the far corner of the room, and guilt prodded her again at the effort he'd taken on her behalf. Kind of him, but not necessary—she was long since used to hauling the cases around.

On her way back down the stairs, Annie couldn't resist a peek at the second story's dance-floor-sized landing. The shades were drawn over closed windows, and each door to the five rooms off the landing was shut tight. Dim and dreary, it resembled a flea market, stuffed with tables, chairs, old trunks, an ancient pedal sewing machine—and what looked to be an old-time player piano.

Maybe people really had danced up here, once upon a time.

Framed photographs also dotted these walls. The oldest were turn-of-the-century, the newest she pegged as 1950s, judging by the crew cuts and horn-rimmed glasses on the men, and bouffant hair and platter-collar dresses on the women.

The whole house was like a treasure chest, full of priceless bits of people and the past, and she wanted to explore it all.

She made another reconnaissance on the main floor. Again, all the shades were drawn, and several rooms had closed doors. She didn't open the shades, though she badly wanted to let in the warm sunlight to brighten the living room and parlor, and shine upon family mementos displayed in curios and on shelves.

A pair of old painted wooden shoes caught her attention, as did fragile silver hoop earrings mounted against red velvet in a shadow box. She couldn't help but wonder at the stories and lives behind those plain, yet treasured objects.

Someday, when she was ready to settle down, maybe she'd buy an atmospheric old house just like this instead of some cute little condo.

The handmade quilts, doilies, and pillows would fetch a good price at any antique mall, but the collection of photos, chronicling some hundred-plus years of family history, fascinated her.

How nice to know who your parents were, and great-great-grandparents, aunts, and uncles, and every permutation of relation in between. How comforting to know you weren't merely a random act of indiscretion and actually had a place to call your own. A place to belong. She bet none of those people, despite their stone-faced stares, would've dropped their kid at a baby-sitter's and never bothered to return.

Annie sucked in a deep breath to clear away those dark, unwanted memories, then collected her grocery bag. This time, as she headed up the steps again, she noticed how the wood beneath her feet dipped inward, worn smooth by generations of footsteps.

Back in her room, she plugged in the refrigerator and unloaded her groceries. After that, she unpacked her camera equipment, laptop computer, and project files.

She paused, then slipped a copy of Lewis's portrait from its folder—the original was stored in acid-free tissue paper in a fireproof safe at her apartment. A young man with wavy brown hair and hazel eyes smiled at her. He was clean-shaven, with fashionably long sideburns, and wore his longish hair brushed back over the high, stiff collar of his dark jacket. He'd tied a jaunty, striped cravat around the neckband of his white shirt. The very picture of a young gentleman—not the sort to commit an act of treason.

The next folder contained photocopies of an unsmiling Gussie Hudson swathed in mourning black, a cameo of Lewis's pretty sweetheart, Emily, and a charcoal sketch by Lewis of his West Point buddy Cyrus Patterson Boone, a future Civil War general.

"You know what happened, Cyrus," Annie said softly, searching for the secrets hidden in those brooding dark eyes—but Boone only stared back with hauteur, guarding his secrets as resolutely in death as he had in life.

She leafed through another file, looking for the letter she'd happened across back in April. The letter Boone had written to his grandson in 1872, forty years after Lewis Hudson had disappeared. The letter that had compelled her to wrangle with Magnusson; the letter she felt certain proved her hunch that Lewis had never deserted, but had been killed . . . the letter in which Boone admitted: *The cost of war touched me but a little, for long ago my innocence died at that place they now call Black Hawk's Hollow, in its dark and cold embrace.*

A short sentence, but almost regretful in tone. It hinted at a guilty knowledge, some dark trauma. Why else would Boone single out this event in his old age, and after a war that cost tens of thousands of men their lives and destroyed the innocence of an entire nation? Army records listed Lewis as last seen around Black Hawk's Hollow—although it hadn't been named that until the late 1860s. To her mind, even that hinted at secrets—why should Boone know the name of an obscure area of wilderness he hadn't been near in over forty years?

The letter convinced her Boone knew much more than he'd told of the night's events. At best, he'd been an eyewitness. At worst, he'd been responsible for his friend's death and then lied to disguise his guilt.

So her goal was simple: go to the place where Lewis was last seen alive and prove he never deserted. She might even get lucky and find Lewis himself, and then she could bring him home where he belonged.

She tucked away the files and got up to open the windows wide, knotting the curtains back to let the room breathe. At once, a strong breeze billowed the faded curtains and the dead, dusty air stirred.

She gave the place a quick vacuum, and found a dusty baby bootie jammed under the fridge. She gazed at it, surprised, before slipping it in her skirt pocket to give to Rik later.

By now, the light had darkened to gold. A quick glance at her watch showed it was after six. She needed to check her e-mail, but the room had no phone jack. Grabbing the laptop, she trooped back down three flights of stairs. Just as she set down her computer on the counter, the phone rang.

Annie reached over and picked it up. "Hello?"

A young woman's voice said, "Oops, sorry! Wrong number—"

"Not if you're calling Rik Magnusson."

In a suspicious tone, the other woman asked, "Who are you?"

"I'm—" What? Annie hesitated, then continued, "I'm a business associate of Rik's. He's out working. Would you like to leave a message?"

"Sure. This is Heather. Tell him I'm coming for the weekend. This is really important, so don't forget."

There was a definite note of envy in that sulky voice.

"I'll let him know," Annie said crisply, then hung up.

Anger, brief and irrational, shot through her.

Well. Surprise, surprise. So there *was* a woman saintly or senseless enough not only to put up with Magnusson's moods, but actually sleep with him, too.

Why hadn't he said something when she'd asked if he lived alone?

Granted, the man's sex life was none of her business, but it would be darn awkward trying to explain her presence when this other woman showed up. God, she hoped they weren't the type to have noisy sex. She was a light sleeper.

Scowling, she looked around until she found a pen and notepad—from Dow's Feed and Seed, of course—and wrote a short note: *Heather is spending the weekend. Perhaps I should wait until Monday to move in? I wouldn't want to intrude on intimate moments or cause trouble with your girlfriend.*

Then, she added: *PS—I'm working at the Hollow.*

Rik slammed the truck door shut, then stalked up the hill toward the Hollow, Annie's note in his fist.

Where the hell did she get off answering his phone, taking private calls meant for him only, and then leaving snotty notes by his coffeepot?

He stopped just outside the woods, cupped a hand over his mouth, and shouted, "Annie!"

"What?" The answer came from a distance, and her voice sounded annoyed.

"I want to talk to you!"

"All right, all right . . . just a minute."

Fists on his hips, Rik waited until she emerged from the woods. She'd changed into a baggy T-shirt, a long skirt that hid her legs, and she wore those butt-ugly sandals again.

She eyed him warily as she approached. "What'd I do this time?"

The resignation in her voice knocked loose some of his anger. He cleared his throat and minded his manners. "I'd prefer you not answer my phone."

"You came all the way out here to tell me that?" She flashed him a look of irritation. "You could've saved yourself the trouble and just nailed a note to the attic door, along with the thousand other edicts you must have."

He stared at her flushed face, taken back. "What are you so pissed about?"

"Me? I don't know. You're the one doing all the shouting. You're the one who just pulled me away from a difficult shot I've spent twenty minutes trying to set up!"

Oh. That.

She was right; he could've waited, and he shouldn't have yelled.

"I wanted to set a few things straight," Rik said.

"Okay." She took a deep, calming breath. "Shoot."

He held up the note and, to his disgust, the heat of a blush warmed his face. "It's not what you think."

She regarded him with those warm, woodsy brown eyes. "Your private affairs aren't my concern. I just don't want your girlfriend thinking you're two-timing her."

Stupid, this rush of anger at her words; an anger

he thought he'd buried a long, long time ago.

"Heather is my daughter," he said flatly.

"I'm sorry I misunderstood." She cleared her throat, then added, "But since you're good-looking and single, why shouldn't I have assumed she was a lover?"

Rik stared at her. He hadn't figured she'd even notice if he were purple or one-eyed or wore tutus—so maybe the attraction he sensed between them wasn't only his imagination.

"You might want to call and explain to your daughter why I'm living in your house, because she didn't sound very happy."

"So what's new?" he said, more to himself than Annie, and looked away from those eyes that seemed to see too much. "And I know how gossip in a small town works. All I came to say is that you don't need to get all huffy and run off to some hotel."

"Oh, don't worry. Remember, not even dynamite can budge me. Now, if you don't mind, I'd like to get back to work."

He took a long, steadying breath himself. "It's almost eight. It'll be dark soon."

"I know that. I'm trying to capture a contrast of light and shadows, which is why I'm here this late and why I don't have much time left. Rik, stop being so protective. I appreciate the thought, but I'm not helpless."

"I've noticed. Look, I don't know why the hell you keep walking over here instead of driving, but I still don't want you breaking your neck in the dark on my property."

"For God's sake, I—" She broke off. "Okay. Then

you can just wait here for me. I should be done in another thirty minutes or so."

Without giving him a chance to refuse or agree, she wheeled about and marched off.

Oh, yeah, hiding beneath those soft, swishy skirts was a woman with an edge, all right. Nothing like his ex-wife Karen, who hadn't any edges to her at all.

Arguing with a woman who didn't back down, but didn't tear him down either, was a new experience. In a way, he liked this about Annie, but didn't care to look too closely at why.

Rubbing away the tightness in his brow, he headed back to his truck. He was just tired and fuzzy-headed from long hours and worries and the heat. Nothing a good night's sleep and a cold shower wouldn't cure. He swung up onto the hood and leaned back against the windshield. A little shade, a little breeze, and the warmth of metal and glass beneath him slowly drew out the tension from his muscles, and he closed his eyes and dozed.

A woman's voice calling his name woke Rik with a start. He sat up, and it took a few seconds before he realized where he was and why—and just who was calling his name.

"Must be nice to fall asleep so easily," Annie said, smiling. She had a backpack slung over her shoulder—one so big that it should've just toppled her right over—and that battered camera hung from her neck, nestled in the valley between her breasts.

He looked away quickly and slid off the truck's hood. "Just resting my eyes. Here. Give me that pack."

She backed away from his outstretched hand. "It's okay. Really."

Unwilling to argue, he raised his hands in surrender and let her heave the pack into the truck by herself and open her own door.

When they were halfway to the house, Annie suddenly arched in the seat, and said, "Oh!" Alarmed, he glanced at her.

"I found this today when I cleaned." She dug around in her skirt pocket, then held up something small and pink. "It was stuck in a crack in the floor, under the fridge. I thought you might want it."

It was a baby bootie, from a receiving set his grandmother had knitted for Heather.

"Is it yours?"

"My daughter's."

Rik went to take it, but when his fingers brushed hers, she snatched her hand back so fast the bootie fell to the seat between them. She turned bright red.

For a moment, neither spoke. With an effort, Rik kept his gaze on the road, but out of the corner of his eye, he saw her reach again for the bootie.

"Just leave it."

His tone was sharper than he meant, and she sank back against the seat, arms folded over her chest.

He slowed the truck as he pulled into the yard. The tension in the cab was thick, uncomfortable. "My ex-wife and I lived up there for a while," he said at last. "After we got married and the baby was born."

A moment passed, then she asked, "How old is your daughter?"

"Sixteen."

He stopped the pickup in front of the house, just as Annie turned to him. Her gaze tracked his face, his hair, then moved lower before she looked up again.

"*Sixteen*? Come on, Rik. You don't look old enough to have a kid that age."

"Eighteen was old enough to be a daddy," he said dryly. When she said nothing, he added, "You can get out. Door-to-door service today."

"Aren't you coming in?"

"Nope. I've got work to do."

"Oh." She hesitated. Then with a quick look back at him, she opened the door and climbed down to the yard. "Good night, Rik."

She shut the door before he could respond. He waited to be sure she was safely in the house, then sat for a moment longer in his truck.

"Shit," he said quietly. "I don't need this. Not now."

With a loud sigh, he drove the truck into the garage, then unchained Buck and let the dog run ahead of him toward the barn. He picked up a stick and hurled it as far as he could into the barnyard.

While Buck dashed after it, Rik untucked the pink bootie from his pocket and rubbed it between his fingers, his chest tightening at how small it looked in his hand.

Not so small anymore, his little girl.

Man, having Annie around was messing with his head enough, and now his daughter had decided to bless him with her presence—which meant she either wanted something from him or had realized it was way past time to make him crazy for a few days.

No doubt about it, Annie would get one hell of a show.

CHAPTER SIX

July 10, 1832, Fort Koshkonong, Michigan Territory:
We have yet to engage the Enemy, despite rumors
that spies have found Black Hawk's trail. My men
tire of building camps and are eager for Blood. Even
Cyrus questions General Atkinson's temerity. Many
companies of Volunteers have disbanded (or what is
left of them, as many have already tired of "glory"
and run off for home . . . would that I were among
them!). General Atkinson talks of marching soon, so
I am entrusting my letters to an Illinois militia man
who is heading home. Mr. Lincoln has kindly offered
to post my package. I know not when I shall have a
chance to write you again.

—LIEUTENANT LEWIS HUDSON,
FROM A LETTER TO HIS MOTHER, AUGUSTINA

"Sorry I'm late for our appointment," Annie said as
she dashed through Owen Decker's office door at the
museum. "I got caught up at the courthouse and
didn't realize traffic would be so bad on a Friday afternoon!"

Owen waved her apology aside as he came to his
feet. "Last rush for vacations. School starts soon and
about now everybody's realized they forgot to go to

Six Flags, see Uncle Joe, or get in a little more bass fishing up at Elkhart Lake."

After several days of Rik Magnusson's monosyllabic grunts, Owen's easy conversation was a welcome relief. Today he wore jeans and a white oxford shirt that suited his quiet good looks. Once she sat, he seated himself.

"Do you have children?" she asked, having noticed he wore a wedding band.

"Two, almost three. My wife and I are expecting a baby in October."

"Congratulations."

"I was a late bloomer." Owen grinned, touching the gray in his hair. "Didn't get married until I was nearly thirty. And yourself? Married?"

It was a question she'd heard often enough before, but this time she didn't laugh it away, even though she returned his smile. "My work doesn't allow time for family."

Surprise flashed in his dark eyes, then vanished. "And how's it going with Rik?"

"It's not."

He gave her a look of commiseration. "I'm sorry to hear he's being difficult."

She didn't want to talk about Rik, and answered coolly, "I do love a good challenge."

Owen got the hint. He cleared his throat. "Let's get down to business, then. I've invited over a friend of mine this afternoon. Krista Harte works at the state's archaeology office and has a background in anthropology."

"Are you an anthropologist?"

"Heck, no," Owen said with a laugh. "I got my bachelor's degree in agronomy. A glorified farmer," he elaborated at her questioning look. "I have over two hundred dairy cattle and own a chunk of land around here."

Annie couldn't help contrasting Rik's dirty boots and sun-darkened skin to this man, in his white shirt and jeans that didn't have any worn spots in their seat or knees.

"You don't look much like a farmer," she said.

"We don't all go around wearing overalls. I own Dow's Feed and Seed, which is where I spend a lot of my days. I have hired hands who take care of the chores at home."

Ah, a gentleman farmer.

"So how did you meet an anthropologist?"

"Bars," came a woman's amused voice from behind.

Annie turned. Owen looked up, his smile widening. "Howdy, Krista."

"Bars," the woman repeated, walking into the office, "are the great equalizers in a college town. There, artsy girls mix with nerdy engineers and, yes, even exalted anthropologists with lowly agronomists."

Owen came to his feet, shaking the woman's outstretched hand. "The only thing exalted about you is your height. Krista and I dated a couple times, years ago," he added.

Annie had already guessed as much. She stood, gauging the other woman, who was certainly striking with her long-legged, broad-shouldered build. A cap of short blond hair topped a rather ordinary, freckled face that, judging by the lines around her mouth and gray eyes, smiled a lot.

After Owen made the introductions, Annie sat

again. "Thank you for coming all the way out here this afternoon for my sake."

"It's no trouble," Krista answered. "When it comes to state history, I'm glad to help wherever I can."

Owen made his way toward the door. "You two talk while I get us some of Betty's wonderful coffee. I know you take yours black, Krista. How about you, Annie?"

"Cream, please, thanks," Annie answered, as he shut the door quietly behind him.

"Owen asked me here because I did my graduate work in ethnic pioneer folklore, mostly Norwegian and German farmers and Cornish miners," Krista explained. "I spent years gathering stories all across southern Wisconsin."

Annie leaned forward with interest.

"I collected a couple dozen from this area, but only three of them are likely to have any relevance to your research."

"That's better than nothing. Do any involve a ghost called Wailing Woman?"

"Yes. I've copied pages out of my thesis so you can go over everything in detail when you have more time." Krista unzipped her leather attaché case, then handed Annie a thick file of papers. "In the first story, the town of Fennimore has a haunting involving a ghostly shape on a horse. The ghost is supposed to be that of John Fennimore, who disappeared during the Black Hawk War."

"Parallels Lieutenant Hudson's disappearance," Annie said, liking how Krista Harte didn't waste any time chitchatting and went right to business.

"I thought so, too," Krista continued. "The second set is a compilation of ghost stories associated with battle sites—Wisconsin Heights and Bad Axe in particular. The Bad Axe has a haunting involving a uniformed figure said to move in great agitation along the river's edge before disappearing. Legend has it he was killed in the battle and is looking for his company."

"Lieutenant Hudson never made it to the Bad Axe."

Krista made a motion with her hand, dismissive or accepting, Annie couldn't tell.

"The other stories are similar, although sometimes the spirit is militia, like at Wisconsin Heights, or a civilian scalped by Indians. Bad Axe also has several Indian spirits, one reportedly a woman looking for her dead child. All of it's high romance, you know. The Victorians loved this stuff."

Nothing so far struck Annie as helpful for finding Lewis. "What about Wailing Woman?"

"I classify her with the Indian women of the battlefields, looking for a lost loved one."

Owen returned with three steaming Styrofoam cups, filling the small room with the scent of coffee. Once they'd settled in their seats again, Annie said, "But the Hollow isn't recorded as a battle site."

Krista nodded. "That's why I've kept this story separate. According to those I've interviewed about the Wailing Woman, including Rik, she's an indistinct spirit who sits on the promontory of the Hollow and does nothing but wail."

"Sounds more annoying than scary," Owen commented.

"I'd have to agree with you." Annie grinned, then turned to Krista. "You're certain this spirit is female and an Indian?"

"Yes, that's a consistent factor in all versions. The

usual account is that she's Winnebago, or Ho-Chunk as they're now called, weeping for a Sioux lover killed by her vengeful family. The Winnebago and Eastern Sioux were known enemies."

"What about the rest of the stories?"

"One has her murdered by a French trapper, and in another, settlers killed her lover and she killed herself in grief."

"Nothing that has to do with the war, then." Annie glanced at Owen Decker, who watched her with a small smile.

"No," Krista agreed. "But the Sioux, Ojibwa, Potowatomie, Winnebago, and Menominee used Black Hawk's revolt as an excuse to whack each other, so there may be a kernel of truth in the first story."

Annie rubbed an eyebrow, thinking. "It might reflect actual tribal warfare during the period. You're sure there's no ties in any of these stories to Black Hawk's Sauk?"

"None I know of, but the Sauk were relocated to Oklahoma, and I didn't interview any of them," Krista said. "My work focused on pioneer folklore and touched only briefly on local tribal lore. I think Wailing Woman is an explanational tale, really. I've been to the Hollow. It's windy up there, with a lot of trees and odd-shaped boulders. Anyone with an active imagination could see shadows resembling a hunched woman, and the wind in the trees sometimes sounds like crying."

Annie opened her mouth to comment, but Owen spoke before she could.

"Maybe," he said. "But when you add it to a missing officer last seen at the Hollow, and that the army camped in the area, it sure sounds like something more than a coincidence."

Encouraged by the interest, Annie plunged ahead. "I would appreciate it if what I'm telling you doesn't go beyond this room, at least not yet. I believe Lieutenant Hudson was murdered and is buried at the Hollow, and I believe whatever happened was important enough for the army to cover it up."

Owen Decker let out a long, low whistle. "That's a live one, all right. You tell Rik this?"

She shook her head. "He's already resistant to my work, and I doubt he'd let me look for buried bodies at the Hollow."

"So what are you going to do?" he asked, brows raised.

Good question. "Deal with it when I have to, I suppose."

"This is also potentially sticky legally," Krista put in. "Nobody can stop a person from digging on his own property, but if you do find a body, the police may treat it as an investigation until forensics can prove the age of the remains rules out homicide. At that point, a trained forensic anthropologist should be called in to excavate the site."

Annie didn't have to strain herself to imagine Rik's response to the local police, county sheriff, and coroner, as well as archaeologists swarming over his land. "The chance of finding any remains is slim."

Krista shrugged. "Anything's possible. I think what you're doing here is fascinating, but it's my job to tell you that history belongs to the public, not a single individual."

Lewis and his story belonged to *her*. To a forensic team, he'd be merely a bag of bones to measure and weigh, an ongoing log of scientific notations. But to Annie, he was family; a man abandoned and failed by the government he'd sworn to protect with his life, and which should've protected him even in death. A man with a very human story to tell.

She should've kept her mouth shut.

Annie glanced again at Owen Decker—and the oddly expectant expression on his face made her uneasy.

Rik leaned back from a column of swirling steam as he drained water off the boiled potatoes. Outside, Buck's barking sounded through the crunch of tires on the gravel. It wasn't his protective bark, but the "hey, buddy!" bark.

A few moments later, Annie came into the kitchen as if on a puff of breeze, skirt fluttering around her legs. He nodded a greeting, then turned back to the sink, tracking her progress through the kitchen by the *thump-thump* of her sandals.

"Mmmm, something smells divine," Annie said, sniffing the air. She stood behind him. To his left— and about six inches away. "What are you cooking?"

"Fried chicken, mashed potatoes, green beans, and biscuits."

"Wow . . . if I ate that much every day, I'd be huge. I really hate people like you, with your warp-speed metabolisms. Nice shirt, by the way. The color's gorgeous on you."

Taken aback by the shift in subject and her chirpy tone, he glanced down at his old shirt—blue denim, nothing fancy—then over his shoulder. Every time he saw her, awareness thrummed low and deep within him. "You're awful cheery."

"A good research day always makes me happy."

Since moving in, Annie had kept a distance between them. His fault, for reacting like a fool when she'd put her hand on his shoulder. Maybe letting her touch him wasn't a good idea, but he still didn't like being treated as if he were diseased.

When she came up beside him, he edged closer. Just for the hell of it.

Her vanilla-scented perfume reminded him of sugar cookies. Man, she smelled good enough to nibble on—and he figured she'd taste like vanilla, too, sweet and rich.

Rik's gaze drifted to her breasts, and beneath her shirt he imagined skin as pale as fresh cream. Forcing himself to look away, he began beating the potatoes with extra vigor.

"I've never seen anybody make real mashed potatoes before." He heard a note of admiration in her voice—and she leaned closer to watch, almost brushing against him. "Mine always come out of a box . . . and that's a lot of potatoes. Expecting company?"

"Yeah. My kid."

"Oh, that's right. I've been busy with Lewis all day and forgot."

Weird way of putting things, but then, she wasn't like any woman he'd ever met.

With one hand still on the potato masher's handle, Rik reached around Annie for the carton of milk on the counter. The instant she realized his arms surrounded her, her gaze locked on his, and her entire body tensed.

Dammit, if that didn't make him want to grab her

hands, slap them on his chest, and yell that touching him was fine and dandy.

He dumped milk into the mixing bowl. "You're invited for dinner, too." He pretended not to see her careful steps back. "Everybody may as well gather around the family table."

She paused. "You're serious?"

"If I say it, Annie, I mean it."

"Thank you." She darted another quick, curious glance his way. "So when's dinner?"

"Heather should be here in about fifteen minutes."

"That soon? I better get ready and dump this stuff, then. I'll be back down in a sec to help set the table." At the door, she turned. "You know, it's a beautiful day outside. You really should open the shades and let the sun inside."

Rik just continued beating the potatoes as she clumped up the stairs. Great. Not even in his house a week, and already she was getting domestic on him.

"Women," he muttered to the potatoes.

When she returned, she'd braided her hair and her lips looked pinker; he was pretty sure she'd put on lipstick, although he didn't want to get caught staring at her lips trying to tell for sure.

After arranging three plates, glasses, and forks on the table, she put her fists on her hips and frowned. "The table could use a little color. There's patches of wildflowers by the road. Can I pick a few?"

"I guess."

"Do you have a vase?"

He snorted. "Annie, in this house there's nothing I don't have. Check the parlor. There must be a couple dozen vases in there. Use whatever one you want."

"Really?" Rik didn't know what to say to her look

of eager delight, so he nodded again. Sometimes she was an easy woman to please.

"I love your place. It's so beautiful, all of it." For a moment, she looked almost puzzled by her own words. "I feel such a strong . . . connection here. Because of Lewis, I guess. Anyway, I'm just trying to say thank you for taking me in."

He looked away, uncomfortable. "You're paying me, remember?"

Not exactly a polite response. Scowling, Rik turned to try again—but Annie had already gone. He stood for a moment, feeling oddly alone, before turning back to the stove.

By the time she came back with an armful of colorful weeds, he had dinner ready.

"I found Queen Anne's lace, chicory, and wild daisies." She settled the blooms into one of his mother's milk-glass vases, one his dad had bought the year before she died. "And look! Foxtail barley." She held the bushy-topped grass below her nose and grinned. "Now I have a mustache just like you, only not as red."

It startled a laugh out of him.

"You should do that more often, you know."

"What?"

"Laugh. You have a beautiful smile."

Before he could find the right words to answer that one, Buck started barking.

Show time.

Annie added the barley grass to the vase, then placed it in the middle of the table and fussed a bit while he waited, his hands shoved into the back pockets of his jeans.

"How's that? Pretty, isn't it?"

Even if they were just weeds, the wildflowers did add a cheery flash of color to the table. When he nodded, Annie beamed with pleasure, eyes sparkling, and it struck him again that she had the nicest eyes, all warm brown and gold and green at once.

He looked away, and as he left the kitchen, Annie said behind him, "I'm looking forward to meeting your daughter."

"Sixteen comes with some attitude," he warned, hand on the screen door. Outside, car doors were opening and closing and Buck was yipping with excitement.

"I remember what I was like at her age." She reached out as if to give him a reassuring pat on the shoulder, but let her hand fall back to her side.

Again, Rik pretended he hadn't seen it and walked out to the porch, focusing on just getting through the next five minutes.

The dark blue Crown Victoria parked in his drive still had its engine idling. Heather, in her too-tight shorts and shirt, stood by the back of the car, pushing her long blond hair out of her eyes. The trunk was open, obscuring the man fetching her bags. The longer Rik could go without having to greet the bastard, the better.

"Hey, kiddo," he said gruffly.

An expression of anger—and envy—crossed Heather's face when she saw Annie, and Rik didn't need to be a mind reader to know what his daughter was thinking.

"Who's that? What's she doing here?" she demanded without so much as a greeting.

Rik shot her a hard look just as the passenger door opened. Karen stepped out, revealing behind her a little boy sleeping in a car seat, and try as he might, Rik couldn't help looking at the swell of her belly before he looked up at her face.

"Hello, Rik," his ex-wife said, smiling her sweet, gentle smile. "How are you?"

"Pretty good," he answered, as he always did. Catching Karen's curious glance at Annie, he added, "This is Annie Beckett. She's renting a room here while working on a book she's writing."

"You must be the woman Heather spoke with on the phone the other day," Karen said politely. "It's nice to meet you, Ms. Beckett."

The trunk slammed shut and a moment later Annie replied, "It's nice to meet you, too. And you, Heather. Your father's talked a lot about you."

The girl rolled her eyes. "Yeah, right."

Karen frowned at her daughter, then looked up at the man who'd come to stand beside her, a possessive hand on her belly.

Rik couldn't ignore him any longer. *Annie, I'd like you to meet the sonofabitch who was screwing my wife while I was working two jobs to support my family.*

"Annie, this here's Owen Decker."

Decker stood in watchful silence, face expressionless, as Annie said, "Hello, Mr. Decker."

"Ms. Beckett." Decker inclined his head in a greeting before looking away, his gaze briefly catching Rik's.

"Dad, get my bags now. It's hot out here, and I'm hungry," Heather complained.

Decker moved toward Heather as Rik started down the steps.

"Not *you*," his once-sweet baby girl snapped at Decker. "I said my *dad*."

"That's enough," Rik ordered. Heather looked at him and opened her mouth to argue, but his stern glare changed her mind. To Decker, he muttered, "I got it."

The man backed away without a word.

"Heather, we'll pick you up Sunday night at six. You listen to your father. It was nice meeting you, Ms. Beckett. You'll have to tell us more about your book some time." Karen's smile was pretty, if forced. Then her husband helped her back into the car and they drove off.

Glancing over his shoulder to make sure Heather was out of earshot, Rik turned to Annie. She looked pale. "What's wrong?"

"Nothing."

"You sure?" She wouldn't look at him.

"Nice family reunion." She turned, giving him a view of her stiff back. "Good thing none of you had a gun handy."

Before he could defend himself, she'd headed into the house. Scowling, Rik watched her go. Well, he had a kitchen full of food waiting, and even if his hunger was gone, he'd go through the motions.

He'd gotten pretty good at that while doing what needed doing. He'd let Karen go, let her be happy. He'd held his head high when he went into town and paid no attention to the looks, to the guys in the bar who slapped his back, pushed a beer into his hand, and told him women were no good for a man, anyway.

By the time he joined Annie and Heather at the table, Rik wasn't in the mood for talking. Heather ignored Annie, talking only to him when she wasn't complaining about the food, the heat, the color of the sky. Anything and everything.

Annie didn't say much either, but for such a bit of a woman, she had a big appetite—she ate four of his biscuits, as if she'd never had hot buttermilk biscuits with honey before.

When dinner finally ended, Rik began gathering the dishes. Without a word, Annie stood and helped. Heather continued to sit, playing with her fork, her insolent gaze daring Rik to ask her to clear the table and make a scene.

He should. A good father would make his kid behave, especially in front of a guest, but tonight he was too tired to play along with Heather's games.

"Thanks." He held Annie's gaze, thankful to see no disapproval in her eyes—just . . . Annie.

"It's the least I can do, after all the trouble you went to in making this wonderful meal." She turned to Heather, who still slouched at the table. "I'm going to the Hollow after cleanup is done. Would you like to come along and watch me work? I have a couple of cameras and a case full of special lenses and filters. If you're interested, I can show you how to set up and take shots."

A spark of interest lit Heather's eyes, but she shrugged and said, "Maybe. Sounds boring."

"It's an invitation, nothing more," Annie replied evenly. "I was about your age when I took up photography. Some people find it interesting, some don't. Your choice—it doesn't matter to me either way."

"Dad, can I?"

Rik nodded, baffled over why Annie would bother with a snotty kid who'd ignored her. "We'll all go. I wonder myself what she does up there all day."

"Ha." Annie suddenly grinned at him. "You just want to make sure we don't talk about you behind your back."

Heather flashed Annie a wary glance. "Yeah, Dad. You stay here."

Rik gently yanked a lock of his daughter's hair. "No chance, brat. I'm coming along to protect Annie from your sunny moods. The poor woman has no idea what kind of trouble she's gotten herself into."

CHAPTER SEVEN

May 10, 1832, Rock River: Much goes through my mind as I sit by the fire and watch the stars. Sleep eludes me, despite the day's march. Army life provides both Toil and Challenge, but it also provides a fellow too many hours to do nothing more than sit and think. What is it I think of, you ask? Soap! And how keenly I miss soft beds and warm food, decent roads and coats that do not itch. My men are gallant souls all and good company, but rough, and I miss pretty girls in pretty gowns and bonnets, their smiles and gay voices and perfumes. I can hear your laughter, Mother, as you read my words. And it is most ironic, where my thoughts wander this night. We men think we are masters of the world, but without the Fairer Sex, their fripperies and frills, we men are a miserable lot.

—LIEUTENANT LEWIS HUDSON,
FROM A LETTER TO HIS MOTHER, AUGUSTINA

Sitting on a porch rail at two in the morning wasn't where Rik wanted to be, but it was better than tossing and cursing in his bed. Between Heather and her sulks, and listening to Annie singing to herself upstairs, his nightly routine was pretty much shot all to hell. He'd tried working on his computer, entering and tracking his stock's daily stats, but Annie's renditions of old Joan Baez tunes kept him from focusing like he needed to. After a while, he just gave up.

Besides, it was too hot to sleep. Not even turning the fan to full blast did any good.

Taking a deep drink of his soda, he tipped his head back and stared at the stars.

Damn. Not a cloud in the sky. No chance of rain.

Even the Hollow was dry and brittle, the little creek down to a weak trickle. Earlier in the evening with Annie and Heather, he'd noticed that right off—before he got busy noticing Annie.

He'd quickly seen how much she loved her work—it showed in her eyes, in her excitement as she explained how a picture wasn't just a picture, but had to have "balance," and had to make "a statement of truth as well as beauty." Even Heather had been impressed, although she'd tried to hide it.

Look through the viewfinder, Annie had said to him, *and tell me what you see.*

He'd seen nothing but fields and trees and neighboring farms.

Look again, she'd said with a smile. *See the colors and lines. See how the brown, triangular field narrows and leads the eye toward the next field, then draws the eye out farther toward the blue sky and green horizon. Like an hourglass. A timeless beauty, isn't it?*

And he'd looked and only said, *Yeah.*

Tonight he'd looked through her eyes and saw his land in ways he never had before—and saw Annie in a totally different light.

The creak of the screen door interrupted his thoughts and he looked down from the stars to see a figure walk out onto the porch; a figure with long legs and curling dark hair.

Rik went still in the shadows. Letting her know she wasn't alone was the right thing to do—but she looked so pretty and soft standing there, he couldn't move. She wore a skimpy pair of shorts and top made of some thin material that molded to her body with every puff of breeze.

Backlit by the moon's hazy glow, she folded her arms above her head and stretched, back arching and breasts thrusting outward.

The moonlight showed every curve of her body, even the shape of a nipple. She had great legs and a sweet, round bottom, and, man, it had been a long time since he'd just enjoyed looking at a pretty woman.

His body responded, and he moved the soda can over his crotch while he let his other foot fall to the porch with a warning *thump*.

Annie spun with a little yelp, one hand to her throat, the other over her stomach.

"Hey, Annie," he said quietly.

"Rik? God, you scared the wits out of me! I didn't see you," she added, her tone cooler. "What are you doing out here?"

"Couldn't sleep."

The warm night breeze carried the sound of her sigh to him. "Me, either. I'm all keyed up, with a million thoughts buzzing around my head. When I'm deep in a book, sleep goes out the window."

"And you figured sitting outside might relax you some."

"That was the plan. So what's keeping you up tonight?"

Like he'd answer that. "Too much coffee."

"Ah." A long silence followed, then she added, "I'm sorry about the comment I made when Heather arrived. You know . . . about guns."

"Forget it."

She came a little closer, trailing a finger along the edge of the rail—she was always touching something. He recalled how she'd touched the rock at the Hollow the first day they'd met; how he'd seen her rub stuff between her fingers, like dry straw and Buck's fur and the thick, stiff leather of a harness strap. She'd even touched the papered walls in his house and the barn's rough old boards, as if they could tell her something.

"Want to talk about it?" she asked quietly.

Rik looked away from her long fingers. "Nope. Karen and I are history, and I don't see any point in dwelling on the past."

"Oh." She smiled her wide, sweet smile. "Well, I don't want to disturb you. I'll head back in."

She was almost to the door before he said, "You don't have to go."

"Are you sure?" She stopped; walked back. Closer this time. He could smell her skin, the shampoo she'd used on her hair. Her top had a dozen little buttons, pearly white and round, and he wondered how fast he could pop them open.

He curled his fingers tighter around the cold can. "Maybe you can tell me about all those places you've been. Your past sounds a lot more interesting than mine."

"Freelancing is a great job, though people always think it's more glamorous and high-paying than it really is . . . and as much as I love to chat about my work, I'm not exactly dressed for socializing." After a moment, she added, "And neither are you."

Rik glanced down at his shorts, cutoffs from an old pair of sweatpants. He didn't wear a shirt. "I'm decent." As long as he didn't move the can. "You're covered."

"You're staring." She leaned against the porch column opposite him.

"Well, I ain't dead, Annie." He liked how she wasn't shy; how she told a man outright what she thought instead of keeping it all buried inside. "Even if dead does seem more your type."

Her body jerked straight. "Excuse me? I'm sure I didn't hear what you just said."

"You heard me," he said, grinning.

Annie arched a brow. "And this coming from a man who doesn't like to be touched. Better look to yourself, Rik, before you start pointing fingers."

That stung. "Never said I don't like to be touched. I'm just not used to it."

"Right."

"You wanna come on over here and test that theory?"

Annie laughed, the honest, fresh sound of it wrapping around him. "Sorry, but I never get involved with my research."

"I'm not research; this Lewis guy is."

"Close enough."

She didn't sound mad, or offended. He didn't know what to make of her, but she sure had his attention— and it was good to know his sex drive still had a heartbeat. "Guess you've had guys making passes at you in the moonlight before."

"A few." She pushed her hair out of her eyes, only

to have the breeze blow it forward again. "And I tell them the same thing I just told you."

"Do they listen?"

"Most of the time. Will you?"

"I'm thinking about it."

Again, she laughed. Rich and low, like her voice. "I'm serious. You're an attractive man, but as soon as I finish my work, I'm leaving. There'd be no point."

"Does there need to be one? It could just be for fun."

For a moment, he wasn't sure who was more startled by his words—himself or Annie.

Then she smiled again, shaking her head. "I can't believe we're having this conversation. Only a couple days ago you told me you didn't want me around."

"Nothing personal. It just takes me a while to warm up to change."

Annie bounced her back against the column; gently, but enough to jiggle her breasts. The aluminum can in his hand made a sharp *clink* as his fingers closed hard around it.

"Primeval lust aside," Annie said dryly, "from what I've seen of you so far, you wouldn't know how to have a casual affair. Everything about you is responsible, rooted—and that generally rules out no-strings-attached sex."

With an effort, Rik looked away from her breasts. "Yeah, like I said—I'm not your type."

She pushed away from the rail and stepped toward him, keeping just out of reach. "Come with me. I want to show you something."

Brows arching, he eyed all those buttons again, the way the soft knit molded to her skin. Though it wasn't an invitation, a guy could dream. "Like what?"

"Don't go there, Magnusson. That's not what I have in mind. Now, come on." She wiggled a finger, motioning him to follow.

Rik didn't move. The cold can had helped, but not enough that she wouldn't notice his semi-erect state the minute he stood up.

"Come on. I won't bite; I promise."

Ah, to hell with it. She was a big girl, and probably had guys with hard-ons making passes at her all the time.

Defiant—and not a little curious—Rik swung himself off the porch rail. To his surprise, she didn't even pretend she wasn't checking out his chest before her gaze slid lower, stopped, then returned to his face.

Rik stood a little straighter, glad the darkness hid the burning heat of his flush. After a moment, he demanded, "Like what you see?"

"I'm a firm believer in equal opportunity leering, and yes, I do like what I see." With a hint of a smile, she added, "I can always look, even if I won't touch."

Annie turned, her hair swinging, then padded away on bare feet. At the door, she stopped and looked back at him over her shoulder.

Rik almost laughed. Christ! Why didn't she just wave a red flag in front of him?

"Are you coming or not?" she asked calmly.

Letting out his breath, Rik followed, but not too close.

The glow from her room provided enough light to see their way up the winding steps, with Annie a pale shape moving before him, swaying hips and long, white legs—and he was pretty sure she was putting more swish into things than usual.

Or maybe he was just doing a first-class job of driving himself insane. No way was he going to get any sleep tonight.

Once in her room, Rik looked around curiously while Annie moved toward a table cluttered with file folders and loose papers, her laptop, a couple of lenses, and the battered camera that seemed permanently attached to her neck.

He remained silent as she handed a paper to him—a painting. At first, he didn't understand, until he registered the old-fashioned clothing. "Your soldier?"

Annie nodded. "It's a copy of a miniature, and the only surviving likeness. Lewis was twenty when it was painted."

Having a face to put to a name made it personal, and Rik wasn't sure he liked that. It was probably just what she'd intended. "Is this what you wanted to show me?"

"Partly. Do you ever wonder how I found out about Lewis Hudson to begin with?"

"No, but I bet you're gonna tell me."

Smiling, she sat on the bed. The springs creaked when she crossed her legs. "I was nineteen, on summer break from college, when I decided to trace my family tree. I found out I was related to a Mrs. David Perrault, who lived in a grand old house in Toledo."

Rik pulled out a chair, straddled it and rested his arms over its back, trying not to look at the pale skin of her inner thighs and just how high those shorts went when she sat like that.

"As luck would have it, she'd just died, but I arrived in time for the estate auction. Old Mrs. Perrault was quite the pack rat, and I found this wonderful trunk of old papers and junk. I made a bid and bought it for twenty-five dollars."

"So how does the old lady fit into this?"

Annie's smile widened. "She was the great-granddaughter of Charlotte Hudson, Lewis's youngest sister, who was only ten when he disappeared. Charlotte lived to the ripe old age of ninety-seven and died in her bed in 1919."

"So you're related to Hudson?" She nodded, and he wondered why she hadn't mentioned this before. It seemed to be an important kind of detail. "And this Charlotte saved all her brother's things?"

"Her mother had." She got off the bed, then handed him another paper, this one a fuzzy copy of an old woman in black. "Augustina Hudson spent thirty years trying to clear her son's name. When she died, Lewis's letters and mementos went to Charlotte. As far as I can tell, Charlotte shoved the trunk in the attic and forgot about it."

"And that's how this all started."

It didn't make sense. He could understand a casual interest—women liked all that touchy-feely stuff—but not dedication like this, even if the kid was family. What was she getting out of it?

Annie, unmindful of his silence, rattled on. "Once I got to know Lewis through the letters, I was convinced he wouldn't have deserted." Pointing to an organized pile of folders, she said, "There were eighty-six letters, and I've annotated every one of them. That pile has copies I've made from books, genealogies, and army rosters. This one has letters from other collections, maps, and lots of pictures."

Rik was pretty sure there were modern murders that hadn't been investigated with such detail. Amazing, the time and effort she'd devoted to some guy dead over 160 years. He hadn't even gotten a decade of loyalty out of his ex-wife.

"Well?" she asked after a moment. "Impressive, huh? You understand now why I'm here, why I want to find the truth and see justice done. Even though Lewis is long gone, I believe his story is of tremendous value."

"To who?"

Her smile faded. "To me on a personal level, of course." She paused, drawing her brows together in a faint frown. "And to anybody who believes time doesn't negate the importance of justice or truth. To anybody who's ever felt powerless or lost, been in love, or dreamed of going home again. It should be of value to lot of people, I think."

He returned the picture of Lewis Hudson to the table, glancing toward Annie. "You've been working on this for ten years?"

She raised her chin. "Yes."

Rik backed away, putting distance between himself and her project—and her expectant, hopeful expression.

At the door, he regarded her for a long moment. "Yeah, it's damn impressive, Annie. But it seems to me all that devotion and loyalty would've been better spent on a man who could return it."

Bleary-eyed and fuzzy-headed, Annie leaned against the turret window, her chin cupped in her hands, and stared toward the Hollow.

It had been almost four o'clock before she'd fallen asleep, only to have the creak and slam of the screen door wake her at five-thirty. She had no idea why that man was sitting on the porch so early in the morning—except that maybe sleep hadn't come any easier to him than it had to her.

It wasn't fair. Why did he have to be gorgeous? And why did she even care what he thought of her search for Lewis?

Too bad all of yesterday and last night hadn't been a dream, including that surprise meeting with Owen Decker. The animosity between those two men had been thick enough to touch.

Frowning, she looked down at the notepad in her lap, full of doodles instead of the paragraphs she needed to write for the photograph of the chicory flower.

At a movement below Annie sat up straight, even as an inner voice denied she'd been waiting for him at all. In the murky dawnlight, she watched him walk from the house with that familiar, easy grace, the dog shadowing his heels.

On impulse, she put aside the notepad and leaned farther out the window. "Good morning!"

He almost dropped his coffee mug as he spun around, then looked up. "Hey, there. Morning."

Hanging half out of the window, like a pining princess in a tower, she called, "Where are you going?"

"Milking."

"Do you ever *not* work?"

"When I'm sleeping."

"And how did you sleep last night?"

A brief silence. "Real good, thanks."

That figured. She said, "Me too. Hey, can I watch?"

"Watch what?" He sounded wary.

"I've never seen anybody milk cows before."

"It's nothing much, and you'll get dirty."

"Rik, please don't treat me like a child."

Another silence. Then, "Make sure you wear something besides sandals and hurry up. I don't have all day."

It took Annie five minutes to dress. When she slipped outside, closing the door quietly behind her, he was waiting for her on the barnyard fence, throwing sticks for Buck to fetch.

When he saw her he slid off the fence, whistled for the collie, then started for the barn. She hurried to catch up through the tall, dew-moist grass that tickled the back of her calves.

"No boots?" Rik asked, as she hustled to match her strides to his much longer ones.

She eyed her red Converse hi-tops. "Nope. But there are washable if I step in something I shouldn't."

His glance moved up her legs, lingering at some point above her knees. "No pants, either?"

"I never wear them." Besides, the denim skirt was sturdy and comfortable.

Then Rik settled his gaze on her chest, and the ends of his mustache widened with a grin. "The shirt's okay."

"Gee, thanks," she retorted, hoping the dim light hid her sudden blush.

She waited until he'd moved ahead before peeking down at her sleeveless chambray shirt, but no buttons gaped open to display her bra's pink lace. She was buttoned schoolmarm tight.

Rik led her to the barn, made of rough-hewn timber and fieldstone, then muscled open the lower doors. The scents of sweet hay and manure surrounded her. Not a high-society scent, perhaps, but it beat stinking city buses and the sour stench of the Dumpsters in back of her apartment building.

The lowing of the cows grew louder when Rik turned on the lights, and the sudden fluttering of wings made her glance in alarm at a fork-tailed bird darting above her head.

"Barn swallow," Rik said. "She has a nest over the door. Don't worry, they won't fly into your hair."

Annie nodded, wishing she'd brought her camera. The dark, warm barn housed other creatures beside the placid-eyed Holsteins. The swooping barn swallows had made baglike nests of mud and grass, and she'd glimpsed the darting sheen of a cat's eyes before it disappeared between bales of hay.

Given time, she could find a hundred different sights and wonders to explore.

She heard another sound from outside the barn and veered toward it. "You have horses, don't you?"

Rik, unlocking cows from their stanchions, glanced back at her and nodded. She moved to the open door and just outside, not ten feet in front of her, stood a dark behemoth flicking its tail. It snorted, and she backed quickly inside.

"That's Brutus, and he's just curious. He won't hurt you."

"What kind of breed is that?"

"Belgians. They're descendants of the horses medieval knights rode into battle."

Naturally, Rik Magnusson wouldn't have aristocratic Arabians or sleek, racy quarter horses trotting about his pastures. No, *he* would have lumbering destriers. War horses.

"Well, Brutus is a magnificent beastie," she admitted, watching the animal plod away. "But what on earth do you do with horses like that?"

"I train them, hire them out, and sometimes sell

foals to the Amish," he answered. "My gang's been used for commercials, resort sleigh rides, and parades all across the state. A couple of times a year, I show them at fairs. This afternoon I've got a wedding in town. The bride and groom want to ride in a horse-drawn carriage to church and then to the reception hall."

She smiled at the image of Rik ferrying around starry-eyed newlyweds.

"Want to meet one?"

When she nodded, Rik walked beside her, then whistled between his teeth. In the enclosed yard behind the barn, one of the smaller horses raised its head. "Come here, Venus. C'mon and meet the lady."

"Her name's Venus?" Annie asked as the horse trotted over, kicking up clumps of dust and dirt.

"Yeah. She's a sweet little horse."

"Little" didn't really fit Venus. She was more like the Brunhilde of horses: massive, splendid, and able to squash mere mortal horses with a flick of her golden tail. She was made of the same stuff as those Germanic women who'd fought beside their menfolk and whupped the Mediterranean butts of Caesar's legions.

"Hey, girl," Rik said softly. "Give me a kiss."

Startled, Annie stared as the horse bumped her muzzle—did a horse have a muzzle?—against the top of his head. He laughed and scratched her chin. Venus curled her upper lip, as if grinning.

"It's her favorite trick," Rik said.

"Don't you worry that she'll . . . bite you or something?"

"I've raised Venus since she was a filly, and you won't find a gentler mare." He petted the pale mane—

almost like a caress, his long fingers slow and gentle. "She's having her first foal within the next three weeks, so I'm keeping a close eye on her."

Annie peeked at the horse's rounded belly. "Do you get a vet when she has her baby?"

"Not unless something goes wrong. I either help out or stand aside, whatever the mare needs. But as much as I enjoy talking about my gang, I've got forty cows that need to be milked. You wanted to watch, so come on."

She did more than watch; she helped whenever she could, asking questions and listening to Rik talk about milk prices and profits, pasture versus forage feeding, feed costs, crop management, and harvest schedules. He explained why he disinfected the teats before attaching the milking-machine cups, and how he had to clean his equipment meticulously, which included hoses, valves, coolers, pumps, and tanks.

"Now you know—" he grunted as he nudged a contrary cow into place—"why dairy farmers don't get vacations."

"How come you just don't hire someone to help you?"

"Because I don't need any help."

That made absolutely no sense. "But if you either hired a few hands or sold some land, you *would* have time to yourself."

"Time for what?" The look he sent her, brief and shadowed, was unreadable.

"Time to live a little! There's a world to see outside your farm, you know."

"Everything I need, I've got right here." His tone put an end to the conversation.

She enjoyed her work, its traveling and challenges,

far too much ever to give it up, but she still envied his self-contained satisfaction, if just a little.

Watching him handle the long teats and swollen udder bags was hardly erotic, but left her wondering what his hands would feel like. Would his skin be rough? Would he be so brisk, so businesslike, when touching a woman's breasts?

She closed her eyes as an image took hold: an image of dark rooms and soft beds, of Rik sweeping her off her feet and his hands moving along her bare skin with teasing slowness, his mouth warm . . .

"Annie, hey!"

Yanked from her fantasy by Rik's impatient voice, she snapped, "What?"

"I said, hand me that rag." He gave her a strange look, then added, "Please."

After doing so, Annie stood beside Rik, helping when asked, fascinated that the gallon of milk she bought from the grocery store started out in a barn just like this.

She'd never drink a glass of milk again without remembering this moment: the dry, sweet smell of hay and raw milk, Rik's hair fire-bright in the morning light slanting through narrow windows, and the muscles of his arms and shoulders straining the faded T-shirt a shade too small.

"What are you doing today?" he asked, dangerously close to one cow's thick hooves. Annie made a nervous gesture, half-shooing him back. He noticed and his mustache hitched up on one side, but he didn't shift his position.

"I'm heading into town. There's someone I want to see at ten this morning." Trying to recall the emergency first-aid courses of her college days, she looked away in time to see the cow beside her raise its tail. She hopped back. "After that, I'm not sure. I'll be photographing the route taken by Atkinson's troops from Fort Koshkonong. That'll take me a couple weeks, so I should get started soon."

"You know where you're going, then?"

"Mostly. I'd like to find some sort of tourist maps, so I thought I'd talk with people at the historical society."

Rik glanced up. Tingling beneath his icy gaze, she said nothing and kept her face blank.

The last thing she wanted was to talk to him about Owen Decker.

Shortly afterward, Annie returned to the house. Since it was too early yet to go into Warfield, she worked for a while on her book. At nine, she saved the file, shut off the laptop and headed downstairs for the bathroom. Heather was still sleeping, so Annie was quiet as she showered and dressed. Then she hoisted a purse over her shoulder, grabbed her car keys, and headed into town.

She slowed as she turned onto oak-shaded Main Street and glanced at her watch. Ten o'clock on the dot.

Annie parked and walked with determined steps through the historical society's front door and into Owen Decker's office. He came to his feet as she said, "Hello again, Mr. Decker."

"Annie. This is a surprise." He cleared his throat. "I don't have much time to talk."

"This won't take long." She sat. He hesitated, then sat as well, with less than his usual grace.

"And what can I do for you?"

"I'll be working along Atkinson's route to the Bad

Axe, and I need detailed maps." Strange, this uneasy feeling he gave her, despite his politeness. "I thought I'd also see if Betty had time to talk with me about the 1932 centennial celebration."

"I believe we have a printed guide with walking tours of the battlefield sites and routes. Betty should be back at her desk soon. She's with my wife at the moment."

My wife.

"You know, we've talked a couple of times, Owen," she said, narrowing her gaze on him. "And it seems you forgot to tell me something important."

He didn't pretend to misunderstand. "I saw no reason to mention it."

"A warning ahead of time that the two of you hate each other's guts might've been nice, but even a quick mention that you were married to Rik's ex-wife would've been enough. You knew I was staying at Rik's place. You knew we'd meet there, sooner or later." She leaned over his desk, close enough to see his freshly shaved beard, the lines around his eyes, and smell his expensive cologne. "What an awkward position you've placed me in."

"Annie—"

"And I have this awful feeling you kept silent on purpose."

His lips tightened. "Ms. Beckett, it's none of your business."

She couldn't argue with his reasoning, yet that faint, oily feeling didn't abate.

"Owen? What's going on in here? What's wrong?"

Annie stood and turned to face Karen Decker, who held a shielding hand over her belly. She looked as delicate, as waxy-pale, as an Easter lily.

"Mrs. Decker," Annie said, nodding toward the woman. Then she turned back to Decker, who hadn't moved from the desk. "I'll go see Betty now."

As she walked past Rik's ex-wife, she heard the woman say, "What was that about? Is it Rik? Owen, what have you done?"

Following a short chat with Betty, Annie drove back to the farm, taking the winding roads at a fast clip. She cranked open the windows to let the wind rush through her hair and blast her face with its dry heat.

God, what would Rik do if he found she was working with a man he hated? At best, he'd be angry with her. At worst he might send her packing, even cause all sorts of complications in her search for Lewis.

Annie took a deep, calming breath. What she needed was a little quiet time in the porch swing. She'd relax with a glass of iced tea and think her way out of this little mess.

But when she arrived back at the farm, it was High Noon at the Magnusson homestead, with a showdown in progress between father and daughter.

"I am wearing this!" Heather's high, strident voice carried clear out of the house and into the yard.

"Over my dead, bleeding body," Rik answered mildly.

"Dad!"

"No. And that's final."

"Hello!" Annie called as she walked into the kitchen.

They both looked back at her. Buck, lying on the rug in front of the sink, didn't raise his head. He just rolled his eyes in her direction, as if this ruckus was old news.

The sight of Rik in a tuxedo—the contrast of tanned

skin and white cotton, of his rugged good looks against the formal, tailored lines—brought Annie up short. My, but he cleaned up nicely.

Heather, on the other hand, wore next to nothing— a bit of black knit fabric with spaghetti straps that showed off her slim young figure to perfection. The girl was lovely, with her pouting child-woman face and fresh skin, and Annie's maternal instincts went on Red Alert just looking at her.

"How was your trip into town?" Rik's curt question cut across the silence. Judging by the high color in his cheeks, he was either hot or angry. Or both. "Did you see who you wanted to see?"

She glanced away, hating this sudden rush of guilt. "Yes, thank you. And don't you both look wonderful. Heather, are you going to the wedding with your dad?"

"Not in that thing," Rik retorted. "You're up front on the buckboard with me and you'll burn parts of your body that were never meant to see the sun."

"I like this dress. God, why do you always treat me like I'm some stupid little kid!"

"Because you're sixteen, not twenty-six!"

"Mom and Owen aren't this strict. Owen lets me dress the way I want."

"Tough. You're my daughter, not his, and under my roof you dress the way I tell you."

Heather glared at Annie. "Do I look like a slut?"

"Heather, I didn't say—" Rik began.

"No," Annie said at the same time. "Although I think that dress is too eye-catching for a wedding. You want to look pretty, but you don't want to up- stage the bride. That's tacky. You don't want anybody thinking that about you, do you?"

Heather glanced at her father, then down at her bare feet and red-painted toenails. "No. It's bad enough everybody thinks that about my mother. I'll go change into something really ugly so nobody will even look at me."

The sound of Heather's angry footsteps faded away in the awkward silence, and Annie turned to Rik. "She's a very pretty girl, and you're right to be concerned, but that didn't turn out quite like I intended. Sorry, I should've just kept my mouth shut."

"Don't take it personally. With Heather, you're damned if you do, damned if you don't. I wish she'd stay home, but there's a few friends—and some boy— she wants to see." He paused. "The divorce was pretty hard on her."

"Growing up generally is."

"And she's in such a damn rush to grow up! Every time a boy comes near her, I wanna grab the little punk and kick him from here to Sunday." Rik ran a hand through his hair, messing its smooth, combed lines. Then he flashed a rueful smile; looking almost shy and sweet. "I know what's going on in the minds of those boys, even if Heather won't see it my way."

Considering he'd been a teenage father, moments like this couldn't be easy and she wanted to do something, anything, to help.

"I can ask Heather if she wants to come along and help me work today."

Rik shook his head, although his smile remained. "Thanks, but baby-sitting a sixteen-year-old isn't what you're here for." Across the kitchen, his gaze caught hers. "You do what you need to do, I'll do what I need to do, and things will work out."

CHAPTER EIGHT

July 5, 1832, Michigan Territory: Savage. What a wonder in this word, and such a puzzle to ponder. How does one determine a Savage? From the garments he wears? I dare say not, as I would not be admitted to fine drawing rooms as I am now. Is it the Color of his skin? That cannot be, as the sun has burned me Red as old Black Hawk himself. Is it the language he speaks? There are men among the troops I cannot understand, yet I do not call them Savage. Is it the God he worships? How, when in this land the Gods themselves are wild and distant. I cannot say what is a Savage. But I am told I must shoot him, lest he shoot me. Thus, when friends and family ask after me, Mother, tell them I am engaged in hunting for Savages. It shall be truth, and oh, it has such a noble ring.

—LIEUTENANT LEWIS HUDSON,
FROM A LETTER TO HIS MOTHER, AUGUSTINA

The first sight to greet Annie when she walked outside early the next morning was Rik's bare chest. He sat on the porch rail, a steaming coffee mug tucked between his thighs, and was slicing an apple with his pocketknife.

Without a jolt of caffeine to bolster her nerves, it was way too early to contend with broad shoulders, nice muscles, and all that tanned skin.

"Good morning, Rik," she managed to say cheerfully enough, shrugging into her heavy backpack and readjusting her camera strap—more to avoid looking at his chest than anything else.

He raised a speared slice of apple in a lazy greeting. "Where you headed?"

"To the Hollow."

"You're not walking over there again, are you?"

His gaze traveled over her body, head to toe, lingering on her breasts—and Annie had to fight back the urge to check her buttons. Again.

"Yup," she said, moving down the porch steps.

"It'd be a hell of a lot quicker if you'd drive."

Annie turned, his unsolicited advice grating more than usual. "I'm getting a feel for what it was like to march while wearing a heavy pack. Lewis was infantry, not cavalry."

Rik's fair brows shot upward. "It'll be hot today. Upper nineties, and the humidity's gonna be a bitch."

"It's not so bad in the woods, and I've brought along water." She tapped the plastic bottle attached to her pack.

He held out a piece of his apple. "Want one?"

Tempting, but she kept her distance. "No thanks."

"Suit yourself," he said, swinging off the porch. "See you later."

Annie waved, then quickly started for the fields, very aware of his gaze upon her. She'd meant to get an early-morning start—it was a long walk and already the heat and humidity wrapped around her like a suffocating blanket—but she'd hoped to avoid Rik.

He was usually in the barn by six and it was much later than that now.

"Get a grip, Beckett," she muttered.

Focus: on her work, on the fields she trudged through. Even if it wasn't prairie, the knee-high alfalfa gave an idea of what it must've been like to march through wilderness at the height of summer in full uniform. In August, when Black Hawk found himself trapped at the Bad Axe River between Atkinson's troops and the steamboat *Warrior*, the weather must've been as ungodly hot as this.

It took a good half hour before she reached the Hollow, and as she walked along the fence line one of Rik's Belgians trailed along beside her, ears pricked forward in curiosity. Smiling, she stopped briefly to stroke its long, flat nose.

At the Hollow, Annie climbed to the promontory and looked across the twisted trees and massive, weatherworn boulders squatting upon its flatter surface. Today, she wanted to photograph the bluffs and capture something of the darkness, the ancient wildness, she sensed still existed here.

The winds buffeted strongly, and she put her pack down to tie back her hair. Even if she'd found no spirits at this place, the wind certainly howled like a maddened thing.

Now, which was the best angle for her shots? The straight plunge to the ground, or the slow, sloping descent into the woods, where the rock curved inward on either side like beckoning fingers?

The first was dramatic, even violent, but the second beguiled with its lines that drew the eye downward and then looped back around into itself. A continuum, almost. An unbroken circle.

Perfect.

Humming to herself, she unpacked her lenses and tripod, then took a sip of water to chase away the ever-present dust and again regretted it wasn't coffee or tea. She hadn't slept well last night after Heather had departed earlier than planned, and under a pall of hostility. The girl hadn't bothered with a word of farewell to her father, much less a hug or any token of affection.

Rik had disappeared for the remainder of the night, and she'd heeded the unspoken warning by leaving him alone.

With a snort of annoyance, Annie stood up straight. Damn—he'd wiggled past her mental DO NOT ENTER zone again.

She set up her camera and, forty minutes later, was satisfied enough with the light to take her shot. Then she sat cross-legged at the top of the Hollow to write for a few hours.

Involved in her thoughts, she almost didn't hear the faint, distant shout carried by the wind.

"Annieeeee!"

Rik. Again? For a man who claimed to be so busy and who didn't want to be bothered, he certainly went out of his way to seek her out.

"What do you want?" she hollered back.

"I've come to get you for lunch."

Lunch? A lame excuse, if she'd ever heard one. But if she ignored him, he'd just come after her. Frowning, Annie stood, struggled into her pack, and picked her way down the Hollow—taking her own sweet time, however.

Catching sight of Rik, she stopped short. He hadn't come in his truck, but on one of his big Belgians. The sight of him on the horse's bare back—so out of time and out of place—sent a shiver sliding down her spine.

"What on earth are you doing?"

"It's called riding a horse," Rik answered dryly. He wore aviator-style sunglasses and had pulled the bill of his cap low, shadowing his face.

"Where's your truck?"

"In the garage. Brutus here needed a little exercise." He patted Brutus's neck while the horse nibbled grass. "So I figured I'd come get you."

"You want me to get up on that thing?" Annie stared at the horse. Its back seemed to loom a hundred feet off the ground, and its hooves looked as big as her head.

"Works best that way."

She ignored the sarcasm as it suddenly occurred to her getting up on the horse meant she'd have to touch him. She edged closer. "Are you sure you want that?"

The tips of his mustache lowered, but he gave a curt nod, then held out his hand.

For a moment, Annie stared at the strong, square palm, those long fingers. His skin was hardened by work and marked with scratches that, in the way of men, went unheeded and undoctored.

"I really don't think this is a good—"

"Stand on that boulder and take my hand," he interrupted, his voice gruff. "You can swing yourself up."

Annie grasped his hand. His skin was warm, dry. She stepped up on the boulder, backpack and all, and with Rik's help swung herself behind him and across the horse's broad back.

"Hold on," he warned, then pulled up on the reins. "C'mon, boy. Let's go."

As the mountain beneath her moved, Annie grabbed Rik's waist and squeezed tight enough to feel every ridge of his ribs. The warmth of his skin radiated outward, and his shirt felt damp with perspiration and humidity. His hair smelled like wind.

"Annie, I can't breathe. Loosen 'er up some—you won't fall."

"Sorry," she mumbled against his shoulder, and loosened her grip—a little.

Her legs stuck out at an uncomfortable angle, and the coarse horsehair itched against the bare skin of her inner thighs. She was too afraid of toppling off a ton of horse to scoot back from Rik. She squirmed; cursing Brutus's scratchy hide, the warm male body in her arms, and the horse's plodding pace.

"How long will it take Brutus to get back to the house? Can he run?"

Rik laughed. "Run? Not unless you want to end up on your butt on the ground. Relax, Annie. You'll enjoy a slow ride."

Intentional or not, his words brought to mind an image of slow, lazy lovemaking. And with the feel of his body against hers, every inch of her tingled. Mmm-hmm, there was nothing like an armful of prime beefcake to make a woman appreciate her basic biological drives.

Annie bit back a smile. The horse ambled along the fence line, and from time to time, Rik patted Brutus's thick, damp neck and murmured to him. The Belgian's ears rotated like radar dishes, as if intent on picking up every word.

After a few minutes, mild resentment took hold of

her that he was talking to a horse and ignoring her. Worse, the press of a moving animal against one of her more erogenous zones made her all the more sensitive to the movement of Rik's muscles beneath her palms, the warmth of his skin, her breasts against his back, and her bare legs tucked behind his denim-clad thighs. In the bright sun, his hair shone with a hundred different shades of copper and gold, mesmerizing her with the intensity of its color.

A bead of sweat coursed down his sun-browned neck to pool in the hollow at the base of his throat. She wanted to catch the drop on the end of her finger—oh, he had a beautiful, strong neck. The sort of neck that invited playful love bites and slow dancing in the dark.

And all she had to do was slide her hands mere inches downward to touch him—persuade him—that he'd be much happier paying attention to her instead of a big, smelly horse.

A tingling ache spread through her. God—wasn't that just like a libido, reminding her at the worst possible moment that it was still alive and kicking.

"Good boy," Rik said again, patting the horse.

That did it. "You prefer animals to people, don't you?"

Rik didn't turn, although his hand stilled a moment before he continued petting the pale mane. "Maybe. Animals don't lie, or pretend to be your best friend and then steal your wife."

Annie stared at his broad back, at the hair curling at the nape of his neck, and registered the anger crackling just below the surface of his even words. "I'm sorry. I had no idea."

He glanced over his shoulder. "You mean Decker didn't tell you?"

A chill of alarm dispelled her languid warmth. "Tell me what?"

"I'm not stupid, Annie. Don't think I didn't notice you and Decker had met before I 'introduced' you the other day."

She looked down. "I didn't know about Decker's connection to you when I first met him, and he somehow forgot to fill me in."

"That's his style. You probably have something he wants—watch your back."

Decker . . . smiling, well-dressed, and ever so polite and helpful. "I can't possibly have anything Owen Decker could want."

"Don't be so sure of that."

All her guilt, building since the morning she'd ignored his phone call, overwhelmed her. Staring at a point between his shoulder blades, Annie took a deep breath and plunged on. "Rik, I have to tell you something."

The muscles beneath her hands went rigid. "I don't—"

"When you first called me and said you'd changed your mind about my visit, I was home, but I didn't answer."

A long silence passed. Tensed, Annie waited for the backlash of his anger—but all he said was, "Why?"

"I . . . well, I didn't want to." That sounded mature! She sighed, and added, "Finding out what happened to Lewis was too important for me to give up."

He nodded, then said again, "Why?"

"Because to me, Lewis is—" She shifted on the horse, suddenly angry and tired of his questions.

"Forget it. It's complicated, Rik, and you wouldn't understand."

"Try me. I'm good at complicated."

Perspiration prickled her scalp and slicked the palms of her hands. God, it was so hot, and the humidity just hung in the air, sullen and heavy. "I'd rather not talk about it."

Or couldn't, without coming across as an idiot. She could imagine the look on Rik's face as she tried to explain.

The silence lengthened, stretching her nerves. Up ahead, she could see a patch of white amid the green trees. The house, at long last.

Rik didn't speak again until they were at the barnyard fence. "You can get off here."

"Okay." But she didn't move. God, it was a long, long way down. "What's for lunch?"

"Beats me."

"Oh." Annie digested that bit of news, anger rising. "So why did you really bring me back?"

"I wanted to get you away from the Hollow." He maneuvered his leg over the horse's neck, then slid to the ground, leaving her to glare down at him.

"I know you don't think too highly of my work here, but you have no right to interfere like this."

Opening the gate to the barnyard, he said, "I'll get us something to eat after I settle Brutus. Come on down."

"No," she retorted. "I think I'll sit up here all day. I rather like the view."

Rik lifted his arms. "C'mon, Annie. I'll catch you. I promise."

Some choice: try to get off by herself and possibly do something stupid enough to get stepped on or dragged, or let this miserable worm of a man touch her.

But already her thigh muscles ached, and her chafed skin had started to sting in earnest, so she grasped Brutus's treelike neck and clumsily maneuvered around until she was draped over the horse's back. From there she slid down into Rik's waiting arms and quickly turned to face him.

If not for her anger, she might have enjoyed having his arms around her. But when he didn't release her, the confining tightness of his hold filled her with unease.

"Okay, I'm safely on the ground. You can let me go now."

He did; a little too quickly and easily, without even trying anything—and this pinch of disappointment was the last straw. The whole situation was ridiculous. It was time to put a stop to it.

"Rik, I meant what I said the other night. I think you're attractive, but while I may be tempted, I'm leaving when my work is done. I won't start anything I can't finish."

"Then I figure you've never finished much of anything before, seeing how you're always on your way to somewhere else."

"I'm sure there's a point to this?"

"Yesterday you told me to live a little, but it seems to me you should follow your own advice."

Annie glared at Rik, who leaned against the fence with that maddening, easy grace. "I have lived, and more than a little. I've seen more of this world in ten years than most people will see in their entire life!"

"That must make it hard on any guys interested in pinning you down for a while."

She folded her arms over her chest, hating how his sunglasses hid his eyes so she couldn't tell if he were teasing her. "Not that this sudden obsession about my sex life is any of your business, Rik, but I *have* let interested guys pin me down a time or two. Quite enjoyably, I might add."

He didn't need to know there hadn't been anyone in a long time, or that her relationships rarely lasted more than a few months.

With a sudden dismay, she realized this was exactly his point.

"You got yourself another interested man right here, even if I'm staying put and still breathing," Rik said. "And just what are you gonna do about that, Annie?"

The casual question left her speechless, and she could only stare at him. He leaned back against the fence, hooking his thumbs in his belt loops, hands framing his groin. A wholly male gesture; a sexual challenge.

Though her voice betrayed none of her fury, her hands shook with the force of it. "You'll excuse me if I decide to pass on your generous offer, since I don't feel I need any 'fixing.' You're an arrogant jerk, you know that?"

He pushed away from the fence. "Maybe. But it doesn't change the fact I want you, Annie."

He led Brutus into the barnyard, leaving her immobilized by shock . . . and something else that slid past the barrier of her anger.

It had been such a long, long time since a man had stirred anything within her—and not a single one of her past lovers had ever said so simply: *I want you.*

*   *   *

After removing the bridle, Rik let Brutus trot off to join his companions. He turned back to Annie in time to catch the shadow of fear darkening her eyes.

Great. He'd just scared the stuffing out of her. Wasn't he one hell of a smooth operator?

"I'm going back to the Hollow," she said suddenly, taking a step back.

He grabbed her arm before she could bolt. "No, you're not."

With a low hiss, she tried to shake free. "I don't believe this! Why don't you just drag me around by my hair?"

"I might. Or I could toss you over my shoulder, so quit making a fuss."

He didn't mean it—yet he eyed her body, gauging her weight. He could sling hay bales that weighed more than she did, so it wouldn't be hard to haul her over his shoulder . . . except she'd probably slug him if he tried.

All the same, he imagined her squirming against his shoulder, that sweet ass of hers right close and her yelling words like "pig" and "barbarian" at him.

"Rik Magnusson, don't you even think about it!"

With his free hand, he smoothed away his grin. "Too late for that."

And too late to hide how his imaginings had given him one hell of a hard-on.

Up the porch he went, pulling her willy-nilly behind—but not holding her so tightly that she couldn't have pulled away if she really wanted to.

Guilt flashed through him anyway, and he could almost see his mother standing right there on the porch, shaking her head at him in disgust.

Shit.

There was nothing high-minded about his intentions, that was for sure. Lust had been chewing away inside him, sharp and keen and constant, ever since that night on the porch.

Man, he wanted to get her alone in a dark room on a soft bed, and pull her long skirt up and up and up. Then he'd give her a hard dose of loving, and a harder dose of reality. A woman fine as her, just wasting herself, was a damn shame.

Inside the house, he dropped her arm and began unlacing his boots. "Don't give me that uppity look. I bet you didn't even take a lunch with you."

"What is it with you and lunch? What does it matter if—"

"You need to eat," Rik retorted. "Otherwise, those winds at the Hollow will carry you clear over to the next county."

Although it seemed impossible, her eyes grew even wider. "You're worried about me?"

"No," he said, a little too quickly, as he headed toward the kitchen. "You strike me as being distracted, that's all."

"I do sort of forget things when I'm working."

From the sound of her sandals, she'd come right behind him where he stood before the open fridge. A shiver took him—probably because of the blast of cool air.

Rik gathered some fixings, then dumped them on the counter. After he washed his hands, he began making a sandwich. "Butter or mustard?"

"I can make my own lunch!" Annie snatched the bread out of his hand. As she mutilated the soft slices with the hard pat of butter, she shot him a quick glance. "That was pretty blunt, what you said back there."

"I don't play games. What you see is what you get."

This time her look was slow and deliberate, moving down his body and then upward again until she caught his gaze.

And the thought hammered him again: there'd be no harm in it if they were both honest, both agreeable and clear-eyed, and Christ, he recognized the need in her eyes right now.

"I'm going to leave," Annie said, so softly he almost didn't hear.

"I know."

Even if she wasn't a woman who could settle down, and he wasn't a man with much to offer, he could still give her something a dead man couldn't, and she could still stay long enough to soothe the deep bite of his loneliness.

Rik rested his hand over hers, fisted as she gripped the knife, and rubbed a thumb over her whitened knuckles. "Try brown mustard. It's good with roast beef and a lot easier on the bread."

Annie turned her face away, as if suddenly shy. "How can you talk about sex and bread and mustard, all at once like that?"

"Because if I don't keep talking, I'll do something I shouldn't."

Annie took a deep breath, pressing her breasts against her shirt, and Rik nearly groaned at the sight. The silence stretched on, and finally he pried the knife away and laid it on the counter. She wouldn't look at him until he hooked a finger under her chin and tipped her face upward. Smiling a little into her wide eyes, he brushed his thumb over the swell of her lower lip—moist and full and meant to be kissed.

"Guess I'm gonna do it anyway," he said, and his voice sounded strangely regretful to his own ears.

Then he slipped his hands into her soft hair, still warm from the sunshine, and tilted her head, bringing his own down until he fit his mouth against hers.

A kiss; just a brush of lips—then a crack in a crumbling earthen wall, and all the needing and the wanting shot through him at once.

Before Rik could stop himself, he'd pulled her close and she just dissolved against him, like heated honey on a biscuit. She soaked right into him, and he slid his hands down her back to her hips, bunching her fluttery skirt in his fingers and sliding it up and up and up.

She made a soft sound deep in her throat, kissing him with such force that he had to lean against the counter to keep from toppling over. When she pressed her hips against his erection, he was ready to hit the floor with her.

Annie's tongue stroked his lips until he opened his mouth and let her inside. Her mouth tasted sweeter than any sugar cookie ever could. His searching fingers found satinlike underwear, and her skin . . . oh, man, her skin was soft and smooth.

"You feel real good," he got out between kisses, his breathing coming fast and hard. "Just like I knew you would. God, Annie, I want you so bad."

She pulled back at his words. The separation registered and he resisted, but her hands firmly pushed against his chest.

"Whoa. Slow down. Rik, I mean it!"

Good going, Romeo. Just what a woman wanted to

hear, how bad he wanted to screw her. Why couldn't he have tried for some romance?

Rik gave the firm, round flesh of her bottom a last, regretful squeeze, then slid his hands out from her underwear and let her skirt fall down around her legs again.

Annie scooted a little distance away, looking too much like a deer cornered by dogs for his comfort. He ran his fingers through his hair, then stared long and hard at the open jar of mustard. "I'm not apologizing."

"No apology required," she said quickly. "I wanted you to kiss me. It's just . . . well, a little more than I expected."

She'd turned pink with embarrassment, but it didn't stop him from demanding, "More than what? I'm not looking for some Sunday school picnic date here, and you know it."

She was silent, then, said, "Rik, I'm not used to men who . . . I mean, what I need is a little maneuvering room here—I need . . . oh, hell, what I need right now is a beer. Too bad I don't drink. Got anything else that's cold and wet?"

Despite his frustration, her flustered expression drew laughter from somewhere deep inside him, a place dry for far too long. "Yeah, I got whatever you want, Annie. All you need to do is ask."

CHAPTER NINE

May 13, 1832: I fear a lady of Good Character should not have such immoderate thoughts, but oh, how I Burn for us to share sweet intimacies, in a little hidden corner of our own, in a little black part of the night. Fie upon them, who would keep us apart! Hurry home, my Love, my Hero, my Heart.

—Miss Emily Oglethorpe,
from a letter to Lieutenant Lewis Hudson

Faced with an overwhelming assault on her senses as well as her common sense, Annie threw herself into her work for the rest of the week, avoiding Rik. She traveled and photographed Atkinson's marsh-ridden route to the Bad Axe, and wrote in a heat of inspiration fueled by anxiety and sharp, restless lust.

That's all it was; just good old-fashioned lust, and she wouldn't mistake Rik's actions for anything more than a man trying to get under her skirts any way he could.

She hadn't expected such fire under all that Nordic ice.

Returning to the farm Friday night, weary and edgy, Annie found the house and outbuildings dark. She didn't know where Rik had gone, but it was a relief not to find him waiting with that watchful look in his eyes.

He'd left her mail on the table, including a FedEx package from a librarian in Oklahoma. Rik might not trust Decker, but so far Owen's contacts had proven to be helpful, and despite their little confrontation, he'd continued to be polite and friendly. This persistent unease she felt toward the man was likely nothing more than guilt on her part.

Annie grabbed the envelope and dashed up the stairs, but didn't open it until she'd taken a shower.

Inside the package were copies of interviews with survivors of the Bad Axe massacre. She didn't expect to find anything related to Lewis there, but she'd read through it all anyway. For a moment, as she glanced out the window into the darkness toward the Hollow, the impossibility of it all overwhelmed her.

How could she ever hope to find Lewis out there? She hadn't a clue where to begin looking. With a sigh, Annie picked up the copy of Boone's portrait and scowled at his haughty gaze.

"The least you could've done was draw me a map with a nice, tidy X on it."

The hours ticked by as she read, sometimes making notations or pulling out files, sometimes tapping her pencil against the table as she stared outside at the splash of stars, wondering where Rik had gone.

A glance at the clock showed it was after midnight. With a soft groan, Annie stood and stretched her cramped muscles. Time for a tea break.

She grabbed a robe to cover her nightshirt—a baroque affair of netting and lace she'd been too weak to resist—in case Rik showed up. Rather than turning on lights, she took a lighted bayberry candle and quietly made her way down the stairs. After several weeks in this house, she'd learned how to avoid all the creaky spots.

In the kitchen, she set the candle on the counter and tossed her robe over the back of a chair. As always, the fussy room made her smile. She'd love to have tea in one of those antique china cups—how else could one *do* tea as it was meant to be *done*?—but instead selected a stoneware coffee mug from Rik's extensive collection.

It struck her as sad somehow that a man who had so many dishes lived alone.

While the water heated, she leaned back against the counter and yawned. Buck, who usually passed his nights on the porch, lay flopped on the floor in front of the bathroom door. He perked his ears when he saw her, but didn't bother getting up.

She glanced at the darkened doorway leading from the kitchen. Rik's bedroom was just off the living room. He usually kept the door closed, but tonight it was open and the room was dark.

Where could he be at this time of night?

Probably picking up girls in the cantaloupe aisle at the local market. She glowered down at her bare toes, not caring a fig where that down-home Don Juan was. Not really.

The whistling of the teakettle broke across her thoughts, and she took the kettle off the burner and began pouring the steaming water into her mug.

"Annie?"

With a gasp, she jerked her hand back and sloshed water over the counter and floor.

"God, Rik, are you making a habit out of scaring me to death? I almost spilled boiling water all over myself!" She peered through the hazy darkness. "I never heard your truck come back. And where *are* you, anyway?"

"In the bathroom."

"In the dark?" She couldn't see any light from under the bathroom door, but Buck blocked most of it. "Don't come out yet. I'm not decent."

"Yeah? Just how not decent are you?"

As she slipped on her robe and yanked the ties tight, she retorted, "Enough that if you walk out now, I'll have to hurt you."

"Damn." After a moment, he said, "Down, boy. Down."

Puzzled, Annie looked at Buck, who yawned. "Rik, the dog's behaving just fine."

Silence. Then, "I bet."

Understanding came on a heated rush of shock. Good God, did he have to be so blasted honest? There were some things she was better off not knowing!

"Okay," Annie said, keeping her voice cool with an effort. "You can come out now; I'm covered."

This time, the silence stretched on a little longer. "We have a small problem here. See, I'm not covered at all."

An image of Rik in all his naked and neatly muscled glory gave her a wicked tickle of satisfaction. Hah! His turn to squirm a little.

"Oh, really?" she drawled. "You mean the only thing standing between me and a naked man is an old oak door with a tetchy lock?"

From behind the old oak door came a muffled snort. "That's one way of looking at it."

"I could stand here all night, you know."

"Enjoying yourself, eh?"

"Yes," she admitted smugly. "And there's nothing you can do about it."

"Bad gamble, Annie."

Point taken. She cleared her throat. "Well, I'll turn around and you can streak back to your bedroom. I won't even ask why you're wandering around in the nude when you know you have an insomniac in the house."

"I have a headache." He sounded aggrieved. "I just went to get a damn Tylenol ... and how come *you're* wandering around nearly naked when there's a man in the house who hasn't been with a woman in way too long?"

"Is that a threat?"

He let out a hoot of laughter. "Only if you want it to be. I'm coming out. No peeking."

Annie flung a look of outrage at the door. "I won't peek! Even though you'd like me to."

Rik made a sound—not quite a laugh, not quite a sputter—then the door opened inward with a sudden violence. Buck yelped, scrambling to his feet. Annie spun around to face the kitchen window—the big, black kitchen window that, in the candlelight, reflected everything behind her as perfectly as a mirror.

Oh, she shouldn't. She really, really shouldn't.

Annie squeezed her eyes shut at the sound of bare feet padding toward her.

"Promise, now," he whispered in her ear. "No peeking."

She shivered at the touch of his warm breath against the sensitive skin of her neck. God, how dare he stand behind her like that, stark raving naked? She answered with a backward jab of her elbow, but Rik was too quick. He laughed again as he moved away.

Miserable puffed-up wretch of a man! It would serve him right if she peeked. If he meant to throw around his sexuality, she had every right to see if he had the equipment to back it up.

Annie opened one eye, then the other . . . and disappointment nipped her. He'd wrapped a towel around his waist; a small towel which managed to cover all the crucial bits but still revealed an impressive expanse of back, chest, legs and one hip. He was tan nearly all over.

And he had very nice equipment. Very touchable.

Her fingers curling against her thighs, Annie looked up—and met Rik's gaze in the mirror of the window. Her breath caught.

"You peeked," he said, his voice low.

She boldly turned, folding her arms aross her chest. "You wanted me to."

"And why would I do that?"

He walked back toward her and her heart pounded with thick, heavy strokes. Here, now, in the candlelight and heat of a midsummer night, she couldn't pretend he'd never kissed her, didn't watch her.

"We both know why, Rik."

"You dodge questions about as well as you've been dodging me all week."

With this man, there was no hiding from truth. He wouldn't allow it. "I needed time to think. I'm not the irresponsible type, and I worry about . . . well, consequences and—"

"I'll take care of you, Annie." His voice was soft but intense, scraping her already sensitive nerves. "I made a mistake like that once, but won't ever again."

"That's not the kind of consequences I'm talking about."

Rik looked at her for a long moment, and she saw the wariness in his eyes. "I'll be honest with you here. My ex-wife pretty much deep-sixed any chance of me falling hard for a woman again. But I've been missing a woman's touch these days. It's been a long time, Annie," he added. "And I want to make love with you."

Even expecting this, his bluntness brought another stinging flush to her cheeks, and she had to look away from his direct gaze.

"I don't suppose anybody has ever told you there's such a thing as too much honesty." She took a quick breath. "But as long as we are being honest, we wouldn't be making love. We don't love each other. It'd be just sex, Rik."

"You call it what you want, I'll call it what I want."

"Why me? Why not some nice, local girl?" Like Jodie, of the cantaloupes. "Someone who'd be happy to settle down and make beautiful babies with you?"

He closed in. Annie tried to back away, but she had nowhere to go—he'd trapped her in a corner. Still unable to meet his eyes, she focused on the ends of his towel, barely held in place with his hand, and not even the shadows of night could hide his arousal.

"Because none of the nice, local girls interest me. You're the one I want."

And all she had to do, to make this wanting a reality, was peel away one finger at a time from the towel and let that wistful barrier fall. There'd be no going back, then; the decision would be made.

"Don't shake like that," he said quietly. "I won't hurt you."

"I'm not afraid."

Liar, an inner voice mocked.

How cool and calm he acted—but Annie knew better. The flame from the nearby candle was reflected in the wide pupils of his eyes.

Fire, under the ice.

"Not tonight," she said quietly, and shivered. "I can't."

Rik's eyes narrowed. "Can't, or won't? Don't lie to me, Annie. I mean it."

A flare of anger mingled with the desire that ached, sweetly throbbing, between her thighs. "I can't. It's ... well, you know, that time of the month."

Instead of retreating, as she expected, he pressed closer; a wall of confining heat. "I can still kiss you."

"I suppose that'd be okay."

Oh, God, yes! She wanted to feel, to taste, his mouth on hers again, the firm pressure, the teasing tongue, the liquid desire ...

He stepped back, and she almost screamed with frustration.

"I'm gonna put on my pants," Rik murmured. "Because if you think your period is enough to stop me from making love to you, you're dead wrong. Meet me on the porch. It's cooler outside."

After he'd melted into the shadows beyond the candlelight, Annie picked up her tea—but her hand shook so badly that she spilled it. She put the mug back down on the counter and then went to the porch to wait.

It didn't feel any cooler to her at all.

When Rik came outside a few moments later he found Annie perched on the rail, in the corner of the porch where he always sat, hugging her knees to her chest.

Christ, she was beautiful ... and she looked so right

sitting there in his corner. Like she belonged.

Annie gazed at him, waiting.

"You're in my spot," he said. As soon as the words were out, he wanted to smack his palm against his head.

"And what makes this your spot, anyway?" she asked, then lowered her chin against her knees to hide a small smile.

Okay. He'd messed up—and she'd noticed—but he could do this. Rik glanced away from her amused gaze, only to find himself in more trouble when her legs snared his attention. He forced himself to look away from the curving thighs revealed by her open robe—thighs that just begged a man to run his hands or tongue along their smooth, pale length.

"Because that's where I sat whenever I came out here with my dad," he said, leaning against the rail which, to his discomfort as well as his relief, was at groin level. "He'd come out for his morning smoke, and I'd come out with my breakfast. We'd watch the sun rise, then go to work. Dad died ten years ago, but I still come out here every morning to watch the sun rise."

"Why?"

He shrugged, uncomfortable with the question. "It's pretty, I guess."

"I think that's reason enough." After a moment, she asked, "And your mother? You don't talk much about her."

"She died when I was fourteen." Even after twenty years, the pain still tugged at him. "She got a bad cold that turned to pneumonia, and then the doctor said the lining of her heart muscles got infected. She died in her sleep."

The soft warmth of her hand settled over his. "I'm sorry."

"Yeah." Something hot burned at the back of his throat, and he swallowed it away. "It was a real tough time. My dad, he was never the same after she left us."

"Left us," Annie murmured, with a shake of her head. He sent her a questioning look, but all she said was, "Do you have any brothers or sisters?"

"Two younger brothers and a sister." He moved his thumb, circling it against the soft, moist skin of her palm. "Erik's in Minneapolis and works in advertising. Lars runs a computer company in Milwaukee, and Ingrid lives in Kansas with her husband and kids. I don't see her much anymore."

"Rurik, Erik, Lars, and Ingrid." Annie raised a brow. "Gee, you wouldn't happen to be Norwegian, would you?"

Rik grinned. "My folks had an attack of heritage anxiety. Us kids were just innocent victims."

"Rurik kinda suits you. The name's more common in Iceland, though."

He curled his fingers around hers, and it pleased him that she didn't pull away. "How do you know that?"

"In my line of work, I pick up all sorts of odds and ends. Makes me a great partner for Trivial Pursuit. Rurik is based on Rorik, a Norse god."

"Mom got it close enough, then. Old Ole changed the spelling of the family's last name, too. Americanized it."

Man, he was out of his mind, talking about spelling when he had a beautiful—and mostly willing— woman all but in his arms. But it had to be her decision to take things further, not his. That was another mistake he'd never make again.

"How about you? Your family?" he asked.

She shrugged. "Not everybody has a family like yours."

Rik waited for her to say more, to explain, but when she didn't, he asked, "I guess you're too worked up over your book to sleep."

"Something like that. I'm so close to finishing the story, and not knowing where—" She cut herself off, then shrugged again. "Things aren't going quite as I'd planned, but I should finish soon."

All the liquid warmth inside iced over at her words. "What was in that package you got today?"

She gave a sigh, tipping her face toward the stars as she squeezed his hand. "A collection of old interviews. So far, there's nothing much." She shifted, then lowered her gaze. "I keep hoping to find something on Boone, because I know he's the key."

"Who's Boone?"

Annie gave him a look, as if he should've known. "A fellow officer."

"And you think this Boone guy killed your soldier?"

"I certainly hope not. They were friends."

Another tug of pain, this one newer. "Trust me, that don't mean a thing." More to steer the conversation away from him than from any real interest, he asked, "Why is Boone the key?"

She glanced at him; a sizzling and sexy look, her eyes half-shadowed by her lashes. "Do you really want to know?"

He didn't, but grinned anyway. "If you really want to tell me."

"How can I refuse such enthusiasm?" Smiling back, Annie pulled her hand from his, then patted the rail. "Come sit beside me. I'll keep the lecture short."

Rik hesitated, then swung his leg over the rail and faced her. He imagined putting both hands on either side of her head, against the siding of the house, then leaning close and kissing all those dead men right out of her head.

Instead, he rested his back against the column behind him, as Annie said, "Boone was the last person to see Lewis, and he changed his story about what happened that night."

Rik lowered his lids, letting her low, throaty voice soak through him. Man, she had the sexiest voice. What would she sound like, crying out as they made love, whispering his name in his ear as her fingers clutched at him . . . ?

"—and on July 29, Boone and Lewis were guarding prisoners at the Hollow when they were attacked by a band of Sauk, who split up to escape. Lewis took off after one band, Boone the other."

Guilt stung him as her soft words cut across his randy thoughts. Forcing himself to pay attention, Rik focused on how Annie's fingers toyed with the belt of her robe, rolling and unrolling it again and again.

"When Boone lost his group, he returned to camp for help. When Lewis didn't come back, everyone assumed he'd been killed."

She paused then and, as if suddenly aware of her mangled belt, dropped it. She rested her hands in her lap and looked at him expectantly.

Rik rubbed a hand over his chin. "Makes sense to me."

"But the Sauk should've been long gone from the

area to begin with. Somebody else must've wondered the same thing."

He raised his brows. "Because . . . ?"

"Because Colonel Zachary Taylor questioned Boone again several months later, and Boone admitted he'd lied. He said Lewis was tired of army life and arranged his desertion to look as if he were killed in the line of duty."

"Makes sense, too."

"Only if you don't know Lewis. And when Taylor asked why he'd lied, Boone said he'd wanted to protect his friend's honor. If he'd really meant that, why change his story? Until then, Lewis was listed as killed in action—a hero's death."

"Could your soldier have lit out, like this Boone said?"

"It's a possibility. Lewis wasn't happy in the army." She brushed back a lock of hair the persistent breeze blew into her eyes. "But I don't believe it. He valued honor, was devoted to his family—especially his mother—and was planning to marry. Deserting would've cost him everything."

"So why did Boone lie?"

"Maybe he screwed up and it cost Lewis his life, but rather than admit it, Boone sacrificed his friend's reputation. Maybe Lewis was killed by friendly fire and whoever killed him was important enough that the army hushed it up.

"Lewis's mother even hired Abraham Lincoln while he was still a lawyer to look into Lewis's situation. Lincoln had served in the volunteer militia with Lewis during the Black Hawk War, but he didn't find anything. He was kind to Gussie, though; told her that her son was a 'good and Godly young man.' She always remembered that."

"What about the kid's father? Didn't he do anything?"

"Joseph Hudson was an old man," Annie said quietly. "Four months after he learned his only son was dead, he suffered a fatal stroke."

Huh. The story actually was kind of interesting—Not enough to spend ten years tracking down a dead guy, but still, there was something to it.

Silence fell between them; an edgy silence flickering with awareness. Her nearness filled him with her fresh vanilla scent. He caught her gaze, and she smiled—sweetly shy—before tipping her face toward the stars again.

"I thought you wanted to kiss me," she said.

"I do."

She didn't look down from the sky. "So what are you waiting for?"

"For you to ask."

"Ask?" That brought her focus back to him. "How?"

She was teasing him, but he didn't mind. He couldn't remember the last time someone had teased him, playfully like this. He liked it. "Whatever works, but you might keep it short and to the point."

Annie giggled and covered her mouth with a hand, as if embarrassed. Then she tipped her head to one side, eyelids half-closed, a smile playing at the corner of her mouth. The breeze blew strands of dark hair across her face, her lips. "Kiss me. Will that do? Just . . . kiss me, Rik?"

"That'll do fine."

Rik slid slowly across the rail toward her, placed

his palms against the wall on either side of her head, and leaned forward.

An easy fit, her lips to his. Soft. Everything about Annie was soft and warm, and kissing her washed away the day's tensions from his muscles, even faded the faint pounding in his temples.

This time, he didn't let out all the wanting and needing at once; he held it back. This time, he wanted to be so close that her breasts brushed against him with her every breath. He wanted to trace the shape of her lips with his own, to taste her, to close his eyes and take the scent of her deep into his lungs. This time he was going to remember the damn romance, even if it killed him.

He gave her choirboy kisses, nibbling her lips until her mouth grew softer still, opened, and coaxed him inside. He wrapped silky-soft strands of her hair around his fingers, all the while touching his tongue to hers, sharing her breath.

"Touch me, Annie."

At his urging, she brushed her fingers along his shoulders. Then, with a low moan, she ran her palms over his belly and ribs, around and around in circular motions all along his chest.

His skin tingling at her touch, Rik kissed her harder. She responded with equal force, making soft and needy sounds, and finally wrapped her arms around his neck and pulled him into her.

And he was sucked in; drowning, swept away by his need. Cramped beneath tight denim, his erection pained him, and he shifted, trying to find some sort of ease. But there was none to be had, so if he meant to torture himself, he might as well do a thorough job of it.

While he worked at the tie of her robe with one hand, he moved his lips to her chin, then to her neck. When he kissed the swell of her breast, neatly revealed by the low neckline of her nightshirt, Annie took a long, deep breath.

"Rik, I don't—"

"Just kisses," he interrupted. "You didn't ask for anything more."

"Oh, God," Annie said, followed by a sound that was both a laugh and a groan. "You never do what I expect. I thought you would throw me over your shoulder, carry me off—"

He closed her mouth with a kiss, then said against her skin, "Remind me to have a talk with you about these fantasies of yours, Miz Beckett."

Her nightshirt was all white cotton and white sheer stuff, and his hand looked big and dark and alien against the delicate fabric and pearl-like buttons. A tug or two, and he'd pop all those buttons right off and send them rolling across the porch.

With surprisingly steady fingers—considering everything inside wasn't too steady—Rik slipped the top button through its opening, then moved to the next, focusing on the buttons and the rapid rise and fall of her breasts. His knuckles brushed against their warm fullness as he moved lower, lingering, shamelessly enjoying himself.

Finally he parted the placket, and the pale, hazy moonlight fell across her bare skin and round, white breasts.

"Jesus," he said reverently, staring at the taut nipples. The hunger inside tightened, and he bent his head, touching his tongue against those enticing tips as she made a sighing sound deep in her throat and whispered his name.

Making out on a porch rail tempted the laws of physics, especially with Annie moving against him, and he eased her back as far as he could, hands again on the side of the house to balance them both. Dipping his head, he tongued her nipples, sucked them into his mouth, then kissed them again, and all the while Annie arched against him, making soft sounds that just made him harder and harder.

"This is so wonderful." Her fingers caught in his hair, holding him close. "We have to stop. I can't ... I'm not—"

He stopped her protest with a hungry, possessive kiss, his tongue making a full circuit over her tongue and teeth and smooth lips. Then he eased back, took a deep, steadying breath, and yanked her nightshirt back together. His fingers fumbled as he refastened the buttons.

Fast and furious, or slow and steady, he ended up the same way: hard and frustrated.

"It's okay," Rik said, not bothering to pretend he could breathe normally. "But when you want to, all you gotta do is ask."

Of course, there was no reason he couldn't do everything in his power to persuade her to say yes— and pretty damn quick, too.

CHAPTER TEN

July 14, 1832, Michigan Territory: I do not take lightly
my duties as an Officer. It is no easy task to direct a
man's Fate. My orders, my decisions, all my actions,
can mean Life or Death. I cannot accept this respon-
sibility with the same ease as Cyrus, but of course
he was born to leadership. He sees our men as mere
Tools, whereas I cannot. When Private Lawton died
of the Dysentery, Cyrus organized the burial detail,
and I wrote the boy's family. It is how we work,
Cyrus and I. He dispenses Orderliness and I dispense
Compassion. He is my Friend, and yet, in this crucible
of Wilderness and War, our differences grow ever
more apparent.

—Lieutenant Lewis Hudson,
from a letter to Miss Emily Oglethorpe

Tuesday afternoon, Annie took refuge in the house
from the heat—a heat so intense that it drained energy, shortened tempers and patience, and made sleep
difficult.

Standing at the kitchen window, a glass of iced tea
in hand, she watched Rik walk his fields and wondered how he could be out there at high noon and
not collapse from sunstroke. No doubt he was sur-

veying the cracked, parched earth and stunted growth of his crops. She wondered why he'd never once mentioned this to her, even in passing.

The possibility that he was hiding the extent of his troubles brought a rush of shame as she recalled how she'd pressed money on him; it also deepened her unease at that growing spark of attraction between them.

He spoke easily of emotional detachment, but men like Rik Magnusson didn't take a woman to bed and then let her walk away when her calendar said it was time to move on.

One of them would get burned here. A hundred times a day, she warned herself against acting on her attraction . . . and a hundred times a day found herself thinking of him, watching him. As she was doing right now.

The sound of an engine and Buck's barking pulled Annie out of her thoughts. She moved to the window overlooking the porch and pushed the curtain aside to see a large van parked in the drive, with the words WKMN-CHANNEL 24 NEWS painted on its side.

A news team? Here?

With Rik far out in the fields, Annie went to greet these unexpected visitors. "Can I help you?"

The man getting out of the van's driver side smiled at her, but a petite, well-dressed brunette shooting around the front answered. "Hi, I'm Janet Olsen of WKMN 24! Are you, by any chance, Annie Beckett?"

"Yes, I am. What's this about?"

"We heard you're investigating an army officer who disappeared in 1832. Is this true?"

"Well, yes, but who—"

"We tried calling ahead, but no one answered the

phone. Do you have time to answer a few questions while we're here? This sounds like something that might interest our area viewers."

Odd; she hadn't heard the phone ring all day. Annie hesitated, then motioned the team up the steps. "You may as well come inside and get out of the heat."

As the reporter, cameraman, and soundman filed past her, Annie glanced toward the fields. Rik was facing the house, hands on his hips, no doubt wondering what she was doing.

But she wouldn't turn away the small blessing of free publicity, even if she probably owed it to Owen Decker.

Inside the kitchen, she chatted with the news crew for a few moments until Janet Olsen decided enough was enough. "Ms. Beckett, I'll need to ask you a few questions so we can decide how to best set up this segment."

"I've done TV interviews before."

The woman looked relieved. "Good. That'll make things easy. First, just who is—or was—Lewis Hudson?"

How strange, to hear his name spoken by someone other than herself!

"Lewis Hudson was a first lieutenant in the US frontier infantry under the command of General Henry Atkinson and Colonel Zachary Taylor, who would one day become the nation's twelfth president."

Olsen nodded. "Good! And what makes Lieutenant Hudson special? Why are you interested in solving his disappearance?"

Why, indeed. "Injustice, Ms. Olsen. After one hundred sixty years, the truth behind Lieutenant Hudson's murder deserves to be told."

With a touch of cynicism, Annie knew she'd hit all the key words when the woman's eyes brightened. Injustice. Murder. Great sound bites.

"Good, very good," Olsen repeated. "Okay. Let's back up here. Tell me a little about yourself."

"I'm a photojournalist. I've published several books on Americana subjects; the two most recent are *The Romance of Route 66* and *Wide Open: The Subculture of American Stock-Car Racing*. I've also written articles for the *Smithsonian* and *American History* and contributed to two pieces published in *National Geographic*."

"I *love* that magazine. I've been reading it since I was a kid. That's great! You must travel a lot."

If she could ever count on a reporter asking one question, that was it—but she no longer bothered to try and debunk the myth that travel was glamorous. "Yes."

After a brief silence, the woman cleared her throat and said, "So tell me about how you first learned of Lieutenant Hudson."

From the corner of her eye, Annie caught sight of Rik approaching the house. She turned her attention back to the reporter. "I came into possession of a collection of family letters—"

"Ah, family, then?"

"He's family, yes." Not that blood ties were all what they were cracked up to be, as she had cause to know. "Lieutenant Hudson's letters led me to believe that he didn't desert, as the army claimed. It's taken me ten years, working when I could find the time between jobs, to track down the evidence to prove that he was murdered and the army covered it up."

"Wow," Olsen said, grinning. She was young. Mid-twenties, fresh-faced and gung ho. "I love conspiracies. The public loves conspiracies—even old ones. This is going to be great! Wayne, don't you think this is going to be great?"

Wayne, the cameraman, nodded.

Just then the sound of footsteps caught their attention, and Annie took a deep breath as Rik walked inside. He took off his sunglasses and tossed them on the table.

"What's going on here?"

"Hello! I'm Janet Olsen of WKMN 24 news and you are?" The woman flashed a camera-perfect smile, giving Rik a quick, appreciative once-over in the process.

Rik didn't return her smile—or her assessment. "I'm the guy who owns the kitchen you're standing in. Annie, I asked you a question."

"They're doing a story on my research." A short, charged silence followed before she added, "I didn't call them."

Rik's gaze met hers, then darkened with understanding.

"Are we causing a problem?" the cameraman asked, his voice pleasant, yet with an edge of aggression that typified most of the media people Annie had ever met.

"Depends," Rik answered, finally looking away from Annie. "This is private property."

"They're only asking questions." She stepped forward, laying her hand over the hard, tense muscles of his arm. "Can we talk? Alone?"

He gave a brief nod and stalked to the parlor. Only then did Annie notice he hadn't taken off his boots—and Rik *always* took off his boots. Unnerved, she still managed to smile at the film crew. "I'll be right back."

"So what's his name?" Olsen asked. "He didn't answer me."

"Rurik Magnusson, and his family, has worked this land since 1844," Annie said with a note of pride.

"Wow," came Olsen's voice as she headed to the parlor. "Let's get this guy to talk to us . . ."

Rik stood waiting in front of a faded tapestry wing chair, hands on his hips, T-shirt molded to his chest by perspiration. Desire took her, strong and sharp. God, she wanted to kiss him right there, despite the camera crew lurking in the kitchen—but judging by the angle of that mustache, she had some explaining to do first.

"Before you start in on me, let me repeat that I had no idea this would happen. But it's *good*. The publicity may help me in the long run."

He stared at her a moment longer. "Decker's behind this."

"That's my guess."

"Do you know why?"

"Does it matter?" She resented his perpetual suspicion of Decker, of her. It even hurt—a little.

"How long are they going to be here?"

"As long as it takes to ask a few questions and shoot some footage. Nothing much. Honestly, Rik, I don't know why you're so upset."

"I don't want this thing of yours turning into some goddamn three-ring circus!"

She took a deep breath, but it didn't cool her anger. "The publicity might bring in new leads, and the sooner I have those answers, the sooner I can finish my work and get out of your hair. Then no more news crews will bother you. That should make you happy."

His lids lowered as his mouth tightened. "I don't like surprises."

"So you've said. But if you continue to interfere with my work, perhaps I shouldn't be here at all."

He said nothing.

After a moment, she took a step closer. "Is that what you want? For me to leave?"

With a derisive snort, he backed away. "And miss nosy reporters in my kitchen? The *thumpity-thump* of your little Birkenstocks around the house? Hell, no."

Something flashed in his eyes; something that, despite his mocking tone, filled her with unease.

"Are you going to ask them to go?" she asked at length.

"No." He sighed, running a hand through his hair. "Sorry."

"Then let's go back in. I'll make it quick and painless."

She returned to the kitchen, Rik silently following. After a round of hurried introductions, he arranged himself against the counter and its backdrop of cabbage roses and lace curtains. The reporter started with her questions again, but Annie didn't miss how often the woman's gaze darted toward Rik.

"We're almost done." Olsen flashed a conciliatory smile. "Just a few more questions. In your opinion, Ms. Beckett, who was involved in this alleged cover-up? You've mentioned several important historical personalities: Zachary Taylor and Henry Dodge, who became Wisconsin's first governor. Any other famous people?"

"Lots of famous people, and some may have been directly involved, but at this time I cannot say as to what extent."

"Can you say who these people were?"

"Brigadier General Cyrus Boone, as well as Abraham Lincoln and Jefferson Davis. As you might already know, Lincoln and Davis fought in the Black Hawk War."

More great sound bites. Big names. Irony. Possible scandal. The reporter all but quivered with glee.

"Just one more question, Ms. Beckett. Is Lieutenant Hudson buried at Black Hawk's Hollow?"

Rik's body stiffened, and Annie suppressed a sigh. "I don't know."

"Then let me put it this way. Do you suspect the body is located on Mr. Magnusson's land?" Olsen pressed.

Annie glanced at Rik, and said firmly, "I can't answer that."

Because he didn't want to send out an open invitation to trespass, Rik refused to let the news crew on the Hollow. He did let them film their interview by his barn.

After persuading him to answer, very reluctantly, a few questions about his family history, the crew interviewed Annie. Rik stood back and observed her confidence, how she played to the camera and made everything sound dramatic and important. She'd done this sort of thing before, and was milking the opportunity for all it was worth. This was a side of her he hadn't glimpsed before and he didn't much like the reminder that she was comfortable in, lived in, a world so different from his.

She looked pleased, though, as did the news crew, while he struggled with anger, wondering what Decker was up to—and if Annie was telling the truth or not. She sure had a way with avoidance, omissions, and half-truths.

After the news crew left, he and Annie returned to the house.

"Do you want something to drink?" she asked at the open fridge, as he stood directly behind her.

"Sure."

As she handed him a can of soda, their gazes met. She quickly moved away, and his chest tightened.

"Annie, we need to have us a talk."

"I know."

"Your soldier . . . Hudson. Is he out there?"

She stood in one corner of the kitchen while he stood in another, like two fighters facing off in a boxing ring.

"Anything is possible," she answered, each word measured and careful. "I don't know where he's buried. I swear it."

Something inside him twisted at her cagey response. "But you think he is."

"It's beginning to look that way."

He'd given her a chance; now he let the subject die. He took several deep gulps of his soda, the carbonation burning all the way down to his belly. After he finished it off, he slammed the can down on the counter and grabbed his keys.

"Where are you going?" she asked as he left the kitchen, a note of alarm in her voice.

"Into town. Catch you later."

"Rik, wait!"

At the front door he stopped. He told himself to keep walking, but he couldn't seem to move. And when she rested her hand lightly on his back, he turned.

"Please." Her eyes pleaded, made him feel like shit for walking away from her, for being angry to begin with. "Try to understand. This is very important to me. I am committed to clearing Lewis's name."

"I sure wish I understood why."

"Because it's the right thing to do! How can—"

"I know that. He was just a kid who got screwed—I get that part. What I don't get is why he means so much to you. Explain it to me. Draw me a picture, Annie."

She stepped back. "Because I'm family. Because I'm all he has. Because nobody cares about him but *me*. Because Augustina Hudson searched for her son for thirty years, and I believe such a bond between a mother and her child deserves no less than my best effort to bring that search to an end."

"There's more to it. What's finding him gonna do for you? How's it gonna make your life better, Annie?"

Her eyes darkened with hurt, then anger. "I do *not* have a yen for a dead man! For God's sake, Rik, after what we did the other night, how can you even think that?"

Their gazes met and held.

Oh, yeah. The other night. The *things* they did—or didn't do. Things he still wanted to do, in spite of the fact she couldn't, or wouldn't, tell him the truth.

But something here bothered him. "How come you don't talk much about your family or friends?"

Her eyes narrowed. The hurt had gone; now she just looked pissed. "For a blunt man, you can be pretty damn obtuse when you want. Your point?"

"That ol' Lewis means more to you than some notch on the scales of justice. I just can't figure out what it is. But don't look all worried; I won't give you trouble about him."

"Not until you get me in bed, anyway."

"You sure don't have a high opinion of me," he said quietly.

"As if you have a high opinion of *me*," she shot back.

"I try to be straight with you. I have since you got here."

All the color in her face was concentrated on her cheekbones. "And what about before I arrived? You called me at the last minute to tell me to get lost, that something had 'come up.' Real original. Why didn't you want me here?"

"Because I like my peace and quiet. I figured you'd mess all that up. Guess I was right."

Without another word, he slammed the door behind him, disappointment souring his already bad mood.

The drive into town didn't take long; he always tended to drive faster than he should. Karen used to get on his case about that all the time.

God, no going *there*—not now. Instead, he mulled over his earlier arguments with Annie, returning again and again to her sharp comment that she could move elsewhere.

He'd laughed it off, but the truth was, she'd brought flowers inside his house and sunlight, and he wasn't ready to let it all go just yet.

Man, he was a fool. Gypsy Annie would breeze right out of his life in weeks—maybe days, if today's news show brought in new evidence as she hoped— and he'd be back where he'd started.

Self-sufficient and successful, he'd thought. But

maybe not, and he had Annie to thank for this sudden, gnawing self-doubt.

By the time Rik pulled into the parking lot outside the downtown feed store, he'd gotten his temper under better control.

There were other feed and supply stores in other towns, but Warfield was his home. If he couldn't walk into Dow's with his head held high, what would his old man say? Magnussons had had credit at Dow's since before his father was even born, and he kept those notepads that came with his bills to remind himself he was the better man, that he was getting on with the business of life.

The counter clerk, one of Heather's friends, was pricing flashlights when Rik walked up to him and said, "Decker in?"

The kid blinked. Warfield was a small town; people didn't forget. Nor did their kids.

"Uh, yeah," the clerk said. "How's it goin', Mr. Magnusson?"

"Pretty good. Listen, tell Decker I need to talk with him."

The kid—Rik couldn't remember his name—looked both excited and alarmed. "Okay, just a minute. He's in his office."

While waiting, Rik checked out the feed prices. They'd gone up—not by a lot, Decker was too smart for that—but it didn't matter. With the weather bad and getting worse, he and a lot of other farmers would soon need to place orders. Then he could kiss his tax savings good-bye.

Maybe a few of his Belgians, too, unless he cashed Annie's checks. He hadn't yet brought himself to do so. Even knowing it was honest money paid for an honest service didn't help clean away the dirty feeling the checks gave him.

"Rik, this is quite the surprise."

Rik took a deep, silent breath and turned. "I need to talk with you. In private."

Decker nodded. Leaving the young clerk standing at the counter staring, Rik followed Decker to the small office in the upper story of the old store, tucked among mountains of boxes and stock. It smelled like dust, dry wood, and engine oil.

Once inside, Decker didn't sit or offer Rik a chair— but he kept the desk between them. Rik wouldn't look at that desk. If he did, he'd only remember something best left buried forever.

"What do you want?" Decker asked.

There was a time when they'd have traded jokes, slaps on the back. But that time was long past. "I want to know what's up with you and Annie."

Decker's brows shot upward. "I'm a married man, Rik. In case you've forgotten."

A red, hot haze burned at the edges of his control. "Did you call the TV station?"

"What TV station?"

"Don't fuck with me, Decker!"

A short, tense silence. Then, "I asked Betty to call; now back off. Annie came to me for help right after she got into town. I'm only doing as she asked."

"She doesn't need your help."

Interest lit Decker's dark eyes. "Did Annie send you to tell me that?"

"No." Not trusting himself, Rik shoved his hands in his back pockets. "And she's Ms. Beckett to you."

"Cut the bullshit, Rik. We both know why you're here. It sticks in your craw that she turned to me and not you." Decker's tone mocked him. "Not that I blame her; she's a smart woman."

Rik dug his hands deeper into his pockets. "Annie can take care of herself. She doesn't need you or me, so don't go acting like you're her damn hero."

"Look, I have no ulterior motives here. She asked for help, and it was within my power to give it. You're overreacting."

"Maybe," Rik said evenly. "But you listen to me real good. I may think she's a little crazy over this soldier of hers, but he's important to her, and that makes it important to me. Don't you use Annie to take shots at me. I won't stand for that."

A silence fell over the room. Then Decker laughed. "A little romance in bloom?"

Rik had said his piece. Now, he turned and headed for the door.

"She's pretty. You always had good taste, if no good sense. What do you think you can offer a woman as worldly as her? The smell of cow shit and years of work that'll put lines in her face and give her old hands?"

Rik stopped, looking at his own hand on the door handle. Not a young man's hand anymore, one hardened by work. Honest work.

"Sorry, *buddy*." He glanced over his shoulder with a humorless smile. "I'm sitting out this round."

He left, shutting the door very carefully behind him—before he lost control of his temper and pounded Decker's face to a bloody pulp.

Back in his truck, he considered driving to a bar in the next county, where no one knew him and where he could sit in the dark, find himself a honky-tonk honey to smile at him, share a beer or two, and set about proving that he had plenty to offer a woman.

But he drove home instead.

When Rik walked into the house, it seemed strangely quiet. He didn't find Annie in the kitchen, parlor, or living room, as he'd expected. He didn't hear her moving around upstairs, either.

"Annie?" he called. He tossed his keys onto the counter, where they slid, jangling, into the coffee-maker—and knocked over the note propped against it.

He froze, not wanting to read it, fearing she'd packed up and moved out as she'd threatened.

With a muttered curse, he snatched up the note and ripped it open—and two little words sent heat roaring through him as he crushed the paper in his fist.

KISS ME.

CHAPTER ELEVEN

April 3, 1832, Jefferson Barracks, St. Louis: I have a
Surprise, and I am saving it until I see you again. I
shall give you a hint . . . it will one day contain all my
Hopes and my Dreams, my Heart and Soul, and yet
is small enough to tuck into a place close to my
Heart.

—LIEUTENANT LEWIS HUDSON,
FROM A LETTER TO MISS EMILY OGLETHORPE

Annie sat on her bed, listening to Rik's steps on the
porch, the familiar creak of the screen door opening,
and then his voice calling for her, followed by silence.

It was too late now to run down the steps and
snatch back her note.

"Annie?"

The first step on the stairs sounded, the creaks
tracking Rik's slow and steady progress.

Shifting on the bed, Annie faced the open door and
pulled at the camisole sticking to her skin. Moments
later, a long shadow fell across the white-painted
wall.

"Annie, you up here?"

She didn't answer. Now, from the doorway, he
could clearly see her sitting on the bed, hugging her

skirted knees to her chest. He ducked through the door, then stopped.

Her heart pounding, she soaked in the sight of him. Heat curled the hair at his neck and temples, and he wore her favorite shirt—the one too many washings had left a shade small—and jeans tight enough to hint at the muscle and power hidden beneath denim.

"I got your note," Rik said.

She took a deep breath of the sweet-scented air blowing through the open windows. "I'd hoped you would."

Rik ran a hand through his hair as he slowly crossed the room. "I figured you were mad at me."

"That comes and goes," Annie said with a small smile. "You have your moments."

"I was out in the fields earlier, and it's hot." He looked at his hands, then back to her. "I should wash up."

"Rik, I don't want a man who smells or dresses like he lives in a department store. I want you just the way you are. I *like* you the way you are."

Several emotions crossed his face—something of pride and doubt—as if he wanted to believe her, but couldn't. It touched her, this crack in his self-confidence. If only he could see himself through her eyes: so striking, so strong and solid, standing in his work clothes against the pristine white of the room, filling it with the colors of blue denim, tanned skin, red knit, and hair the color of old gold.

On a sudden inspiration, Annie unfolded her legs and slid off the bed. "Can I take your picture?"

His eyes narrowed. "Why?"

"Because you're beautiful," she said simply, and watched a flush spread across his cheeks. "Please,

Rik? I want to remember you just the way you look right now."

Her words—and their implication—hung between them. Then he glanced again at his hands. "I'm not too clean."

"You're not ashamed of the work you do, are you?"

He stiffened, chin rising. "Hell, no."

"Then what's the problem?" When he didn't respond, she picked up her camera. "May I?"

"I guess."

"Don't pose," she said, focusing.

She could tell that once he shook off the awkwardness of facing a camera, he'd photograph like a dream. The camera loved the vivid energy of his wariness, and the man had no bad angles. When he folded his arms across his chest, making the most of his lean, muscular build, she grinned.

"Perfect. If *Playgirl* ever comes looking for farmer hunks of the Midwest, you be sure to give them a call."

He laughed as she'd intended, and Annie snapped the photo, hoping she'd captured that delightful contrast of prickly pride and humor.

"Does that mean you're gonna ask me to take off my shirt?" His blue eyes gleamed with laughter—and a challenge.

"*Carpe diem*—go for it." She wouldn't pass up a chance to eyeball that delectable body.

With one hand he pulled the shirt over his head and tossed it aside. God, he had an utterly kissable, strokable chest—and she remembered that night on the porch, the texture of his skin and hair, the lines and curves of his muscles beneath her fingers.

She ached to touch him again.

"Maybe I'll unsnap my jeans—do this hunk business right." He grinned, his mustache widening, and opened his zipper to reveal plain white briefs against brown skin and an arrow-straight line of golden hair leading her gaze right down to the main event.

As the heat closed tight around her, Annie raised her camera. "A dairy farmer exhibitionist: now that's something you don't see every day. Don't enjoy yourself too much; I'm on to you, you know."

"Oh, I'm intending for you to be on me."

A sharp thrill shot through her. His direct stare reflected the unwavering persistence that had fueled his Viking ancestors over the North Sea and helped his pioneer kin tame a wilderness—and now all that inborn persistence was focused on the pursuit of only one goal: herself.

She was doomed!

Grinning, Annie ducked behind her camera and aimed at six-feet of to-die-for male, circling until she had him in full light. No hiding Rik in coy shadows; no brooding, bad-boy shots: this man was golden, kissed by the sun and wind, and he belonged in the honest, uncompromising sunlight. His looks could handle that sort of truthfulness.

Annie took several more shots, then Rik put his fists on his hips, legs spread, and grinned—a little boy's grin on a man's body.

Desire curled through her, and she swallowed. "I see you're getting into things."

His eyes lit with wicked humor. "I figure I'll be getting into things real soon, yeah."

Before she could respond to that crude bit of wit, he'd moved closer. Through the viewfinder, Annie watched him advance until his body blocked her lens and everything went black. An urge to run seized her, but she stood her ground as he slipped Old Faithful over her head.

"What are you doing?" She eyed him, his half-open jeans, her camera now in his hand.

"It's my turn to take pictures of you." He turned the camera around, and examined it. "I just push this button, right?"

With more calmness than she could claim, Annie arched a brow. "It's somewhat more complicated, but yes, pushing that button will take a picture."

"Smart ass." He brought the camera up and Annie, who'd wielded Old Faithful since college, found herself on the opposite end of her own lens—and not sure what to make of it. "Take your hair down," he said, voice low and suggestive.

For a moment, she hesitated. Then she reached up and pulled her hair free of its clip, letting its heavy, warm weight fall around her shoulders, where its inner strands at once adhered to her heat-dampened skin.

"Real nice . . . now unbutton your shirt. Slow and easy."

"Wait a minute." Her worry faded, a sudden suspicion taking its place. "Are you asking me to strip at camera-point?"

"Not asking. Telling."

She snorted. "No way am I letting you take pictures like that of me."

"You were taking pictures like that of *me*."

"It's a different situation and—"

"Like hell it is."

"Well, you can take off your shirt and it's no big deal . . . wait, that's not right. It *is* a big deal . . . oh, damn. What I mean is, you have a very attractive chest—"

"So do you," Rik interrupted again. Fiddling with the lens, he made a sound of satisfaction. A grin slowly widened his mustache. "Give me one good reason why you won't unbutton that shirt for me."

"For starters, I might get famous one day, and you'll sell the pictures to some tabloid for a million bucks, then write a sleazy memoir all about our sweaty sexcapades on sultry summer nights—"

She stopped, clamping her mouth shut.

"Hey, don't stop. I want to hear more about the sweaty sex part."

A blush heated her cheeks. "Rik!"

"C'mon, Annie. Let a guy live out a fantasy or two."

She stared at him, astonished and intrigued. "You have . . . fantasies about me?"

"Oh, yeah. Most of 'em involve me watching while you take off your clothes."

"You know—you're right," she said as an image flashed to mind: Rik tossing her over his shoulder and masterfully striding toward a summer field all a-flower with daisies and chicory, making love to her amid the scent of crushed grass and the lazy music of droning bees. "If we're going to have a fling, we should do it right—fantasies and all."

Under the unwavering eye of her own camera, she unbuttoned her camisole. Halfway down, she heard a familiar click and whir, and on the next button, her fingers fumbled.

"Let the shirt hang open—just like that. Don't move."

Rik edged closer and took another picture. Then he

smiled and pushed the camisole from her shoulders. She clasped her hands before her, and the shirt fell around her back and waist like a shawl, leaving her only in a red-satin bra and floral skirt.

"Christ, you're beautiful," he said after a moment, lowering the camera. His gaze roamed her body, from her bare toes to her head.

Annie moistened her lips, hardly believing this was happening. "What next?"

At her soft question, he cocked his head to one side, as if carefully considering his options. "Take off your skirt."

She hesitated, then eased the skirt down, heart thudding and faintly breathless. "And now?"

Rik motioned with the camera. "Lie down on the bed."

Annie turned. Such a pretty bed, high and narrow, with its buttercup yellow chenille spread and soft fringe brushing the floor. Slowly she walked to the bed, then sank down. The mattress springs creaked as she drew up her bare legs.

"Aren't you going to kiss me?" she whispered. "I asked."

"Oh, yeah," he answered and snapped another shot. He aimed the camera at the foot of the bed. "First I'll kiss your feet and ankles. Then I'm gonna run my tongue right up those pretty legs to your knees." He moved the camera as he talked, the lens tracking his route. "You ticklish behind your knees?"

Annie smiled. "I'm going to plead the Fifth on that one."

"That's answer enough." The camera moved higher. "I didn't figure you as the red-satin type, Annie, but I sure do approve." Up, up the lens moved.

"I'll kiss my way up your belly and then I'll have to do something about that nice bra. You may as well. slip a strap off your shoulder now."

She did as he asked, aching with the need for him to do all that he promised—and so much more. The hard ridge of arousal under his jeans only made her ache sharper, deeper.

Fear dwindled to nothing before the power of her need.

"You'll let me keep one of these pictures," he said softly.

"Maybe." Annie let her smile widen. "You'll have to work for it, I think."

"I'm up to the job." He grinned back. "Turn toward me. I want to see your face."

"You just want a cleavage shot," she said, turning to her side. The weight of her breasts pushed against the bra and she hugged her arms against her stomach to give him some serious cleavage.

"Oh, man." He groaned over the camera's *click-whir*. "You are the sexiest woman I have ever known."

Propping her head on her hand, she looked at him—and his half-open jeans. Oh, my. No mistaking what he had in mind for her. She shivered a little with anticipation. "You've known that many women, huh?"

"I haven't exactly been celibate since my divorce." To her delight, he flushed. "But my mother always said it's quality, not quantity, that counts."

"Such an un-macho statement." She laughed, sinking back against the feather pillows. "And I don't think sex was what your mother had in mind when she gave you that lecture, Rik."

"Probably not," he admitted, his gaze boldly checking out her breasts. "Now, how about you do something with that other strap."

She slipped her finger beneath the red satin, eased it over the curve of her shoulder, and the bra gaped, shifted—but didn't fall.

"One more picture," he said, standing above her.

Unable to resist the lure of his half-open fly, she rolled to her knees and tugged his zipper down, fingers trailing along his erection. He made a low sound as he took his last shot—a highly compromising one, should anyone ever see it—then put the camera carefully on the floor. Annie shifted to her knees on the bed and wrapped her arms around his waist, kissing his chest. His skin was salty and warm, the hairs tickling her nose.

"Kiss me, Rik. Right now."

He bent, his mouth taking hers in a hard, impatient kiss as his hands slid into her hair, drawing her upward. When she tangled her fingers in the thick warmth of his hair, his grip tightened, and he lowered her back onto the bed. The mattress creaked beneath their combined weight, and the bumpy, soft pattern of the chenille spread tickled the bare skin of her back.

Releasing his hold, Rik moved down toward her feet, parting her legs to accommodate his body. She sighed as he kissed her arches, the curve of her heel, her ankles. He pressed hot kisses to her calves and when he reached her knees, his mustache brushing the sensitive skin, she squealed in protest.

Rik grinned from where he nestled neatly between her legs, his hands on either side of her hips. His darker skin contrasted sharply against her pale thighs. "I haven't even tried tickling you. Man, it don't take much to send you over the edge."

"I can't help it!" She pushed at his shoulders—but not very hard.

"Let's see what kind of noises you make when I kiss you here," he murmured, then bent and kissed her thighs. The ends of his hair skimmed her skin and she startled at the touch, as soft as it was. But when he pressed a kiss against the satin at the juncture of her legs, his breath warm, she melted. Her muscles softened, eased around him, and she closed her eyes, sighing again.

Lost in the pooling warmth and desire of his touch, she didn't open her eyes, not as he kissed his way up her stomach, not as he kissed a circular path around her breasts, coming close to—but not touching—her nipples.

As Rik trailed his wet tongue up along her neck, he moved his hands under her back and, with one quick movement, freed her of her bra. Kissing her mouth again at last, he tossed the bra aside. In her mind's eye she could see it, scandalizing the cool white floor with its hot red satin.

"Look at me, Annie." His voice was low but urgent, and as she slowly opened her eyes again, his hands cupped her breasts. Her sensitive skin roused beneath the touch of his rough palms and this time, a soft moan broke free.

In the sunlight, his hair shone like fire and his eyes—clear, deep blue—held her mesmerized as his hands slowly and steadily worked their magic.

"What do you want?" he asked. "Ask . . . just ask, Annie."

"I want you naked." Her low voice came from deep in her throat as she pushed his jeans down, and a few short seconds later his clothes joined her bra.

Annie let out her breath on a long sigh. God, he was beautiful, in his blunt, male way. She touched his erection; tentatively at first, then more boldly as the hard heat in her hand excited her.

She wanted more than kisses—she wanted sweet aches and sizzling needs, the feel of his rougher skin against hers. Rik's hot mouth on her breasts, his fingers easing toward the aching place between her legs. She wanted—

"Ask, Annie," he whispered. "Christ!"

Moving her hips against his hand, she said, "I want you." But that wasn't right. Her eyes fluttered shut as she struggled for better words, to give him what he needed, what she wanted. "Make love to me, please!"

As she spoke he surged over her, his kiss consuming as he quickly rid her of her panties. Then his knee nudged her legs wider apart and all her world was filled with Rik: wide shoulders, chest gilded with red-gold hair, the rigidity of his arms as he held himself above her.

"Christ," he said again, his voice tight. "I almost forgot. You're making me so damn crazy I can't even think."

The weight and warmth of his body disappeared as he grabbed his jeans, searching the pockets until he found a condom.

Then he moved back over her. But this time, his urgency was tempered by gentleness as he cupped her face. "You sure about this?"

Annie brushed the tips of her fingers against his cheeks. "I'm sure, Rik, so long as you understand what we can give each other."

"You mean besides a good time?" he grinned, but the heat had faded by a few degrees from his eyes.

"I have nothing to offer beyond friendship, and some playful, sweet sex. I can't give you more than that. I *can't*. Do you understand?"

For a moment he went absolutely still, then murmured, "I don't need anything more."

A sadness stole over her even as she smiled and traced his lips with her finger. "I knew you'd say that."

"Annie." Rik gave her another muscle-liquefying kiss. "I can't wait."

"Don't. Come inside," she answered, pulling him down toward her. "Please."

Without hesitation, he slid inside—cautious at first and then, as she gave a long, low sigh of contentment, he filled her, soothing and agitating at once.

"God," he breathed, head back, eyes closed. "God, you feel so damn good."

The raw desire in his voice, on his face, augmented her own in a blast of sensation: the heat of his damp skin, the salty taste of his neck and the rock-hard muscles of his arms, the incredible blue of his eyes and the thick, hard feel of him, inside her. Right . . . so very, very right.

Raising her hips, she urged him to move, and he did so. Not slow and steady, but with deep, pumping thrusts that left no thought beyond joining with the tight spiral of pleasure until release unwound them both, dizzied and breathless, a few quick moments later and only seconds apart.

He lay upon her in a hot press of male flesh, sweat pooling between their bodies. Rivulets tickled her sensitive flesh, trickling down her sides.

"That was nice," she said softly, threading her fingers through his warm hair.

He made a low noise against her cheek, then kissed her ear. "That was a near-death experience. I swear my life flashed before my eyes." He raised himself on his elbows, grinning, his color still high.

At that smile, and his tenderness, she froze. A sense of unease spread within her, slowly and darkly, like shadows slipping across the sun. "I suppose you have to leave now . . . you probably have work waiting."

She began to move from the bed, to put a quick, safe distance between them, but he grabbed her hand.

"Nothing that won't wait for another hour or so. Don't go. Stay with me, Annie."

Stay with me.

So very tempting. He only meant now, this moment. For a brief second, she wanted to stay for much longer than a night or two.

Firmly, she pushed that thought away.

"Hey, it's my bed. If anybody leaves, it should be you," she said lightly.

He smiled. Then his mouth claimed hers again as his hands cupped her breasts, chasing away all her doubts and fears, and this time—oh, yes, this time— she got slow and steady.

With Annie finally asleep, Rik stood and stretched. After burning up the sheets in the hot attic with a woman who, in the flesh, left all his fantasies in the dust, the fan's cool air against his skin was a welcome relief.

It had been so long since he'd known this body-draining satisfaction. He hadn't even realized how much he'd needed Annie—her soft touches, the mind-numbing sexual release—until he'd made love to her.

He stood for a moment just looking at her, lying

facedown on the bed and sleeping deeply. Light and shadows played across the fair skin of her back. His gaze tracked her rounded heels and calves and the firm, smooth hill of her rear; the valley of her back that rolled upwards toward her shoulders. Hair the color of oak leaves in autumn spilled across the pillow. His gaze rested finally on the peaceful profile of her face, and something soft, something warm, washed over him.

He wanted to lie back down beside her, to know again the comfort of a body curled against him, a familiar face on a pillow next to his.

But he had work to do. For a man of the land, work was never really done, which made it a hard life for some.

It sure wasn't a life for someone like Annie—and she'd made sure he understood that before letting him make love to her.

Rik bent slowly and gathered his scattered clothes. He didn't dress right away, letting the fan blast him with cool air. He walked the room, working off the sluggishness until he came to Annie's table—and the pictures kept in place by rocks she'd pulled from the pile of fieldstones in back of the old barn.

The Hudson kid had been a good-looking guy; the sort to appeal to women. He looked romantic. And rich. Briefly, Rik flipped through the other copies: the dowdy old woman, the backstabbing buddy, and the cute blonde with the big smile. Then he turned his attention to the stack of letters, also held down with a chunk of rock.

With a glance toward Annie to make sure she still slept, Rick moved the rock aside and picked up the letters. Printed on one side was a translation of the spidery, formal writing photocopied on the reverse. He read Annie's translation.

I should fight for this land were it mine . . .

The first words grabbed his interest and Rik sat down, still buck-naked. After he read the entire letter, he looked again at the picture of Lewis Hudson, aware of a deep, inner twinge of respect for the kid.

A paragraph from the next letter, underlined by Annie, made him smile:

Tell Mrs. Howard that I dream every night of her Ginger Cakes. Oh, I vow I shall eat a Mountain of them when I am home. I am counting every day. Until then, the thought of one Morsel, of even the merest Crumb, is enough to get me through these dreary days of marching, marching, marching . . .

Rik quickly thumbed through the letters, noticing that Annie's soldier hadn't written all of them.

Oh, Emily, not even thirty years have dulled my Grief . . .

About half of the letters were from the old lady and the girlfriend, Emily. Emily's letters, despite the old-time phrases, reminded Rik of Heather—until one sentence caused him to raise his brows.

I Burn for us to share sweet intimacies . . .

Christ! He'd always thought women back then were sexually repressed—but this one sure hadn't been the shy sort. Rik grinned and gave a thumbs-up to Hudson's portrait.

No wonder Hudson was smiling.

Just a lovestruck young guy with a lot of big dreams and a habit of thinking too much. Rik could relate, as he too had been a kid with a few dreams. The 160 years between him and Hudson didn't matter so much, really.

The last letter stunned him, even though he knew the whole story from Annie:

Lieutenant Lewis Hudson has unlawfully abandoned his post and duty as an officer and shall hereby forfeit by his actions all honors, all privileges, and payments due to him by the United States Government. Let it be understood that should he be found and brought to trial, his actions constitute treason and he shall be subject to full justice. What personal effects Lieutenant Hudson left behind, I am returning to you, his family. I share your sorrow and your loss at this unhappy turn of events. May God grant you strength to forgive your son this shameful deed.

Bullshit!

Taken aback by the force of his anger, he glanced again at Annie. She'd stumbled onto something, alright, and he couldn't help but admire her dedication to Hudson. God, what he wouldn't give to have a woman at his side who'd show him loyalty like that.

He returned the letters to the exact place where he'd found them, the rock on top, and then quietly dressed—all the while watching Annie, trying to contain the deep, drawing need she'd awakened.

Once dressed, he crossed the room to the door, stopping only to pull the sheet over Annie's beautiful body, his fingers lightly brushing against her soft skin. Then he kissed her cheek and went to work.

CHAPTER TWELVE

July 27, 1832, Michigan Territory: This is no way to fight a war. The marshes sicken us, the hills confound us, the forest hides God knows what Dangers within its depths and the prairies which hide nothing at all. We know not which way to turn, where we go. General Atkinson cannot decide to Advance or Retreat. Rations are low and my men grow more restless with each passing day. We are our own worst enemy and I cannot speak, to anyone, how I fear disaster awaits just beyond the next hill or tree.

—Lieutenant Lewis Hudson,
unsent letter to his mother, Augustina

The next day, Rik returned to the house for lunch earlier than usual. As he walked through the door, a mechanical rumbling roar greeted him. He stood for a moment, boots in hand, listening to the sound of Annie vacuuming in the parlor. Then he dropped his boots and stripped off his work clothes.

He'd wash up first, then go kick that vacuum into the corner and make love to her right on the parlor floor, beneath the grim gazes of his grandpas and grannies.

The cold water he splashed on his face sent a revitalizing shock through him. Turning, Rik pulled a clean pair of shorts from the laundry basket sitting on top of his dryer—and tumbled a bra to the floor.

He stared at it, water drops tickling his skin as they rolled down his neck to his bare chest.

Just a bra.

Nothing he hadn't seen before. By sixteen he'd mastered the tough-guy art of unfastening hooks, so bras weren't a big mystery—even if this one was an eye-popper. All white, with small pearls sewn on the flower design of the lace; a bra meant to be flaunted and removed with randy reverence.

And he was more than ready to be reverent.

He headed toward the parlor, eager to see what bra Annie might be wearing right now, and stopped short in the doorway, grinning. She was singing to herself, doing some sort of cha-cha with the vacuum, bobbing her head and swishing her hips in an energetic rhythm.

Man, what that woman did for a Dirt Devil.

Rik silently enjoyed the view until she pivoted and saw him. Surprise flashed across her face, then embarrassment as she switched off the vacuum with her toe.

"You're trying to scare me witless again, aren't you?"

"Nope. Just admiring the way you wiggle those hips."

A blush tinged her cheeks as she glanced at the clock. "It's not even eleven. What are you doing back so early?"

He advanced. "Why do you think?"

"*Now?*" She grinned. "After yesterday afternoon and yesterday evening and this morning, too?"

"You know, I like how you only wear skirts." Tugging her against him, Rik grasped a fistful of the gauzy stuff and pulled it upward. "Handy."

"Not to mention cooler in hot weather."

"You'd be even cooler if you take it off," he suggested helpfully, then kissed her, sliding his free hand into the back of her panties to cup the smooth warmth of her bottom.

What he liked even more than her skirts was how she didn't play games. She shot straight about her needs, and he never had to guess if "yes" was really yes or if "no" was really no, as he'd had to with his ex-wife.

With Annie, he had no doubts. At least, not where sex was concerned.

"The bedroom?" she whispered against his neck, teasing him with her tongue. When she tickled his lobe, he went from semiaroused to rock-hard in a second.

"What's wrong with here? That spot on the floor in front of old Ole looks good to me."

She glanced at the oval photograph beneath filmy beveled glass. The white-haired old man, his white beard flowing over a black coat, glared back at them as if to say: *Don't even think about it, boy.*

"I doubt old Ole would appreciate us making whoopee under his nose," Annie said, her words nearly matching his thoughts.

"I figure he'd be glad to look at your backside instead of Auntie Clem's hat."

"Who?"

"My great-aunt Clementine." Rik eased the elasticized waistband of her skirt down her hips. When she didn't smack him, he finished the job and let the skirt rustle to the floor. She wore bright green panties made of some sheer, sparkly material that didn't hide much at all. He pressed his hips against her, trying to ease the ache. "She's the old gal that looks as if something died on top of her head."

Annie laughed as she slipped her hands beneath the waistband of his shorts. "Shame on you! Hats like that were all the rage in her day . . . oooh, my oh my, what have we here?"

She closed a hand around him, stroking him with a slow, easy back-and-forth rhythm that made him suck in his breath.

"You know us guys," he managed. "We only think about one thing."

"I'll let you in on a little secret." She squeezed him, then gently ran her nails along the underside of his erection. "Us girls think about it a lot, too."

"So let's skip thinking," he said as he slipped her T-shirt over her head. "And get right down to the doing part."

She wore a bra that matched her apple green panties, and he could see her dark, stiff nipples beneath that sheer, sparkly stuff. He bent, tonguing her nipple through her bra while she slid her hands into his hair, sighing, and held him close.

While Annie moaned softly, he fumbled at the back of her bra, searching for hooks.

"This one's a front-loader," she whispered.

Rik laughed, then had to kiss her again. "You're funny and sweet, you know that?"

She made a goofy face. "Just a laugh a minute."

At her words, something inside him gave a weird catch, but he was too busy liberating her breasts to examine it. He tossed the bra aside and it landed with a thump on the back of the floral sofa, over one of Grandma Alice's hand-tatted doilies.

Then Annie slid to the floor, taking his shorts and briefs with her, and anticipation punched his hots for her up another few degrees.

Rik slipped his hands into her hair and urged her forward. When her mouth closed over him, hot and wet, her tongue stroking him delicately, he closed his eyes tight and dropped his head backward. The sensations swept over him, demanding and intense, building with each teasing kiss. But as he began to reach his peak, he pushed her away.

"Not yet," he muttered.

Not until he made her cry out as she had this morning, when he'd made love to her in his bed while the early sunlight flickered across her bare, soft skin. He wanted to hear how he pleasured her before he let himself go.

He lowered her to the carpet, claiming her lips and mouth with such heated urgency that a moment passed before he registered the push of her hands against his chest. At once, he broke the kiss.

"Roll over," she said breathlessly, eyes shining, her smiling mouth wet from his kiss. "On your back."

Arching a brow, he rolled over—right in the line of old Ole's grumpy stare. He laughed, choking off abruptly when Annie straddled him.

"What's so funny, huh? This?"

"Christ, no," he said, with a deep groan of satisfaction as she took him inside. "But great-plus grandpa is watching."

"Well, then, make him proud."

Again he laughed, and as she moved against him, he had a fleeting thought that sex should always be like this—fun and sweaty, serious and intense. So good he wouldn't care if he died right then and there. So hot his whole damn brain melted into a white, hazy fog of pleasure.

He let her ride him until he sensed the hot slide to climax begin, then he rolled her over and began pumping, in and out, faster and harder, until he caught the rush and came with a muscle-shaking violence that left him limp and winded.

When he opened his eyes again he realized he lay sprawled across Annie. She didn't complain, but he quickly rolled off her to the parlor floor, puffing, surrounded by all the frilly stuff his female relatives had collected over the years—and the family photos. Even if all those eyes really couldn't see him and Annie lying like this on the floor, it still gave him the sensation of being watched.

After a moment his gaze settled on his parents' wedding portrait and, beside it, his and Karen's. He stared at those foolishly young faces as Annie's fingers played along his chest.

"You look far too grim for a man who just did what you did. What's wrong?"

"Nothing."

"Rik. Please. Don't make love to me and go quiet like this and then say nothing is wrong. I'm the paranoid type. Was it something I did? Or didn't do?"

He tipped his head toward her amd smiled. "Nah. Just looking at my wedding picture. I don't come in this room much anymore. Guess I'd forgotten how young I was."

Annie hitched herself up to her elbows, studying the photo with a somber expression. "You were both little more than children. Your parents must've had a fit."

"Dad was pretty pissed, that much I remember." He sat up, draping his hands over his knees. "Karen's parents never liked me. They'd wanted her to do better than a farmer struggling for every buck."

"Do you want to talk about it?"

Rik looked down at the floor. "Don't see the point."

"It helps sometimes, that's all."

"You really want to hear?" he asked, glancing up again.

"If you really want to tell me."

He smiled a little at her wry answer. "Me and Decker were friends since kindergarten. We did everything together, even chasing girls, and by our sophomore year we were both crazy about Karen. But she couldn't make up her mind about which one of us she wanted. I wish I could blame Karen and Decker for everything, but the truth is, the blame's spread around pretty evenly."

In the picture, he was standing stiffly in his rented blue tux with the ruffled shirt, and Karen in the dress she'd borrowed from her sister, a veil pinned to her long hair. They stood with hands clasped, looking back at the camera, more dazed than happy. His friends had gotten him half-drunk and he hardly remembered the ceremony, except that it was hot and he'd nearly puked on the minister's shiny black shoes.

"And to say Karen chose me over Decker would be pushing it, since we got drunk one night, and she ended up pregnant. I did the right thing and married her, but Decker swore I got her pregnant on purpose. Hell, I was seventeen and stupid, but not that stupid. He never would see it my way, though."

"You tried to make things work."

"We both did, and we were doing okay until my dad got lung cancer. Heather was four and Karen was on me to get a place of our own, but Dad needed me. Erik and Lars were away at college, and Ingrid had just gotten married, so it wouldn't have been right to leave." He fell silent, the faint echo of all those angry words and tears ringing in his memory. "Dad had run up some debts from modernizing the farm, and Decker's old man was after us to sell. But Dad wouldn't hear of it, so I took a factory job working nights to make enough money to keep us afloat."

Remembering always left him tired and angry. He'd done all the right things, made all the right choices, and everything had still gone wrong.

At the touch of Annie's hand on his, he took a long breath and continued. "When Dad got real sick, it was hard on Karen being alone, taking care of a kid and Dad, too. She liked to be taken care of herself, and I couldn't give her that. She wanted another baby, but I wanted to wait. We started fighting, and I remember thinking I didn't know her anymore. She wasn't the Karen I'd married."

"Maybe you just grew up?" She slipped her arms around his waist and squeezed him, surrounding him with the smell of Annie and vanilla. Such a peaceful, pure smell. "You never had much of a chance to be a kid, did you?"

"Nope . . . had to raise my brothers and sister after Mom died, and I was twenty-four when I took over the farm after Dad's death. Things were rough. I was still working days and nights, and when Heather started kindergarten, Karen got a job. At first, it helped a lot."

Rik finally looked away from his wedding photo. "When she started working nights after I quit the factory, I should've seen what was going on. We didn't need the money, but she wanted to work and because she seemed happy, I didn't say anything."

"How did you find out?"

"Lars and his wife came down to visit and were watching Heather, so I dropped by the restaurant to surprise Karen." Rik closed his eyes for a moment, and turned his face away from Annie. Even all these years later, the shame and pain still hurt too much to share. "I wanted to take her out to a hotel and fire up the romance, you know, because it was flagging some after ten years. Man, was I surprised to find she'd been off her shift for hours, gone next door to the feed store and Decker's office."

"Oh." After a short silence, Annie asked softly, "Was the divorce her choice, or yours?"

"Mine. I'd put her through some rough times, and she deserved to be happy. It was Decker she wanted, and I wasn't gonna stand in the way."

"That was very generous."

"Yeah. Wasn't it, though."

"But you're still angry."

He frowned. "Being mad won't change what happened. Like I said, I did what I had to do and let her go. End of the story."

"I hope that's true, Rik, and you're not keeping any anger bottled up inside, because that'll bring you nothing but grief. Believe me, I know all about it."

"Don't lecture me, Annie." He sent her a sharp look. "And what do you mean, about—"

"Did you confront Decker?" she interrupted.

His fingers tightened involuntarily. "No."

"Why not?"

He turned toward her then, glaring, regretting he hadn't just kept his mouth shut. "I had a kid to think about. Do you think I was stupid enough to cause trouble with her new stepdaddy?"

The phone rang—a timely interruption.

"I gotta go answer the phone."

But before he could move, Annie came to her feet in all her naked glory. He could only stare at her, dazed and irritated and admiring—and knowing he was gawking like some green kid.

"I'm already up, Rik. I'll get it."

"You're not even dressed. It's my phone, I'll—"

"No!"

Shit—what had gotten into her? One minute she was soft and warm, the next she was all snarls and claws like a half-wild barn cat.

With a growl, he flopped back on the floor and closed his eyes. "Fine, dammit. You go answer the phone."

Annie had only insisted because she was expecting a call, one she didn't want Rik answering. She shuddered at the thought. In this instance, Rik's timing for romance was lousy.

On the fifth ring, she picked up the phone. "Hello?"

A too-familiar voice boomed cheerfully, "Hey, Annie!"

With a furtive glance toward the parlor, she whispered, "Decker, I can't talk now."

Without another word, she hung up. She hesitated, then switched off the ringer as well, just to be safe.

"Who is it?" Rik called.

"Nobody. Wrong number."

Returning to the parlor, she found Rik already dressed—at least, as dressed as he'd been to begin with—and holding her panties and bra. Self-conscious, Annie snatched the garments from him and dressed. As she fit the bra in place over her shoulders, the elastic snapped, absurdly loud in the silence.

"Somebody just hung up, huh?"

She didn't care for the directness of his gaze. "Yes."

"You're lying."

The heat of guilt rushed through her. "What?"

"I lived with a champion liar, so I know a bad liar when I see one."

Annie looked away. "I want . . . I wish you wouldn't be so quick to assume the worst of me. But you won't ever trust me, will you, Rik?"

"Trust is something that don't come easy to me anymore. But I'm trying," he added after a moment, and she looked up to see his jaw muscles clench. "God, I am trying."

"I can't finish my work here without your help. I need your trust, and I wouldn't *ever* do anything to deliberately hurt you, Rik. I—" She stopped before blurting something she had no business saying, then finished bitterly, "Oh, for God's sake, it doesn't matter! Once I find Lewis, I'll be out of your hair—"

"Stop saying that, dammit!"

He stalked from the parlor, his back stiff, leaving Annie behind, stunned by the force of his anger. She yanked on her skirt and hurried after him, and found him at the kitchen sink, hands fisted against the counter as he stared out the window.

"Rik, you know how important this book is to me. Why are you making it so hard?"

But she knew. God, she knew.

He took a deep breath, as if clearing his head. "You gotta understand, honesty is real important to me. I can see why we both weren't truthful with each other at the start, but that's behind us now. From here on out, Annie, don't lie to me anymore."

The sudden pain in his eyes sliced through her. She wanted to tell him everything, but as she'd sensed from the start, Rik and Decker had unfinished business between them, and she didn't want her search for Lewis—or even Rik himself—to suffer because of it.

"Well?" Rik demanded, his tone almost belligerent.

"You're right. But sometimes honesty isn't always best, and now is one of the times."

Rik fixed her with a piercing, Nordic stare. "Does any of this have to do with Decker?"

On a long sigh of defeat, she said, "Yes."

"I thought so." He turned away.

"Rik, please! Try to see it from my side. I'm sorry about what happened between the two of you, but Decker has been very helpful, and I need him."

"Why?"

"He knows a lot about the Black Hawk War and the area's history, and that saves me time. I don't have much to spare. I have to leave by the end of September."

Rik said nothing—and a dark, fretful fear rose within her.

"Maybe Decker isn't above causing a little trouble between us just because he can," Annie continued, keeping her voice even. "But I've already warned him against doing so."

"He doesn't care about you or what you're doing.

He wants to use you to get back at me."

"You're wrong." God, she hated this tunnel vision of his! "Decker is genuinely interested in my work. But if you give him a chance to goad you, he'll take it. And you give him plenty of chances, don't you?"

His eyes narrowed, his color high. "Annie—"

"Honesty, Rik," she interrupted. "You want it, but can you handle it? Can you handle me telling you why you've forgiven your ex-wife for cheating on you, but not your ex–best friend?"

"No!" He pushed away from the sink. "This isn't about me or Decker. It's about why *you* keep going behind my back!"

"I'm protecting you, Rik," she finally said as he walked away from her. "In the only way I know how."

At the door he turned, his expression changing to something almost like . . . wonder. "Me? You're protecting *me*?"

"I'd be more open with you if I knew it wouldn't anger or hurt you. But we both know that can't happen. I can separate you from Decker. I can work with him, even knowing what he did, even not liking him. But you can't do the same, can you?"

"Was that Decker on the phone?"

She paused, then said, "I *am* going to see Decker today. Is this going to cause a problem between you and me?"

For a long moment he looked at her, and then his chin rose with that damn-the-world pride of his. "No."

Annie walked up to him. "Prove it."

At first he looked puzzled, still angry. Then, gathering her in his arms, he pulled her close and kissed her. A long, hard, possessive kiss. He locked her against him, didn't let her breathe, slipped his tongue inside her mouth, and kissed her until she became light-headed, engulfed. Overwhelmed and panicked within his confining, narrow hold.

But Annie fought back her fear, the smothering sensation of being closed in and trapped, and let the kiss soften as it eased the edge of his anger and distrust.

Finally, he let her go.

"You better get back to work," she said quietly. "I have to do the same."

"Yeah." He ran a hand through his hair, not looking at her. Then he turned, dressed again in his work clothes, and stalked out the door.

As the sound of his footsteps crunching on the gravel faded away, Annie sagged back against the doorjam.

She'd been the worst kind of fool. Any woman with half a brain could see Rik Magnusson was a family man. Fiercely loyal, protective, and territorial.

He needed a woman just like him to stand at his side—and she wasn't capable of that. All her life, she hadn't lived in one place long enough to learn how other, normal people managed to succeed at this love-and-commitment business.

How could she have let herself believe this thing between them would be only a casual fling? Believe that he couldn't fall in love—or that he wouldn't want to hold her here, possess her completely.

CHAPTER THIRTEEN

May 3, 1832, Jefferson Barracks, St. Louis: A ceaseless wonder to me, our Friendship. Cyrus and I see through different Eyes, yet we remain true Friends and I value him as I value no other Man. This night, we talked of the future, and I declared I shall follow Father's wishes and pursue a life in Law and Politics. Cyrus wishes to remain with the Army. It is his Life, he swears. It is no surprise, as it is no surprise Cyrus cannot see this War through my Eyes. Those who stand to gain from claiming this land, and its vast wealth, cloak their Cause beneath Noble words and speeches that stir the Heart against the Sac. Cyrus tells me falsehoods or nay, we know our duty and must obey. I know my duty, but you taught your Son too well, Mother, and I value Truth overmuch to care for this duty of mine.

—Lieutenant Lewis Hudson,
from a letter to his mother, Augustina

Later that afternoon, Annie ran Owen Decker to ground at his home, a trendy two-story affair on a thoroughly modern farm with outbuildings shaped like airplane hangars. The place reminded her of factories, of big business—nothing at all like Rik's farm, with its layer upon layer of history, each generation leaving a mark, a memory, for the next.

She parked her car in the drive and followed the walk along a well-manicured lawn, then rang the doorbell. A childish yell sounded from inside the house, followed by a woman's voice. The door opened to reveal Karen Decker.

"Ms. Beckett," she said in surprise.

Annie opened her mouth to respond, but before she could, a dark-haired little boy chirped, "Hi!"

"Well, hello to you, too." She smiled down at the boy, who wore a *Tyrannosaurus rex* T-shirt and baggy shorts. A handsome child, like his father. She glanced back up. "May I come in?"

At her question, Karen recollected herself and stepped back from the door. "I'm sorry. I . . . wasn't expecting you."

"I've come to see your husband," Annie said, shutting the door behind her. "Mrs. Michlowski said he's here."

The house was ferociously air-conditioned, and Annie saw she stood just off a cheery living room with toy cars and Duplo building blocks strewn across its floor. Nice, but it lacked the charm of Rik's place.

"Yes, he's here," Karen Decker answered after a moment, as her son wrapped himself around her hips, accentuating her pregnancy. "Sweetie, don't squeeze Mommy so hard." She smiled. "At this point, it doesn't take much to put a strain on my bladder. Jason, can you go upstairs and tell Daddy there's a lady here to see him?"

"Okay!" The boy, eager to help, raced off, and Annie listened to the thump of his small footsteps running on the floor above.

"How's Rik?" Karen Decker asked at length. Something sad, even guarded, shadowed her blue eyes.

Hardly the epitome of a sultry Scarlet Woman.

"Fine," Annie said. "He was heading to the barn when I last saw him. Working. You know Rik."

At that, Karen managed a true smile, and it made her look younger; more like the girl in the wedding photo. "He does work hard."

Footsteps sounded through the strained silence; a heavy tread trailed by a light *pitter-patter*. Father and son, coming down the stairs. Annie glanced up, then back at Karen Decker.

"He's a good man," Karen said softly.

Her tone was strangely both defensive and regretful, and Annie didn't know if she meant her current husband or her ex-husband.

"Ah. Annie," Decker said, coming forward, his son balanced on his hip. He wore khaki trousers and a polo shirt, sharp and handsome as usual. "I tried calling a couple times—"

"Rik was home, so I turned off the ringer," she interrupted.

An awkward silence followed, as Decker glanced at his pale, wide-eyed wife and handed over their son.

"Why don't we go upstairs to my office." He kissed his wife, caressed her round belly as if in comfort, then ruffled his son's hair. The little boy laughed. "This way."

Annie followed, smiling again at Karen Decker— who didn't smile back—and winked at Jason. He had a sudden attack of shyness and buried his face in the crook of his mother's neck.

Decker's office turned out to be a typical masculine affair of dark paneling, gun cases, and hunting-theme artwork. Once they were seated, he said, "Does Rik know you're here?"

Odd, how Decker always referred to Rik as Rik, but Rik never called Decker by his first name.

"Of course he knows I'm here. I'm just renting a room in his house; he doesn't have any say in my life. He doesn't think much of my work and couldn't care less if I see you."

Decker leaned back in the chair, one dark brow raised, watching her. "Is that so?"

"Yes," Annie answered, her tone clipped. Despite everything she'd said to Rik earlier, she didn't quite trust this man, and if she gave the impression she and Rik were uninvolved, maybe Decker would back off. "As he's told me a hundred times already, he's a very busy man and doesn't have time for my nonsense. Of course, he used a more colorful turn of phrase."

"I'm sure he did," Decker said, still watching her with hawklike interest, as if deciding whether or not she was a snack worthy of his attention. "So. Why are you here?"

"First, I want to thank you for alerting the local media to my story. I do appreciate it, although in the future I'd prefer you let me know ahead of time."

He smiled. "It was a sudden whim. I had Betty call. I also asked her to call you, but she must've forgotten. Betty *is* getting on in years."

Just like the reporter had "tried" to call, no doubt. "I also want to talk to you about General Cyrus Patterson Boone. Specifically, if he ever came to this area later in his life."

"I haven't heard that he did. But several of his descendents came to the Bad Axe in 1932 for the memorial ceremony. There was a write-up about it in a few local newspapers at the time. We have copies here in the museum. Talk to Betty about it."

"I may do that, thank you."

Tipping his head, Decker regarded her with a knowing gaze. "Why are you asking about Boone, anyway? The man's reputation is spotless. He was one of the Union's finest generals, despite his feuds with Lincoln. He married a society belle, had a half dozen kids, and died a very rich old man."

"I'm asking because Boone and Lewis were friends, but my research shows Boone also deeply envied Lewis." She paused, satisfied by the sudden, closed look on his face. "Boone came from old money, and Lewis didn't. Lewis excelled at West Point, while Boone finished toward the middle of his class. Lewis outranked Boone after graduation, even though Lewis was younger by a year. Envy can make a man do strange things."

Decker went still, then arched a dark brow with indifference—but Annie didn't miss the tightening of muscles around his mouth. "Your point?"

"Stop antagonizing Rik."

On a burst of laughter, Decker sat back. "I have to tell you, it would drive Rik crazy if he knew you were here trying to fight his battles for him."

"So there's a battle to be won after all, Owen?"

Anger filled his dark eyes. "I'll see you to the door, Ms. Beckett."

After being politely escorted out of the house, Annie climbed into her car with a sinking feeling in the pit of her stomach.

Rik didn't hide his dislike for Decker, but only now did she see what lay beneath Decker's gentlemanly façade—and saw that she had somehow reawakened an old and bitter rivalry.

Maybe the tunnel vision had been hers all along, and not Rik's. Maybe she owed him an apology.

When she pulled into the drive at the farm, she saw Rik running toward the older barn, the one his great-great-grandfather had built. Its gray timbers, worn by time and weather, still stood strong enough to provide a warm, dry home for the Belgians.

Alarmed, she rolled down the window and called, "Rik, what's wrong?"

"Nothing!" He turned, jogging backward. "Venus just had her foal. Come see her!"

With a burst of excitement, Annie quickly parked the car and ran toward the old barn.

"Rik, where are you?"

"Back stall."

His voice came from the depths behind a huge green-and-yellow John Deere tractor, combine, and corn picker—a very scary-looking device, and she carefully inched past it.

She joined Rik where he stood just outside the stall, intently watching the mare and her tiny, wobbly-legged new foal. The air smelled thickly of sweat, and Rik's blue shirt and arms were specked with stains she'd rather not identify.

But all that paled to nothing beside the wonder of this newborn creature, with its big eyes and springy little tail.

"Oh . . . she's beautiful," Annie whispered, amazed.

"Yeah," Rik said, pride ringing clear in his voice. He rubbed a gentle hand along the mare's flank. "I knew you'd give us a pretty baby, Venus."

Annie watched, thinking it sad he'd been denied

the chance to live with his own daughter and watch her grow. A man like this was prime father material. And prime husband material.

She looked away from Rik's happy face, her gaze catching his soiled shirt. "Your shirt's a mess."

"Yeah. Venus needed a little help there toward the end. We'll wash up," he said.

"We?"

Rik grinned at her; that boyish grin that made her breath catch.

And more.

Her heart made a hard, solid thump, a punctuation point to the obvious.

Oh, God. How had this happened? How had she let it happen? So busy fearing he'd fall in love with her, fearing he'd be hurt when she left . . . she hadn't even seen the danger to herself until now.

Too late. And too impossible. All of it, impossible.

Blind need drove her into his arms, a need fueled by panic as much as a need to hold him close, to have the heat of his body chase away the sudden chill inside her.

He grunted as she threw herself at him and stumbled back against the stall, holding her close. Then he kissed her; fierce and possessive—not asking why, not asking what was wrong or right, only giving her what she needed.

Then he pulled back, kissed her nose, and grinned again. "Let's wash up and have us a celebration."

After a last check on Venus and her foal—nursing noisily, tail twitching with eager delight—Annie took Rik's hand in hers. They walked back to the house, swinging their entwined hands like a couple of kids.

There was nothing childish about that gleam in

Rik's eyes, though, and he stripped off his shirt before he even reached the cellar door. He barely waited until she was within the cavelike place before he had her up against the cool, damp wall and yanked her shirt free.

Annie shivered at his touch. Or maybe it was the cold, creepy cellar . . . not exactly a primo spot for a seduction. She tried concentrating on the pleasure curling through her as Rik kissed her breasts with his hot mouth, and not how many spiders and other creepy-crawlies lurked about, waiting gleefully to burrow into her hair.

"What's the matter?" he murmured against her ear, and she shivered again.

"I hate the dark. And skittery things with lots of legs."

He laughed then, his quick hands making short work of her clothes. She helped him along until they both stood in the cellar with nothing on but their socks. Rik stripped off even those, but she wasn't so brave and dashed up the steep, rickety stairs for the bathroom.

Rik followed right behind her, with a smart smack on her bare behind. She squeaked, then his warm body pressed against her as he cranked the water full blast into the tub.

"For you, I'll even do Mr. Bubble," Rik said, dumping a shocking amount of the stuff into the tub.

"*Mr. Bubble?*" As she eased into the warm, wildly foaming water, Annie sent him a questioning look—and a quick peek at the powerful erection jutting toward her. "You don't strike me as a bubble-bath kind of guy."

"It's Heather's," he said, one corner of his mustache

hitching up as he noted the direction of her gaze. "How is it?"

Annie cleared her throat, hoping he meant the water temperature. "Why don't you come in and find out yourself?"

"Guess I will." Rik maneuvered around her, then sank into the water and stretched out against the back of the tub, his head resting against the tile. "Jesus, this feels good . . . but I know what'll make it feel even better."

"Men," she said, laughing. "You are so predictable."

"Part of our charm," he agreed, as she settled against him, kissing him deeply, unmindful of anything until Mr. Bubble got a little out of hand and Rik had to shut off the water.

Then he returned to his lounging position and pulled Annie back against him. She settled against his wet, soapy chest with a contented sigh. His tub was big and deep enough to spiff up several kids at once—or two adults who wanted to mix a little sex with their soap.

With Rik's erection nudging her back, Annie scooted up his chest. She shot him a playful grin, then gathered a mass of bubbles and arranged it over her breast.

"What are you doing?"

She scooped up more bubbles over her other breast. "Always wondered what it'd be like to be a forty-quadruple D." She eyed the two bubble mountains on her chest. "So, what do you think? Are we working toward another male fantasy here?"

Behind her, Rik's body shook with silent laughter. He flicked the bubbles away, his hands cupping her breasts, thumbs massaging her nipples. "I'll pass on this one."

She sighed, squirming a little at the sharp threads of desire winding through her. "I thought all men were hot for really big boobs."

"Some of us are just hot for whatever boobs are at hand," he said, kissing the side of her neck.

"Hmph." His mustache tickled and she jabbed him gently with her elbow. "That wasn't very romantic."

"Hey, I'm pretty much your standard-issue male and like boobs on principle. Size doesn't matter."

Sloshing in the water, Annie turned. She eyed his crotch, then the bubbles surrounding him.

Rik laughed. "Better not."

"Spoilsport. It's *my* turn to play out a fantasy. Why can't I have Mighty Dong?"

"*Mighty Dong?*"

"Super Dong?" She grinned. "Captain Penis?"

"Honey, I think that ranks as blasphemy."

The gleam in his eyes alerted her, but he dunked her too quickly for her to react. As she came up sputtering, he squeezed shampoo in his hand and pulled her close.

"I'd wash out your mouth with soap, but I'm feeling lazy."

"No fair. You're bigger than me," she grumbled, as his fingers worked the shampoo into a rich lather, massaging and caressing as he did so. "Do I get to dunk you?"

"You can try."

"You bet I—"

"Annie. Hold that breath."

She got out a yell before he dunked her again, but couldn't protest further—he continued rinsing her hair and the water kept running into her mouth. She waited until he'd finished before making her move. She grabbed his ankles and yanked, but he didn't fight back at all as she pulled him under. He surfaced with a laugh, spitting suds and shaking his hair like a wet dog.

By this time, half the water in the tub had sloshed over onto the floor, so Annie ran more water as they soaped each other's bodies clean. The touches, wet and slippery, lingering and deliberate, left her aching to make love to him, to take that hard, wholly male part of him deep inside and unwind that knot of desire, tightening with every moment they played.

"The tub's big enough for some hanky-panky," she whispered, nibbling at his earlobe, fingers tight on his shoulder as she moved over him and rubbed against his erection.

He only grunted, his hands hard on her skin as she lifted her hips and settled down slowly, taking him inside bit by bit.

Suddenly he stiffened. "Wait. Shit! I'm not—"

Annie kissed him quiet, uncaring.

But Rik pulled out of her, with a glare that should've sizzled her on the spot. "What the hell's the matter with you? Do you want to get pregnant?"

"Of course not!"

Cool denial, over a flash of images: Rik's smiles and gentle hands, his touch warming her to the core, the newborn foal nursing beneath the mare's satisfied, maternal gaze—and for the briefest moment, Annie imagined Rik at her side as she nursed a beautiful, golden Viking baby at her breast.

The cold inside her began to spread again. God, how foolish could she be? This life—this man—

wasn't for her. She had no business even fantasizing about it.

"You're right," she said, standing, the water rolling off her body in little waterfalls and drips. Rik's gaze on her was hot, hungry. "I guess we got a little carried away."

He pushed up, still erect, and kissed her. She sensed that his hard, abrupt kiss was meant to tell her something, but she didn't understand and hadn't the courage to ask.

Rik grabbed several towels and they dried each other off. Then, still without a word, he took her hand and drew her to his bedroom. She loved his room: so big and airy, with its sky-blue walls, old spindle bed, and hand-stitched summer quilt. Even in the coldest Wisconsin winters, Rik's bedroom would offer summertime cheer and warmth.

When he moved to draw the shades over the windows, Annie said, "No. Don't shut out the sun."

After getting the condom in place, he lowered himself on the bed over her; his body a wall of tense heat. He made love to her slowly, gently, coaxing her to a climax several times with his mouth, then his hands, before he finally slid inside and let himself go.

Afterward, holding him in her arms, Annie fought back tears.

She wouldn't make matters even worse by crying.

When they'd cleaned up again, Rik made grilled cheese sandwiches in his underwear. Annie didn't think she'd be able to eat a grilled cheese sandwich with a straight face ever again. Once they'd eaten, she enticed him up to the second floor to help her clean. He protested until she said, "I promise to make it worth your while. There's five beds up here."

"Four," he reminded her, blue eyes bright with interest.

"That's still quite enough!"

He helped her open all the doors and windows wide. Finally she asked him to push the old player piano farther out onto the floor so she could dust it.

Then, throwing the rag aside, Annie plinked out the chords of "Chopsticks."

"How's that?" She grinned at him. "Pretty impressive, eh?"

Rik returned the grin and edged her out of the way with his hip. He played a few chords as if warming up and then, with a flourish, launched into an energetic, rhythmic ragtime song. She watched his long, work-roughened fingers fly across the keyboard, and when he finished, she stared at him, wide-eyed with shock.

"My God. I had no idea you could do that! You don't—"

"Look the type?" Rik finished her sentence, his tone wry. "I only know a couple songs. Mom taught piano to bring in extra money, and I learned from her. I haven't played since Heather lived here." He ran his fingers along the keys in a plaintive, discordant string of notes. "Mom sure loved this old piano."

"You still miss your mother a lot, don't you?"

"Sometimes." He didn't look at her. "I was just a kid when she left us."

Annie kissed his cheek softly, then whispered, "Do you have a picture of her?"

He turned, pointed. "Right there. Mom and Dad both."

Annie walked over to examine it. A buzz-cut youth, a sturdy young woman with hair as starched as her dress. Both blond and clean-cut. Sunny. She traced the faces with her finger.

"A lovely couple. What were their names?"

"John and Laura."

"And these must be your brothers and sister... your parents made some very pretty babies. I bet they'd be proud of you."

"I should fix this thing." Rik looked away and ran his fingers over the yellowed ivory keys again. "I gotta go call Heather. Our deal is that she names all the fillies, and she'll be mad if I don't tell her Venus had her foal. Then I'll get my tools and come back. Don't go anywhere."

"Oh, I won't." She watched him walk toward the stairs, back straight with pride, even with all the hurt inside he wouldn't let go—and she ached to see him smile again. "If you can get this old player piano to work, we're turning off the lights and dancing in the dark. All night long."

Rik glanced over his shoulder and grinned. "You're gonna kill me yet—but I'll die a happy man."

Then he made his way down to the kitchen. Yawning, tired and content and warm from making love with Annie, he dialed the phone.

Decker answered, and just like that, Rik's peaceful mood shattered.

"Get Heather," he said coldly.

"In a minute. I need to know if you've seen Annie lately."

Rik said nothing.

A pause. "Oh, that's right, she's living with you. Must be nice having a pretty woman around the house again."

"I want my daughter on the phone now."

"Sure. As soon as you give Annie a message for me."

"I'm listening." Pencil scratching against the note-pad, Rik wrote down a series of names and numbers. No way would he give the bastard the satisfaction of knowing how much he hated that Annie had asked for Decker's help before she'd asked for his.

Then he talked with Heather and somehow ended up agreeing she could bring a bunch of her giggly friends with her when she came to visit on Friday.

After he hung up the phone, he fetched his toolbox and spent the next hour flat on his back on the floor or crawling about the innards of a musty old piano. He got the rollers working while Annie chattered away and tidied the second floor. For the first time since his dad had died and Karen had left, the landing glowed bright and shiny.

"All this wonderful stuff!" Annie burst out at one point, kissing him so fast he hadn't a chance to kiss her back. "My God, I could spend years exploring it all. Do you have any idea what a lifetime of stories you have up here?"

He'd only grunted an answer, because until she'd let him see it through her eyes, it'd been just a lot of dreary, broken junk.

By the time he'd finished chores and dinner, and by the time he and Annie had tested each of those four beds and one braided rug—first base in room one, second base in room two, home run in room four and a time out in room five—it was dark enough to dance, Annie nuzzling his neck, bare and warm in his arms.

And all night long, all through the dark house rang the echo of off-key ragtime music, murmurs, and laughter.

CHAPTER FOURTEEN

July 17, 1832, Youngstown, Ohio: You must not, my Dear, tell me not to worry, for I am a Mother and it is my sole Right and Duty as a Mother to worry about my child and especially when that child, no matter how tall and handsome and strong, is far away and engaged in Dangerous Pursuits amid blood-thirsty Heathens.

—AUGUSTINA HUDSON,
FROM A LETTER TO HER SON, LEWIS

"You know, you'll have to keep your hands off me while Heather is here," Annie said.

It was early evening, and he and Annie had finished dinner. She'd cooked—nothing fancy, just spaghetti and a salad—which left him with the chore of loading the dishwasher.

Rik looked at her, admiring the slim lines of her ivory knit dress. Its long skirt drew his gaze downward to her bare feet. She'd painted her toenails with some of Heather's baby pink polish.

A guy was in deep when he found a woman's toes sexy.

"Nothing kills dirty thoughts quicker than a bunch of giggling girls."

"Good point," Annie admitted, walking toward him as he started the machine. "It's only for a few hours. I think I can keep my hands off you for that long."

"Keep looking at me like that and we'll never make it out of the kitchen," he said, amused, not missing the direction of her gaze. It boosted his ego. Just a bit. "I'm thinking the table looks just about the right height and it's long enough, too. Come here, woman."

"Oooh, I love it when you get barbaric," she teased, then came into his arms and tipped her head for a kiss.

But before he could do more than slide his hands down her back and pull her close, Buck gave a loud woof and dashed toward the entryway. At the door, he revved into his barking-his-head-off routine.

Rik glanced at the clock, reluctantly dropping his hands from her curving bottom. "Six-thirty. One thing I'll give the bastard, he's punctual. Buck, shut up!"

Together, he and Annie waited on the porch as the dark sedan drove closer, its engine humming as the driver shifted into park. Then the doors opened, ejecting five girls into the yard, all of them giggling.

Rik suppressed a groan. Man, it would be a long couple of hours.

An electrical whine sounded as Decker lowered the driver's side window. "What time do you want me to pick them up?"

"I'll drive them home myself," Rik answered curtly.

Decker nodded. "Sounds good. See you later, Heather."

Heather, far too busy with her friends, didn't respond. Probably on purpose.

"Heather, somebody's talking to you," Rik said, loudly enough to interrupt her.

Startled, she looked at him, then at Annie. "Huh? Sorry, Dad. I wasn't listening."

"Not me." He pointed to Decker.

Heather grimaced as she flounced around. "Okay. We're here. We're thankful. You can go now."

Rik gave her a look that let her know her lapse in manners would be dealt with later. With a sulky expression, Heather turned away.

Acting as if her rudeness were no big deal, Decker leaned further out the window, and said, "Annie, I'm still getting together the names you asked for, regarding Boone. I should have a complete list ready within the next couple days."

It was stupid, and the girls were watching, but Rik moved closer to Annie and rested his hand low on her hip. Decker, who looked like he might've said more, snapped his mouth shut.

Annie didn't move away, even though her body tensed at Rik's touch.

"Thank you, Owen," she said, politely enough. "I'll give you a call in a few days, then."

He raised the car's tinted window, turned in the yard, and rumbled away down the drive.

The girls swarmed together, and Rik did his best to ignore how a few of Heather's friends darted bright-eyed looks his way, giggling when he noticed them. It was something he was getting used to: Heather had told him her friends considered him "hot."

"Dad, can we go see Venus now?"

"You know the rules. No yelling, no going in the stall, and no sudden moves. Venus is still nervous." He glanced at Annie. "You want to come along?"

"Sure," she answered, and now the girls turned and stared at her. They didn't bother hiding their curious, measuring looks. More giggles erupted, then whispering.

"No, she's not!" Heather said, a little too loudly. "She's just living in our attic."

Rik glanced at Annie and saw a smile tugging at her lips.

"Hey," he said. "I want to introduce you girls to Annie Beckett. She's a writer and a photographer. Annie, these are my daughter's friends—Maggie, Erin, Bethany, and Tamara."

The girls—who all dressed the same and wore their hair long—said hello, accompanied by another round of curious looks.

"What do you write?" asked dark-haired Tamara.

Rik approved of her. She was brighter and more mature than most of Heather's cronies.

"Documentary nonfiction," Annie answered.

"Bo-o-o-ring," droned Erin.

This one, on the other hand, he considered a few pints short of a gallon.

"Not really," Heather broke in, to his surprise. "She's working on this cool mystery about a soldier who disappeared on our land ages ago. You should see him. He's kinda cute."

"There you go: Lewis Hudson, teeny-bopper idol," Rik whispered in Annie's ear and moved aside quickly to avoid her jabbing elbow.

Once in the barn, the girls "oohed" and "ahhed" over the filly, like they always did when facing a cute baby-thing with wide eyes and a clumsy gait that came from not yet understanding how to work those long sticks attached to its body.

"My God," Annie said quietly, moving close against him. "Just days old and look at her hop around like that!"

Raising his voice, Rik asked, "Have you decided on a name for her yet, princess?"

Bouncing excitedly, Heather said, "We talked about it on the way over. Tamara says I should name her Titania."

"That's a nice name. Tamara, are you a fan of Shakespeare?" Annie asked.

Tamara looked puzzled. "I was thinking of the boat. You know, the movie about the *Titanic*? But that didn't sound like a girl's name, so we came up with Titania."

"Ah," Annie said.

"Did Shakespeare write about a Titania?" Heather asked.

"Yes, in *A Midsummer Night's Dream*. She was queen of the fairies."

"Sounds good to me, princess. Is that what you want?"

His question spawned a hurried, whispered conference and then Heather said, in a lofty, British accent, "Yes, and I hereby name thee Titania." Giggling again, she added, "Titania the Too-cute. Oooh, look at her! Isn't she so, so sweet?"

"That's my cute limit," Rik said with a grimace. "Heather, Annie and I are heading back to the house. Are you girls coming?"

"Can we stay in the barn?"

"Sure, but not too long. You don't want to make Venus nervous."

With Annie at his side and Buck trotting along at their heels, Rik set a leisurely pace back to the house.

As they approached it Annie stopped to take a deep breath and said, "I love it here. It smells so fresh, and the quiet is pure bliss—even to a dedicated city slicker like me."

Rik opened the gate. "I couldn't live anywhere else. This is where I belong. Wouldn't even care if someday, when my time's up, they buried me beneath that big old oak in the backyard." At his words, her smile faded, and she looked away. "What's wrong, Annie?"

"What you just said, it made me wonder . . . oh, never mind. You'll only think it's stupid."

Rik caught her arm and pulled her to him. "Nothing about you is stupid, Annie. Now tell me."

She looked embarrassed. "I was only thinking how much I hope Lewis had a chance to make love to a woman before he died. It seems so awful, that he might not have ever known what it's like to . . . to have what we have, I mean." She looked away again, her cheeks pink. "See? I told you it was stupid."

Rik paused, unsure what to say. "What about the girlfriend?"

"Oh, they never would've been left alone long enough for that," Annie answered, as they began walking again, and she caught his hand in hers. "Besides, Lewis was too much the gentleman to compromise her reputation. He would've done the right thing and waited until they were married."

"He was a soldier, and there must've been a friendly female or two around the fort." Not that Rik cared if Hudson ever got lucky, but he hated seeing Annie sad. "The kid probably got laid a time or two."

"You are so crude!" She smacked him lightly on the arm. Then she laughed, and that was all that mattered.

Still, it left him thinking and wondering, too. Thinking he should take the time to enjoy what life had to offer, or else what was the point? Annie sure had a way of making him look at things in a different way.

On the porch, they watched the sun settle over the wooded bluff of the Hollow. Annie leaned against the main column, tracing her finger over the heart and initials carved into the wood long ago. In the sunlight, with her flowing pale dress, she looked like an angel.

Rik came to stand beside her and she gave him a heavy-lidded, nonangelic glance. Damn. One look, and whoosh! He was all afire for her again, ready to make love to her in a heartbeat. Even though he knew this was only because of the newness, he marveled at its power.

"Who was the ardent swain?" she asked, tapping her finger against the crude letters.

"Great-grandpa John. He proposed to Great-grandma Ilsa right where you're standing."

She looked up, smiling with delight. "Really?"

"It's a tradition. Grandpa Edward proposed to Grandma Alice here, and my dad proposed to my mom here."

"And you proposed here, too?"

His smile faded. "No. Maybe that's why my marriage went bad. I broke tradition and didn't get any of the family magic."

Annie looked out toward the Hollow. "Well, it's a very lovely and romantic spot."

He moved in closer, until he could smell her sweet vanilla scent, until the breeze blew strands of her hair into his face, and until he could soak in the warmth of her body.

"I guess it's safe for me to stand here," she said.

"You won't be doing any proposing to me."

Her tone was light, playful, but Rik thought he heard something more. Maybe he was just reading into her words things he shouldn't.

"I'm thinking about one," he said, and she jerked her head around to stare at him, wide-eyed with alarm.

"I'm proposing to kiss a pretty lady, if she'll let me."

She smiled then. "What about our peanut gallery?"

Rik glanced toward the barn. "Not a peanut in sight."

"So we're safe." She turned toward him and he wrapped his arms around all her soft warmth and drew her close. She always smelled so good, so bright and shiny. He kissed her; a long, deep kiss he hoped she understood didn't just mean sex.

Still, Annie pulled away after a moment, her eyes half-closed, cheeks flushed. She ran her fingers along his face, tracing the line of his jaw, his nose, his lips.

"You are a remarkable man, Rurik Magnusson," she said, then startled him with a light smack on his ass. "And distracting. You almost make me forget why I'm here to begin with. I have to go: Lewis awaits, and I really must get some work done today."

He nodded, and watched her walk away.

Damn it all to hell, if he hadn't just been thrown over for a dead man. Again.

Working in her makeshift darkroom—the attic's tiny bathroom—Annie heard the girls return to the house an hour or so later. She could hardly miss them; they sounded like a small invasion.

She swished her prints around in the chemical

trays, watching the images slowly seep inward, ghost-like and indistinct. She was developing the last roll of film she'd taken at the Hollow—which she should've done days ago.

She sighed and began pinning up the prints to dry. Even though she needed to be in Montreal by October for a travel brochure shoot, she couldn't find the energy to plow through the most mindless of tasks, much less begin searching for Lewis in earnest.

Finishing this book meant she'd have to say good-bye, and despite all her talk of truth and justice and familial duty, her interest in Lewis was mostly self-serving. She didn't need a high-priced shrink to make the connection for her. In her life, nothing lasted; places and people came and went. But for the last ten years, she'd shared the bond and love between Lewis, his mother, and Emily. It had helped fill the empty little place inside her that nothing else had filled.

Until now.

Sudden tears stung her eyes.

"Idiot," she berated herself.

That didn't help, either.

Just then the sounds of an argument carried to her, despite the closed door and two flights of stairs. A deep male voice and strident female complaints. Annie glanced up from the tray, but resisted the urge to go downstairs.

It didn't concern her, and Rik hardly required her opinions on Heather. He understood his daughter's moods were partly because she was unhappy, embarrassed, and confused by what had happened between her parents.

A sudden, rapid pounding of feet on the steps warned Annie the battle had come to her door anyway. She quickly pinned up the last print, then let herself out of the darkroom.

A moment later, Heather stormed into the room and launched herself across the yellow chenille spread.

"Uh-oh," Annie said, then asked as she was meant to, "What's wrong?"

"He hates me! He doesn't even want me around!"

"I take it 'he' is your father?"

"He won't ever listen to me. He never lets me do anything fun and or—"

"Heather! Get down here right now and don't bother Annie with this crap!"

"It's okay," Annie called, as the first step creaked under the weight of his foot. "You don't need to come up. Heather isn't bothering me, and we can have a talk."

A brief silence. "Five minutes. Then she gets her butt back down here."

Turning to Heather, Annie saw the girl's mutinous bottom lip—and the sparkle of tears in her blue eyes. "*Der Führer* has spoken," Heather said bitterly.

Ignoring the bait, Annie asked, "Why are you upset?"

"He won't let my friends spend the night. He said he has too much work to do. Work, work, work," she spat. "He never has time for me. God, no wonder my mom ran away. Even Owen has time for me. I told him so, too!"

Oh, boy.

Annie sat on the bed beside the girl. "Did you ask ahead of time if your friends could spend the night?"

"No, but what difference does it make? It's not like we have school tomorrow. We don't want to go back to Mom's house. We want to stay. I won't get in the way." Heather gave her a pleading look. "Can you talk to him?"

Double oh boy.

"Heather, try and look at it from his point of view. Having four girls drop in out of the blue isn't convenient, no matter how much you swear you'll stay out of his way."

"I wanted him to take us for a hayride, like he did when I was little, but he said he doesn't have time." The tears spilled over. "Fine. If he doesn't want me, I won't come here ever again!"

"Of course he wants you," Annie said.

"No, he doesn't. He never did. He had to marry my mom, you know."

"I know." She gave Heather's hand a squeeze. "Your dad loves you, but making difficult demands on him isn't the way to make him prove it. You're very lucky. I wish I'd had a father I could have fought with, like this."

Heather stared. "Are you an orphan or something?"

"Not exactly. Just one of those kids left to the state to raise."

She laid it bare in a matter-of-fact voice, that old, restless hurt. How could a mother not want a child? Or, more to the point, not want her? Had she been too stupid or ugly? Cried too much? Who was her father, and why hadn't he cared, either?

"That really sucks," Heather said, still wide-eyed. "So, like, did you live in an orphanage?"

"A series of foster homes. I wasn't a well-mannered child. Since I couldn't get mad at my mother, I got mad at everybody else, which didn't make me very lovable or adoptable."

Time had a way of dulling even painful anger and fear, the childish fantasy that her parents had searched for her but just couldn't find her. She'd mostly come to terms with it, but doubted the remaining tiny spurts of anger and betrayal would ever completely fade.

"And in high school," Annie added, "the popular kids voted me the kid most likely to die young."

"Whoa," Heather whispered. "Were you, like . . . I mean, did you do drugs and stuff?"

"Yes, until some people helped me see that I could hurt myself all I wanted, but it wouldn't make me feel any better about myself or punish my mother for abandoning me. Then I got lucky. When I was fifteen, a social worker hooked me up with a volunteer who helped me change my life."

"Like a big-sister program?" Heather asked, a small frown creasing her smooth skin.

Annie nodded. "Lucy Cantor was an amateur photographer who helped me find something to focus on besides my anger. I got into a drug-rehab program, landed in a decent foster home, and improved my grades enough in my last year of high school to win a college scholarship. I got my life in order, and never looked back."

"That's so sad!"

"Heather, a lot of things happen to kids that are beyond their control—like the situation with your mom and dad. You don't have to like it, but it's your choice how you deal with it. Waste your life on anger, or move on and find your own happiness."

The girl glanced away, blinking back tears. "It's so

hard! I try not to let it bug me, but everybody still talks about it, about what my mom did . . . And my dad, he didn't even try to fight for her or anything. He just let her go."

"Making yourself and your parents miserable won't magically fix any of that. Your mom and dad will still be divorced, your mom will still have found another man to make a new family with, and your dad will always be a hard worker. He can't help that."

"But he used to have time for me," Heather said softly.

"He still does—but you're too old to make demands like a little kid. That only upsets your dad and makes you unhappy. Believe it or not, having parents who love you enough to sometimes drive you crazy is a good thing." Annie grinned, then poked Heather with her elbow, to keep the girl's tears at bay. "You better get going. I think we've blown our five-minute limit."

Heather bounced off the bed. As Annie stood, the girl exclaimed, "Dad, I was just going down. You didn't have to come get me!"

Annie spun to see Rik in the open doorway, in the shadows. Of course, he knew all the creaky places on the stairs as well as she did—and how to avoid them should he so choose. How long had he been there?

"I didn't hear you come up," she said flatly.

"Guess you two were too busy yakking."

Clearly aware of the undercurrents in the room, Heather glanced between the two adults, frowning.

"Get in the truck, young lady, and no more tantrums. I won't put up with that crap, and you know it."

Heather opened her mouth, then took a deep breath

instead. "Can I have a sleep over with my friends? Not next Friday, because I have to baby-sit Jason, but the weekend after that?"

Rik looked over the top of his daughter's head toward Annie. "I can swing that, if it's okay with your mom."

"Promise?" Heather demanded in a tone of suspicion.

His face softened. "Promise."

"Will you take us to the mall?"

Rik hesitated, then nodded. "Sure—I'll even take the whole mob to one of the big malls in Madison. You can shop where all the swanky college kids do."

With a squeal, Heather threw her arms around his neck and squeezed. "Thank you, thank you! I can't wait, this will be so awesome! Can we buy clothes for school? Maybe some new CDs? I'll ask Owen for the money, if you want."

Annie had to look away at the expression on Rik's face. "We'll talk about that later, Heather. Go down to the truck now. Your friends are waiting."

"Okay." Heather turned to Annie. "You haven't finished your soldier's book yet, have you?"

"No." Annie still hadn't moved from the bed, feeling as if the room was webbed with electrical currents and any move she made would be dangerous.

"Cool! I hope it takes a long time—I don't want you to go yet. See you later, Annie."

Annie listened to the sound of Heather's footsteps as she raced down the stairs, leaving her alone with Rik. For a long moment, they stared at each other across the room.

"You'd better go, before they decide they can drive themselves home."

"Yeah." He shifted, then said quietly, "Thank you."

She managed a flippant smile. "Hold that thank-you until after you get my therapy bill."

He still didn't move.

Annie broke the standoff by turning away. "I'd better get back to work."

She walked to the table and pretended to look at files, then listened to the sound of his receding footsteps and finally the crunch of gravel as he drove the truck away. The wind carried the sound of youthful laughter back to her.

Forty-five minutes later she heard the truck return, but Rik didn't come back to the house. At the turret window, she pushed aside the faded curtains and watched him stride toward the barn.

Cows to milk. Horses to settle and feed. A new mother to check on.

Well, what did she expect? That he'd come rushing back to her over a sob story better left forgotten? She was as bad as Heather, tempted to make unreasonable demands so he would prove she had a place in his life.

Bad idea. Rik owed her nothing. He had his priorities, she had her own, and she'd best remember that.

Determined to get those priorities straight, Annie sat at the table. She turned on her laptop, then opened the book file and scrolled to where she'd left off:

Here, at this tower of rock which will one day be called Black Hawk's Hollow, Lewis spends his last night. Here is where his journey takes an unforeseen turn: the journey that began in a wealthy household in Ohio, continued onward to the heady excitement of West Point, and finally to the loneliness of a frontier fort, ends here in mystery.

Ugh. That wasn't what she wanted. Too melodramatic.

She retrieved one of the newly developed photos she'd taken of the Hollow and stared at it, willing the Goddess of Inspiration to hit.

As always, her eye was drawn to the curving rock, bent like fingers beckoning inward. Maybe she could do something with that image: *the ancient stone tower beckons Lewis Hudson to his fate* . . .

God, that was even worse.

She gazed again at the photo. Not fingers; maybe arms. Sheltering arms . . . embracing arms. . . .

Sudden cold sliced through her, and she dropped the picture to the table, goose bumps rising on her skin.

Within its dark and cold embrace . . .

"Oh, my God," Annie whispered. She bolted down the steps, shot through the door, and ran for the barn, shouting for Rik.

CHAPTER FIFTEEN

July 29, 1832, Michigan Territory: I am sick. Sick at heart and weary of this War. With each passing hour, my belief in our Cause rots further away. Where is there honor in slaughter, in the violation of Innocents? Can murder be just, as long as one's skin is White and the other Red? Can I call any man Friend, who commits such acts? I am angry and afraid. So afraid, Mother, that when it will matter most, I shall fail my duty as a Man and a Christian. Before I fall asleep upon the ground and dream of things I pray you shall never see or hear or feel, I remind myself that one must do what is Right and Just, and the <u>Consequences Be Damned.</u>

> —LIEUTENANT LEWIS HUDSON,
> UNSENT LETTER TO HIS MOTHER, AUGUSTINA

Rik was cleaning his milking hoses and cups for the night when he heard Annie screaming his name. He dashed from the barn, a hundred disasters running through his head. He saw her coming along the road, taking the long way around to avoid the Belgians in the barnyard.

Whatever it was couldn't be life-threatening, then.

"Over here!" he hollered back. "What's wrong?"

She waved her arms at him, shouting something that wasn't clear until she came closer: "I've found him! I know where Lewis is buried!"

At her jubilant reply, he went still. Of all the disasters he'd imagined, this wasn't one of them.

Not yet, dammit.

A few moments later she arrived at his side, her face flushed from excitement and running. "Did you hear what I said? I found him, Rik; I know where he is!"

"Yeah, I heard you. Hold on—wherever he is, he's not going anywhere. Come in the barn and sit down before you pass out. I've got a can of soda."

"No! We have to go to the Hollow, we have—"

"Just wait a minute." He clamped his hand over hers. "Calm down first, then we'll make a plan and go from there."

"I was writing and looking at pictures, and everything just clicked!" She all but skipped beside him. "Boone, that bastard, he *did* draw me a map with an 'X' on it!"

Once inside the coolness of the barn, she sat down and let out her breath in a long sigh.

"What kind of map are you talking about?" he asked.

"Not a deliberate one, believe me."

She took the soda he pressed into her hand and drank deeply, the muscles of her throat moving fluidly—an unexpectedly sexy image. She'd changed from the dress into her camisole and gauzy skirt, and Rik's gaze trailed lower to the damp cotton sticking to her breasts, the lace and small buttons.

Funny thing about Annie—she often dressed to be undressed, in his opinion.

"Boone wrote a letter in 1872," she said, interrupting his randy thoughts. "Basically saying the deaths he'd seen in the Civil War didn't bother him because he'd long ago lost his innocence at 'that place they now call Black Hawk's Hollow, in its dark and cold embrace.'"

Maybe it was late. Maybe he was tired and out-of-sorts from the day's events, but Rik didn't get it. "So?"

Her eyes gleamed with excitement. "I was sitting at my computer, looking at the photos I'd shot at the Hollow a couple weeks back, trying to get the words to match. One shows the rocky ledges curving down and inward. Like fingers, I thought. Then it came to me it looked like arms, like an embrace."

Rik gave a low whistle and arched a brow. "He's buried in the coulee?"

"It makes sense. You could easily hide a body under cover of darkness in a shallow grave. The rock would shelter the grave from the wind and bad weather."

"I'll be damned." He thought of all the times he and his brothers had played around there, unaware a dead man lay beneath their feet.

Then he remembered the first time he'd taken Annie to the Hollow, and how she'd asked about mines and caves.

"Let's get some shovels. I want—"

"You knew he was buried here all along," Rik interrupted, his voice hard.

She met his gaze squarely, even as her face drained of color. "I suspected as much, yes. I hoped I could find his body and take him home where he belongs. I haven't exactly lied to you, Rik."

"But you haven't exactly been honest with me, either."

"No." She looked away. "I decided not to say anything until I was certain he was here, and by then I'd hoped you would have warmed to the idea. I wanted to tell you everything, but you didn't make it easy, you know."

"And I'd like to trust you, Annie—but you're not making it easy, either."

She slammed the soda can against the concrete floor and stood. "Where are your shovels? I'm going to look for Lewis."

"It'll be dark soon." He grabbed her arm as she pushed past him. "You're not going up there by yourself at night."

"So come with me."

"Hell, no. There's other things I want to be doing with you in the dark, and digging dirt isn't one of them."

Her face pinkened with anger and challenge. "Sleeping with me doesn't give you the right to tell me what to do. Remember, it's just sex. Isn't it?"

He tightened his hold. "It's more than that, and you know it. Now, c'mon—I've got work to finish up, and I'm not letting you outta my sight."

"Let go of me *now*!"

God, he was sick and tired of all this! Rik dropped her arm and said, "Go on, then. I don't give a damn where you go."

He wanted her to stay, to make soothing noises, even apologize. When she turned and marched off, leaving him standing alone, a hazy, hard-held fury exploded.

"Don't you walk away from me!"

At his shout, she stopped short. A few, quick strides brought him to her side. Annie stared at him, wide-eyed. For a split second he hesitated, then he locked his arms around her hips and hoisted her up over his shoulder with a grunt.

"What are you doing?" she asked incredulously, squirming and trying to smack his hands.

"I'm tired of you running away from me for *him*." Holding her was like holding on to a wet, angry cat. "Jesus, Annie, how do you think that makes me feel?"

She grew still. "And this will make you feel better? Carting me off like a sack of oats?"

It didn't, but no way was he going to admit that.

"Are you telling me you're *jealous* of Lewis?"

Rik grimaced as he headed for the ladderlike stairs leading to the upper haymow. "I wouldn't call it that."

"So what would you call it?"

"I'd call it none of your damn business!"

He could almost hear the wheels turning in her exasperating, imaginative female brain.

"Well," she said, her tone subdued, "you're right. I got a little overexcited. You can put me down now."

"Nope."

"Rik, I mean it. Your shoulder's hard as a rock and digging into my stomach, and all the blood is rushing to my head."

Strangely, his blood was busy rushing elsewhere.

"Don't tell me you're not enjoying this," he answered, and, despite his residual anger, grinned at her sputtering denial. "I've heard a few of your fantasies, and getting carried off is one of 'em."

"Like hell it is!" Annie let out a breathless shriek as he pretended to let her slip, and her fingers clamped into his skin like grappling hooks.

"Put me down, you oaf!" She still sounded mad, but more of a grumbling-mad than a you're-dead-meat sort of mad.

Playing up the moment as He-Man, Rik said, "Shut up, woman."

There was a shocked silence. "*What* did you say to me?"

"No self-respecting oaf is gonna let his woman backtalk him like that. You heard me: shut your sweet little mouth."

Another long pause. "If it's my turn to play out a fantasy, then you have to do it right. You can't say 'shut your sweet little mouth' like you can't wait to get under my skirt. You have to say, 'Silence, wench!' " She made her voice deep and gruff.

He cleared his throat and rumbled, "Silence, wench!" As an added flourish, he lightly smacked that pert little ass next to his cheek, then started up the narrow steps to the second floor.

"Clark Gable made this look more romantic," she complained. "I keep bumping my nose on your butt, and now my ears are ringing . . . hey! Are you taking me up the *stairs*? Ouch! Rik, watch my head! Getting brained is *not* part of my fantasy!"

He laughed, and as they reached the upper floor, he tried not to bump her against anything . . . or topple backwards. She wasn't exactly a featherweight, but since he valued his hide, he didn't dare huff and puff or grunt.

"Oooh," she said. "A haystack—how classic. I like how you think."

"Who says I'm thinking?" He dumped her on a

mound of dried hay, which was more prickly than it looked and sent up a cloud of chaff.

She sneezed. And again. "This isn't supposed to be part of the fantasy, either."

"Sorry. The oaf forgot to plan ahead and bring a blanket," Rik said, standing above her, hands on his hips.

Annie smiled. "The delicate maiden will allow him to make it up to her."

"Lucky guy." Rik folded his arms over his chest, knowing she liked that. "So what does your barbarian or pirate or—"

"Viking."

He started to laugh, but her stern glare stopped it cold. "Okay—and what does your Viking do next?"

"He ravishes his plundered virgin all night long and gives her a couple dozen orgasms."

Rik gave a hoot of laughter. "How about you give me twenty minutes and I'll see if I can make you a happy woman a time or two."

After pulling a condom from his pocket, Rick unzipped his jeans, eased her skirt out of the way, and then covered her body with his. He slipped his hand between her legs, her moist warmth telling him she was ready. Which was a damn good thing, because all that wiggling she'd been doing had him hard and hot for her, too.

He pushed inside her, and closed his eyes at the overwhelming sensations shooting through him from head to toe.

"God," he whispered, kissing her hungrily. "Baby, what you do to me . . ."

Annie wrapped her arms and legs tightly around

him, pulling him closer as she made little moans that drove him wild.

"Harder," she urged, matching his increasing rhythm. "Oh, please, oh, please!"

Moments later her harsh gasp sounded in his ear; his own shout of release echoed amid the rafters and unsettled the birds, sending them swooping and soaring. Breathing hard, he and Annie lay tangled together, bits of hay sticking to their bodies.

On a long, sliding sigh of satisfaction, she said, "I don't think that was twenty minutes."

Rik groaned and rolled off her onto the hay. "This Viking's had a long day. Cut him some slack."

Annie curled against him, nuzzling her head against his neck in that way of hers. "Hold me," she whispered. "I want you to hold me like you'll never let me go."

A strange, half-forgotten tenderness touched him at her words. He wrapped her in his arms and pulled her close, fingers brushing along the bare skin of her back and bottom. She played her fingers across his chest and shoulders, lulling him while he listened to the drone of the flies, creaking crickets, and the whippoorwills singing their songs.

The peacefulness of the moment soaked into him. He liked this, and wanted it to last—a little longer, anyway. He just wasn't ready yet to let her go.

"We can go look for your soldier tomorrow," he said, smoothing back her hair. Man, she was so beautiful. Letting her go would hurt. Just the thought of it made his chest squeeze tight. "The coulee's not that big. If he's there, it shouldn't take much more than the morning to find him." He paused, then said, "You feel up to it?"

"It's long past time I let it go," she answered, drowsy.

Rik wasn't sure what that meant, but after overhearing her conversation with Heather, he had an inkling of what Hudson meant to her. For her sake, he hoped the kid was at the Hollow.

"I gotta finish up a few chores. You look tired, so why don't you stay up here and rest until I'm done? Then we can head back to the house."

"Okay." She sighed, moving into the warm place where his body had been. "Don't forget to come back for me."

At the stairs, he looked back at her. She lay curled in the hay like a sleeping kitten, half-shadowed by hazy, dust-mottled rays of sun slicing through cracks in the barn's planking. The fist inside his chest squeezed tighter. "No chance of that."

By the time Rik returned, Annie had tidied up and spent some time thinking as she watched the birds dart and flutter above her. He'd been truly angry earlier when she'd insisted on going to the Hollow. Looking back at it now, it had been a foolish notion, but she'd been too excited to think rationally.

Still, his reaction worried her. It was more than anger; there was something else she couldn't quite understand. He denied it was jealousy, but it certainly looked that way to her.

Annie sighed. The man baffled her half the time, but, God, he knew how to make love. She closed her eyes, still feeling the low, thick thrum of desire. She ran a finger over her lips, remembering the taste of him, the almost rough urgency of his lovemaking.

How sweet of Rik to go along with one of her sillier

fantasies. Who would've expected he'd have such a streak of playfulness? She couldn't help wonder what other frivolous but titillating games they might play.

Her smile faded. Whatever those games were, they'd have to be quick about it. Her time here was fast drawing to a close.

The thump of heavy boots sounded on the steps, and then a head of tousled red-gold hair emerged. As Rik came to stand beside her, the darkly golden beams of the setting sun stroked his hair with fingers of light. She longed to do the same.

"Ready?" he asked.

She nodded, then grasped his outstretched hand and let him pull her to her feet. "I'm hungry," she said.

"Me, too. How does something icy cold sound?"

"Closest thing to heaven on earth."

"Then let's hit the Dairy Queen."

"I do like how you think." Annie grinned. "I could go for a grape Mr. Misty—jumbo size."

A short while later, she sat beside Rik as he drove the pickup into town. He took the drive-through, and ordered a grape Mr. Misty for her and a jumbo vanilla cone for himself. With the windows rolled down and night settling in, they drove back along the dark, winding country roads.

"You know," Annie shouted over the wind and a classic rock song playing on the radio, "this is the closest thing I've had to a date in ages!"

Rik grinned, driving with one hand while he fought a losing battle against the ice cream dripping down his cone. "Guess I'll have to take you out for a real date one of these days. Restaurant, wine, fancy clothes—the whole deal."

One of these days.

Her mood darkened a little, although she continued to smile and chat as if nothing was wrong, as if the tears she held back didn't make her throat ache.

Distracted, she didn't notice at first that Rik was taking a roundabout way home.

"Where are we?" she asked, not recognizing any landmarks.

"It's a surprise."

"Oh?" Sluuuuurp. "What kind?"

"One that goes with Dairy Queens and pickups." He waggled his eyebrows, and Annie laughed.

"You have got to be kidding."

"Nope." He slowed the truck, pulled off the road and into a thick clump of trees, then shut off the engine. "You ever make out in the flatbed of a pickup?"

"Um, not that I can recall, no."

"Good," he said, his tone smug.

He opened her door and helped her down, then led her to the back of the truck. She peered around the dark woods, listening to insects and sensing the fluttering of unseen wings around her.

"Are you sure we won't get caught?"

Getting caught would be awful . . . although the possibility *did* add a provocative twist of the forbidden.

"Doubt it. Not much traffic on this road."

"Well, your white truck stands out like a beacon. What if some cop comes by?"

"He'll get an eyeful." Rik hoisted her into the back of the pickup. "There's a blanket. Make yourself comfortable."

She spread the old wool blanket on the bed, then settled back as Rik climbed in beside her. She looked up at the sky, filled with the brilliant flash of stars and the shimmering curve of the moon.

"Isn't that a sight," she murmured, taking in a deep breath of pungent woodsy air. "The stars aren't this bright in the city. Out here, they light up the night."

He lay down beside her, hands behind his head. "Sure do."

"Did you really bring me out here to make out?"

In the dark, his teeth flashed white. "If you want. Or we can just lie here and talk."

Annie propped herself up on her elbow and gazed at him. "You are something else, Rik. It makes me think and wonder."

"And what are you thinking and wondering about this time?"

"Oh, more nonsense—like where I'd be now if I'd met and fallen in love with someone like you ten years ago."

Silence settled between them; insubstantial, yet solid as a wall of stone.

She shouldn't have said that—but somehow, it seemed important to do so. Liberating, even.

"And where would you be?" he asked at length.

"Maybe . . . happily married with a couple of kids and a minivan. And a house and garden of my own, with lots and lots of tulips and snapdragons, and I'd write children's books. I wouldn't make much money at it, but that would be okay, because I'd be happy."

"You seem happy now, Annie."

"Yes." She smiled at him, at the truth of it. "Yes, I am."

"I'm glad to hear it." After a brief silence, Rik added, "I guess life hasn't always been easy for you."

"No." She rolled over to her back again, then laced

her fingers behind her head, as he did. "A lot of people didn't think I'd amount to much of anything, and predicted I'd end up just another statistic. I proved them all wrong, and I'm proud of what I've accomplished."

"You should be. You're a hell of a woman, Annie Beckett, and don't let anyone ever tell you otherwise." He rolled over and kissed her quick and hard. "Who was your mother?"

Surprised by the question, Annie tipped her face toward him. "I can't remember the last time somebody asked me that."

Rik continued to watch her. "Do you know her name?"

A moment passed before she said, "Shasta Sue Beckett. That was her name . . . still is, I suppose, unless she's dead. When I was nineteen I tried finding her, but it was as if she'd just disappeared. I really shouldn't complain, though. At least I know my mother's name, which is better than the blank line on my birth certificate where my father's name should've been."

At length he said, "I'm sorry."

"Yeah . . . nineteen was a pretty bad year, except for later that summer. That's when I found Lewis. Did I ever tell you Gussie searched for her son for over thirty years?"

"Yeah," Rik said quietly. "You told me."

"That's real love—the kind that deserves a shrine or something. It's why I want to write this book, I guess."

When he said nothing, she turned her head and looked at the strong profile of his face. On impulse, she asked, "Do you think you'll ever get married again?"

"Ain't that a loaded question." His voice was low, a shade wary. "I don't know. I've been so busy these last five years that I haven't given it much thought."

"Mmmm," she said. "You mean you've kept yourself busy so you wouldn't have to. I'm sure there are dozens of women in Warfield who'd be more than happy to help you lick your wounds and soothe that wounded male ego."

"Meaning exactly what?"

Uh-oh. The "wounded male ego" part hadn't gone over well.

"Meaning we all have to live with the past. You've used your work to isolate yourself and avoid messy old emotions."

"Christ," he said in disgust, sitting up. "I didn't bring you all the way out here just so we could fight. We can do that at home anytime."

"Are we having a fight? I thought we were talking. You said—"

"Getting criticized wasn't what I had in mind." Rik glared at her in the moonlight. "And don't get me wrong here; I think a lot of you—but you ain't exactly a blue-ribbon example of well-adjusted womanhood, you know."

"Yes. I know." But his words hurt, anyway. "All I'm saying is that you'll never be able to move beyond your hate and pain if you don't let it go and make peace with Owen Decker."

"I have made peace with the bastard—I haven't killed him yet, right? Dammit, don't you stand in judgment over me! I loved Karen. I thought Owen was my friend. They took my trust and made it shit.

Made me wish some days that I could just die, instead of crawling out and facing everybody who'd take one look at me and knew I couldn't even—"

As he cut himself off, Annie looked away, her stomach knotting with tension and sympathy. She understood the pain of rejection all too well.

"What do you care, anyway?" he said when she didn't answer.

Don't make me care, she wanted to shout. *I won't; I can't.*

"I shouldn't care," she said quietly.

"Right . . . and it's not like you're gonna stick around."

Annie looked away. In the following silence, he pretended to look at the stars while she hid her shaking hands in the folds of her skirt.

"We better head back. It's getting late."

Annie sat up as he swung himself out of the flatbed. "You're angry with me. I'm sorry. I enjoyed going to the Dairy Queen. I enjoyed the ride here, and I think I'd have liked making out under the stars."

Rik took a long breath and ran a hand through his hair. "Maybe I overreacted some," he said, each word careful. "Anything to do with Decker pushes my hot button. I'm not so much mad at you as I'm mad at . . . I don't know. But I don't feel much like making out. Maybe we can come back here some other time."

But they wouldn't. She'd had a once-in-a-lifetime chance to neck with Rik Magnusson under the stars, and she'd lost it.

"Maybe," she said anyway, smiling at him as he lifted a hand to help her out of the back of the truck.

"Sorry I jumped all over you like that. Guess a kiss

would be okay." He pulled her close. "Sorta like a rain check."

Annie couldn't hold back a bubble of laughter as she pressed against him. "Or sorta like kiss and make up, hmmm?"

His mustache stretched wide in a returning smile; then he bent and kissed her. His kisses devastated her, turned her knees to mush. Annie rubbed against his body, as if by doing so she could spark something more between them.

But not this time. Rik broke away before she had a chance to kindle much of a flame; a bit of curling steam was all she'd managed.

Still, Annie held on, unwilling to let him go. She looked up at the bright splash of stars, twinkling as if to some cosmic beat, then back at Rik. She smiled slowly. "Can you hear it?"

He arched a brow. "Hear what?"

"The music of the stars. Dance with me, Rik," she coaxed, rocking her hips to the natural rhythm of rustling leaves, creaking branches, and a steady drone of crickets.

"That's some imagination you got, Miz Beckett."

"My chief talent." She slipped her arms around his neck, his lovely, nibble-inviting neck. "Humor me."

"Wait a minute." He unwound her arms despite her protest, then reached inside his truck and twisted the ignition key to start the radio. He fiddled with the dial until he found a song that suited him—Ben E. King's immortal *Stand By Me*.

"My imagination's no match for yours," Rik said as he drew her close again. "You gotta draw me a picture, Annie, every time."

She nuzzled his neck as they moved to the pure,

plaintive music. In the small clearing, in the pale glow of the moon and the stars, it was as magical a moment as she could hope for, in its own bittersweet way.

Rik moved his hands from her shoulders down to her hips, while she twined her fingers behind his head, playing with his soft hair. Resting her head against his shoulder, she pressed soft kisses along his throat, imagining the strong, steady beat of his blood in the vein beneath her lips. With the tip of her tongue, she traced a heart against his skin.

Something hard bumped the back of her legs, and she realized he'd slowly backed her against the side of the pickup. She didn't protest when he opened the door, lifted her inside, and made love to her on the front seat, with all its confines and awkward angles, to Heart's *Crazy On You*.

Afterward, sated and sleepy, she snuggled close to Rik as he drove back to the farm, the music turned down low, the dashboard glowing with an eerie green color. Resting her head against his arm, she fell asleep and the next thing she knew, he was waking her up.

Once in the house, Annie went to Rik's bedroom and began to undress. For a moment he watched her in silence, then said, "What are you going to do about Hudson?"

She glanced at him before pulling her camisole over her head. "I'm going to the Hollow and dig around until I find his body."

"By yourself?"

"If need be. I can manage by myself," she said, as his body tensed. God, he was going to be difficult about this, after all. Disappointment made her voice bitter. "I've been doing so all my life, because I learned early that if I didn't, nobody else would. The only person I can ever depend upon is *me*."

He sent her a dark look. "What about ol' Lewis? Bet he's never let you down."

Outside in the distance a lone vehicle roared past, just as anger roared through her. "No, he hasn't."

Seconds ticked by as they stared at each other across the bed, with its crisp, turned-back sheets of tan percale.

"Yeah . . . dead's pretty safe, I guess," Rik agreed, striding toward the door. "Good night, Annie. Sweet dreams."

"Where are you going?" she called after him, even as he left the bedroom, killing the lights behind him.

When he didn't answer, she listened to his footsteps, the *click-click* of Buck's nails as he followed his master, then the creak and slam of the screen door.

She flinched.

Fine. He could act like a big baby. She'd just let him sit and sulk outside while she went upstairs to her white-tower room, to the work she should've long since finished. Rik was right. What did any of this matter? She would be leaving in a few days.

But she sat on the bed and hugged Rik's pillow against her, breathing in his scent.

Finally, weary of waiting, of the strange, hollow loneliness pressing upon her, she pulled on one of his T-shirts and went out to the porch. Rik sat in his usual spot, with Buck sprawled at his feet.

He silently watched her approach, the lines of his body taut with anger and hurt pride.

Oh, that pride . . .

"Come back to bed, Rik," she said softly, laying her hand on his shoulder. "It's late."

At her touch, he began to pull away. Then, to her

wary surprise, he rubbed his knuckles gently across her cheek.

"We'll have to deal with your leaving, Annie. You know that."

"I know."

But she couldn't bring herself to ask what, exactly, he meant by "deal with."

CHAPTER SIXTEEN

June 24, 1832, Rock River: Oh, is it not a fine thing, this Business of Living? More so, when Danger is at hand. I expect we shall cross the Sac trail soon. It is our chance at last for a good fight, so we may bring this sorry Affair to a merciful end. But fear not, Sweet Emily, Death cannot touch me whilst I wear the tenderness of your Love as a shield! I swear I shall not allow it. Yet, I must admit a soldier's life holds many Hazards, and should Heaven decree we not meet again, know that I am ready to meet my God in good conscience. Know that I shall think upon you at the last. Know that even Death shall not unmake what we have made. Know that I will wait upon you, howsoever long it may be. Know that I love you, always."

—LIEUTENANT LEWIS HUDSON,
FROM A LETTER TO MISS EMILY OGLETHORPE

The day dawned bright and hot, and Rik waited until after he'd made a pot of coffee to wake Annie. She wore nothing beneath the sheets, providing him with a tantalizing peek of bare shoulders and curving back. She slept on her side, her face half-hidden by the fall of her hair.

If only he could let her sleep, and skip this whole day.

Rik bent to brush back her hair, kissed her shoulder, and whispered, "Time to wake up, honey."

She yawned, then stretched, one hand keeping an iffy hold on the sheet—to his disappointment.

"This is the plan." Rik handed her a steaming mug. "After I finish the milking and feed the horses, I'll come get you and we'll drive over to the Hollow."

Annie took the coffee and met his gaze. "Okay. I'll do some writing this morning, and maybe make a phone call to the mayor's office in Youngstown and ask about reburials."

He leaned down and gave her a quick peck on the cheek. "I'll be back in a couple of hours."

Knowing Annie was impatient, Rik hurried as much as possible—in his experience, a cow just couldn't be rushed—and returned to the house by nine. He changed out of his work clothes and washed up, then called for Annie. She *thumpity-thumped* down the steps in a flash.

"Are we going now?"

"Yup. Got everything you need?"

She nodded. "My camera bags are by the door. Let's go."

The short ride to the Hollow passed in silence, mainly because he couldn't think of a single thing to say. Digging up dead men wasn't something he did every day. But Annie needed his help, and as much as he wished she'd never find the kid—or at least not find him for a good long while yet—he wouldn't be a jerk about it.

He parked the truck and, while she hauled out her equipment, he retrieved the shovels from the back.

"You ready?" he asked.

"As I'll ever be." Annie took a deep breath. "Let's go find Lewis."

Together they walked to the foot of the Hollow, where the sloping rock curved inward to a natural shelter. It was about six by eight feet in total, and filled with dead leaves, brush, rubble, and fine, sandy soil washed down from years of past rains.

"If you were hiding a body, where would you bury it?" Rik asked.

She walked around the coulee, then stopped and pointed to the most sheltered area within the enclosure, where the rock wall was highest and curved most. "Right here."

Rik briefly met Annie's gaze. "Then that's where I'll start digging."

The kid could be buried two feet under, or ten. Without another word, he picked a spot, aimed, then placed his boot on the shovel's top and sliced its tip into the soft earth.

She sighed when he did so. After a moment, she picked up the other shovel and went to the opposite side of the coulee and began digging.

Despite the early hour and the cover of the trees, the heat and humidity soon grew unbearable. Rik peeled off his T-shirt and tossed it aside. The gauzy material of Annie's skirt clung to her hips and legs, and her own T-shirt might as well have been painted on. He wanted to tell her to sit down and take it easy, but knew better.

"How are you doing over there?" he asked.

She didn't stop digging. "Hot."

Rik waited for more, but she was too focused on finding Hudson to turn and smile at him—or any other sign that would tell him she remembered he still existed. He turned back to his own patch of freshly turned dirt and started digging again, with a little more force than before.

Nearly an hour passed, and he'd turned up nothing but rocks and old roots. Light-headed from heat and thirst, he figured he'd give things another five or ten minutes, then call it quits until early evening brought cooler temperatures.

Just then, his shovel hit something. Probably another damn rock, but he slowed all the same. Using the tip of the shovel, he gently pushed dirt to either side of the pale object showing through the black dirt. Then a little more, to provide a better look.

He hunkered down, put the shovel aside, and used his fingers. With a cold jolt of shock, he saw that he wasn't touching stone or wood. The porous surface, roundness, and stark white color all told him he'd found bone.

His heart pounded like the die-cut machines in the factory where he'd once worked: *boom-thump-boom-thump-boom*.

With the back of his hand, Rik wiped away the perspiration dotting his forehead. Then he brushed away more soil to reveal the unmistakable holes of eye sockets.

Lewis Hudson . . . seeing and feeling the warmth of the sun for the first time in over 160 years.

Rik stood, swallowing despite his dry mouth. "I think you better see this."

At his words, Annie turned. Her gaze went first to his face, then to the hole behind him. Even as she paled, she said, "What is it?"

"I've found him."

He couldn't think of how to break it gently. At first, he wasn't sure Annie had heard him. No relief or happiness crossed her face, as he'd expected. Then Rik saw her trembling hands. She slowly came forward. Her gaze didn't leave his face.

"Are you sure, Rik?"

"It's a skull. I'm sure about that much."

Blinking rapidly, she moved around him and looked down. Rik stood behind her, rubbing her shoulders, giving what comfort he could.

After a long moment, she whispered, "The end."

Before he could respond, she turned abruptly into his chest, weeping. Startled, he wrapped his arms around her, making *hush-hush* sounds, like he'd done with his daughter when she was little.

"What's wrong?" Her tears wet his already damp chest, and all he could think was, *Christ, what had she expected to find*? "Annie, talk to me. Draw me a picture. Make me understand."

"I don't want *that* to be him," she whispered. "I thought seeing him like this wouldn't matter . . . but it does! I know you think I'm just—"

He stopped her words with a hard kiss. "Don't say it."

Once her weeping faded, Rik turned, with Annie in his arms, and they both gazed silently at the skull. He couldn't help but think of the portrait of the smiling kid with the friendly eyes, or hear the "voice" from those letters he'd read.

Letting her go, he knelt and carefully brushed away more soil. "Okay, kid. Let's find the rest of you."

Annie dropped to her knees beside him, sniffling, tears making rivulets on her dust-covered cheeks. Without speaking, they cleared away the black earth that entombed First Lieutenant Lewis Hudson, sometimes using fingers, sharp sticks, and even Rik's pocketknife.

"Careful," Annie said, picking up a small object in her hand. "We should start putting all the dirt in a separate pile. There's evidence here we may be missing. This looks like a military button."

With dirty fingers, she cleaned it until Rik could plainly see the large, round shank button with the letters "US" on top.

"His mother gave him a gold cross," she said. "I have a description of it in one of the letters. If we find that, we'll know for certain this is Lewis, although with this button, I'm positive."

They had reached the clavicle and upper ribs, flattened inward by the weight of the ground above. Rik thoroughly examined every clump of dirt, and found a blackened thing he thought was a cross, but turned out to be just an old root.

"What's this?" Rik asked a few minutes later, holding what looked like a leaf, but was old leather, hardened and rotted.

"I have no idea. It doesn't look like any standard military gear I've seen." Annie took it from him, gently poking at the lumpy mass until it opened. She gasped, then whispered, "Oh, my God."

Rik peered at the tiny thing in her palm, and sunlight glinted against a dull gleam of gold. A ring. Plain, nothing special.

She looked up, her gaze distant and unfocused. "So that's what he meant."

"What?" he coaxed.

"Something Lewis wrote to Emily in one of his letters." Her eyes closed as she quoted from memory,

" 'I have a surprise, and I am saving it until I see you again. I shall give you a hint . . . it will one day contain all my hopes and my dreams, my heart and soul, and yet is small enough to tuck into a place close to my heart.' "

Rik softly swore around the sudden lump in his throat.

Annie opened her eyes again. "I have to call the police. It's the right thing to do."

He nodded. "I'll get a tarp from the truck so we can cover him up."

As he stood, Annie grabbed his arm. "I'd like to wait until tomorrow, though. I want a little time to . . . to take pictures, and make notes."

But her tear-stained face and pleading eyes told Rik she needed to say good-bye to the kid in her own way. He sighed. "I'll wait here until you're done with your pictures."

"But you've got work to do."

"I can spare a few hours. Annie, don't argue. Just . . . do your thing, okay?"

She nodded and smiled uncertainly, then moved away, camera in hand. Rik sat close by as Annie set up and snapped photos for the book that now had an ending. He helped from time to time, but mostly he just watched, his frustration growing with every passing moment.

Disaster should come in a sudden flood, wiping out everything in the blink of an eye. It wasn't supposed to inch closer, so a guy could watch it coming. Anticipate it, twist himself into knots pretending nothing was wrong, or that he could do something about it.

But he *could* do something; he could ask her to stay. Right—give up her globe-trotting job, one that any idiot could see she loved. Give it all up to be a farmer's wife.

Decker's words came back to taunt him. The bastard had a point. If Karen had been so unhappy, how did he stand a chance with someone like Annie?

It was just sex, dammit; that was all it was meant to be.

Abruptly, Rik pushed himself to his feet. "I gotta get something to eat and drink. I'll cover him with a tarp and we can come back after dinner and after I finish my chores. It'll be cooler by then."

She hesitated, "But—"

"I'm not giving you a choice here, Annie."

Not looking at all pleased, she nodded. "All right. I'll pack up while you get the tarp."

True to her word, she was ready to go by the time he returned with the bundle of black plastic. She helped spread it over the grave, then they hunted around for rocks big enough to hold it down.

The ride back to the house passed in silence, while Annie stared out the window. Not in any mood to talk, Rik didn't bother trying to crack through the quiet.

Rik spent the rest of the afternoon working in the barn and tending the Belgians, whose daily practice he'd neglected lately. The familiar, hard work forced him to concentrate on the tasks at hand and kept him from thinking too much. Right now, he didn't want to think at all.

After dinner, Rik settled the horses in the barn for the night, then headed back to the house. He glanced up at the turret window to see Annie leaning out, elbows on the sill, her face cupped in her hands.

He raised his hand in a salute. She waved back, and

he called up, "You ready to head to the Hollow?"

"I thought you'd never ask!"

Ten minutes later, Rik found himself back at the Hollow, lounging with his back against the sun-warmed rock while Annie sat beside him on an old tree trunk that had fallen over decades ago, and typed.

Tap-tippity-tap-tap. Her fingers flew over the keyboard. Finally, curious and a little bored, he came to stand behind her and looked over her shoulder.

"Mind if I read?"

"Uh-unh," she said, not taking her eyes from the screen.

Since the screen was small Rik leaned closer, and caught a whiff of vanilla-Annie scent. While he'd been out working up a sweat, she'd taken a shower. Self-conscious, he backed away, but stayed close enough to see what she'd written:

It is silent, the darkness thick and close except for a small fire. Uniforms cling in the heat, like melted wax to skin. None can see what will transpire within the embrace of this rock. There are no roads here. No trains or auto-mobiles or airplanes. No houses. There is nothing but silence, and the shot rings out loud and sharp and pro-fane . . .

"You think he was shot?" Rik asked.

"I'm guessing. I can always change it later," she said, with no break in her typing.

The grave is a raw gash. It hurts me to see it, as if the shovel has cut through my heart as well as this earth. This was a mother's hope, a father's pride, a young woman's love. He lies deep within the ground, white bone against black earth. No loving hands arranged him in a pose of peaceful sleep. Unkind hands flung him here like refuse to lie tangled, unquiet. This pretty, wooded glade is now hallowed ground, and the earth and rocks and trees all reverberate with the violence done here . . .

Rik had read enough. Chilled in spite of the heat, he moved away.

But she was right. For a moment, all his troubles and worries shrank to nothing. Considering what one man had lost here, how could he not be grateful for a sunny day? Or the simple prettiness of a wildflower at his feet, the daughter he'd made, and the woman before him who said she liked him just the way he was? For whatever time he had left with Annie, weeks or days, he would be thankful.

At least he'd give it his best shot. It wasn't as if he hadn't known this moment would come; she'd made it clear from the start she wouldn't stay.

He sure knew how to pick them.

While she continued typing, Rik returned to his makeshift seat. In the hot sun he dozed off and on, awakened once by the soft touch of fingers against his cheek. Half-asleep, he'd thought Annie leaned close, kissed his temple and whispered, "I love you."

Only a dream.

He startled awake again to the sounds of Annie packing her gear—the thump of lids, the click of fastenings. The sun was setting, the woods darkening, and he pushed himself away from the rock, massaging his stiff neck muscles.

"Ready to go home?" he asked.

"I can't."

Rik rubbed the back of his head, certain he hadn't heard right. "What was that?"

"I can't go back." She raised her hands in a helpless sort of gesture. "I can't leave him alone out here tonight, not like this."

A few days ago, her words would have angered him. Now, they only left a dryness in his mouth. "Are you telling me you want to camp out here tonight?"

"I'm sorry." She looked away. "You don't have to stay."

Rik snorted. "Like I'm gonna leave you alone in the woods with a dead man. Give me more credit than that, Annie."

"But this has nothing to do with you, and you've already done so much. I can't ask—"

"I make my own decisions. I'll take your things back to the house, then get blankets, pillows, and a flashlight. We'll sleep in the truck. How does that sound?"

Her answer was to walk to him, take his face between her hands, and thoroughly kiss him, stirring a hot arousal. But she stepped away before he could do anything about it. Taking a deep breath, Rik helped carry her cases to the truck and, for the second time that day, made only a brief stop at his house.

Besides gathering the items he'd mentioned, he also asked her to pack food while he took a quick shower. The dirt from the Hollow seemed ground into his very pores.

As he packed the truck, Rik caught Annie watching him. "What?" he said, and checked his jeans to make sure his fly was zipped.

She smiled. "You're a true-blue good guy, you know? Why are you doing this for me?"

"Ah, it's nothing. Get in," he replied, uncomfortable with the praise, yet pleased, too.

He drove farther into the woods than usual, bouncing over rocks, deep ruts, and fallen branches, until the headlights illuminated the familiar rocky tower looming above them.

"This is as close as we're gonna get. I don't want to wreck the undercarriage on my truck."

"This is perfect." Annie cuddled close as he switched off the engine. The silence—or as much of a silence as could be found in a woods full of birds, insects and animals—gathered close around them. "Are we going to stay in the cab, or in back of the truck?"

"In back. More room to stretch out and move around." He grinned at the "move around" part, and she rolled her eyes at him—but she smiled, too.

Her smile turned into a frown. "Um, what about bugs?"

"It's been too dry for mosquitoes, but we can always come back into the cab if bugs get to be a problem."

She ran her hands along his chest, then slipped one hand lower to rest against his fly—and he shot from soft to hard in a heartbeat. "Let's go to bed," she whispered. "But first I want to make sure the tarp is still in place."

Rik grabbed the flashlight and opened the door, shaking his head. Man, all she had to do was rub his dick and he'd follow her anywhere.

The Hollow had always been creepy at night. Now, it was worse. The flashlight's yellowish beam picked up the black tarp, flapping as the breeze eased under the plastic through the gaps between rocks.

"Looks covered," he said. "Let's go."

Forget subtle, he had a hard-on begging for some serious attention. Placing his hand on the small of her back, his fingers on the curve of her butt, he gave her a slight push toward the truck.

Annie turned to him. At first, he thought her angry, but she began yanking his shirt from his jeans with an unmistakable urgency. Then she took the flashlight from him and dropped it to the ground. Its light flickered from the jostle, and blinked out.

Taken aback, Rik stood still as she fumbled with his belt, then pulled down his zipper.

"Christ," he finally managed. "*Here*?"

In the dirt? The rocks and twigs would gouge his knees and hands, and poke her soft backside.

"Here," she whispered, her hands inside his underwear. He sucked in his breath at her firm, determined touch. "Now."

Rik closed his eyes. God, her hands were sliding along his erection, squeezing, teasing him, and he thought his knees would buckle right there. "Okay . . . okay, baby. Slow down, so I—"

She stopped his words with her tongue, sliding it deep in his mouth while her hands continued stroking his penis. Rik groaned, and she pulled back. "Love me," Annie whispered. "Love me hard and deep and make it last forever."

Forever.

In just seconds, he had her on her back on the forest floor, her skirt up around her hips, and he pushed inside her, raising her legs over his shoulders so he could go deeper yet.

Annie made a low sound in her throat, then whispered, "Yes, oh, God . . . yes . . . yes . . ."

Something of her desperation moved him. Or maybe it was only the mood that had dogged him all day, an uneasy mix of mortality and lust and gratitude, that drove him to touch her, to leave her with a memory she would never forget.

The night breeze was sharp, the scents of the forest sharper yet. Her fingernails hurt his back, but he didn't care. Nothing mattered but being inside her, all tight and hot and wet, giving her pleasure and finding release.

Pumping hard into her, listening to his own rapid breathing, her increasing moans and whispered urgings, Rik strained to connect, to find, to hold on to something just beyond his reach. Almost there—and she was sobbing his name over and over again, when the climax rocked him, his body shuddering, helpless to contain the explosive force of pleasure. Her legs slid from his shoulders, and her arms, warm and soft, drew him down and close, until he smelled vanilla and earth and leaves.

"Thank you," he whispered against her throat. "God, thank you."

"Again," she said on a long sigh.

Breathing hard, his heart thudding like crazy, he murmured, "Annie, sweet Annie, give me a minute here."

But instead of lying quietly in his arms, she laughed and sprang to her feet. To his amazement, she peeled off her shirt, then her skirt and soon stood before him, bare and beautiful in the shafts of moonlight shining through the swaying branches.

"What's gotten into you tonight?" he asked, once he got his tongue to work the way it should.

"You mean besides you?" she teased.

He grinned back, despite a sudden, sharp stab of sadness. "Besides me."

"I need to feel alive and safe . . . and wanted." She dropped to her knees beside him, trailing the fingers of one hand down his chest to his dick, and that good ol' boy rose to the occasion. "Do you want me, Rik?"

Always.

Off went his clothes, thrown aside with urgency. He pulled her to the ground again, surged over her, and she wrapped her legs and arms around him. He kissed and massaged her breasts, teasing the nipples until they stiffened into taut, hard peaks. When she moved her hips to take him inside, he couldn't hold back his deep, low groan of need.

Then he knew nothing but the slow burn and tightening pleasure. He heard only her short, harsh breathing, coming faster and faster until she climaxed with a high gasp and he followed, moments later, emptying himself inside her again.

A twinge of pain—a stick jabbing his hand—pierced through his haze, and brought him back to full awareness. He raised his head from the warm crook of Annie's neck.

"Oh, shit," he muttered, resting his forehead against her warm, tousled hair.

"What's wrong?" She nuzzled his neck, like she always did after their lovemaking.

"I didn't use a rubber."

Maybe great sex short-circuited his brain, because he didn't even give a damn. So what if she was pregnant? That's what sex was for, to create life—and right now, the idea of making a baby with Annie appealed to him.

He'd like a son someday.

Rik closed his eyes as weariness rolled over him, his muscles slowly relaxing.

And Annie would probably want to name the poor kid Lewis.

"I'm sure it won't matter. We only did it twice."

His eyes snapped open, his muscles tensing again. "Once is all it takes. Promise me something." In his arms, her body also stiffened. "Promise me, Annie, that if you end up pregnant, you'll tell me. Don't hide it or lie or . . . anything else."

"I won't get pregnant, Rik; I'm sure it's—"

"Just promise—that's all I ask, dammit!"

Silence followed his harsh words; a silence broken only by the winds whistling and moaning through gnarled tree branches high on the Hollow. Wailing Woman was getting one hell of a show tonight.

"I promise," she whispered.

Relieved, Rik sat up. He sucked in a deep, steadying breath, then looked around—and swore again. "I don't believe this. We just screwed each other not even two feet from a dead man."

After a short, surprised pause, Annie laughed. "I think Lewis is beyond being shocked."

"Gives me the creeps." Rik shivered, and then, to his surprise, laughed as well. "Let's head back to the truck before we do something really crazy. Looks like the flashlight's busted. Here's my jeans and your shirt and skirt, but I can't find my underwear—"

"It'll wait until tomorrow," Annie said, molding her body against his back. "Forget it for now."

And so he did. A naked woman rubbing her breasts on a man's back was likely to make him forget just about anything.

Once settled comfortably in the flatbed, on soft pillows and wrapped in a sheet, Annie fell asleep almost at once.

For Rik, sleep didn't come so easily for a change. He ached with exhaustion, wrung out from the day's events and the round of howling-wild sex, but he couldn't wind down.

For a long while he watched Annie as she slept. Brushing aside a strand of her curling hair, he rubbed it between his fingers, and then kissed her forehead.

Just sex, he'd sworn; no messy stuff. He didn't even think he had it in him, to fall for a woman again.

"Did anyway," he whispered, knowing she couldn't hear.

In her sleep, Annie made a snuffling noise, wriggling deeper into the pillow. After pulling the sheet more closely around her half-clad body, Rik pulled on his jeans and slipped away.

He needed to walk, even if he had nowhere to go. No hiding what he felt for her, no burying it in work—and no avoiding that he had only a few short days to persuade her to stay.

Moonlight soon revealed where his restless walk had taken him: to the coulee.

No surprise there.

Somehow, everything about Annie began and ended right here, with Lewis Hudson.

Rik hunkered down beside the tarp. In the strong breeze, the plastic rippled and swelled. The tarp pushed against the rocks holding it down, as if something beneath struggled to break free.

The thought raised the hair on the back of his neck, even though he didn't believe in ghosts. He didn't have to. The ghosts of his own making, and hers, were trouble enough.

"Time to let her go, kid," he whispered to the straining tarp. "She belongs with me now."

Somehow, he expected an answer. A sign—something, anything—from a man who was long, long past caring about Rik's problems.

Feeling stupid, he stood and walked back to the truck. Sliding beneath the cotton sheet, he gathered Annie's warm body in his arms. A burst of pure thankfulness shot through him, that this woman had touched his life.

Without Annie, he'd still be in the dark, blind to the only truth that mattered: that his life was better, and brighter and softer, with a loving woman at his side.

CHAPTER SEVENTEEN

[The Black Hawk War] had its origins in avarice and political ambition . . . was prosecuted in bad faith and closed in dishonor."

—THE LIFE AND ADVENTURES OF BLACK HAWK,
BENJAMIN DRAKE, 1838

"This is Janet Olsen with WKMN News. Over one hundred sixty years ago, this peaceful patch of woods was the site of a terrible tragedy in a senseless war."

Annie repressed an urge to roll her eyes at the reporter's expression of faux gravity.

"Today it is the site of a major investigation, as the Sauk County Sheriff's Office and forensic experts try to determine the cause of Lieutenant Lewis Hudson's death, and just who buried him in this desolate place in 1832. With me now is author Annora Beckett, whose unswerving dedication and tireless ten-year search for the missing soldier has finally paid off. Ms. Beckett, can you give us a little background?"

After nearly a week of this, Annie could do it on autopilot. Over the reporter's shoulder, she saw Krista Harte laughing with another anthropologist as they painstakingly cleared Lewis's remains—measuring, drawing and photographing everything.

Smiling at the camera, Annie provided her standard answer—her conspiracy theory, the loss of a gallant, idealistic young officer, and the dumb luck that led her to the grave, which had nonetheless earned her the admiration of the local police.

The reporter thanked her, then looked into the camera. "In a moment, we'll talk with the forensic anthropologist on site. But right now we have with us the president of the Warfield Historical Society, Mr. Owen Decker, who has helped bring the long-ago tragedy to the public eye. Mr. Decker, would you care to comment on what the local citizens of Warfield think of all this?"

Owen Decker stepped in front of the camera. He smiled at her, but she didn't smile back, because while it seemed that half the county swarmed over the Hollow, the Hollow's owner remained conspicuously, stubbornly, absent.

Not that she blamed Rik. Within hours of her call to the local police, the Hollow looked like a war zone, bustling with a small army of law officers. Then the news crews arrived in their vans, soon followed by local newspaper reporters and curious townsfolk. And Owen Decker had quickly turned the high-profile situation to his advantage.

Rik avoided the reporters whenever he could, but she didn't know for how much longer. The phone rang often now, and just this morning, as he'd returned from his chores, he'd been all but ambushed by Ms. Olsen. Then a stray bunch of teenage boys looking for mischief had spooked the Belgians, and one of them ripped a long gash in his flank by running against the barbed-wire fence.

Rik had lost his temper and kicked the news crew

out of the yard. But Annie doubted Rik had seen the last of Janet Olsen, whose interest in the story extended to an interest in Rik.

"Hey, Annie," Krista called, waving. "How's it going?"

After Krista's initial lecture—she wasn't happy that Annie and Rik had "compromised the integrity" of the site—she was always willing to answer Annie's questions.

"Not too bad," Annie said. "Almost done with Lewis?"

"No way," answered the forensic anthropologist, Rupert Jackson, a tall, thin man with a bald crown and a ponytail of gray-brown hair. "But we should clear the pelvic region today. So far, looks like a bayonet thrust to the chest is what killed him. No official statement until we get him back to the labs, though."

Yesterday Krista had found the cross, proving Lewis's identity beyond a doubt. The cause of death, however, came as a surprise. Annie had expected a bullet.

"Are you sure it was a bayonet?" she asked.

"You betcha. I've seen my share of battlefield remains," Rup said, stepping up out of the gravesite. "Time for show-and-tell, kids."

Curious, Annie moved closer, as did a young cop and a woman from the local newspaper.

Rupert rummaged around in a large box stored off to the side, mumbling to himself, then pulled out a rifle and bayonet.

"Do you always come to work armed with bayonets?" Annie asked with a grin.

"I do when I'm working with battlefield remains. This is an exact replica of the flintlock rifle and bayonet a US infantryman would've carried in 1832." He glanced at the cop. "Don't get all twitchy; the firing mechanism has been disabled."

Rup then picked up a small Styrofoam cooler and handed it to Annie. Puzzled, she asked, "What is this for?"

"Hold it to your side . . . yes, just like that. Now hold on real tight. I'm going to do a little demonstration here. Don't worry. I'll aim for the cooler, not your heart."

Understanding dawned, along with alarm. "Wait! I don't—"

Before Annie could finish, he plunged the bayonet into the cooler with a soft *thuck* sound. The force of the thrust knocked her back against an oak.

The reporter squeaked in shock, and the cop winced and murmured, "Ouch."

"It would've been that sudden, that quiet." Rup smiled, his pale eyes bright. "The deep marks on the ribs and vertebrae indicate a lot of force in that thrust. Whoever killed your soldier did it just like this. Lieutenant Hudson didn't die instantly. It'd have taken thirty seconds, maybe even a full minute, for him to hemorrhage to death. He had time to look his killer in the eye. And the killer could've watched the life fade right of his eyes, too. Nasty, nasty business."

Hands shaking, her palms damp, Annie stood still as Rup yanked the bayonet from the cooler. She stared for a moment at the neat slice in the Styrofoam, then placed the cooler gingerly on the ground.

"One gallant cooler, sacrificed to science," Krista said, shaking her head. "Rupert, did you have to scare her?"

Rup only laughed, then swung back down into the grave.

"Sorry about that," Krista said with a sigh. "I should've warned you that Rup kinda gets into his work. So, any luck on your end proving who might've wielded that bayonet?"

"No proof," Annie answered. "Just hunches."

"It's been a long time." Krista mopped her sweaty neck with a faded bandanna. "You'd be lucky to get to the truth now. But you never know," she added cheerfully. "You found Lieutenant Hudson against all odds."

So she had.

And she wasn't sure it had been such a good thing, now.

It was bad enough to have died as he had, but now he was on display for ogling media, scientists, and anybody who could squeak past the cops, standing bored and hot in their uniforms. Fearing vandals, guards had been brought in to watch the site around the clock, and that included local police supplemented with volunteers organized by—surprise, surprise— Owen Decker.

Since he was president of the Historical Society, Decker's presence here wasn't unexpected, yet Annie knew he also couldn't resist poking his nose around simply to irritate Rik. As she watched, Decker offered to fetch Rup Jackson for Ms. Olsen.

"How are you holding up to all this madness?" Decker asked her, as Rup trotted off to entertain the Channel 24 crew, rifle and cooler in hand.

"Just fine, considering the part you played in manufacturing this 'madness,'" Annie said. "You were pretty quick with those phone calls, Owen."

He looked hurt. "Why won't you believe my intentions are good? This is one of the most exciting events our community has seen in years. It's an important piece of state history, not to mention a fine human-interest story. I wouldn't be surprised if the bigger stations pick it up in a few days."

"Great," Annie said with a scowl. "Rik's jumping out of his skin as it is, and he's really upset about what happened with his horse. There's no reason for these people to go anywhere near the house or barns. They shouldn't even be parking in the fields! I realize the corn doesn't look like much, but being smashed by dozens of tires isn't helping any."

Decker looked properly sympathetic. "Warfield's a small town. Most folks feel like family, that they have the right to be involved. And there's nothing like a news camera to draw out every gossip in a fifty-mile radius."

"I still think you could act as if you're enjoying it all a little less and—"

"Rup!" Krista's excited shout interrupted Annie. "Rup, get over here. Quick!"

The ponytailed anthropologist came on the run—along with everybody else. Annie poked the young cop's shoulder. "What is it?"

"They've found another arm."

Stunned, Annie could only stare at him. Finally, she said, "What did you say?"

"Looks like your soldier didn't die alone, Ms. Beckett."

"Hey, Annie!" Rupert yelled. "Got any idea what John Doe this arm might belong to?"

"None at all," Annie said, pushing her way through to the site. She hunkered down at the edge of the grave. Its precise, sharp edges looked as if a giant knife had cut a neat square out of the earth. An earthy version of a coroner's postmortem incision. Inside, in an undignified sprawl of bones, lay Lewis.

And somebody else.

Rupert pointed his pen at several long, thin bones. "Ulna and radius. Significantly smaller than your boy who, by the way, was a big guy. Articulated, too. Looks like both of these poor bastards were buried shortly after death."

Annie continued to stare at the bones, sifting through her mental file cabinet. "I can't think of any other infantryman or officer who went missing. The militia suffered some losses at the Heights, but all bodies were accounted for."

"Could it be Sauk?" Decker asked.

"Oh, jeez," Krista sighed. "I hope not. No offense, Annie, but that would open a whole 'nother can of worms."

Annie didn't have to ask why. In recent years, the Native American population had grown more vocal regarding the treatment of their ancestors' remains.

"Nothing we can do about that," Rup said, as the TV camera swung toward him. "Hey! Get back before you collapse the site wall. Officer Dave, can you prod these people back at least five feet from the edge?"

Obligingly, Officer Dave herded everyone back—including Annie, relegating her to just a part of the mob.

Still numb from the shock of this new discovery, the urge to get away from the people, the camera, even the Hollow itself, overwhelmed her. Annie spun around and headed back toward the house, ignoring Decker and Krista and Ms. Olsen calling after her.

Even before she arrived at the house, she heard the sound—a sharp *wham-bam-wham*. As she drew closer, she saw Rik on the garage roof.

"What are you doing!" she shouted above the hammering and loud music blaring on the portable radio—the unmistakable voice of the Boss, Bruce Springsteen.

"What the hell does it look like I'm doing?" he yelled back, each word punctuated by the slam of the hammer.

"Are you mad at *me*?" This was too much. She needed someone to talk to, a shoulder to cry on. She needed *him*. *His* shoulder.

"I'm not mad at you."

"Oh, sure. That's why you're beating the hell out of your roof."

"I'm nailing shingles, Annie. What do you want? Aren't you missing all the excitement at the Hollow?"

"I needed to see you."

Up on the roof, high in the air, he stood and flung his arms outward. She gasped in alarm. "Here I am. You've seen me. Now you can go, and I can get back to work."

"I don't think so!"

Annie marched toward the ladder and climbed to the roof.

"Get down—you've got no business being up here!"

"Same goes for you, *lover*."

Shirtless, he knelt on the roof beside a stack of black shingles, a half dozen boxes of nails, and several hammers. Inching along the ungodly hot, steep incline of the roof, Annie snatched up a hammer, and said, "All work and no play makes Rik a very cranky guy, so

I'll tell you what: I'll help. All you have to do is give me a crash course in roofing."

"You want to *shingle*?" He looked completely, utterly, baffled.

"I need to pound something—because if I pounded what I want to, I'd end up in jail."

A slow, reluctant grin cracked his face. "You're my kind of woman, Annie."

"Right now, I'm not sure that's a compliment," she retorted, but grinned back.

Rik provided a few basic instructions, then they went to work, kneeling side by side, their hammers rising and falling in a companionable rhythm. Up, down, up, down . . .

Annie peeked at Rik, at the sheen of sweat on his skin and the strong muscles of his arms and back bunching fluidly with every movement.

No wonder sex popped to mind whenever she came near him. How could she not want him, every single hour of the day?

She forced her attention back to hammering. It was very gratifying, really. No wonder men were into the whole tool thing. Sawing something to pieces or pounding little metal spikes into a hard piece of wood had a certain edge over crying, eating chocolate, or spending money.

Several minutes passed before Rik asked, "Who're you mad at?"

"It'd be easier to ask who I'm *not* mad at," she grumbled. "I am so tired of cameras."

"I thought you wanted the attention."

"I did . . . and I still do, but it's not what I'd expected, you know? Lewis was a *human being*, and that's what I wanted people to see. But all this news exposure is just dehumanizing him, making him into a hot byline and a bunch of forensic gobbledygook!

"That whole incident with the news crew this morning, and how Vanguard got hurt . . . I am so sorry for all the trouble I've caused and I really, really don't like how I'm always tripping over Owen Decker," she finished quietly.

Rik looked up. "Decker's at the Hollow now?"

"Yes."

"I told you to watch your back."

She glanced down at the roof, saying nothing.

"Annie, look. Don't get all worked up. Vanguard is fine, and all you did was get caught between me and Decker," Rik said after a moment, his tone careful. "It pisses him off that all this is going down on my land and not his. So he's gotta push his way in here, or else I'd get all the attention and look good, and that wouldn't set right for that game he likes to play."

Amazed, she squinted against the bright sunlight toward him. "You know what he's up to?"

"Always did." He gave her a wry look. "I'm not the only one who needs to make peace with the past. He can't let go of proving he's the better man. The better husband, the better father, the better farmer. The better whatever. You name it."

Shaking her head, Annie said, "One of these days, the two of you should settle that score before somebody really does get hurt."

Rik merely grunted as he grabbed another sheet of shingling and started nailing it in place.

"So who are *you* mad at?"

He gave her an irritated shrug. Translation: I don't want to talk about it. Not important. Who cares. It's nothing.

Although this was plainly not the best time for a talk, she couldn't keep quiet any longer about what had just happened at the Hollow.

"There's something else."

He glanced at her, waiting.

"They found another body with Lewis."

Rik straightened. "Didn't see that one coming, did you?"

"No." She began hammering again, with a vengeance. "There weren't supposed to be any—" *BANG!* "—surprises or—" *BANG, BANG!* "—complications to threaten my neat theories."

"Hate those complications, don't you."

It wasn't a question. Annie stopped to glance at him, then quickly looked away from what she saw in his eyes.

After a long moment, Rik said, "Who is it?"

"I don't know. Rup and Krista haven't cleared enough of the body to even determine if it's male or female."

"But you have some guesses."

Rik could read her like a book—he was oddly perceptive for such a rough, blunt man.

"It's probably nothing earth-shattering," she admitted. "But I have a feeling our Mystery Skeleton is Indian. Lewis and Boone were guarding Sauk prisoners that night . . . which is something else that's always bothered me."

She put down the hammer again. "I'm no military expert, but don't you think it's strange that two officers, and not some lowly grunts, were on guard duty that night? Wouldn't it be risky to have both your first and second lieutenants away from their command, especially when you were out in the middle of nowhere and even your scouts were lost?"

"You've got a point there."

"What if the whole guard story was as much a lie as the desertion story?" Annie asked. "Boone lied through his teeth about Lewis. The proof of that is back there in the dirt."

"With somebody else."

"Or more than one. Who knows what they'll find?" She twisted around until she faced the Hollow. "God, Rik, what happened that night?"

A dozen scenarios came to mind, not all in Lewis's favor. Maybe it was simple and straightforward: Boone killed Lewis while trying to prevent a desertion, then panicked and buried him, later drumming up a story when under pressure from Taylor.

"But maybe," she said out loud, looking at Rik, "maybe something else happened at the Hollow. Rik, where did Old Ole say the fire circles were? Do you remember?"

He pointed toward the house and yard. "All around down here. It was flat and grassy back then."

"So why were they guarding prisoners at the Hollow? It's awfully secluded up there."

"What are you getting at?"

"I don't know." She sighed. "But Lewis was an idealist. Maybe he tried to interfere where he shouldn't have and ended up dead."

"Like protecting someone?"

"Bingo," Annie whispered.

"I bet you a Mr. Misty that body's not only Indian, but female."

"I don't like where this is heading." She grabbed the hammer and a shingle and began pounding,

pounding, pounding . . . until Rik's hand stopped her.

"Hey. Take it easy. I can think of a better way to work off your frustration." The light tone of his voice contrasted with the oddly tense lines of his face.

Annie blinked at the image that flashed to mind. "You're not serious, are you? On the *roof*?"

"Hell, no," Rik said, with a crack of laughter. "The only shows I put on are behind closed doors."

"Well, why not work off some frustration?" she asked, tossing the hammer aside. "And if friendly little Ms. Olsen pops by again, this time she'll get a clue that you're mine."

Rik's eyes gleamed. "She is kinda cute."

"She's way too young for you."

"Jealous?"

"Maybe," she admitted, lifting her chin. "But don't let it go to your head, Magnusson."

In the house, Annie went straight for the sink and drank a glass of water in a few thirsty gulps. "I hate, *hate* this waiting. I don't know what's taking so long. I wish Rup and Krista would finish up everything tomorrow."

"You're in that much of a hurry to get outta here, huh?"

"Finding Lewis is what I came here to do." She sent him a cautious look. "I will finish this. I will take him home. If it was part of *your* family out there, would you just leave him, just forget—"

"I understand you have to take him home," Rik interrupted, watching her with an almost . . . expectant expression. It left her cold. "I'm even glad for the kid. Really. But what are you gonna do after that?"

She didn't look away. "Rik Magnusson, right now,

all I care about is having you show me how to work off a whole lot of frustration."

His gaze darkened. A moment later, he smiled and asked, "Got anything in mind?"

"Just the basics." They'd made love dozens of times already, but talking about it, anticipating it, filled her with a heated, aching desire. Relieved that she'd distracted him, she gave him a slow smile. "Who's turn is it for a fantasy?"

"Mine."

"How come it's always your turn?"

"It's my turf." Rik's smile widened to a wolfish grin. "And my kitchen table looks pretty good right now."

"The *table*? In broad daylight with the windows wide-open?"

"You're the one who's always opening the blinds." He walked toward her. Quickly, Annie moved out of his way, keeping the old table between them. "And Buck will bark if anybody shows up."

"Your mother would be appalled you're even thinking of this," Annie said, scooting fast to avoid his sudden grab.

"Maybe." His blue eyes gleamed with intent. "I seem to recall my dad chasing her around the kitchen a time or two."

"Oh, I see." She laughed. "We're playing tag."

"That's right. And I'm 'it.' "

"Lucky me." On a wicked inspiration, she unbuttoned her camisole as she walked, revealing Rik's favorite bra—the one with all the lace and pearls.

He took a quick breath, then lunged toward her. Annie squeaked, darting to the other side of the table in the nick of time.

"Hah! You'll have to do better than that, Magnusson."

"Just warming up." Already shirtless, he upped the stakes by popping open the snap of his jeans and pulling the zipper down. The swell of his erection filled the narrow denim "V."

Annie risked a quick glance south, and swallowed. "You play dirty. Shame on you."

"You started it." He stalked her round and round in a circle, both their bodies tensed, alert—until a twitch of his muscles triggered a laughing dash around the table.

After several laps, Annie slowed, and then circled the table once again, trailing a finger provocatively along its polished oak. "The farmer in the dell," she sang in a low, breathless voice. "Hi-ho, the dairy-o, the farmer in the dell—"

His snort of laughter cut her off. "Jesus, Annie!"

She moistened her lips, slowly, enjoying the flash of desire in his eyes. "It fits."

"You know the second verse?"

Annie froze. "Um, I—"

"The farmer takes a wife."

Rik launched himself across the top of the table, sliding like a runner stealing a base. Annie shrieked as his hand seized the tail of her open camisole.

Outside, upset by the commotion, Buck started to howl.

She shook free, leaving Rik holding only a bit of white cotton and lace. "Maybe. But he'll have to catch her first."

"This farmer is no fool," he said with that feral smile. "All's fair, as they say." His shoulder muscles bunched for attack.

Annie yelped and dashed from the kitchen, laughing as she shoved chairs in her wake to slow him down.

Rik hurdled the chairs, so close behind her she could feel his breath. She ran to the parlor, Rik hot on her heels, winding around the chairs and sofa, upending pillows, rattling the crystal, and knocking Old Ole off center.

Cornered next to a massive potted fern, she feinted to the left, then darted low, just barely avoiding his grasp, and headed for the living room.

"Dammit!" Rik laughed behind her. "This is worse than catching chickens!"

"Now there's romance for you," she gasped. In the middle of the room, she stopped short and grabbed the TV remote from Rik's chair. "Stop right there . . . come any closer and you'll never see Mr. Remote again!"

Rik skidded to a halt, eyes wide. "Talk about playing dirty. That's it: no quarter given now."

He had her. She couldn't escape this time.

But Annie ran full tilt past Rik anyway, laughing as his arms and hands closed hard around her.

She twisted and bucked as Rik, cursing, struggled to hold on to her. Her knee connected with his belly and he let out his breath in a loud *ooph!* and almost let her go. But he managed to hang on, and hauled her wriggling and giggling toward the bedroom.

There, he heaved her onto the bed, where she bounced quite high twice, then pinned her to the mattress with his body before she could roll away.

"Man, you're something, Annie. I can't remember the last time I had this much fun." He moved his hips against hers, breathing fast. "Wanna wrassle, wild woman?"

Annie grinned up at Rik.

"Well? What do you say?" he asked, nibbling on her lips.

I love you.

Briefly, she closed her eyes, holding back the sudden burn of tears. "Only if I can be on top."

"You're always on top."

The farmer takes a wife . . .

How could she want to laugh and cry like this?

In a deliberately light tone, she chided, "The Farmer in the Dell needs to loosen up, be a little more liberated."

Rik laughed, rolling over until she straddled him. "I think the farmer's in a heap of trouble."

"You have no idea."

She wrestled with him, not with all her strength, but not making it easy for him, either. She fought as he got her out of her clothes, wrecked the bed to get him out of his jeans, and tumbled with Rik to the floor in a tangle of sheets and summer quilt and clothing.

Having discovered—by accident—that Rik was ticklish under his arms, she used this tactic with merciless glee to free herself and scrambled toward the bed.

Again, he moved too fast for her to escape. As she climbed onto the mattress, stripped of its sheets and blanket, Rik snagged her ankle and pulled her toward him. Facedown on the bed, she had no chance to move before he covered her body with his. Annie gasped at the shock of his entry—sudden, hard, and deep—but as he moved within her, pleasure spread,

aching and demanding, and she arched back against
him, wanting more.

"Gotcha," he whispered raggedly as he thrust into
her from behind, sweetly thick and unrelenting. "And
I think I'll keep you. For a little . . . while yet."

"Rik, no," she moaned.

"Yes." A deeper thrust, sending shocks of pleasure
shimmering through her body. "God, yes, Annie!"

Too far gone to protest, to remind him she couldn't
stay, Annie arched her head back, eyes squeezed shut,
the intense pleasure shooting through her until she
sobbed his name, over and over again.

Later that night, Annie sat with Rik in the living
room. He quietly watched the evening weather report—the marks of exhaustion on his face as plain as
the faint scratches from her nails on his skin—while
she pored over Krista Harte's dissertation and the
Oklahoma interviews.

The news came and went, and Annie looked up
from the sea of papers surrounding her only to watch
the five-minute news highlight of herself at the Hollow. She was glad Rik wasn't in a talkative mood. Her
nerves were still far too raw for any more confronta-
tions.

When a light snoring from the armchair caught her
attention, Annie glanced up. Rik had fallen asleep, the
TV remote in a place of honor on his stomach.

The sight filled her with a sweet longing she didn't
dare look at too closely.

Tempting as it was, she couldn't stay. Life with Rik
was as alien as life on Mars. Once the novelty of sex
faded, they'd find they had nothing in common. He
was a workaholic . . . and what would she *do* here?

With Lewis's story at an end she should start thinking about her next project, and God knew where that would take her, or for how long.

Rik wasn't exactly blessed with an abundance of patience, nor did he strike her as the type who'd put up with a long-distance relationship.

A sudden thought took her: he'd skipped a condom during that little tussle earlier, too.

God, what if she were pregnant?

Panic set in with a vengeance. She had to close her eyes and breathe deeply, several times, before it passed. Then, to make sure it didn't come back, she focused on the papers before her and retreated to the past.

While Rik continued to snore away beside her, Annie stretched out on the floor and read until her eyes grew strained. She skimmed lots of interesting insights into Native American life in the early part of the century, but nothing relating to Lewis or Boone. Five more pages—then she'd call it quits for the night and try to herd Rik into bed.

She turned the next page, started reading—and sat abruptly, heart pounding.

"Rik." She shook his foot. "Rik, wake up!"

He jerked awake, his reflexes fast enough to catch the remote before it fell to the floor. Within seconds, his gaze went from sleepy to clear and alert. "You found something."

"I think so! It's an interview with one of Black Hawk's great-grandsons. Listen to this." She read from the page: " 'My grandfather's sister lost a grand-daughter at that place and my grandfather told the soldiers they had murdered this daughter of his blood and that a white soldier tried to help her but he was killed. The soldiers at the fort, they would not hear my grandfather's words.' "

He whistled, low. "You got it, honey."

"Maybe." Quickly, Annie scanned the pages again, her hands shaking. "It doesn't say where or when, but it must've happened around the battle at Wisconsin Heights."

"That's bad?"

"Yes. Atkinson's regulars were still cooling their heels back at Fort Koshkonong. The 'soldier' who'd tried to protect the woman must have been some poor fool of a militiaman who got in the way of a barrage of lead shot."

"But you can't be sure of that."

She shook her head, her mind reeling with flashes of insights, thoughts, and possibilities. Even without verifiable proof, this rang true. "Lewis was a Galahad in the flesh. It would be just like him to try and stop the rape of a female prisoner."

"And get killed for his troubles. Human behavior," Rik sat foward, shaking his head. "It sure don't change much over time."

"And it makes sense. The army was riddled with egos and rivalries. Alcoholism was rampant, tempers short, fear and frustration ran high, and men had been away from women for a while. A bad combination."

"So maybe Boone got drunk, went after a little fun, then argued with Hudson and killed him."

She looked at him, blinking back her sudden tears. "My God, Rik. I think you're right . . . Boone killed his own friend in some ugly dispute over a woman."

"Shit like that happens all the time. All you gotta do is read the newspapers." For a moment, his eyes darkened with an old pain, then he said, "If we could put two and two together, somebody else must have. Why didn't the army go after Boone?"

Annie frowned. "The silence could've been politically motivated. Ambitious men often used wars to launch political and military careers. Boone's family had money and clout; Atkinson himself might've protected Boone. Or maybe nobody wanted to ask questions, and so the problem just . . . went away."

"So now you got all the proof you need, right?"

"Not really. Nothing strong enough to accuse one of the Union's most respected generals of murder." She began gathering the papers into their folders. "But nobody said I can't pose a few questions and make people think."

"And this means you've wrapped up the book."

Her hands stilled a moment; then she resumed filing. "Pretty much. There's just a few loose ends to tie up."

After a moment, Rik said, "You ready to hit the sack? I'm beat."

She nodded, and together they turned off the lights in the house one by one, and then slipped beneath the cool cotton sheets. Annie edged close to Rik's tense body. She waited, hoping he would relax, roll over, kiss her, and take her in his arms. God, tonight she needed to be held.

But he made no move to touch her, and all her fears and doubts came back in a rush, leaving her no peace.

"Lewis wrote a letter to his mother the day he died," she said into the darkness. "He never sent it, but the letter was with his personal belongings and the army eventually sent everything back to his family."

When he didn't answer, she took his silence as a signal to continue.

"When he wrote that letter, he was upset. It's always sort of haunted me. Now I know why."

"What did he say?" Rik asked at last.

" 'Before I fall asleep upon the ground and dream of things I pray you shall never see or hear or feel, I remind myself that one must do what is right and just, and the consequences be damned.' " After a moment, she added, "He underlined those last three words."

For a long while, they lay in the darkness and the silence, until Rik said, "Looks like when it mattered, he did the right thing."

"But the consequence was his *life*! And everything that mattered most to him."

She shivered and Rik drew her body close to his at last. "You were right all along, Annie, and now he'll be recognized as the hero he really was. The good guy wins, even if it took a long time."

"Thank you for understanding." In the darkness, she made little circles on his chest with her fingertip, over and over again. Then, gathering her courage, she whispered, "Rik, we need to talk. I have to tell you—"

"Don't. I don't want to talk about your leaving. I don't want to talk about Lewis. I'm too tired." Abruptly he let her go and rolled over, his back to her, a chasm between them. "Just . . . go to sleep, Annie. Whatever it is you have to say, it can wait." He hesitated, then added quietly, "Please."

CHAPTER EIGHTEEN

November 28, 1832, Youngstown, Ohio: Please accept our deepest gratitude for sending home our Dear Boy's last letters. Forgive me, but I must I plead another kindness, Sir, and ask for a little letter to tell us how it was with our Boy when you saw him last. Was he cheerful, in good health and sound of mind and Heart? We have heard tales, Sir, tales which do not bear repeating.

—Mrs. Augustina Hudson,
from a copy of a letter to Abraham Lincoln

Rik headed for the kitchen and the sound of Annie's cheerful voice.

"*Bonjour! Monsieur Wagner, s'il vous plaît.*"

He stopped short in the doorway, staring at her back. French? What was this?

"*Oui, je m'appelle Annora Beckett. Merci.*" She leaned over the counter, jiggling a foot. "*Bonjour!* Hello, hello, Randy! It's Annie. I got your message and yes, I'm running on schedule. I'll be in Montreal by October."

Rik walked the rest of the way into the kitchen, and Annie turned quickly, the phone still to her ear. Over the table, their gazes met and locked.

"Um, yes . . . I'm looking forward to working with you, too. Say, I can't talk now. I'll give you another call in a few weeks, okay?"

She hung up the phone, gave the receiver a slow, deliberate pat, and then looked up at Rik. "I'll pay you for the long-distance charges before I leave."

Rik didn't trust himself to answer. He headed for the coffeemaker, and poured a mug full.

"I'm sorry about all these calls." Even as she apologized, he heard the dial tone as she picked up the phone again. "There's so much to do, and time's getting short."

Still, he said nothing, struggling to bring his sudden fury under control.

"Yes, I'll hold," Annie said behind him, in a businesslike tone.

The silence ticked by, second after second, before she said quietly, "You look like you're in bad mood this morning, Rik."

He turned then. "Why shouldn't I be? I've got dozens of strangers underfoot, getting in my way and knocking on my door at all hours of the day, the damn phone never stops ringing, and now I got a bunch of Indians picketing in my fields!"

Annie blinked, as if surprised. Then she hoisted herself up to the kitchen counter and started swinging her bare feet. "They want the woman's remains returned to her tribe for proper burial, that's all. And they're not picketers, Rik, they're activists."

"Like anybody can ever prove what tribe she belonged to," Rik retorted. "It's more like a bunch of people using a pack of reporters for their own private gripes."

"No, it's more like a bunch of people trying to do

the right thing, even if you think it's ridiculous." She glared at him. "Just like you think my conspiracy theory is ridiculous."

Too bad he couldn't bang his head against the kitchen cupboard and howl out his frustration. He'd made just the one comment yesterday, and she was still mad about it. "All I said was that you should be thinking it *might* not be a cover-up—"

"Give me a break!" she interrupted. "We have two people dumped in a secret grave—a woman with a crushed skull and premortem injuries to her arms and ribs, and an officer bayoneted to death, even though his family was told he deserted. You tell me Lewis wasn't trying to protect her and that he wasn't killed because of it. You tell me the army—"

"I'm not telling you anything," he snapped, holding tight to his temper. Sleep had been scarce lately, and her defensiveness and his bad mood weren't just because of a few reporters and picketers. *Activists*.

Christ, what a mess.

That morning, film crews from Madison and Milwaukee had arrived to get a piece of the local action. With one word to the cops he could clear out the Hollow of at least the activists, media, and busybodies. But for Annie, annoying media exposure was still better than none at all, and as Decker kept harping, history belonged to everybody.

Like hell was he going to come out looking like a bad guy.

"Rik."

He glanced up. "What?"

"Don't do this to me . . . don't do this to yourself," Annie said softly. "You knew all along that I have to leave. I can't—" She cut herself off, then said, "Yes, I'll still hold, thank you."

Rik took a deep, calming breath to keep from yanking the phone out of her hand—or yanking the whole thing out of the wall and throwing it in the trash. "You can't what, Annie?"

"For God's sake, Rik! You—"

"Da-a-a-d!" Heather called from the second floor, over the tinkling of an out-of-tune piano and pealing giggles. Rik looked up, then ran a hand through his hair.

"What?" He couldn't help the irritation in his voice.

"Are we ready to go to the mall yet?"

"No!"

Silence. Then, "Okay. You don't have to yell."

Man, he had a headache.

And why had he agreed to take Heather and her friends to the mall, with this crap going on at the Hollow, and him and Annie fighting?

"Somebody just shoot me," he muttered, then glanced at Annie, still cradling the phone between her shoulder and ear.

In the days since Krista and Rup had cleared out Hudson's remains and sent them to a lab in Madison, Annie had spent hours on the phone with city officials in Youngstown and with the Department of Veterans' Affairs, arranging for a reburial with full military honors.

"Give your phone ear a break," he said, a sudden inspiration striking him. "Come along with us to the mall."

"Rik, I'm waiting for at least a dozen calls. I can't go anywhere."

"You bought an answering machine," he said. "Let it take them."

"The whole reason for this trip is so that you can spend some bonding time with your daughter."

"Yeah, I know." Giggles erupted upstairs again. "But I'd like you to come with me. I'd really like it a lot."

She frowned. "How long will you be gone?"

"All afternoon." The enormity of it overwhelmed him, and he repressed a groan. "Please?"

With a shadow of a smile, she hung up the phone. "Are you scared of a bunch of girls, Rik Magnusson? A big, tough guy like you?"

Rik opened his mouth to deny it, then admitted, "Damn right I am." More giggles, the *twitter-twitter* of whispering. *They* were coming down the stairs. "Please, Annie?"

"How can I say no?"

Fifteen minutes later, he'd packed Heather, Tamara, and Erin in the backseat of his pickup, with Annie in front beside him, and then they were off.

The girls insisted on turning the radio to some rock station and playing it loud. Rik didn't mind, since it drowned out their unending chatter.

Madison may have been voted one of the best places to live, but Rik still hated cities. He hated the rude drivers, and despised malls most of all. Store upon endless store of the same overpriced junk, and the human traffic was even worse than the street traffic outside.

It put him on edge as they entered—all these people and the noise and activity—and made him appreciate his farm all the more. Nothing flashy, his place. No designer this or that, no perfumes that cost as much as his grocery bill—just enough work to keep a body from being so bored they had to wander around like zombies.

Annie slipped her hand over his with a slight squeeze, interrupting his thoughts. "I hate these places," he said.

She smiled at him; a smile missing her usual sunny warmth. "You're out of your element, country boy. But don't worry. This reformed mall rat will take care of you."

Rik snorted, just then noticing his daughter had veered for a store with display windows hawking more sexy underwear than he'd ever be lucky enough to see in his entire lifetime.

"Oooh," Annie cooed, like one of those cozy, content mourning doves always perched on his porch. "A Victoria's Secret! Let's go."

Rik dug in his heels, as best he could amid a bumping, jostling crowd. "I'm not going in there."

"Oh, come *on*, Rik." She tugged his arm. "We've both been a little stressed lately. It'll be fun."

Considering his mood, torture was more like it.

"I'll let you help me pick out a little something." She flashed him another tentative smile—and he just couldn't say no to her.

"I'm not touching a damn thing in here," he warned in a low voice as they crossed the threshold into what was definitely Alien Territory. Every muscle in his body tensed.

Heavy perfumes, satiny and lacy bits in a rainbow of colors hanging from padded hangers or displayed on mannequins—the whole store was packed with stuff designed for the sole purpose of making men go crazy.

And the prices!

Glimpsing a tag on a racy number in leopard-print satin, he nearly swore out loud. He couldn't imagine Annie spending that much when his sole intention would be to get it off her in as few seconds as possible.

While Heather and her friends exclaimed over a rack of neon bras, Annie picked up a purple bit of nothing, and said, "What do you think?"

"I can't say out loud what I'm thinking," he retorted, trying not to imagine what she'd look like in the clingy, shiny garment with its thread-thin straps and neckline that would plunge nearly to her navel.

Lust and anger warred inside him, twisting his guts into a knot. Couldn't she see what this was doing to him?

"Rik," Annie whispered. "Relax."

In public, in front of the girls, pride demanded he pretend nothing was wrong. He glanced around, caught the interested gaze of a young salesclerk, then turned back to Annie. She was watching him, smiling, but it didn't reach her eyes. "Relax? I'm the only guy in this place."

"It doesn't insult your masculinity at all. Trust me on this. And here." She draped the purple thing over his hands, her fingers lightly stroking his skin for a moment. "If you won't help me pick out anything, you may as well make yourself useful."

Rik didn't protest, even if it left him holding something no self-respecting man would be seen touching in public. Or, at least not in the presence of said man's staring teenage daughter and her wide-eyed friends, who were poking each other with their elbows.

But it sure was soft, the smooth fabric catching on

the rough skin of his hands and, man, it would slide off Annie's body with a whisper . . .

He had to close his eyes, fighting back the gray despair threatening to roll over him. When he opened his eyes again, he saw his daughter bearing down on him, carrying an item he was damn sure she had to be at least eighteen to even touch.

"I'm buying this," Heather announced in her "dare to say no" voice.

He eyed the black bit of lace. "What for?"

"Because it's so awesome!" Heather held it up against her chest and the dull ache between his brows grew to a hammering throb.

No, no, no. His baby was *not* a sexual being. No way. Never.

"You have enough money to pay for it?" he demanded, rubbing his eyebrows. "Because I'm not spending over thirty bucks on that."

Heather's nose went up. "Owen gave me money. He said I could buy whatever I wanted."

Christ, he did *not* need this. Not now. "Heather—"

"Hey!" It was Annie, suddenly at his elbow. Briefly, her gaze locked with his. "Heather, that is so pretty! You should try it on first, though. It can look great on the hanger, but feel and look terrible when it's on. I want to see if this sleep shirt fits, so let's go into the dressing room together. You girls stay here and keep Rik from running his fingers through the panties on the table."

Though Annie smiled, her tone was firm. Heather opened her mouth to speak as Tamara and Erin started giggling behind him, but Annie hooked

Heather's arm and yanked her toward the dressing rooms.

Saving him, he knew very well, from saying something he'd only regret later.

"Was that necessary?" Annie demanded moments later, as she and Rik's daughter squared off against each other in the perfumed dressing room.

The girl eyed her. "What?"

"Don't you 'what' me, Heather. Playing your father against your stepfather like that is wrong. They have enough bad blood between them without you adding to it."

A look of shock crossed Heather's face and her eyes, a darker blue than Rik's, widened. "Like you have any right to tell me what to do!"

"No, I don't," Annie agreed, her tone low and terse. "But your father, despite having a very bad week, agreed to let you and your friends stay the night, and he agreed to drive you to the mall. Don't repay him by making him feel like a loser."

As suddenly as it had come, the girl's defiance crumpled. "I didn't mean to."

Annie sighed. "Give your dad a break here, okay? You know he's having money problems because it hasn't rained, but he'll buy that bra if you insist. But you'd better have a good reason for doing so."

Heather looked down at the bra. "I guess I don't need it."

On impulse, Annie reached over and brushed a lock of the girl's long hair from her eyes. "I know it's hard for you right now, especially with your mom ready to have another baby." She could tell she'd hit a nerve by the girl's high color; in this respect, she was every inch her father's daughter. "But hang in there. Believe me when I say that making other people unhappy just because *you're* unhappy is no way to deal with problems."

"I hate it that Mom is pregnant. It's so gross! I don't even want to think about them doing it together, and I hate how *he* won't leave her alone," Heather said with a shudder.

Annie took a deep breath. The dressing room of a lingerie store was not the best place for a confessional. She should pat the girl on the head, spin her around, and march her right back outside for her father to deal with.

But along with abandoned soldiers no one else cared about, she had a weakness for confused young girls.

"Heather, your mom and stepfather love each other. There's nothing 'gross' about it. Making love, and making babies, is a natural expression of that kind of love."

"Right. Like Mom *loved* my dad while she was sleeping around with Owen."

"I'm not saying what she did was right, or that it didn't hurt a lot of people, including you and your dad. If she was unhappy, she should've asked for a divorce. But as much as it pains me to admit this, adults can be pretty stupid. And sometimes, doing the right thing isn't at all easy."

"I want to live with my dad," Heather said, looking up again. Tears brimmed, but didn't spill over. "With Mom and Owen, I'm just a free baby-sitter. My little brother's okay, for a kid, but it's like . . . like I don't belong anymore."

"Have you talked with your dad about this?"

"Oh, sure! Like he'd agree. He doesn't have time for me now. I'd just be in his way."

"Give him the benefit of the doubt, Heather, and sit down and talk with him. He can't read your mind."

After a moment, Heather whispered, "But then Mom would think I hate her."

"It's a tough situation, but talking about your feelings will help make it a little easier. Okay?"

The bowed blond head nodded once. "Okay."

Annie gave her a quick hug. "We'd better go. Be nice to your dad, now—maybe even offer to visit the tool section in Sears."

As Heather looked up, a dimpled smile flashed across her face and something inside Annie made a funny little twist. But before she could push open the dressing-room door, Heather said, "You like my dad, don't you?"

"Well, yes. He's a decent guy."

"No, I mean you *like* him. You know!" She rolled her eyes. "I see how you look at each other."

"Oh? And how is that?"

"Well, my dad looks at you like he'd like to eat you up." The girl grinned; a cheeky, mischievous grin. "Do you guys—"

"Heather, there are some questions you shouldn't ask," Annie interrupted in a warning tone. Then she took the girl's shoulders, spun her about, and said, "Out, out, out!"

When they emerged from the dressing room, Annie almost smiled at the naked look of relief on Rik's face.

"It doesn't fit, Dad," Heather said, shrugging nonchalantly. "I'll put it back, and then we can go."

Annie, however, bought the negligee, and, to her

amusement, Heather actually asked her father if he wanted "to go to Sears and look at tool stuff or whatever."

With a straight face, Rik declined his daughter's offer and agreed to let the girls range ahead, with orders to meet him and Annie again in a couple of hours.

That left her alone with Rik—along with her perfumed Victoria's Secret shopping bag with its purple sweet-nothings inside, and a tension so thick she could almost see it shimmering between them.

"I'm hungry," Rik said, looking away. "Do you want to shop, or get something to eat?"

Neither really appealed, but they couldn't stand here like this for the next couple hours. "Are there any good restaurants around here?"

"A food court," he said. "A bunch of fast-food joints around a big cafeteria."

Annie made a face. "Better than nothing, I suppose. Are you sure you don't want to go to Sears?"

He smiled at her. "You put her up to that, didn't you?"

"Guilty," she said, catching his hand in hers. His fingers closed around hers tightly. "We had a little chat in the dressing room."

"I figured as much. She looked mighty guilty when she came back out." He hesitated, then added, "You didn't have to do that. She's my kid. I may not be much for raising her, but—"

"Oh, Rik, that's not true, and you know it."

He looked over her shoulder at some distant point. "I wasn't around much when she was little. Then I didn't say a word when Karen asked for full custody, because I figured that's the way it was done. I thought

I was doing the right thing, but ended up letting another man raise my daughter."

Side by side, they wound their way through the crowd and headed toward the food court.

"Even good people make mistakes," Annie said at last. "Don't beat yourself up over it. You made a mistake, and you're trying to make up for it now. That's all that counts. Besides, could you really have managed joint custody? Running a farm on your own, with a small child around?"

"I could've made an effort," he answered tightly. "More than the one I made, anyway."

"That still doesn't mean you're a bad father. Heather is upset about the gossip, about the tension between you and Decker. She has mixed feelings about the new baby, but that's to be expected, isn't it? Otherwise, she's pretty much a normal teenager."

"Nothing at all like you were?"

Not the subject she wanted to discuss. Keeping her gaze focused straight ahead, she said evenly, "I didn't have a father or mother in my life, or even a stepparent, who cared about me. Photography saved my life, Rik, and working on Lewis Hudson's story helped me put a lot of my anger into perspective. Or at least it helped me channel it toward a more worthwhile effort."

"Your parents were idiots to throw away a kid like you."

They'd arrived at the food court—a large, noisy cafeteria of fast-food restaurants, just as he'd said it would be.

"For all I know, my mother may have thought she was doing me a favor by abandoning me. My father probably never even knew I existed." Annie glanced around. "Oh, boy. Welcome to heart-attack central. I'd much rather be sitting in your kitchen eating biscuits with honey."

"I'll make some tomorrow morning when I cook breakfast for the girls." With his hand on the small of her back, he guided her toward one line. "I'm leaning toward Taco Bell. That okay with you?" When she nodded, he added, "I'm buying."

"You don't have to. I can pay my own way."

"I know that, Annie, just like I know you can take care of yourself. But I want to pay for your lunch anyway."

While they waited their turn in line, Annie's gaze lingered on Rik's broad shoulders and the golden hair curling at his nape. He didn't appear to notice, but quite a few women were sending admiring gazes his way.

At times like these, she wanted to grab him and shake him silly, and shout that there was nothing wrong with him: not as a man, a husband, or a father. He didn't have to prove what a great provider he was—even it only meant buying her a taco.

But she kept her mouth shut. He needed to see it himself, and after the stress of the past week, she wanted to steer clear of any talk that cut too close to the personal.

An elbow poking her arm interrupted her thoughts and she looked up. Both Rik and the counter clerk were watching her expectantly.

After their order had been filled, she followed Rik to one of the few open tables, squeezed between a mother with three young children—all of whom had an allergy to chairs—and a group of adolescent boys greatly amused by their repertoire of body noises.

Rik looked pained, but did his best to ignore the situation. Annie sat and took a big bite of her taco.

"Why did you talk Heather out of buying that bra?" Rik asked suddenly.

Annie sighed and licked a dribble of hot sauce off her finger. "I pointed out that it's not nice to play you and Decker against each other for a thirty-dollar bra nobody will ever see, especially since you're worried about money."

He treated her to the Magnusson Chiller Stare. "Who says I'm worried about money?"

"I recognize stunted crops when I see them." She kept her voice low. "And it hardly escaped my notice that you refused to let me visit until I offered money."

"You've got no right butting into my business."

"Don't be a hypocrite," she snapped, then shot a quick look at the woman with all the kids—but the woman was too busy containing chaos to notice anything around her, including a mild spat brewing. "I earned the right to be concerned when I went to bed with you."

His color still high, Rik said, "My problems aren't that bad. I've survived worse."

Annie raised a brow. "But . . . ?"

He scowled. "But I don't want to have to sell any of the Belgians. That's why I agreed to take your damn money. Insurance against disaster, I guess."

"Thank you for being honest," she said. "And I don't want you to have to sell Brutus or Venus or her new baby. I'm glad I could help you out in some way, considering the mess I've made of things this week."

"Yeah . . . what did you tell me? No trouble. I wouldn't even know you were around. Girl Scout's honor, you said."

She recognized the words from those first letters they'd sent way back in spring. "I told you, I never anticipated this sort of response."

He took a bite of his burrito. "Don't try and tell me you're unhappy about it."

Shifting on her chair, she glanced at him and then away. "It's not so black-and-white, Rik. I'm glad for the attention, yes, out of a sense of validation for Lewis. And it can't hurt to have a ready-made audience when it comes time to find a publisher for this project."

He raised a brow, as she had. "But . . . ?"

"But I don't like sharing him," she admitted. "Not like this. It feels so . . . intrusive! And I hate losing control over the situation."

"You seem to have pretty good control over everything. You found the kid, you got a handle on what happened to him, and now you're taking him home like you want." He shrugged. "What else is bugging you?"

Annie put her drink down with more force than she intended, sprinkling the table with soda. "Probably the same thing that's bugging you. Now that I've found Lewis, I'll be leaving soon."

His eyes narrowed a fraction, but no other emotion crossed his face. "Not before I get a private showing of that purple thing you just bought, right?"

The nonchalance didn't fool her.

"This isn't easy for me either, you know," she said, with a quick glance at the people around her. Of all the places to get into this, why here?

With a napkin, Rik wiped his mouth and mustache. "Don't make it hard, then. Take the kid home and come back."

Annie dropped her gaze to her half-eaten taco. "I'm not the kind of woman you need."

"And what kind of woman do I need?" he asked mildly.

"Strong. Committed and . . . rooted. Just like you."

"You're strong, and women don't come much more committed than you." He paused, then added, "I figure we've been pretty good for each other. It could work."

Annie briefly closed her eyes. God, she'd seen this coming, had known this moment would arrive.

"You can't pretend you don't like me some," Rik continued in the same even voice.

"I like your wonderful house. I like your farm. I like the deep ties to your family and history, even Lewis's history. And I like you very much, but—"

"I know I scare you, Annie. Why is that?"

Her stomach knotted with a sudden, all-too-familiar fear. "Because I don't know how."

A long moment of silence passed before he said, "I'm not following you here, honey."

"It's too much." She still couldn't look at him. "Like wanting a quick dip in a pool, only to drown in an ocean."

No, that was all wrong. What a stupid thing to say!

"What I mean is," she said, looking up at last and meeting the full force of those blue eyes. "I want . . . I guess I'm looking for what Lewis had: to be so important, to be so loved, that I changed a life forever. But I'm afraid I don't know how . . . how to love like that."

This time, Rik glanced away. "You've made me see a lot of things differently. Isn't that enough to start with?"

"Rik, I won't deny that lately I've thought about settling down, but I've never had that kind of life. It's not you I'm afraid of, it's *me*. My feelings for you, and that you may be asking me for something I'm not capable of giving."

"You could try."

"But that's just it! I've never, ever made a lasting bond with another person, not the way you mean. Not the way you deserve."

"What about Hudson? I'd call that a hell of a lasting bond."

She eyed him. "Is this a trick question? As you pointed out once, he doesn't count; he's dead. Remember?"

"It tells me you've got what it takes. But Hudson doesn't have what you're looking for, and what you've made him into isn't real." He frowned. "Life's just too damn short to be afraid of living."

His words spread a glow within her; as if a light she'd let go out a long, long time ago had suddenly rekindled again.

But that light wasn't strong enough, or bright enough, to chase away all the doubts and fears. She'd lived with her shadows for far too long to let go of them so easily.

"I don't want to hurt you," she whispered, meeting his gaze. Neither looked away. "The idea of even *trying* terrifies me. You don't deserve to be hurt like that again. My God, you—"

"I," he said quietly, "am a grown man. Take your best shot, Annie. So long as I see it coming, I can handle it."

There it was. Her choice: the easy way out, or the biggest gamble of her life.

"I can't," she finally said. Then, as his eyes widened with something like shock, she added in a rush, "I can't answer you now. I . . . I have to think about this more."

He nodded, even smiled a little. "When you make up your mind as to what you want, just ask. You've got to make this decision yourself. I won't force it on you, but I'll be waiting."

A good answer. The right answer. Yet somehow, his words dampened that little light struggling within her.

Then Rik leaned across the small table, across the half-eaten ruins of their lunch, and surprised her with a hard, full-tongued kiss. A kiss crackling with heat; a kiss that so possessed her that all the noise and faces, motion and places, faded away, leaving nothing but Rik.

CHAPTER NINETEEN

April 9, 1842, Springfield, Illinois: I regret I can do no more for you at this time. Without evidence to contradict Captain Boone's official report, a Case cannot be made. I shall, Madam, continue to address this issue as Opportunities arise. I clearly recall Lieutenant Hudson and believed him to be Fair, Trustworthy and Loyal to his Oath and his Country. I saw nothing in his actions to indicate he would abandon his men to the perils of the enemy or a hostile Wilderness. He seemed a Good and Godly young man.

—ABRAHAM LINCOLN, ATTORNEY,
FROM A LETTER TO MRS. AUGUSTINA HUDSON

All the way back home, Rik mulled over his conversation with Annie, while the girls in the backseat kept up a constant yakkity-yak, going on about "awesome" clothes and the cute boys they'd flirted with, and gushing over their spoils amid the rustle of paper bags and shrink wrap.

He glanced at Annie as she stared out the passenger-side window, and wondered again what he'd have to do to prove what she meant to him.

A woman like her, proud and scared all at once, would take a lot of patience and gentle handling. And while she might still run off and break his heart, it was a risk he was willing to take.

Annie turned from the window then, caught his gaze, and smiled. A warmth spread deep inside, and brought to mind the sexy lingerie she'd bought and what he wanted to do with her the minute he got her home.

"Dad?"

Or, the minute he got her alone without the girls underfoot. "Yeah?" Rik asked, meeting his daughter's eyes in his rearview mirror.

"Thanks for taking us to the mall."

Surprised by this rare show of politeness, it took Rik a moment before he said, "You're welcome, princess."

Annie moved her hand to his free hand, which rested on his thigh, and squeezed it. When he glanced at her, she winked—and trailed her fingers up his leg. He swerved the pickup when her fingers lightly caressed the denim over his dick.

"Dad! Jeez, you drive worse than Mom!"

"Sorry, girls." He gave Annie a grin as she pulled her hand back, folding both hands on her lap like a prim old lady in church. "I didn't want to hit that squirrel."

Annie laughed. "What a guy—you're quick. Good reflexes," she added, with a smile meant only for him.

After that Rik drove faster, eager to get home and find a spare ten minutes to finish what she'd just started. But when he pulled into his drive, the sight of a news van parked by his barn curdled all those warm liquid thoughts.

"Dammit! I am sick and tired of these people thinking they got free rein of my place."

Now he couldn't hustle Annie off to the barn for a little horizontal refreshment.

His anger intensified as he slammed the pickup's gear into PARK. Evading Annie's restraining hand, he walked fast toward the barn. Several men were smoking, leaning against the red wall, and threw their cigarettes aside when they saw him. A cameraman and a suit moved toward him, but backed up quick enough when they realized he didn't have a friendly greeting in mind.

"I'm not gonna warn you people again," he snapped. "This is private property, and you got no business being here. I've tried to be a good guy about the Hollow, but I draw the line at my home. You get the hell outta here before I call the cops."

"Do you know who we are?" demanded the guy in the suit, his pretty-boy face looking as offended as if he'd just stepped in a cow patty.

"I don't care. Get lost. Now."

"I'm Brett Cassidy with the Chicago CBS affiliate and it is my job to keep the public informed—"

"The public doesn't need to be informed in front of my barn."

"Perhaps you don't comprehend the significance of this story to the nation's history." Pretty Boy didn't know when to give up, and his tone translated "you don't comprehend" into "you ignorant hick." "The murder of Lieutenant Hudson involves nearly a half dozen important historical personalities. We just interviewed Mr. Owen Decker over at the Hollow, and—"

"And I asked you what any of this has to do with my barn," Rik interrupted.

"We want a personal angle," Pretty Boy said, reversing his tactics and flashing his pearly whites. "Chief Black Hawk fell victim to modern progress, as you have—"

"What the hell are you talking about?"

"—and since you own one of those small farms being sacrificed to big business, we thought you might appreciate the chance to make your plight known to the American people," the man finished, as if Rik hadn't spoken.

"I'm not in danger of losing my farm!"

"Not according to Mr. Decker. We mean no disrespect, Mr. Magnusson, but the difficulties facing the American family farm are hardly a secret. Besides the fact that it will gain you much-needed money, what are your feelings about the petition for the sale of Black Hawk's Hollow?"

Anger burned at the last thin thread of his control. "*What* petition?"

Pretty Boy looked at him as if he were an idiot. "The petition started by Mr. Decker and Ms. Beckett, asking the state of Wisconsin to buy Black Hawk's Hollow as an historical site."

That inner thread snapped. Rik grabbed the man's suit lapels and slammed him back against the barn.

"I won't tell you again," he said into the man's startled face. From the corner of his eye, he saw several of the crew move closer. One man placed a restraining hand on Rik's shoulder. "Get off my property, or I'll call the cops. You comprehend the significance of that?"

"Of course," Pretty Boy said coldly. "Let go."

Rik backed away, shaking off the hand on his shoulder. He stared at them, waiting as they packed their equipment in sullen silence, not missing the muttered "stupid prick." But he didn't move until the van shot back toward the road amid ricocheting gravel and spitting dirt.

He turned toward the house. Anger now warred with a bitter disappointment. He expected Decker to pull a trick like this.

But Annie?

She'd gone behind his back time and time again for the sake of Lewis Hudson, but if she was in cahoots with Decker, trying to steal his land—and stealing it was, no matter how noble Decker made it sound—this he could not forgive.

He started back toward the house, knowing he owed her the benefit of the doubt and, if nothing else, a chance to explain herself.

The sick grinding of his belly worsened the closer he came to the house. The girls still sat in the back of the pickup, their eyes bright with excitement. Annie just looked worried.

"What happened?" she asked.

"I chased them off." Rik glanced at Heather. "Girls, you go on into the house. I need to talk to Annie."

He didn't miss how their smiles and excitement faded, replaced by surprise. They looked at Annie as they scooted out of the truck, but not even Heather questioned his order.

"What's wrong?" Annie asked once they were alone.

The concern in her brown eyes seemed so real, her hand on his arm so warm, so soft. "Tell me about the petition, Annie."

Confusion crossed her face, along with wariness, and Rik had to look away.

"Petition?" she repeated. "I have no idea what you're talking about."

"You swear?" he asked, looking up again.

Her eyes narrowed. "You think I'm lying."

Rik hesitated, trying to find the right words. "It wouldn't be the first time, Annie."

"So what breach of faith have I supposedly committed?"

Rik heard anger in her soft voice. "That reporter said you and Decker started a petition asking the state to buy the Hollow."

"And you believe a *reporter*? A total stranger?"

His patience unraveled completely. "Don't make me look like the asshole here, Annie. All I'm asking is that you tell me the truth—if you even know what it means."

Annie's head snapped back as if he'd hit her. At once, he wanted to call back those words. He even stepped forward, as if he could grab them out of the air.

"Well," she said softly. "I don't have to make you look like an asshole. You're doing a fine job of it all by yourself." Her face pale and pinched with hurt, she turned and walked to the porch. From the steps, she faced him. "I don't know anything about this petition. If Owen Decker said I did, then he's lying . . . and damn you, Rik," she whispered. "Damn you for believing him over me."

"How could I be sure?" he demanded. "It's not like you won't do anything for Lewis Hudson. You as much as said so. And why would you care if I lose a few acres? You told me I should sell off some land, anyway."

She looked down at him. "I like the idea of Lewis

being memorialized in the place where he died. He deserves that. But I didn't have anything to do with it."

Bitter understanding pierced through his haze of anger, sharp as a knife in the back, at what Decker had intended—and like a blind fool, he'd played right into it.

With a low curse, Rik wheeled around and headed for his pickup. He hoped the bastard was still holding court at the Hollow, because the time had come to settle the score once and for all with his old boyhood buddy.

"Rik, where are you going?"

At the door of his truck, Rik turned. Annie wore a look of alarm below the pale anger. "Where do you think?" he shot back. "Keep the girls in the house."

"Rik, don't! Please, you—"

He slammed the door and roared the engine, cutting off her protest, and then floored the accelerator. Before long, his rearview mirror showed Annie's car closing on him fast.

Too bad she hadn't listened—but nothing would make him go back now.

The number of cars and trucks at the Hollow forced Rik to park down the road. He was striding fast toward the Hollow when Annie drove past, parked her car, and ran to catch up with him.

"Rik, don't you do anything stupid! Stop!"

But he didn't stop, even when she hauled back on his arm. Just ahead, Decker stood with the Indians, nodding seriously as a short, barrel-chested guy with braids talked and gestured.

Decker glanced up as Rik pushed his way through the small group of placard-carrying activists. Since he wasn't gentle about it, his progress was marked by shouts and angry muttering.

"Rik, I'm glad you're here." Decker's eyes gleamed with an unmistakable pleasure—and anticipation. "I was explaining my plan for the Hollow, and everybody agrees it's the right thing to do. I came by earlier to talk to you, but you weren't home."

And just like that, Rik was on the defensive.

"Maybe it's the right thing to do," he said into the sudden silence. "But not the way you did it. You owe me an apology, Decker, for going behind my back. It comes down to stealing—and that's something you're real good at."

Another silence, this one shot through with whispers.

"And we both know why you did it," Rik continued, as the Indians moved back cautiously, scenting blood in the dank, woodsy air of the Hollow.

"Owen?"

It was Karen. Rik didn't look away from Decker, but he heard her come up behind him.

"Owen, you told me Rik had agreed to this idea."

Rik closed in on Decker, who didn't move, or look in the least bit worried.

"You bastard," Rik said quietly.

"This place belongs to the public, for all generations," Decker answered at last. "Had I come to you with the idea, you would've refused to listen because you hate my guts. You assume everything I do is to get back at you, but you're wrong. I'm taking action to preserve the Hollow with its place in the history of our state. If you'd try to live farther ahead than the next day, you'd understand I'm working for the general good, not trying to steal anything from you."

"That's a lie," Rik said flatly. "And you know it."

"Hey," said the young cop on guard duty—Dave Harrison, Don Harrison's youngest. "Everybody back off. We don't want anything getting out of hand here. Mr. Magnusson, Mr. Decker, maybe you want to take this matter some place more private."

"Nah," Rik said. "I have him right where I want him. Seems fitting I take down one lying bastard where another figured he'd gotten away with—"

Decker swung at him, hard.

Anticipating it, Rik ducked and launched a punch in return. His fist grazed Decker as he feinted to the right.

A woman screamed, but no one moved to prevent the fight—not even Harrison, a hometown boy who understood what this was really about.

Circling Decker in the clearing, Rik heard Annie call his name.

Of course she'd try and come between them.

"Rik, don't do this!" she pleaded, pulling at the back of his T-shirt. "You'll hurt each other. It isn't worth it. None of this is worth it!"

"Let them be."

A quick glance over his shoulder showed Karen, her face white and drawn, take Annie by the arm and pull her back.

"Let them be," his ex-wife repeated. "This has been a long, long time coming."

No kidding.

The camera crew closed in just as Decker struck at Rik's knees. Rik avoided the kick, but doing so opened him to attack. Decker launched himself hard at Rik's gut, knocking them both to the ground.

Years ago, they'd mock-fought like this for fun, but

Decker's punches weren't playful now. Rik rolled back to his feet. Decker followed. Rik struck again. His fist connected with Decker's jaw in a solid, meaty thud, and Decker sprawled backward in the leaves and dirt.

Decker had more weight, but Rik had his anger. It blunted the pain of the blows raining against his face, ribs, and gut. He hammered back as hard, as furiously, until he rammed his shoulder into Decker's belly. Decker went down again, with Rik on top of him. Pinning Decker beneath him, Rik launched one last, satisfying punch before Harrison moved forward, pulling Rik back by a fistful of knit shirt.

"I win this round," Rik said, gulping for breath, as Decker glared up at him through the sweat and dirt and blood on his face. "And I want you to apologize to Annie—"

"Fire!"

Rik looked up. One of the Indians jabbed a finger toward the sky.

"Fire! Jesus, look at that smoke!"

Rik followed the pointing finger to see a black column of smoke spiraling skyward like an angry wraith.

Right over his farm.

"My daughter and her friends are back there!" Rik briefly locked gazes with Annie, standing white-faced beside Karen.

"You better come with me," Harrison said, shoving Rik toward the road. "The rest of you people stay put."

"Owen, I am *not* staying here if my daughter is in danger!" Karen's voice was high with fear.

Rik ran for the squad car parked by the gate. Behind him, car doors slammed, engines revved, and voices shouted.

As Rik slid into the squad, Harrison slammed it in gear and shot toward the road. Rik spared a quick glance over his shoulder, and saw Annie yank open the back door of Decker's car.

"I've got a ten-twenty-four at Black Hollow Farm on Magnusson Road," Harrison said into the radio as he sped toward the house, siren wailing. "Request ETA for assistance."

"Ten-four. Fire and rescue units are already en route. ETA ten minutes."

Harrison glanced at Rik, but said nothing. Both knew ten or fifteen minutes was too long. In this wind, it'd take only seconds for dry, weathered wood to catch.

Rik swore as Harrison turned onto the drive and approached the house and barnyard. In the time it had taken to notice the smoke, the dairy barn was burning out of control and already spreading toward the old barn.

How had this happened? With the dry spell, he'd been so careful . . .

The news crew! The men with the cigarettes they'd thrown aside before leaving, and he had been too angry to register the danger.

"There are the girls," Rik said, pointing. "Thank God they're okay."

Heather and her two friends huddled on the porch, teary-eyed and frantic. Heather ran down the steps before Harrison even brought the squad to a halt in front of the house, the locked wheels sliding in the gravel. Rik kicked open the door and stepped out, and Heather threw herself at him.

He held her close enough to feel every precious bone in her body.

"Daddy! The barn's on fire! We . . . we didn't see it right away because we were watching TV and Erin was on the phone with Brad. I called the fire department, but I didn't know what else to do! Ohmigod, I'm so scared! The horses . . . Venus and her baby and all the horses!"

"It's okay, princess," he said, as Decker's car roared into the yard beside him. Decker stepped out, wiping his bloody nose with his sleeve. Karen and Annie followed.

"You get these girls across the street to Roger and Janine," Rik said to Decker. "Now."

Decker nodded. Karen gathered her weeping daughter close against her and rubbed a soothing hand along Heather's back, while Annie pulled Tamara and Erin into a fierce, protective embrace.

With Heather and the girls safe, Rik turned toward the barns. For a few brief seconds, shock and dismay held him frozen. Already the flames were shooting up along the old gray planking of the barn his great-great-grandpa had built.

Nothing would save the buildings, or anything inside. The tractor and equipment he could replace, but the Belgians . . .

"Aw, Christ," he whispered, running toward the fence. "My horses . . . I gotta get my horses!"

"Rik, no!" Annie screamed behind him.

"Wait," Harrison yelled at the same time. "It's too dangerous! Wait for the fire trucks!"

Rik vaulted over the fence, then ran flat out toward the old barn. It wasn't too late yet. He had time.

At the sound of running footsteps behind him, he glanced over his shoulder.

Harrison.

Rik motioned him back angrily, until he realized Harrison meant to help. He flashed the young cop a look of gratitude. With Harrison's help, he pushed open the doors of the old barn, and at once smoke gathered in his throat, thick and bitter.

"They're panicked," Rik shouted over the sound of high-pitched neighs and powerful hooves banging against wooden stalls.

"I can handle horses!"

Harrison was a farm boy, too. Still, calming a rearing, two-thousand-pound animal would be tricky.

"Just try and drive them toward the door," Rik ordered.

Coughing, eyes stinging from the smoke and blasting heat, Rik yanked the first stalls open. He and Harrison yelled at each horse, slapping their hands against powerful hindquarters. Vanguard and Marigold bolted for the door, but Brutus wouldn't move. He kicked, massive hooves lashing at the stall behind him and barely missing Harrison's head.

Harrison yanked a saddle blanket from the stall, then climbed up the outside wall and threw it over Brutus's eyes. "That should calm him down. I'll lead him out. You get the next two!"

At a strange popping sound, Rik looked up, coughing hard. The roof was going. Already the back of the barn was on fire—where he kept Venus and her foal.

Harrison would have to take care of Napoleon and Tiberius.

Hunkered low, he ran for the back stall, hardly able to see through the smoke—his John Deere was nothing but a hulking blur—but he could feel the violent vibrations on the wood as Venus kicked the stall, her whinny high-pitched and frightened.

Heat blasted him, drying and tightening his skin, as if it were suddenly too tight for his bones. He fumbled at the stall bolt, then flung the door wide. He caught Venus's halter and pulled her forward, but she wouldn't budge.

"Come on," he begged. "Run, run, dammit!"

Something crashed to the floor near him, hissing and crackling, and Venus panicked. Her heavy body slammed Rik into the stall headfirst. Pain shooting through him; he slid to the floor.

Shaking his head to clear it, he pushed himself to his knees just as he heard Harrison call his name.

"Here!" The word hardly came out before Rik doubled over, coughing. Smoke, thick and acrid, filled his lungs. Then Harrison hauled him up, and Rik handed Venus off. "Get her out. I'll take the filly!"

Harrison wrapped the blanket around Venus's head and led the horse away. At once, both were lost in swirls of dark smoke.

Now he had to find Titania.

The fire roared as loud as a freight train. He could hardly see more than two feet in front of him. On hands and knees, he crawled around the stall, trying to find the foal.

Just as he was about to give up and run before the burning rafters crashed down around him, his hand brushed something soft. He felt along farther, fingers finding long legs, then a head.

She moved weakly as he grabbed her. Dragging the limp, heavy body, he crawled along the floor and stayed close to the line of stalls, knowing they would lead him to the door. Only a few feet more.

Christ, he hadn't known a fire could spread so fast!

Rik didn't dare breathe the searing, toxic air. He concentrated all his strength on dragging himself and the filly toward what he prayed was the door.

Dammit, he *wouldn't* die like this. Not now.

Picturing Annie's face, as if she were standing just a few feet in front of him, guiding him, he crawled until he could go no farther. As the smoke overcame him, Rik coughed uncontrollably and everything around him began to fade away into a roaring, whirling darkness.

The filly slipped from his grasp as he pitched forward. The instant before he hit the cement, he saw a shape floating toward him through the smoke, as bright as an angel.

Then there were hands—many, many hands—and the blinding blue and white of the sky and sun. Clear air, and pain, and, finally, a sudden, complete blackness.

CHAPTER TWENTY

December 24, 1832: Dearest Gussie, I should not write for fear of causing you greater sorrow, but who else shall know of my Loss if not you? It is the eve of our Lord's birth, a time of contemplation and joy to all but myself. I hear HIS footsteps outside. I hear HIS laughter. I had hoped to behold HIM, have him clasp me to his breast. But he shall not come. I shall not see his Dear Face again, hear the Joy of his laughter. I cannot weep. Inside, all is a furnace of Rage. How dare time march forth toward a New Year and not bring with it my Lewis?

—MISS EMILY OGLETHORPE,
FROM A LETTER TO AUGUSTINA HUDSON

"I'm sorry, but rules are rules. The only visitors allowed in the ICU are family."

Annie stared at the burn unit nurse. She'd driven all the way to University Hospital in Madison, where Rik had been transferred after he'd been pulled from the burning barn, only to be stopped outside the door to his room.

Rules—stupid, institutional, bureaucratic rules! God, she'd had enough of those to last her a lifetime.

"Please," she said tightly. "All I want is to see that he's all right."

"I'm sorry." The nurse, an older woman, looked sympathetic but firm. "He's off oxygen, but we've given him medication to help calm him and let him rest. Between the effects of a mild smoke-inhalation injury and some superficial burns, what he needs most right now is sleep. Try to understand that."

Annie glanced away, the antiseptic smell of the place making her nauseated and light-headed.

"You don't look very good, hon. Try and relax. We're keeping him overnight just to be safe, but he's going to be fine. He'll come home a little sore and hoarse, but that's all. Now, I suggest you go home and ... hey!"

A tall man in a suit, his tie pulled loose, pushed past both Annie and the nurse.

"Excuse me, sir, what do you think you're doing?" the nurse called, leaving Annie and going after the man. The nurse grabbed the man's arm, and he turned.

Annie froze, staring.

Gold hair, blue eyes ... the resemblance was unmistakable.

"My name's Lars Magnusson. My brother is here. I want to see him now!"

A dark-haired woman hurried toward Rik's brother. Small and well rounded, she also wore a suit. "Lars, please! Calm down!"

Annie stepped back quickly toward the door, trying to make herself as small as possible. She did not want these people—Rik's family—to see her. Oh, God. She couldn't face them, not now.

The woman grasped Lars Magnusson's hand, her face pale with fear. "This is my husband ... can we see Rik? Is he all right? We drove down from Milwau-

kee as fast as we dared and we're just . . . nobody
could tell us anything, not even how badly he's in-
jured or—"

The nurse smiled. "He's doing very well. Come this
way—"

Poised at the burn unit's door, Annie glanced one
last time over her shoulder at Rik's brother, and at the
concern and fear on his face.

"—you can visit for a short while. He's been quite
popular," the nurse continued. She glanced over her
shoulder, then frowned. "Hey, where did the other
young lady—"

Annie quickly slipped through the door, just as
Rik's brother turned. As the door swung closed behind her, she all but ran toward the hall.

Once she felt certain no one had followed, she
paused a moment to catch her breath and try and control her sudden panic.

Eyes closed, she took a deep, steadying breath.

Dear God.

Rik had almost *died*.

Never, ever would she forget the terror of waiting
for Rik to emerge from the burning barn. She'd run
after him, only to be yanked back by Owen Decker.
While she'd fought and kicked to get free, Sergeant
Harrison and several of the Indians, who'd come from
the Hollow to help, had pulled Rik from the flames.
He'd collapsed only a few feet from the door, the foal
beside him.

Then the fire trucks and ambulances arrived, and
the hellish hours that followed had seemed to drag
on forever—and still there was no end in sight.

People stared at her as she walked back through
the hospital to the parking ramp. With her wild hair,

scrapes, and sooty clothing, she probably looked as if she should be in the ER.

"Annie! Annie Beckett, hey!"

Annie turned and watched Owen Decker limp toward her. For once, he didn't look neat and polished. Although he'd cleaned up, the bruises and cuts from his scuffle with Rik—and her—were livid against his skin.

"What are you doing here?" she asked.

The steady stream of people split around them, fluid as a river flowing around an island.

"Why do you think? I've come to see Rik."

"You can't, not unless you're family. They wouldn't let me see him."

Decker regarded her for a long moment, then he said with quiet urgency, "I didn't mean for any of this to happen. You have to believe me."

"Why should I?"

"Because it's true," Decker insisted, and the fear in his dark eyes looked real. "I never thought . . . I didn't want anybody hurt!"

Annie sighed, too tired to stay angry. "But if you hadn't been so eager to interfere, those men wouldn't have been smoking at the barn in the first place."

"I never gave anybody permission to go near the house or outbuildings—"

"It wasn't *your* right to give permission about anything at all," Annie interrupted. Weariness threatened to push her knees out from under her, and she was aware of a hollow and airy sensation, as if she weren't entirely residing in her own body. "You just don't get it, do you?"

He said nothing.

"Thank God Rik will be fine, and that none of the

cattle or horses were lost. If Rik, Sergeant Harrison, and those two Indians hadn't been able to get the Belgians to safety, and if that little horse had died, I don't think I could even look at you."

"You asked for my help. Or have you forgotten?" He grabbed her arm as she pushed past him. "You seemed pleased with the media attention."

She stopped short. "What do you want me to do, Owen? *Thank* you? Come on. You can lie to yourself all you want, but we both know why you did what you did." She pulled against his tight grip. "Now let me go. I never want to see you or talk to you again."

Leaving him standing there ashen-faced, Annie walked away. But on the drive back to the farm, Decker's words haunted her, and a leaden guilt crowded closer and closer until she had to open the car window, taking in great gulps of air.

The guilt worsened as she drove down the road to Rik's house and saw the blackened ruins of the barns—and the half dozen or so people who'd gathered at the roadside to gawk at this latest disaster. Warfield would be humming tonight.

And, of course, there was one of the ever-present news vans, cameras primed for action.

As if they hadn't already done enough damage. Though they were only doing their job, Annie couldn't ignore the anger surging through her.

For a woman who made a living with a camera, it was a most unfamiliar feeling.

A police officer—an older fellow with a graying crew cut and a paunch—stood guard over the property. She slowed the car as she approached him, then rolled down the window.

"I don't want anyone near the house." Out of the

corner of her eye, she glimpsed a cameraman and reporter trotting toward her. "I'm not answering any questions, and I'm not saying a thing about Rik. They can call the hospital."

"Yes, ma'am. I'll see to it that nobody bothers you. Hey!" he shouted. "Get back! The lady doesn't want to talk."

As she turned into the drive, she glanced in her rearview mirror and saw the cop deep in a discussion with the reporter—a heated discussion, judging by those jabbing fingers.

Once inside the house, Annie fed Buck and hugged his warm, furry body for Rik's sake. She then called the Deckers, hoping to catch either Karen or Heather, but no one answered.

After hanging up, she stood for a long while in the kitchen, unable to summon even a flicker of energy to move. God, how empty and quiet the house seemed without Rik.

Into that heavy silence, the phone rang.

She made a grab for it, thinking it might be Rik, but then drew her hand back and let it ring until the answering machine picked up.

"Ms. Beckett, this is the Youngstown mayor's office calling. We wanted to let you know you can proceed with your plans for Lieutenant Hudson's interment. Both the VA and city council have agreed to cover the costs of the burial. Please call back soon. We'd like to arrange an interview with our newspaper and local television stations." The woman's voice paused. "It's a beautiful thing, what you've done here, and we'd like to share it with the people of our city."

Then came the mechanical *click* as the call was completed, and Annie had to get out of the house to escape the sudden suffocating silence that followed. She ran to the porch, letting the screen door slam behind her.

A beautiful thing, indeed.

Taking in a deep breath, smelling the acrid stench of smoke still thick in the air, she gazed at the charred buildings. Pale, ashy dust covered everything. Between that, and the dry, stunted crops and heavy gray clouds in the sky, the farm looked bleak and death-like.

A detached part of her knew Rik's insurance would allow him to rebuild. If he'd had to lose anything, at least it was only buildings. He could've easily lost his entire herd, every one of the horses he was so proud of or, God forbid, even Heather, who'd been so close to the fire.

But nothing eased her stinging guilt. Rik had trusted her, and this was what had come of it. After a moment, finding no peace even here, Annie returned to the house.

The phone was ringing again.

"Hey, Lars," came a gruff male voice. "It's Erik. Karen just got a hold of me to tell me what happened and said you'd already left for Madison. I'm hoping you're staying at the old house. If you're there, pick up." A pause. Then, "I'll leave a message for you at the hospital, in case you're there, but if I miss you, I want you to know Marcia and I are driving down to Madison tomorrow. Tell Rik to hang tight. We'll get everything squared away."

Annie took a long, deep breath.

Time to go, then.

His brothers and sister and in-laws would rally around Rik, and his neighbors would drop by with casseroles and salads and offers of help. Even if she could find the courage to stay and face Rik, he wouldn't need her. And the last thing she wanted to endure was the censorious glares of the entire Magnusson clan.

If Rik's brothers came to the house and found her still here, they'd assume God only knew what about her relationship with Rik. The thought of trying to explain, to excuse her part in the fire . . . she couldn't do it.

She had no reason to stay. Her job here was done. She'd found Lewis and cleared his name, and that would have to be enough. For now, at least.

Annie trudged upstairs to the attic room, careful not to brush against anything and leave the black smears of soot. She showered, then threw away the clothes she'd worn—they were ruined, and she could never bring herself to wear them again. After that, she packed and carried everything to her car. She made several more phone calls and even tried the Deckers again, hoping to talk with Heather and say good-bye. But the phone only rang and rang.

Finally, as the sun began to set behind the gray clouds still hoarding their rain, she sat at the kitchen table, wrote out her last check to Rik and then, after a brief hesitation, wrote a short note as well:

I won't be here when you return. I'm taking Lewis home, as you know I must. It is the right thing to do. Besides, I can't face you or your family after what happened today. Maybe you can't face me just yet, either, so I thought I would provide us both with a little time and distance. Perhaps, after enough time has passed, we can talk again. Until then, please accept my deepest apologies for the pain I've caused you. Don't worry about Buck, the horses, or the cows. Janine and Roger are taking care of things until your brothers get here. I'm glad Titania is all right. I'm leaving you a check. I only wish it could be more. I owe you so very, very much.

She propped the letter against the coffeemaker, then walked through Rik's house one last time. Under the silent gaze of generations of Magnusson eyes, and with unshed tears of anger and grief burning at the back of her throat, she shut each door, closed the piano, and pulled the shades down over the windows.

"I want you to rethink this, Mr. Magnusson." The doctor stood in the doorway of the hospital room, flanked on either side by a nurse, as Rik slowly pulled on a pair of jeans.

Jeans that Annie had brought yesterday, along with his wallet and keys—and some idiot nurse had sent her away.

"Don't care," he whispered. It hurt to speak. "Going home."

To Annie. Knowing her like he did, he had to leave now and stop her from doing something foolish and panicky. He could only hope he wasn't too late. If he hadn't been so doped up yesterday, he'd have sent Lars to the farm after Annie.

"I can't sign your release," the doctor snapped.

Rik nodded. Fine. He motioned the man to move, so he could get out of this lousy little room, with its closed smells of sickness and beeping gizmos.

The doctor didn't budge. "How are you getting home?"

"Call a taxi."

"All the way to—" The doctor glanced down at the clipboard in his hand. "—Warfield? That'll cost a bundle."

"I don't care." Lars and Sheila were staying in a hotel in Madison, but Rik didn't want to involve Lars in this. Not yet. "Call me a taxi. Now."

The doctor nodded at the nurse beside him, the older one in pastel scrubs who'd found Rik out of bed a little while ago and, like some tattling kid, had gone for the doctor.

With a disapproving glance, the nurse did as ordered, and a half hour later he was on his way home in the back of a bright yellow taxi driven by a guy who couldn't have cared less that his passenger didn't talk back.

The ride did cost plenty, but to Rik's surprise, the driver refused payment. "Looks like you had some seriously bad karma play out here, mister. I wouldn't feel right, taking your money. Good luck."

Before Rik could protest, the driver pulled away.

He stood for a moment in the yard, looking first toward the empty place by the garage where Annie always parked her car, then at his ruined barns. Finally, with a deep breath, he walked slowly up to the porch. The door was unlocked, and when he pushed through Buck greeted him with joyful barking, leaping on his chest and licking his chin.

A nice welcome home, but not the one he wanted— and he knew at once that Annie had left.

The house was dark, closed up, all the sunshine gone with her.

Almost without realizing it, he glanced toward the coffeemaker. Sure enough, she'd left behind a neat, folded square of paper.

Instead of going right to it, he pulled out a chair at the table and sat. Buck rested his head on Rik's knee, gazing upward with a soulful expression.

It sank in then that she'd really gone, and wasn't coming back.

"Jesus," he whispered, then wished he hadn't. It felt as if a steel pipe, not a plastic tube, had been rammed down his throat in the ER.

He rose slowly to his feet, every damn inch of his body aching, then walked to the counter and picked up her note. Something fluttered to the floor. He bent with a groan and picked it up. A check.

This time, the bitter pain had nothing to do with singed lungs. With careful movements, he pulled out his wallet and placed this check with all the others he hadn't cashed—and wouldn't, especially now.

Then he read the note. And a second time.

Torn between anger and disbelief, he sat again at the table. Part of him had known she'd run, but part of him—maybe the bigger part—had hoped otherwise. He didn't blame her for the fire, but he did blame her for this. For leaving him.

Rik closed his eyes, blinking away a sudden blurring. God, he was tired. And he hurt. Everywhere.

He looked skyward, more from reflex than anything else, and whispered, "Kid, when I said it was time to let her go, this wasn't what I had in mind."

Outside, a rumble of thunder answered him.

It took a second or so for the sound to penetrate his grim thoughts, then he heaved himself to his feet and walked to the window.

It *was* thunder. In the sky, clouds roiled together, electricity sparking within. He went out to the porch, taking in a lung full of air that smelled of rain—and burnt wood—but couldn't bring himself to look at the barns again, or where his horses huddled under the shelter of trees in the pasture.

He watched the clouds gather and the wind pick up. Rain slashed down in gray, hazy sheets at first, while lightning cracked and thunder rumbled. The rain came down so hard it poured out the eaves of his house and over the sloping roof of the porch like waterfalls, washing away the smell of burnt wood and flattening the hay in the fields with its weight.

"Too late," he said to himself. "Dammit, it's all too late."

When the violence of the storm had passed, Rik walked into the yard, tipping his head back and letting the warm, gentle rain fall on his upturned face and drench his T-shirt, his jeans, his skin. If he squeezed out any tears then, nobody but him had to know.

The rain had soaked him thoroughly before a grumbling in his stomach reminded him he hadn't eaten any real food in way too long. Not feeling up to cooking, he grabbed an apple. If he peeled it and chewed it to a pulp, swallowing might not hurt so bad.

Unwilling to stay in the dark, quiet house, Rik sat on the porch steps and watched the rain fall over his ruined barns and thirsty earth. With his pocketknife, he carved away the peeling in a long, winding red curl.

Then Buck, flopped at his feet, surged upward and started barking. Soon Rik heard the sound of an approaching car.

Heart pounding, he started to stand. Had she changed her mind? Come back? Then he remembered her note, the darkness of his house, and sat down heavily.

Lars and Erik wouldn't show up for a while yet, either, so it must be some damn reporter or gawker.

His hand closed tight around the knife, just as a dark blue Crown Victoria pulled into the yard.

Well, hell. This was one visitor who wouldn't get a red carpet welcome.

Decker opened the door and stepped out into the rain, but he didn't move away from the car.

For a long moment Rik stared at him, then he turned his attention to the apple and carved out a sliver of meat. "Get lost," he said, hating that his voice sounded so hoarse, so weak.

Silence, except for the pattering rain on the car, on the roof. When Decker didn't leave, Rik looked up. "I said, get out of here."

"Not until we talk," Decker answered at last.

"Not interested." Swallowing hurt like a bitch, but no way would he let on.

"Where's Annie?"

He shrugged. "You tell me."

Decker stared. "You mean she's gone?"

Rik nodded, gouging out another piece of apple, and briefly imagined he wasn't stabbing his knife into the soft fruit of an apple, but into Decker.

The thought brought him to his feet, fast. "You better go."

Decker walked forward. "No. We need to talk. Or I do. I've come to make amends, Rik."

"Too late for that."

"It's time we buried this hate between us."

True enough—but not now. Not with something red and angry and hot pushing at the back of his brain; something primal and violent. He closed his fingers hard around the knife's handle as Decker took the first step up to the porch.

"Bad idea," Rik warned.

Decker, sporting an ugly shiner and a split lip, glanced at the knife. He hesitated, then continued up the steps. "It's now or never."

Rik looked away, keeping a tight focus on slicing the apple and acting as if nothing was wrong. But he knew how close Decker stood: close enough to feel the heat of his body, to smell his aftershave and sweat. Rik's gut knotted, and the red pushing at the back of his eyes intensified.

"You were fucking my wife behind my back," he said. "There's nothing you can say that I want to hear."

"I love Karen."

Rik gave a soundless laugh. "And I didn't?"

"Not like I did. Like I still do."

"You wanted her because I had her." He chewed the apple and swallowed, glad for the pain. "When the marriage ran into trouble, you took advantage of that."

"I wasn't the one who made her unhappy and confused," Decker shot back.

"No," Rik agreed after a moment. He pitched the half-eaten apple aside. Then, carefully, he wiped the knife clean on his jeans. "But she was my wife, not yours. Then you had to go and make trouble between me and Annie, and that puts me in a piss-poor mood, Decker."

Rik looked up. The only thing standing between him and Decker was the porch column, with its peeling white paint and crude carving made by a long-dead, lovestruck ancestor.

A heart. A stupid heart.

The red, angry thing inside exploded and Rik plunged the knife toward Decker. With a dull thud, the blade slammed into the wooden column, right above the carved heart and not even an inch from Decker's neck.

The man flinched, but didn't back away.

"I didn't know Annie would . . . look, I am responsible for what happened here." Decker raised a hand, then lowered it. After a moment, he shoved both hands into his trouser pockets. "I have wronged you deeply. I couldn't admit that I wanted to make you look bad so I'd look better. I didn't want to see myself like that, until someone showed me in a way I . . . couldn't ignore."

Rik stared at Decker, over his white-knuckled, shaking hand still grasping the knife. "What are you babbling about?"

Decker took a deep breath. "Karen left me. She told me she didn't want me anymore because of what I did to you, then she packed up the kids and left."

Looking down, Rik yanked his knife out of the wood, folded its blade away, and returned it to his pocket. He should feel something at Decker's admission. Surprise, satisfaction. Anything. But what he'd done—or had almost done—left him too weak-kneed and numb for anything but fear.

After a moment, he trusted his legs enough to carry him around the other man and down to the middle step, where he sat down hard, paying the rain no mind and taking deep, steadying breaths.

Why the hell didn't Decker say something? Jesus

Christ, he'd nearly stabbed the bastard, and he just stood there.

"I had time to think when I was home alone last night." Decker settled on the step beside Rik, but a foot or so away. The rain soaked his fancy shirt and plastered his dark hair to his face. "My place sure is big and empty without Karen and my boy."

"I know the feeling," Rik said.

For the first time in years, he looked at Decker— really looked at him. He saw the gray hair, the lines around his mouth and eyes, and then glanced down at his own hands. No, not a young man's hands anymore.

Decker shot him a guarded glance. "I figured you'd gloat. What goes round comes round, and all that." When Rik said nothing, he added in a rush, "I want Karen back, but I also want to break this circle of hate. I'm tired of being the bad guy, the scumbag who stole the wife of a man who'll always be better than him."

As Decker's voice cracked with emotion and bitterness, Rik faced him. "Even when we were kids, you made everything a competition. It was just stupid games back then, but I sure wish I knew where it went so wrong."

"Do you ever miss what we had, Rik?" Decker's eyes were so dark they were nearly black. "When we were kids?"

Rik didn't look away. "You were my best friend. We did everything together. Sure, I miss it." He paused, sleeving the rain out of his own eyes. "But we can't ever have that back."

"Yeah, I know." Decker slumped forward, and sighed. "What Karen and I have, it's good. I don't want to lose her, and I don't much like the man I see myself becoming. I can pay you for your barns, if—"

"Forget it. I don't want your money." Where had that red anger gone so suddenly? How could it have just scattered, like smoke in a breeze. "What are you going to do now? Are you going after Karen?"

"I thought I'd give her a few days. She's pretty upset."

"She's got a temper all right, if you push her far enough."

"And you?"

Rik glanced at Decker. "You know I got a temper."

"No, I mean, are you going after Annie?"

Rik almost smiled at the irony of it; him and Decker sitting side by side, soaked, battered, and glum, mooning over their fled womenfolk.

He glanced down at his hands and flexed them. "If Annie doesn't want to be with me, why should I go begging after her?"

All that was left now was self-pity, gray and drippy like the sky. He wanted to wallow in it; submerge himself in it, wrap it around his hurts.

Decker gave a snort of derision. "You always had more pride than good sense, and you never had a clue about how to handle women."

This time, Rik did smile. "Good sense? You're the one sitting in the rain next to a guy who considered poking a few extra holes in your hide."

Again, Decker hunched over, knotting his hands together. Very softly, he said, "Would you have?"

"I thought about it." His smile fading, Rik focused on the distant line of trees at the Hollow. When Decker said nothing, he added, "You wanted me to."

At that, Decker looked up. "Maybe. Maybe I

wanted you to hurt me back . . . to fight back, just once."

"Christ," Rik swore in disgust, in anger—and an odd twist of grief for the friendship they'd shared, and lost.

This time the silence stretched longer, while the rain began to level off and he and Decker sat lost in thought.

"You don't get it yet, do you?" Decker asked at length. "That Annie went away because she wants to be with you."

"What kind of candy-ass philosophy is that, Owen?"

Decker tipped his head to one side. A grim smile crossed his face, causing his cracked lip to bleed. "You're not stupid. Figure it out."

Rik stood, ignoring his aching muscles, the raw burning of his throat, the pounding headache, as the slow realization filled him with a cold fury.

"Forget doing the right thing," he said, his voice rising. "I'm tired of being the good guy. I'm tired of waiting. She's got no right to walk away from me like that. I'm not letting her."

Rik reached out his hand. Decker hesitated, then let Rik pull him to his feet.

"Thanks," Decker said, wincing. "You pounded me pretty good. It never used to hurt this bad before. Either you've learned to fight, or I'm getting old."

Rik released Decker's hand. "Maybe a little of both."

"Do you know where Annie is?"

"No, but it can't be too hard to track a woman with a hundred-sixty-year-old corpse."

Decker smiled. "Good luck, Rik. Hope it works out."

"Better keep some of that luck for yourself." Above them the clouds began to break apart, and a filmy ray of sunshine streaked through the humid haze. "I mean it, Owen. Don't let Karen down like I did. You screw up your marriage, and I swear I'll hunt you down and beat the shit outta you. Again."

"Thanks for the warning," Decker said dryly. "Now get the hell out of here and go fix your own damn mistakes."

CHAPTER TWENTY-ONE

June 6, 1862, Youngstown, Ohio: Oh, Emily, not even thirty years have dulled my Grief and still I search for my son in every chance met Stranger's face. I shall ache for him, I think, until my very last breath.

—MRS. AUGUSTINA HUDSON,
FROM A LETTER TO MRS. EMILY (OGLETHORPE) LASSITER

It was over.

Ten years of work ended here—in a hotel room not much different from dozens of others she'd stayed in, and then tomorrow morning she'd be rushing through another airport with her bags, amid a sea of strangers.

Yes, life was back to normal.

Annie stood at her window in the hotel set in the noisy hubbub of Youngstown's business district. Looking out across a sunset skyline of sleek modern office complexes alongside older, elegant buildings, she watched the traffic and pedestrians below for a long while, then dropped the curtain over the window.

The governmental bureaucracy had come through. Lewis had been laid to rest with full military honors earlier that afternoon, and his record cleared of the desertion charge—and it warmed that cold place inside her, if only a little.

"I brought him home, Gussie," she whispered to the silent room, wishing Lewis could know he hadn't died for nothing.

But ghosts didn't exist. If they did, then maybe this pervasive sadness, this weariness, would leave her.

Annie sank to the bed. Even knowing it was pointless, she rang the front desk. "This is Annie Beckett in room 432 calling for messages. No, I only want messages from Rik Magnusson. Oh . . . I see. Well, thank you, anyway."

Of course Rik hadn't called. It's not like she'd had the guts to call and tell him where to find her.

Restless, trying to ignore the sensation of the walls pressing in upon her, she pushed up from the bed and crossed the room to the table where she'd set up her files and laptop. A neat pile of notepaper lay beside the computer.

In the early hours of the morning, when sleep wouldn't come, she'd typed the last sentence of her book. Now all she needed was a sense of satisfaction of a job well-done. But it eluded her, along with the sense of triumph, of validation, that also should've come with the offer from Idlewild Press to buy her book.

They'd offered far more money than she'd hoped for, yet she'd only said, "I'll need a little time to think about it."

She'd reached her decision, but hadn't yet brought herself to make the call that would mean letting go of Lewis for good. With a sigh, she leaned back against the table, picked up the notepaper, and read:

Angry and shamed by what this war has made of him, of his men, Lewis tries to order his thoughts in a letter that will never be sent. Many of the men have been drinking whiskey, and as Cyrus heads toward the bluff against orders, Lewis goes after him.

There are two women, one badly beaten. Lewis doesn't think twice about placing his body between Cyrus and the women. Angry words follow; perhaps shoving, then Cyrus has a rifle in his hand and Lewis experiences his first inkling of fear.

But Lewis will not back down. He is an officer and a gentleman, with a duty to uphold, and the consequences to his friendship be damned.

"Lieutenant, you will stand aside—"

"I will not—"

"Lieutenant Boone, you will put your rifle down! That is an order!"

The end comes quickly. Only the reverberation of metal piercing flesh and bone is heard. Then, a harsh gasp of pain, of shock.

The violent thrust impales Lewis against a slender pine and brings two friends face-to-face on a dark, moonless night. Lewis lives long enough to understand, long enough for Cyrus to see the pain and rage reflected in his eyes before death dulls them. Long enough for Cyrus to realize what he has done—and what no one must ever know.

Only guesses and hunches; she could prove nothing. Her book would list just the facts, and soon Civil War historians would be hotly debating Boone's guilt. What she knew in her heart, she had written down for her eyes only. This way the truth existed somewhere, in black-and-white, no matter how briefly.

But Lewis's last moments were his own, too private ever to share—and with slow deliberation, Annie tore the paper in her hands, again and again, until only shreds remained.

Then she turned and picked up the phone again, a new resolve brimming within her.

Rik had been so very right. Life was simply too short to waste on fear. Either he would want her or he would not; either she would be strong enough to love him as he deserved, or she would not—but she could no longer stand not taking that chance.

She let the phone ring until the answering machine kicked on. How eerie, listening to her own voice on the greeting message.

"Hi, Rik. It's Annie. I just called to talk . . ." She trailed off, uncertain. "I'll try again later, since I'm leaving Youngstown tomorrow. Hope everything is okay with you. Give me a call back at—" She glanced at the telephone, then gave him the number. "Take care. Talk to you soon."

After closing the curtains and blinds and instructing the concierge she didn't want any calls—unless it was Rik Magnusson—Annie crawled into bed, still dressed, hoping to snatch a moment of badly needed rest.

But sleep wouldn't come.

After tossing and turning for several hours, she gave up. She brewed a little pot of coffee, turned on the television, and started surfing channels.

". . . the story of Lieutenant Lewis Hudson," came a reporter's solemn voice, catching her attention, "which has deeply touched the citizens of Youngstown."

Annie sat straighter, glancing at the clock. Ten o'clock already? She turned back to the TV, which showed a dozen or so people gathered at the ornate iron gate of the cemetery.

Then the camera returned to the reporter: "It's a tale that goes beyond the lure of conspiracies, beyond the seductiveness of secrets, and the tragedy of human greed. Perhaps what has touched us, quite simply, is hope—"

The camera cut to six tall, well-built young servicemen—much the same age Lewis himself had been—carrying the flag-draped casket. Briefly, Annie closed her eyes as a memory she'd never forget flashed to mind: the muted colors of the stone markers, the smell of freshly cut grass, and the steady *click-click-click* of the honor guard's polished shoes, sharp and rhythmic on the concrete.

"—a hope that goodness will always triumph over evil," the reporter continued. "No matter how many years, even centuries, have passed. And although the entire truth behind this young soldier's story may never be known, it has left us with another valuable and undeniable truth, which is that it's never too late to bring home those who have given their lives in the service of our country."

The camera cut away and she watched again the knot of middle-aged Vietnam vets, stuffed into their old uniforms, with unashamed tears on their faces, snap to attention and salute as the honor guard and casket moved past. Again, tears burned her eyes.

At least one generation understood the cost of war. These veterans had come not only to honor Lewis, but all their buddies lost in the jungles of a foreign land.

Perhaps some of those buddies had yet to return home.

"One woman determined she could make a difference," said the reporter's voice, as the camera showed Annie standing by the casket and accepting the folded flag.

While the reporter's voice droned on, she gazed at the screen and the stately old tomb of the Hudson family, last opened in 1919 to welcome Lewis's youngest sister back to the bosom of her family. Today, she'd brought Charlotte's big brother home, too.

The news feature had been tastefully done, she decided as she turned off the TV, and respectful. She looked over at the folded triangle of the flag lying on the bedside table. It had been given to her as a courtesy, more than because she was a distant relative.

How many stars had been on the flag when Lewis had died for his country? Quite a few less than fifty.

From the flag, her gaze moved to the phone. Why hadn't Rik called? Even if he'd been in the barn when she'd left her message, he should have returned to the house by now.

At midnight, when Rik still hadn't called, she checked with the main desk for messages—of which there were several, but none from Rik Magnusson.

Puzzled, and worried, she rang the farm again at midnight. Once again, she reached only the machine.

Either Rik wasn't home or he wasn't taking her calls.

If he wasn't taking her calls, why? Her note hadn't been a good-bye. She'd intended it for space, for a cooling-off period. A time to think everything through with their heads, not their hormones.

Of all her dark and oily doubts, one loomed larger than the rest: Rik had never once said he loved her. Or that he even needed her.

Had he? Even just a little? Maybe she only wanted

to believe his feelings for her ran deeper than they truly did.

She knew so little of love. The only real example she'd had came from the letters between Lewis and Emily—but Rik wasn't a Lewis, and she certainly wasn't an Emily.

Maybe she should have told him she loved him. Told him to his face, not in a whisper while he slept. But she'd been too afraid.

Now what?

She could get busy and start a new project. Her calendar was full; she had a book offer to consider, several weeks to prepare for her Montreal trip . . .

Her mind blanked, any future without Rik looming as a cold, empty void.

Sinking back onto the bed pillows, Annie turned the TV on again to chase away the silence, and muted the volume so she wouldn't disturb anyone in the adjoining rooms. In the small hours of the morning, exhaustion overtook her at last, and she slept.

She dreamed of the farm.

Sitting on the front porch swing, she listened to the starlings and whippoorwills, killdeer and robins sing all around her, and the breeze smelled of sweet hay and earth and fresh rain. The breeze caressed her face as she swung back and forth, while the chains went *creak-click-cre-e-a-a-k*.

Suddenly the swing's noise changed to a *BANG-BANG-BANG*.

Annie jerked awake, blinking rapidly in the fuzzy state between sleep and wakefulness.

The impatient pounding on the door came again.

She swung out of bed with a quick glance at the

clock—it wasn't even five in the morning yet—and called, "Hold on!"

Annie peered through the peephole, then stepped back, forgetting to breathe.

Rik . . . *Rik* was here!

Fingers trembling, she unhooked the security chain and opened the door. For a moment, speechless, she could only stare.

He looked tired. And angry.

"Hi." She stood still, at a loss over what to do or say as she soaked in the sight of him, from work boots to snug, faded jeans and red-cotton shirt, right up to a grim face with a day's growth of beard and blood-shot eyes.

She ached to hold him, to kiss away those lines of exhaustion.

"I woke you up," Rik said.

Annie heard the roughness of his voice, and her own throat tightened in sympathy. "I don't mind, really. I just . . . didn't expect you."

He held up a piece of paper—the note she'd left him.

"Oh." She sighed. "You'd better come inside."

Rik followed her into the room, and she could almost feel his stare behind her; that too-blue, too-intense Magnusson Chiller Stare.

To break the silence, she turned and said, "How are you feeling?"

"I've been better."

"Your voice is hoarse." He shrugged her concern off, and she added, "You look okay. The burns—"

"Are no big deal," he interrupted impatiently. "I'm fine."

"You came after me," she whispered at last, to put

this miracle into words, and make it more real.

Nobody had ever come after her before.

"You knew I would."

Annie frowned, opened her mouth to deny it, but said instead, "How did you find me?"

"I called the newspaper and TV stations." He crushed the note into a ball and tossed it on the bed. "I've been driving all night, and I'm too tired to play games, Annie. I've come to take you home, where you belong." He paused, then added, "Even if it means I have to haul you all the way back over my shoulder."

She blinked again, unsure of his mood. "You're mad at me, aren't you?"

"You're damn right I'm mad!"

"So . . . that was a threat," she said, eyeing him warily, even as something like joy tickled inside. "And not a marriage proposal?"

CHAPTER TWENTY-TWO

April 28, 1832, Fort Armstrong: It does nothing but
rain. Shall I never see the Sun again?

—Lieutenant Lewis Hudson,
from a letter to Miss Emily Oglethorpe

How the *hell* had the M-word come into this?

Suddenly on the defensive, Rik settled for a safe
response: "What?"

"You heard me."

That gleam in her eye meant trouble. He cleared his
throat, and winced in pain. "We have some unfinished business."

"Such as?" She moved, putting the bed between
them.

Man, that bed looked good—and so did Annie. It
hit him hard, how much he'd missed her. He wanted
to pull her close and kiss her like crazy, but he wasn't
so dead tired as to miss the tension in the air.

She didn't exactly look mad, but she didn't exactly
look happy to see him, either. He'd driven all this
way, going over in his mind again and again the
things he'd say—pissed off one minute and terrified
the next. And now all of those preplanned speeches,
all those painfully rehearsed romantic phrases, went
pop into nowhere.

"You left me," he said, his tone cold and accusatory. "While I was lying flat on my back in a hospital and pumped full of God knows what kind of shit, you left me."

She glanced away, two bright spots of color staining her cheeks. "I know. I'm sorry."

"Why did you run?" he asked, gentling his rough voice as much as he could. "That's what it was, Annie. The first chance you got, you ran off. Why?"

Letting out her breath, she sat on the bed. "I had to bring Lewis home."

"Bullshit." After a moment, he joined her, and at once the scent of her wrapped around him. He'd even missed her perfume. "You could've waited. I would've come with you. Hudson was important to you, and that made him important to me."

Annie didn't look at him as she whispered, "I wanted to stay, but then there was the fire and you were hurt, and I knew your family was coming." She glanced at him, then quickly away again. "I was afraid you and your brothers wouldn't want me around. As each hour went by, the feeling just got worse and worse . . . so I decided to make things comfortable and leave. I had to bring Lewis home, and I thought that would give us both time to think things over."

"And what do you need to think over?"

She shot him a look of amazement. "We're very different, Rik."

"Yeah. So?"

Uh-oh. Wrong answer. Amazement turned to narrow-eyed anger.

"Have you given any thought at all to the future? *Our* future?"

ALL NIGHT LONG 355

"Yeah," he said again, this time defensive.

"Beyond sex?"

"You know, men don't always think with just their dicks."

"And why should I believe otherwise? Why should I think there's more between us than sexual compatibility? I'm not giving up a job, changing my whole life, for good sex. You haven't even told me you love me, Rik!"

Damn. Now she'd gone and thrown the L-word into things, too.

"Neither have you," Rik retorted. He warily added, "This is the unfinished business I was talking about. We need to work things out."

"Fine," she said with a shrug. "You work it out in Wisconsin, and I'll work it out in Ohio. Some women might not care about moving in with a man without a word of commitment or a single 'I love you,' but I'm not one of them. Once we work it out, then maybe we'll go somewhere. Or maybe not. I can take care of myself, Rik. I don't need a man to do that for me."

"Dammit, I know that! But you're still coming back with me."

"No, I'm not."

He glared at her, baffled by the angry challenge in her voice. "Like hell am I letting you walk out of my life again, Annie."

"And just what are you going to do about it?"

Then out of his mouth came the words he hadn't thought he'd ever say again: "Do you want to marry me?"

Annie edged away, eyeing him. "Take two . . . is this a pop quiz or a proposal?"

"Just answer the damn question!"

Rik squeezed his eyes shut with a deep growl of frustration. Real smooth. Christ, this had to be love. In the room with her only five minutes, and already she'd short-circuited his brain.

But he knew what she wanted.

"Because if that's a proposal," she said, her voice pitched a little high, "it's not a very romantic one."

Ah, to hell with pride and all the right words.

Rik slid to one knee beside her and, ignoring her startled look, took her hand. "Annie, you're making me crazy here. I can't do romance right like most other guys. All I can say is, I need you in my life and I want you to stay with me. Marry me. It's all in your hands, honey. Your choice."

She laughed.

Heat flashed through him. Here he was, on his knees, for Christ's sake, and she was *laughing*. "Annie—"

"Yes," she said. "Oh, yes, I would love to marry you, you ornery, barbarous Viking oaf."

Somehow, he hadn't exactly pictured her accepting his proposal using words like "ornery" and "barbarous" and "oaf."

Rik frowned. "You could've just said yes, without all that other stuff."

She touched his face and ran a finger over his lips. He went still at her touch, forcing himself not to grab her, toss her back on the bed, and make love to her.

"But I like all the other stuff. You wouldn't be you without it. I've missed you so very, very much, Rik."

Okay—now this was more like it.

"You," he growled, pushing himself to his feet. "My house feels like a tomb. Even Buck's moping." He sat on the bed, content for the moment to just hold her hand. Staring down at their entwined fingers, he added, "I missed you, too."

At that, she looked away. "I needed you to come after me."

"I know," Rik said, as quietly. "Honey, I won't ever leave you. I promise, and you gotta promise to trust and believe me, and not make me prove it like this. No more running away."

Her cheeks colored bright red again. "I want . . . I'm still a little scared, Rik."

"You can do it. I know you can." Touched by her whispered admission, he rubbed her back. He didn't know if it helped ease her fears, but her muscles relaxed at his touch. "You want to be with me, right?"

She nodded, scooting a little closer.

Oh, yeah—this was defintely much more along the lines of what he'd imagined during his long, lonely drive.

"Well, I'm not going anywhere. I've got a hundred and fifty years' worth of ties to that farm. You stick with me, and I guarantee I'll stick with you. As I see it, you've brought the kid home, so now you may as well attach yourself to my cause."

That earned him a glare. Thank God; he hated seeing Annie in the dumps. He wanted her laughter and fire, all her sunshine and colors and funny way of looking at life.

Then she gifted him with a slow smile. "I had one of those bolt-of-lightning revelations yesterday."

Rik eyed her with a sudden wariness. "Am I going to like hearing this revelation?"

"Mmm, I think so. I realized that all my life, I've been searching for something. I thought I'd found it in my work, or that I'd find it by bringing Lewis home. But I was wrong. What I've been searching for my whole life, Rik, is *you*."

Silence followed her hushed words, and Rik could only gaze back at her, at her warm brown eyes, sweet face, and smile. He cupped her cheek with his palm, and she turned into his hand, kissed it.

"Maybe I've been waiting for you my whole life," he said, and the words sat right on his tongue.

"You mean that?" she whispered, eyes wide.

"Yeah." He smiled and trailed a finger across her lips, over her cheek, then down her neck to the softness of her breast. "But I'm getting mighty tired of waiting, Annie. Especially about some things. Let's go home."

Sudden tears sprang to her eyes.

"Shit, honey, I'm sorry. That sounded stupid and crude and I didn't mean . . . I—"

"Oh, Rik, hush up," she interrupted, laughing, then kissed him hard. "When you said 'home,' it reminded me of something and made me a little sad, that's all."

He let out a breath of relief. "Want to tell me about it?"

She tipped her head to one side, regarding him with a solemn expression. "Do you believe in destiny, Rik?"

"It depends. Why?"

"Do you realize that if Lewis hadn't been murdered, we'd have never met?"

At the question, his heart skipped its regular beat. Then he brushed aside a lock of her hair, tucked it behind her ear, and frowned. "The right thing to say, I guess, is that I'm sorry he died, but I can't." He kissed her soft lips. "Not if it means I can't have you."

He kissed her again, then pressed her back against

the rumpled white sheets and eased away her black dress, her bra and panties, until she wore nothing at all.

"I'm going to make love to you," he whispered, kissing the warm, moist valley between her breasts, right where he imagined her heart beat for him and him alone. "And show you what you mean to me in the best way I know. Then we're going home."

After a long trip through Ohio, Indiana, and Illinois, Rik pulled into his drive by early evening.

"Oh, my God," Annie said, shaking her head. Even though she'd known what to expect, the charred remains of the barn packed a dark, sickly punch to her belly. "I think it's worse than I remember . . . wait, what's that? A wall?"

"Yeah," Rik said. Every time he spoke in that raspy voice she ached to hold him close. "While I was off running after you, my brothers and a few neighbors hosted an old-time barn-raising. The local lumberyard donated trusses and wood. The crew'll be back next weekend to put up the rest of the frame, so I can get my cows back inside."

"Do you need money? I have some saved up, and I have a book offer," she said, suddenly remembering. "I haven't accepted it yet, but I can, if you—"

"I don't want your money, Annie," Rik interrupted as he stopped the truck. "Seems like every time I turn around, you're shoving money at me." He reached behind him and pulled out his wallet. To her shock, he pressed each of her checks, creased from the wallet and warm from the heat of his body, into her hand. "You can just rip those up."

Annie stared at the checks in her hand. "Why did

you take them, if you never meant to cash them?"

He shrugged. "Because it made you feel better to give me money—but it never felt right for me to use it."

"I'd like the money from Lewis's book to go to your farm," she asked, slipping the checks into her purse. "It would help me feel like I've made amends for the damage."

"The insurance covered all that."

From the very start, she'd been wrong about Rik. "I'm sorry I tried to bribe you like that, when we first met. It was wrong of me."

"It's okay; I guess I deserved it. I was acting like a bastard. Annie, you can go ahead and take that money for the book. You can do whatever you want with it. But do it because you *want* to, not because of anything you feel you owe me. The circle's closed, honey. Nobody owes anything to anybody."

Strange words. She glanced at him as he helped her from the truck. "What do you mean?"

"Everything is the way it's supposed to be now," he said. "Let's start out clean. Let's say the fire here burned away all the bad stuff, and left nothing but the good."

His words brought a smile to her face. "Have I ever told you how much I like how you think?"

He grinned back. "A time or two. Come on—let's get something to drink and sit on the porch and watch the sun set."

A few moments later, after suffering the enthusiastic welcome of an excited collie, they stood on the porch side by side, Rik straddling the rail while she leaned against the main column.

Annie took in a deep breath of familiar scents, and

it filled her with a swell of sweet contentment. "The minute I saw the farm and your house, I fell in love with it."

"And what about me?"

"Well, it took longer to fall in love with you." She laughed at his frown. "You were kinda testy, you know."

"Me? Testy?" His brows shot upward. Then he grinned. "Testy. I like that word. It's got a bite to it."

"Yeah, right—some bite. I learned real quick that you and your dog were two of a kind: all attitude."

"So when did you figure you were, you know . . ." He paused, that delightful flush staining his cheeks. "Warming up to me?"

"You mean when did I fall in love with you?" she asked, amused. With men like Rik, you had to read between the lines. When a woman said "I love you" to a man like this, he'd only respond with "Me too" or "Yeah."

Rik glanced away and shrugged. "Yeah."

Her smile widened. "I'm not sure. It sort of came sneaking up on me. But I did think you were gorgeous from the first time we met."

"Yeah?" He sounded pleased, surprised. Even a little smug.

"Yup, despite your bad attitude, I couldn't help but notice you had one fine behind." As he sputtered with laughter, she added more seriously, "But I think I fell in love with you when you came for me on that horse, when you told me you wanted me. No one else had ever said that before, or at least not like you did. I do love you. I couldn't say it before, face-to-face, but I do."

No longer laughing, Rik looked at her, his color still

high—and ran a hand through his hair. "That makes me one damn lucky guy."

She smiled at his discomfort, his evasion, then turned a little toward the post. The magical post, the one with the heart. She frowned suddenly. "I don't remember seeing this before."

Just above the heart Rik's great-grandfather had carved, she saw a deep cut in the wood, perhaps half an inch long.

Glancing to where she pointed, Rik shrugged again—but she detected a sudden tension in his muscles that warned her from probing this subject. At least, not now.

"So, what you said ... about being lucky. What were you trying to tell me?" Annie asked softly. Then, as a gentle nudge, "Draw me a picture, Rik."

"Oh, yeah." Rik glanced at her, mustache widening in a small smile, then pulled out his pocketknife. "I forgot where we're standing."

He looked at the column for a moment, then slipped the blade into the cut—Annie didn't miss how it was a perfect fit to his knife, but wouldn't say so— and carved a new heart above the old one. It was a bit lopsided, but big enough when he'd finished to hold the words: RIK LOVES ANNIE.

"There you have it," he said, putting the knife away. To her surprise, he hoisted her up to the porch railing and then went down on his knee.

"You already did this part." Annie laughed. "Or are you trying to look up my skirt?"

"Don't get smart. I didn't do it *right* the last time." He cleared his throat, frowned, then gathered her hands in his. "Annie Beckett, I want to look into your pretty eyes for the rest of my life. I want to wake up beside you for all the mornings we've got left. I want to hear your laughter in this old house, and I swear to God, I'll shrivel up and die if you don't say you'll marry me." He made a face. "How's that for romance?"

Tears and laughter fought inside her, and holding them back left her throat tight and painful. "Again, yes! I'll marry you, Rik . . . you are everything to me. Everything," she repeated with a soft force.

Friend. Lover. Partner. And their love was the thread that stitched them into an unending circle.

He stood, and kissed her. Gently at first, then more insistently, gathering her close, running his hands with lazy intent along her back and bottom. "Welcome home, Annie."

"I'm never, ever leaving you again." She sighed happily, yanking his shirt from his jeans.

"I think we'd better take this to the bedroom," Rik said. He took her hand in his, and pushed open the door. "Come on back inside."

EPILOGUE

April 15, 1836, Columbus, Ohio: It is with great joy that I write to tell you I have been safely delivered of a Daughter. Oh, how beautiful she is, Gussie! We have named her Catherine and I am in awe of each tiny finger, every curl of hair on her dear head. Richard wept when he first held her in his arms. As did I. In truth, I am most weepy these days. The Doctor declares it is because I am of a delicate Constitution and overcome with fatigue. Perhaps this is so, but perhaps it is because for all my Joy and Contentment, for all that I dearly love my Husband, I cannot help but remember and ponder at how different our lives might have been had Fate bent a kinder eye upon us all. These words I write are between you and me and Heaven alone. Richard is my life and so now, Catherine. Yet, between you and me, Dear Gussie, a part of me will always belong to Lewis. A part of my Heart that, once touched, was marked forevermore. He was loved. He is missed, if only by a handful of souls upon this Great Earth.

—MRS. EMILY (OGLETHORPE) LASSITER,
FROM A LETTER TO AUGUSTINA HUDSON

Rik rolled out of bed, eyeing the empty spot beside him and the indentation of a head still visible on Annie's pillow. He grinned, wondering where Annie had run off to this time.

Since Heather had moved in with them, finding time for hanky-panky required a lot of ingenuity, along with a dash of nerve and luck. With Heather at a friend's house for the night, he'd seized his chance to make love to Annie in the soft sunlight of early evening.

Whistling to himself, he pulled on his jeans and then checked for Annie in the living room. When he didn't find her there, he headed to the parlor. He found a pile of her books on the floor, but no Annie.

Rik paused to admire the newly framed picture hanging on the wall across from Old Ole's scowling portrait. Right next to Auntie Clem and her ugly hat, he'd placed their wedding picture.

Annie had looked so beautiful that day, she'd brought tears to his eyes. She'd worn an old ivory-beaded flapper dress she'd found in one of the trunks on the second floor. He'd worn his tux, and they'd married right on the front porch of the house on a crisp and cool September afternoon, with only a few friends and family as guests.

Erik and Lars had come, and even Ingrid had driven up with her brood. Owen and Karen, who'd worked out their problems before the birth of their son, didn't attend, of course. Owen had sent a present, though—a long, silver knife engraved with the wedding date and both Rik's and Annie's names. Owen had enclosed a note with it: *This one's for the cake*. Rik had laughed when he'd read it, much to Annie's puzzlement.

He checked the kitchen next. She'd been there, leaving behind a pot of freshly made coffee and, propped beside it, a sheet of folded paper in some soft pinkish color. Rik picked up the note, taking in a whiff of vanilla scent, then opened it:

Dear Rik, have I told you lately how much I love you?

Smiling, he leaned back against the counter.

Have I told you how much I love even the sound of you and Heather arguing? How I love the sound of her giggle when she talks on the phone with her boyfriend? Or how much I love how you're accepting the fact your little girl is growing up, but still fighting it every step of the way? Have I told you how sexy you are when you get that helpless look on your face?

He chuckled, in spite of the pang of anxiety over the reminder of Heather and her boyfriend. Try as he might, he couldn't help wanting to scare the living shit out of the boys Heather brought home. Any kid dating his baby girl had better have the balls to stand up to him and look him in the eye—and tell the truth when he demanded it.

He returned to Annie's perfumed love note:

Have I told you lately how I love your quiet support and understanding in overseeing the sale of the Hollow to the town? For being patient with my indecisiveness on whether I want to write children's books or open a photography studio of my own? Have I told you how much I loved our honeymoon, and how I shall remember it forever and always?

Oh, yeah—they'd had a grand time on that honeymoon. Great food in little restaurants tucked away in the countryside, peaceful walks along the shores of Lake Michigan, and of course, great sex in that white, lacy room in the inn.

Lovingly, his gaze tracked the breezy handwriting of the last sentence:

And have I told you how happy I am that you brought me home again?

Something squeezed his throat tight, and a moment passed before he refolded the note and tucked it in the back pocket of his jeans.

"Annie!" he called, walking to the stairs that led to the attic room, which she was busy turning into an office. "You up there?"

"I'm out on the porch."

Rik turned, grabbed his denim jacket, and went after his wife. He found Annie standing at the rail in one of her airy skirts and one of his T-shirts, looking out across the fields with their brown stubble of harvested corn.

"I got your note," he said, as he always did when she left her little love letters for him to find.

"I knew you would." She smiled back at him, her hair tousled from their lazy lovemaking, cheeks flushed pink.

A swell of tenderness rose within him as he stepped behind her and pulled her into his arms, and frowned at the touch of her chilled skin against his bare chest. "Where's your sweater? It's October, not the middle of summer."

"Oh, it's not that cold." She tipped her head back against his shoulder, still smiling, and accepted his quick kiss. "And a jacket's no use if you don't wear a shirt under it, dearest."

He snorted. "You make me so hot I could stand in snow buck-naked and not even notice." She wrinkled her nose at him—so he had to kiss her again—and then he added, "What are you doing out here?"

"Admiring the view. God, this place is beautiful in the fall. You Magnussons never do anything halfway. Even if Ole was a mean old codger, he must've had a streak of romanticism to settle here."

Rik gazed out over the top of her head, absently rubbing his chin across the softness of her hair.

He tried to see it through her eyes: how the golden light of the late autumn sun gilded the countryside as far as the eye could see. In the yard, the yellow maple had shed her mantle of leaves in wild abandon, but the prissy old oak still kept a firm hold on her rusty brown cloak. The gold-coin leaves of the aspen, beside the scarlet fire bush, cast a kingly splash of color against the white planking of the garage.

"There's more, you know," she said, her soft words pulling him from his thoughts.

"More what?"

"A little addition to my note. But I wanted to deliver it personally."

Rik raised a brow, intrigued. "Yeah? And where is this little addition?"

"In a place tucked close to my heart."

Ah, a game of hide-and-seek! He liked Annie's games.

Stepping back, Rik ran his gaze over her. The only pocket he saw was on her T-shirt, stretched taut over one breast, and Rik gently cupped his hand over that soft, warm mound. Even though they could both hear the crackle of paper, he said, "Hot or cold?"

Annie laughed. "Definitely hot."

Grinning, he slipped his finger inside the pocket, letting his fingers brush against her breast and rub the stiff peak of her nipple before he snagged the slip of paper.

When he pulled it out, he glanced at it for a moment, curiosity nipping.

"Go on," Annie urged. "Open it."

Slowly, Rik unfolded the small note:

And have I told you that you're going to be a father? Or how happy I am to be contributing to the next generation of Magnussons at Black Hollow Farm?

He grabbed a column for support, holding it so tight that the newly carved heart gouged the palm of his hand.

Annie watched him, her woodsy-colored eyes full of joy and uncertainty. He opened his mouth to say something, but his happiness got all tangled with the wonder, and the words got stuck somewhere between his brain and the tip of his tongue.

"Are you happy about the baby?" Annie asked, a frown creasing her brow.

"Yeah," he managed, then cleared his throat and

said more loudly, "Annie, honey, you sure know how to knock a man off kilter. When?"

"Late May."

"Spring. I . . . oh, man, a baby." He ran a hand through his hair, with something damn near like panic. "Heather's gonna read us the riot act on baby-sitting, you know."

"I know."

He couldn't help but remember all the good times fatherhood had brought him before—and all the mistakes he'd made.

But he'd learned a few things in the sixteen years since he'd held his firstborn, when he'd been a green, scared kid himself. "This time, nothing's gonna be more important than my wife or my kids. I promise you that."

"I know."

He kissed her forehead and slid his hand down to her stomach. "I'll hire someone to help me around the farm, if you want."

"Why? I can drive a mean John Deere," she said, trying to look serious. "And I'm learning to say 'teat cup' without laughing." But she laughed a little, anyway. "Pretty soon, I bet I'll be milking cows faster than you ever could."

"So what are you saying, Annie?"

She kissed him; a loud, smacking kiss. "I'm saying, you've got me! What else do you need?"

Rik laughed. "Just another kiss." She obliged, with plenty of enthusiasm. "And maybe a sandwich. Making love to you leaves me hungry."

"Can it wait?"

"Well, you're eating for two now—" He sucked in

his breath as her hands cupped him through his jeans. "It can wait."

"Rik?"

"Yeah?"

"Tag." She smacked his rear. "And you're 'it'!"

AUTHOR'S NOTE

Sometimes, a book is the result of an idea that's incubated for years.

When I was fifteen, my family and I were out for a Sunday drive in the country and passed by a historical marker commemorating the Battle of Wisconsin Heights. A battle in *Wisconsin*? My interest was piqued, and over twenty years later, that historical marker became the foundation for *All Night Long*.

History has always fascinated me, the good as well as the bad. The Black Hawk War of 1832 isn't well known, and while hardly a glowing moment in American history, it should be remembered—if nothing else than for the hundreds of men, women, and children massacred at the Bad Axe. My main sources for research were John Wakefield's *History of the Black Hawk War*, published in 1834, and Cecil Eby's *That Disgraceful Affair: The Black Hawk War*. The historical facts as presented in *All Night Long* are true, although Lewis, Emily, Cyrus, Augustina, and the events involving them are fictional. Ironically, Abraham Lincoln and Jefferson Davis really did serve together in the Black Hawk War, but it's doubtful they ever met.

My family emigrated from Belgium to Wisconsin's

Door County in the mid-nineteenth century and
farmed there for over a hundred years until my
grandfather sold his farm in the 1980s—so I didn't
have to look too far afield for my inspiration for Rik
Magnusson.

I must thank the Belgian Draft Horse Corporation
of America for their assistance; the Wisconsin Dairy
Producers; Jude Higgs for answering my "horse questions"; and forensic anthropologist Leslie Eisenberg of
the Wisconsin Burial Sites Office for answering questions like: "So, let's say I find this body..." Blame
me, not them, for any mistakes or creative license I
might have taken.

Dear Reader,

As we all know, every bride is beautiful—but a bride left at the altar is a force to be reckoned with. In Tanya Anne Crosby's latest Treasure, *Happily Ever After*, we meet Sophie Vanderwahl. She's been waiting for three long years for her wandering fiance to return. But when she discovers his indiscretions, she sets off to find him—determined to give him a piece of her mind. So she boards handsome Jack MacAuley's ship, and begins a journey of discovery—for Jack is everything her husband to be is not...handsome, irresistible, powerful and faithful in his love.

A modern-day Montana cowboy, a peerless heroine, a love story you'll never forget...this is what makes up Cait London's latest Contemporary romance, *Sleepless in Montana*. Hard and haunted, Hogan Kodiak is an outsider in his own family. Love has burned him in the past, and he's determined not to let sassy Jemma Delaney under his skin. But when passion overcomes caution, Jemma and Hogan embark on a romance that just might shake the Kodiak family to its very core.

In Avon Romance, we're first off to Scotland with Kathleen Harrington's *The MacLean Groom*. Rory MacLean is ordered by the king to wed Joanna, the fair daughter of the rival MacDonald clan, only to discover that his bride has run off!

And if you love Regency-set love stories, don't miss Margaret Evans Porter's *The Seducer*. Highborn Kerron Cashin is tantalized by the local innkeeper's daughter, Ellin Fayle, but when they're caught in a compromising position he must decide if he should be honorable and wed the country lass.

Enjoy!

Lucia Macro
Lucia Macro
Senior Editor